To Sheila,
 I hope y
book.

[signature] '24

Dear Sis'
For you, w/ Love
xx
'24

RYSZARD

Ryszard

A story based on a true account.

Marcia   Wakeman

Gymea Publishing

Published by Gymea Publishing

www.marciawakemanauthor.com/

ISBN   978-0-646-86387-0

Dedication

To Dad, who at times was defined by his past. May you rest in peace. And to my grandchildren, may you learn from GG's story.

> *"Hope is being able to see that there is light despite all the darkness."*
> *Desmond Tutu*

RYSZARD

Prologue

My bones creak as I sit on an old chair up against the wall, the summer heat warming my back. I rub my arms with cold fingers, then carefully peel away a band-aid from the new scratch on my forearm, to inspect the small wound.

It has stopped bleeding, but the band-aid is saturated with blood. I fold it into a tight, small parcel and sigh. These days I seem to bleed and bruise easily. Something to do with the medication I'm taking.

As usual, the retirement village is quiet. I lie my head back against the warm bricks and close my eyes. In the distance a lawn mower drones monotonously. Nearer, a frog croaks in the drainpipe next to the bedroom window. Insistent and unrelenting, it begs a mate to join the chorus. It takes me back to the warm summers in Poland. Before the war. When my brother Jo and I played for hours along the riverbank near our home.

I remember the cool breeze off the river, ruffling my hair, and I laugh to myself when I recall the games we used to play. Especially, the frogs we caught hiding in the bulrushes.

Part 1

1939

Chapter

1

"Keep blowing, keep blowing!" Jo whispers excitedly.

We lie near a pool in the reeds. I have a straw stuck up a frog's bum and keep blowing until it inflates into a ball. It squirms and wiggles as I lower it to the water while holding onto its back legs.

"Let it go now!" orders Jo, releasing his frog as well.

The frogs flounder about on the surface, escaping bubbles of air farting from their bums. Dragging themselves along, their web feet frantically paddling under the water, they try desperately to dive to safety. But the air keeps them afloat. Jo's frog reaches the far side and finally dives. Mine just flaps around for a while until it disappears into the reeds.

"I won! You owe me fifty groszy Rys! You want to win it back?" He snickers.

"How?"

"A rematch. Another frog race, Rys."

I eye him suspiciously. He always catches the biggest frog. I'm tired of losing. I roll onto my back and sigh.

"Nah, I don't feel like it."

I prop myself onto my elbows and watch the wild ponies grazing along the riverbank.

It's a beautiful summer's day, the breeze wafting gently along the river, lightly rippling the surface of the water.

My attention is caught by the small grey stallion munching

grass, lifting his head from time to time to keep watch on us. Grinning, I lean towards Jo.

"Go and sneak up behind him and hit him with a stick for an extra fifty groszy!"

Jo grumbles, "Nah, you do it. That grey bastard gave me a nip on the back last time, for getting too close to his mares!"

"Okay." I hiss over my shoulder as I crawl towards the horses. "I'll do it, but It'll cost you a zloty plus the fifty groszy I owe you."

I ease my way through the bulrushes and crawl up the embankment, slowly creeping along the back of the ridge. I approach the stallion from behind, picking up a stick on the way and step softly towards his flicking tail.

I whack him hard.

Swivelling around, his top lip quivering with fury, he rears up, his forelegs beating the air above my head.

I jump back so quickly I lose my footing, landing on my ass as his hooves thud down near my feet. He rears again, neighing his fury.

Frantically, I scramble to my feet. And run!

Clambering over the ridge, slipping and sliding on the long grass, I bolt towards the fence surrounding the football field.

The stallion pounds the earth behind me.

He's gaining on me.

Snorting, almost in my ear, his hot breath raises the hairs on the back of my neck.

Panic-stricken, I glance over my shoulder. Straight into a mouthful of bared, yellow teeth.

Desperate, heaving a breath, I run faster.

I can outrun the bastard! I'm sure I can! I have to! The fence is right here! I've made it!

I reach for the top railing, and as I'm about to fling myself over it, the collar of my shirt is yanked backwards. My feet hit the ground with a thump, buckling my knees. The horse holds on tight. Sticky foam drips down the back of my neck, drenching my shirt. My legs scrape the ground, and my feet start to pedal as he charges along the fence towards a pile of rubble.

He skids to an abrupt stop, shaking his head. And me. I quiver like a plate of jelly. My arms flap madly as he flings me in a wide arc. I land face down on the pile of broken bricks. Winded, and gasping for air.

Safely in the background, Jo is laughing himself silly. Furious and humiliated, I stagger to my feet.

Snatching up a chunk of brick, I let it fly. But I miss the bastard.

Neighing and snorting his victory, he rears up once more and pounds the earth. Sniggering, he trots off to his herd, his tail flying in triumph.

I swipe at the blood on my elbows and wrists.

Jo runs up to me in fits of laughter. Bending over with his hands on his knees, he gasps for air, tears streaking his face.

"Hit...hit...hit him again! I'll double the bet!" he wheezes.

"Nah," I grunt, rubbing my arse.

#####

My name is Ryszard.

I'm 12 years old.

I live in a city called Sochaczew, near Warsaw, the capital of

Poland. At the hub of an extensive railway system that transports goods all over Poland, Sochaczew is a main export centre for farm produce and farming supplies.

Flowing past the edge of the city and through the neighbouring farmlands, the Bzura River irrigates the flat fertile land which produces corn, potatoes and cabbages.

I live with my family in a two-storey red-brick house with two attic windows. Ma's pride and joy is the neatly manicured garden. At its centre, red tulips sprout from a circular bed. Pink roses climb a trellis over the front door. Ma cultivates all kinds of flowers and vegetables. Supplying our neighbours with potatoes and turnips.

I share a long attic room with Jozef, my older brother. We sleep on wrought iron beds along one wall with an old set of drawers on the other side, leaving the rest of the space to play in. The beds are separated by a narrow table holding a small oil lamp that burns all night. Jo fears the dark. I never tease him on account of his terrible nightmares.

The attic can be either cold or very hot, depending on the time of year. Ma makes sure we are warm by giving us extra feather eiderdowns and hot water bottles in winter, and in summer she opens the two small windows, allowing a refreshing evening breeze to flow through, cooling the room.

My two younger sisters, Zaneta and Angelika, share a small bedroom below us, the space mostly taken up by a double bed.

Cluttered with their belongings, their room is always untidy. Their latest drawings cover the bedroom walls, pinned up in every available space. Woollen yarn is stuffed in baskets and off-cuts of fabric are piled high on a chair. Pencils are scattered over a small desk and onto the floor, a trail of pencil shavings leading towards an overflowing bin.

When Auntie Alicja comes to visit, which is quite often, she sleeps in the double bed with the girls. Sandwiched between them she snores like a bear, smells like a cat and takes up all the room. Begging to sleep downstairs on the sofa, they complain to Ma.

"Pease Ma … Please!"

"Girls! Stop complaining!" snaps Ma. "The parlour is for guests and special occasions and is not a spare bedroom. Your Aunt Celina slept in that bed before she died, God rest her soul, and your Auntie Alicja likes to sleep in it, as it reminds her of our older sister. You will just have to put up with Auntie's snoring!"

My poor sisters despondently trudge upstairs to suffer once again.

My parent's room is furnished with a carved four-poster bed, matching wardrobe and dressing table. Every week a vase of freshly cut flowers is placed next to a pitcher and wash basin on the rosewood washstand. A silver framed mirror hangs above it, making the bedroom look very grand. Pa bought it for their wedding anniversary two years ago, from the department store he has managed since I was a baby. The bedrooms are above a formal parlour, where my parents entertain their friends.

A spacious kitchen, where we mainly live, faces the backyard. Pale blue cupboards are set against bright blue geometric patterned wallpaper. A sink with a pump handle faces a large bay window housing herbs growing in small clay pots.

Light and airy, the kitchen is dominated by a scrubbed

wooden table and six chairs. The floorboards are swept morning and night and the cooking stove is always alight, with a kettle simmering on the hob.

Ma collects porcelain plates, each one decorated with rural scenes or flowers. They are displayed along the walls or on top of cupboards. Three more expensive plates, edged in gold, take pride of place, carefully arranged above the centre of the dresser.

Jozef, Jo, is my best friend. We're only eighteen months apart, almost like twins in a way. Short like Ma's German side of the family, we both sport blond hair and green eyes like our Pa. Our younger sisters have brown eyes and straight black hair, the same colouring as Ma.

When it rains or snows Jo and I play soccer in the attic, using a tightly wound and taped paper ball. Ma hollers from the bottom of the stairs about the noise, then stomps up the narrow staircase to stand in the open doorway.

"Stop the racket!" she shouts at the top of her voice.

Panting, Jo and I fall on our beds spluttering apologies and grinning sheepishly. Ma gives us a lecture on how destroying the house and that one day we will fall through the floorboards. We know it by heart. She slams the door behind her as she leaves.

We listen for her to return to the kitchen, then jump up and start the game all over again, trying to be quiet, until we forget.

Jo and I also play soccer on a sports field with the local boys, usually after school. We're not in a community soccer club, run by a coach, but in teams Jo and I put together every time we play. Sometimes with only seven players and sometimes with eleven a side. We have a great game when we get that many.

#####

One afternoon Pa, looking angrier than I can remember, walks into the kitchen. He throws the newspaper on the table. I sneak a peek at the headlines. 'WAR' in huge letters, is splashed all over the front page.

"The bloody Germans have declared war on Poland!" Pa thunders.

Ma gasps, her hands covering her mouth. Her knife clatters into the sink forgotten amongst the potato she was peeling. The girls whimper, clutching at Ma's skirts. Jo and I silently edge closer too, wary eyes on Pa. Seeing he has scared us, he lowers his voice, but is still very angry.

"They bombed an airbase on the Hel Peninsula!"

We all grow quiet.

Listening. Ma sits at the table, preparations for the meal put aside, and stares at Pa, her face ashen. Jo slips into his chair opposite, his eyes wide. The girls begin to cry, tears streaming down their faces. I study my father's grim face, my head swimming. *WAR! What does that mean?*

Will Pa go to fight? Will we be invaded?

For nine days we wait to see if the Germans will invade. Uneasiness pervades the city. Everybody is in a hurry. The train station becomes crowded. People are leaving, their luggage piled high on trolleys. Shops begin to close, their windows boarded up with wooden planks, but we go on with our lives as if nothing has happened.

Pa says we should wait and see what happens. Our allies have promised to support us and stop the invasion.

Jo and I still go to the sports field after school to meet up with our friends.

One Friday afternoon, we make two teams with eight players per side and run onto the field. Jo shout orders. Filip and Jan, stand astride in the goal mouth while. Jo dribbles the ball, setting up an attack.

Plane engines roar above our heads.

Looking up we spot planes flying low in formation and begin to cheer. Jumping up and down with our hands in the air we call up to the sky, cheering the British planes.

"The Allies have come! They are here!" shouts Jo.

Air-raid sirens begin to wail in the city.

Air-raid? But…

Suddenly afraid, I look up at the planes, really look. And notice crosses on the wings. I look at Jo in horrified disbelief.

"They're Germans, not British!" Jo shouts. "Take cover!"

Then all hell breaks loose.

The German bombers fly low, spewing out bomb after bomb. We run to the edge of the field and dive into a deep ditch.

Burrowing our bodies in against the steep sides, we tuck our legs up to our chests and bury our heads between our knees.

A bomb explodes on the soccer field.

The younger boys scream in terror as another bomb explodes closer to the ditch. We press ourselves deeper into the mud, covering our ears.

It lasts minutes but feels like hours.

Finally, the bombardment stops.

Squinting through grit filled eyes, Jo and I look over the edge to see the smoky image of the last German bomber fading into the distance.

"I think it's the Do-17. A bloody big bastard!" Jo hoarsely

whispers.

Hearing rapid gun fire, we look up to see a Messerschmidt, a small German fighter, strafing the ground with its machine guns. It is flying over the soccer field, towards the ditch. Wrapping my arms even tighter around my head, I duck down and pray to the Virgin Mary to protect us. I look up to see Jo still peering over the edge, watching the plane coming closer.

"Get down you idiot!" I yell, yanking his shirt.

He squats down as bullets whiz over our heads. The barrage only lasts a moment before the plane lifts away and follows the bomber towards the horizon.

My ears are ringing, and I taste dirt in my mouth. Jo and I turn to face each other as billowing smoke drifts our way, filling our nostrils with an acrid stench. Thick flakes of ash fall around us, landing on our heads and shoulders. We are filthy, our clothes covered in mud.

The ground shakes from more explosions in the distance.

We scramble out of the ditch and peer down at the boys, still hiding there.

"Is anyone hurt?" Jo shouts.

Our friends slowly stand. Dazed.

They stare at us. Stunned.

"Our homes!" Jo yells.

He takes off running, back towards town.

"Oh my God! Ma and the girls!" I yell as I run after Jo.

His face is deathly white. We run as if a squadron of Messerschmitt is chasing us down.

Chapter

2

Weeding her garden, Ma hears planes approaching. Thinking it's the Polish air force, she doesn't take much notice, but when the roar of the engines tells her they are flying unusually low, she looks up and gasps. Instead of the Polish insignia of red and white squares, these planes have the German iron cross painted on their wings.

Throwing down her trowel and racing into the house, she makes the sign of the cross, begging the Virgin Mary to save her family. Dashing to the kitchen window with a feeling of dread, she clings to the sill and peers through the glass. Bursts of machine-gunfire pepper the ground, mowing down neighbours running towards their homes. Many fall to the ground, dead and bleeding, their groceries spilling over the pavement and into the gutter.

The Messerschmitt climb up to the sky, leaving a clear path for the German bombers to rain their deadly cargo onto the houses. Buildings are blown apart. Gardens and roads are suddenly a bewildering maze of smouldering craters. Billowing smoke from raging fires turn Sochaczew into a terrifying hell.

"Zaneta! Angelika!" Ma screams. "Take cover in the cellar!"

Zaneta and Angelika are sitting on the floor in their bedroom, knitting scarves.

They look around in confusion when they hear the air raid siren, followed by the explosions. Screaming with fright, they drop their needles to the floor and run around in circles, flapping their arms like distressed ducklings. Ma dashes up the stairs and pushes them out into the hallway.

"Get to the cellar! Now!" she screams at them again to be heard over the deafening noise. "We're under attack!"

The girls scamper down the stairs, Ma following close behind as the house shakes with every explosion, plaster dust raining on their heads.

Yanking up the cellar door, Ma flings it back with such force it smacks down hard, leaving a dent on the linoleum floor. She grips the back of their dresses, shoving them down the steps ahead of her.

"Get going! Get going!" she yells, grabbing the trapdoor behind her and slamming it shut.

The bombardment is unrelenting. Two doors down, a house erupts into a huge fireball, hurling pieces of slate, burning timber and broken bricks into the air. The shock wave rocks our house on its foundations, throwing Ma and the girls onto the cellar floor, coating them in dust. Coughing, they lift their heads to face each other, only to scream as another huge explosion booms above their heads.

Finally, the house settles with the occasional thud of falling timber.

Ma and the girls sit up and gaze around in bewilderment.

"Mama, are you okay?" Zaneta cries out, grabbing her mother's trembling hand.

Ma heaves in ragged breaths, "I'm alright Zaneta. How is Angelika?"

"I'm fine ... I'm fine!" Angelika splutters, spitting dirt from her mouth.

"We must get out!" exclaims Ma.

Still coughing and wiping their faces with their dresses, the girls clamber up the stairs only to find the door jammed from the outside. They look at each other in a wild panic and begin to scream. Ma mounts the steps behind them, yelling for them to stop. She grabs their arms, shaking them into silence.

"Don't just scream, you silly girls! Call for help!"

Hammering on the trapdoor with their fists, they start yelling.

"Someone please help!"

"We're stuck down here!"

"Help! Help!"

Struggling for air, they choke as thick smoke billows around them.

Gasping for breath, Ma sinks down on the step, clutching her chest.

#####

Jo and I dash into our street. Then skid to a halt. We stare in disbelief at the horror around us. For a moment we think we're in the wrong place.

House after house is either on fire or razed to the ground. Thick grey smoke streams into the sky, blocking the sun. Fires erupt amongst the rubble as walls crash to the ground.

We hear the sirens of fire trucks in the distance. People are screaming and running out of their homes. Some are in shock and stagger around, not knowing where to go.

It's a scene from Hell!

I stand there wide eyed, breathing hard.

Jo grabs my arm and drags me along. "Come on! Don't stop! We need to get home!"

We race to our house, slowing to a stop, our mouths gaping.

Our home is gone!

Black smouldering timbers have fallen on top of crumbling walls. Furniture burns where it lies. I recognise the sofa, and Ma's sideboard. They're piled high in a corner of what used to be the parlour. Burning. We jump back as more timbers crash to the floor and demolish the kitchen table. Our beds are on the top of a jumble of bedroom furniture in the middle of the room.

Ma and Pas' wardrobes and expensive gilded mirror are smashed to pieces, all mixed up with the broken shards of Ma's precious plates.

Clambering over the smouldering wreckage of what was once the kitchen we frantically call out, thinking the worst.

"Where are they?" yells Jo.

I scramble to where I believe the cellar door is and can just make out faint voices coming through the rubble. I desperately clear a mound of bricks and mortar away.

Jo joins me but it's piled high. The cellar door is completely jammed.

Jo squats down and thumps the exposed floorboards.

"Are you all okay!"

A faint voice calls out from the cellar.

"No! Mama has collapsed on the stairs! There is a lot of smoke! Get us out! There is a fire! Get us out now!"

Pan Kalinski, our next-door neighbour, appears at his back

doorway rubbing his face. He squints against the smoke haze, looking befuddled and confused. Scratching the top of his balding head, making his remaining hair stick up on end, he takes a swig from a vodka bottle and glances our way. He slowly lowers the bottle, his eyes growing wide with astonishment.

"Are you okay boys?" he yells. "Where is your Ma?"

"We're okay! But Ma and our sisters are trapped in the cellar," I yell back. "We need help to get them out!"

Wearing a grubby plaid shirt half tucked into worn, faded corduroy trousers, he stumbles down his broken steps.

Hitching up his waistband, he grabs a shovel standing upright in a garden bed and swings it over his shoulder. Draining the last few drops, he tosses the empty vodka bottle towards a pile of garbage. After a few more steps he stumbles over a pile of broken bricks, landing on his knees. Heaving and grunting, he struggles to stand, his fat stomach wobbling with the effort.

Gasping and swearing, he leans on his shovel.

"Don't worry! I'm coming! I'm coming!"

Shouting in a booming voice, he staggers over a pile of timber and lumbers toward us.

"I'm here to help Pani Muszynska! I'm here to help!"

Pan Kalinski, Jo and I work steadily, tossing aside bricks. We expose a smouldering beam lying across the cellar door and wedge bits of timber under the charred wood, rolling it to the side. Running out to the garden, Jo finds another shovel and helps the big man clear the remaining debris from the cellar door.

Tendrils of smoke filter ominously from the trapdoor,

making us even more frantic until it's cleared. Pan Kalinski sits on his haunches and pries the door open with his bare hands. As he lifts it, broken mortar slides down into a heap near our feet. Billowing black smoke escapes from the opening. Holding his free arm across his face, Jo reaches for the girls. They fall onto the floor where they lie coughing and sobbing with relief. Pan Kalinski pulls the door open further, slamming it right back with a crash.

Straining, he lies down and reaches into the cellar, his large balding head and shaggy beard disappearing into the hole. He sees Ma struggling up the steps, trying to grasp the railings along the wall.

"I've come to rescue you Pani Muszynska," he shouts. "Do not worry, I've come to rescue you! Come on up, Panni Muszynska. I'm here to rescue you!"

He grabs our mother's outstretched arm and guides her out, grunting and sweating as he pulls himself up onto his knees.

Ma emerges covered in grey dust, fighting for breath. Tears run down her grimy face as she clings to Jo and sobs, her dress torn and singed in places.

Gently, Pan Kalinski leads her to a garden bench, near the overturned bird bath, and both sit down wearily.

Jo places a bucket under the garden pump and fills it halfway, then sets it down at Ma's feet. We watch her wash her face and pat herself dry with her apron. Slowly she looks around then stands to face the wreckage of her home.

"Oh my God! Oh my God!" she gasps. "Sweet Mary help us!"

We turn to gaze in horror at the destruction.

Angelica clutches Ma's arm, "There's nothing left!

Everything is burning! Our house is gone!"

We survey the rest of the neighbourhood, aghast. It looks like Armageddon. The end of the world.

Nearly all the houses in our street are on fire with our neighbours desperately trying to put them out.

We hear anguished cries and grief-stricken screams amongst the bombed houses as the injured and the dead are discovered.

Fire trucks, parked along the adjoining street, flash red lights into the smoky gloom. The firemen try desperately to extinguish a huge blaze engulfing a large apartment block. The flames reach high into the sky, filling it with ash and smoke.

"Bloody Krauts!" roars Pan Kalinski as he pulls himself off the bench and looks up, shaking his fist in the air.

Ma pats his arm.

"Now, now Igor! You are frightening the girls

And think of your heart. You could put a strain on it by shouting like that. Sit down and take a few breaths."

A few minutes later, Pan Kalinski slowly stands and gently pulls Ma up. She kisses his cheek, making his face glow red.

"Thank you, Igor for helping the boys."

He kisses her hand and shambles back to his shabby house, which surprisingly escaped the bombing and mounts his back steps, slamming his door behind him.

We find more buckets in the garden shed, fill them with water and wander through the wreckage to put out small fires. The one in the parlour has died down to smouldering embers, but we allow the fire in the collapsed cellar to burn.

Ma stands on the charred back steps, pointing to the shed.

"Find the wheelbarrow! Fill it with anything you can find. I'll fetch your Pa!"

Looking a lot older than her thirty-three years, Ma clutches the stone wall for support as she walks unsteadily past the neighbours. She looks forlorn. Destitute. The back of her dress is stained black from soot. Her sleeve is torn in places and one of her stockings has rolled down to her ankle.

We watch her walk away, her feet dragging.

"Can I go instead, Mama?" Zaneta calls out.

Ma turns to face her.

"No... No, Zaneta. You stay with the others. I'll be alright!"

She wipes the tears from her cheeks and smooths back her hair; and stands a little taller. My heart aches for her.

We managed to find two cooking pots, a frying pan, kitchen utensils, our winter coats, some clothes for all of us, a few framed photos, a ball of string and the girl's sewing baskets. The rest of our household goods were either too big to carry or were destroyed in the explosion. I find my soccer ball and place it, still pumped up, on top of the pile in the barrow. I put a small piece of Ma's mirror into my pocket to give to her later.

Ma gets a lift with Pan Wojcik in his old truck. He is heading into town to look for his daughter who works at the same department store as Pa. An hour later, she returns with Pa covered in blood, holding a cloth to his head.

Rushing up to him, Jo grabs his coat sleeve.

"Pa! What happened?"

Pa draws in a long breath, taking the cloth away we notice the gash above his eye.

"We heard the air-raid siren, and were heading for the basement," he recalls. "When the store was hit, I stayed back to help some of the stragglers who were injured from the blast.

I was the last to go down the basement steps when there was another explosion out the back. I think it was a fuel tank. Anyway, something hit my forehead and I'm lucky it didn't strike my eye!"

We look at the blood still trickling down his face. Pa wipes his forehead and cheek, then looks down, regarding us affectionately with his green eyes.

As Pa turns his gaze and looks at the wreckage his face turns white, his eyes awash with tears.

"Antoniya! Our lovely home! Did anything get saved?" he asks in a croaky voice.

"Only what's in the wheelbarrow Papa," Angelika answers for Ma.

Wiping his eyes Pa looks at the barrow, shaking his head in disbelief.

Ma grabs his arm.

"Wladyslaw," she pleads, "we should go to my sister's farm!"

Pa picks up a cup belonging to a tea set, a wedding present from his mother, and places it carefully into the wheelbarrow. He slowly shakes his head.

"I must report to my old cavalry unit," he says firmly. "There is no time to lose."

We all speak at once.

Pulling at his arm, Ma argues with him and starts to cry. Pa pats her hand.

"Don't worry, Antoniya dear. I'll be alright. I'll get a lift with Tomasz. Go to the farm with the children, and I'll get back to you there with news. I must join my old regiment, my dear. I must fight for Poland. It's my duty."

"Please Wladyslaw, stay with us!" Ma implores, looking up at him.

He pulls her into a hug, placing his chin on top of her head. "Now, now Antoniya! You will be safe with your sister. The boys will look after you and the girls."

She continues to cry with her face buried in his jacket. I look away, feeling sad for my mother. It looks like she'll have to cope on her own.

I remember overhearing Pa and Uncle Tomasz planning to re-enlist if the Germans invaded Poland. They talked about it a couple of weeks ago well into the night, while drinking vodka in the parlour. But they both delayed joining the army. The war didn't seem real. It was the bombing today that spurred my father to join up at last.

Incredulous, I look at him. I can already imagine the German tanks grinding along the city's streets and the Luftwaffe bombing us once more.

Pa is abandoning us to our fate.

How can he, Uncle Tomasz and the Polish Army honestly think the Polish cavalry, who still use horses, can defeat the German tanks?

How can Pa be so stupid, believing we won't be in any danger at Auntie's place or, that the Polish army could push back the Germans without help from other countries?

Ma sits quietly on the stone bench, staring at her wrecked garden. Uncle Thomasz pulls up in his old, beat-up Fiat 508 with the front headlight smashed in and a deep scratch along the bonnet.

Pa slides into the passenger's side and greets our uncle with a handshake, slamming the door shut. We stand amongst the ruins in silence while Ma turns away from him, tears running down her face.

I curse my father under my breath.

As the car moves slowly up the street, exhaust smoke spilling out the back, I keep my thoughts to myself and once again wander around the ruins with Jo.

Panni Wojcik, a kind, stout woman walks across the road and sits next to Ma. Holding her hand, they talk quietly.

After a few minutes Ma calls out, asking if we collected any eiderdowns. Being children, we hadn't, believing it wasn't important.

Digging around the wreckage we find five smoke-soiled quilts in an overturned cupboard and put them on top of the pile.

Wearily, we follow Ma and Panni Wojcik back to her house, pushing the laden barrow in the fading light. The sunset is a deep red glow through the smoke haze. Golden rays pierce deep purple clouds. I sigh. On another day it would be spectacular, but right now, its beauty is lost on us.

Ma insists Jo and I wash outside, using the pump. She scrubs the dirt out of our clothes and hangs them to dry in front of Pani Wojcik's kitchen stove, still lit from the evening meal. Wrapped in our eiderdowns, smelling of smoke, our stomachs full of Pani Wojcik's potato soup, we gaze into the flickering fire and whisper about the day's events.

Zaneta yawns and Ma tells us all to lie down.

"I know it's uncomfortable, but this is the warmest place in the house. It will be cold tonight," she whispers, tucking the bedding around us, kissing us on the brow.

"Now try to sleep, all of you," she soothes. "We have a big day tomorrow."

Rising unsteadily to her feet, with her back towards us, she grasps the kitchen bench and leans heavily against it. Dipping her head, she weeps silently, her shoulders heaving with each sob. I roll onto my side and stare at the backdoor leading outside. Tears run down my face as I imagine my home as it used to be with Ma's garden in full bloom and the front door painted a bright red, against a backdrop of flowering pot plants.

I pull the covers over my head and drift into a restless sleep.

CHAPTER

3

Next morning, we take turns pushing the wheelbarrow to the station, to catch a train to Auntie's place near Tomaszów Mazowiecki, about a hundred kilometres southwest from Sochaczew. We've been visiting Auntie for as long as I can remember, staying for weeks in the summer holidays.

Reluctantly, we leave the wheelbarrow outside the station. Bundling our belongings into our eiderdowns, we tie them with string, making five sacks for each of us. As we walk off, Ma gives the wheelbarrow an appreciative pat. It has served her well the last few years.

The platform is overcrowded with people, their belongings stuffed into suitcases, baskets and sacks. Far too many cram into the carriage, sitting squashed in seats or in the aisles, peering vacantly into space or out the windows.

We push our way to the back where an old man moves his battered suitcases into the overhead baggage rack, allowing Ma and the girls to sit down. Jo pushes the girl's sacks under the seat as I wedge the remaining three along the aisle.

The children are unnaturally quiet. They cling to their parents, staring, bewildered, around the carriage. The only sound is the urgent whimpering from hungry babies, hushed and soothed by their mothers.

Ma slumps against Zaneta who holds her close. Angelika takes her hand. Jo and I stand in the aisle, grabbing the back of their seats as the carriage begins to jerk forward. The train crawls along the tracks, picking up speed as we leave Sochaczew behind.

I stare through the carriage window to the smoke covered sky. A stench of burning fills the destroyed city. Eerie light filters through the smoke-clouds. My heart sinks. Deep sorrow gnaws at my chest. I look around the carriage and notice most of the passengers staring out the windows, many weeping openly for their lost homes. Their lost lives.

Silently, I curse the Germans.

As passengers disembark at stations along the way, Jo and I are relieved to find seats on the carriage floor, with our knees up and our backs against the seats.

The trip takes most of the day.

The train slows to a stop and the engines hiss into silence. We stand and stretch, then look outside. Only to find it's not Tomaszów Mazowiecki, but a small-town kilometres away from our destination.

I recognise it from previous trips. The conductor makes his way through the carriages, shouting instructions.

"The railway lines were bombed further up the line. You will have to make your own way to the city!"

Disembarking onto the narrow platform, passengers jostle for space, pull on overcoats and organise luggage.

In this chaos, Ma helps us put the sacks on our backs and slings a smaller bag and her own sack over her shoulder.

Normally we would have made a fuss, groaning and complaining loudly. But we are too tired and weary to protest at the news of more German destruction. Instead, we stoically descend the platform steps and march along the bustling main road already full of army trucks, tanks, jeeps and fleeing people.

The convoy of trucks passing us is German.

The enemy.

Murmuring rebelliously, we all move off the road and allow it to pass. A few old men spit on the ground, muttering to themselves and cursing under their breaths.

We stand on the verge of the road and stare as the trucks speed past with little regard for the hundreds of refugees. People scatter as the vehicles plough through the throng. The drivers blast their horns and shout obscenities.

German soldiers, in the back of the trucks, glare back at us. A couple of Krauts gesture rudely at Ma and the girls.

Jo swears under his breath, and I imagine giving them the finger. But only in my imagination, knowing I could get shot if I do so.

Within an hour the tired girls start to cry.

Ma tries to distract us by talking about farm, making us laugh when she recounts the antics of Auntie's cats. But Ma's starting to limp, and her stories soon stop.

We sit down now and then to rest on the side of the road. When Jo pulls Ma up to continue the journey, she finds it hard to stand.

Taking off her shoes we see her heels rubbed raw with bloody blisters. Carefully she places her shoes back on wincing with pain.

Zaneta takes Ma's smaller bag and drapes it over her shoulders.

Jo and I split the contents of Ma's sack and add it to our own, including her quilt. We carry the four sacks without complaint as the girls support Ma, each holding onto an elbow. A small group of women and children walk with us, dragging suitcases or pushing prams piled high. A couple talk to Ma about their homes and their men going to war. A large woman complains about the lack of good coffee available in the shops, followed by an animated discussion about the price of bread.

A canvas covered farm truck trundles up the road behind us. The driver honks his horn for us to clear the road. We're too slow, and he is forced to stop. He pokes his head out the window, waving his arm, shooing the group of women and children out of his way.

"Come on. Hurry up, you lot," he calls out in Polish, with not a hint of a German accent. "Out of my way!"

Ma is tired.

Her feet hurt something awful.

She's afraid of the Germans.

Already grumpy and desperate to get us to safety, anger boils up inside her. She turns to face him.

Hands on hips, her sore, aching feet braced, she stands her ground.

"Come on ladies," the driver pleads. "Before another bloody German convoy comes along."

He rubs his face with his grimy hand. "My farm is on the other side of the city, and I want to get home before dark."

"You want to get home before dark!" Ma growls, "before another German convoy comes along!" She mimics sarcastically. "So do we, mister, but unless some kind gentleman with a truck stops and gives us a lift, we have no hope of that."

She hobbles to the side of the cab and thumps on the door.

"Mister, look at us! We're women and children who've been bombed out of our homes, not some passing church parade!" She reads pity in his face, and reins in her burst of temper.

"We're in dire need. Children will die if we can't get them to safety."

Ma reaches up and grabs his arm.

"Please sir," she pleads, "it's too far for the little ones to walk, and they're too heavy for us to carry."

The women crowd in behind Ma, backing her up, adding their pleas to hers.

"We're not asking much. All we're asking for is a lift into Tomaszów Mazowiecki." calls out one lady, her head wrapped in an old scarf.

"That's right, mister, just as far as Tomaszów Mazowiecki" calls another. "Do it for the children, and we'll bless you forever."

"Please, sir, my mother lives in Tomaszów Mazowiecki. It won't even take you out of your way," pipes up a young woman.

"Imagine if these were your children?" Ma adds.

Overwhelmed, the besieged Polish farmer gazes into the grim, pleading faces of the desperate women and children.

He nods. Slowly. More in understanding of what the German invasion has done to his homeland, than in acceding to their pleas, but that's all the agreement Ma needs.

"Thank you! You're a good man." she says, shaking his hand.

"Thank you!"

"Blessings on your head, sir!"

While the other women chorus their fervent thanks, Ma gestures to Jo and me to help the women and their children climb into the back.

"Quickly," she urges. "In case he changes his mind."

She and the girls clamber up, only when she's sure their companions are safely aboard.

Sighing with relief, Ma sits on the hard bench built along the side, kicks off her shoes and examines her heels once more.

Exhausted, our sisters slump beside her, rubbing their arms. Jo and I are the last to climb in, swinging the sacks off our backs onto the floor. Wedging them under the wooden seat, we sit down. I rub my shoulders and move back a bit, allowing more leg room for Jo. A woman bangs the truck's cab. The driver grates its gears, throwing us all sideways. Ma yells at him to be more careful.

The weather is changing. Glancing at the sky I see dark clouds building up. Wind billows the canvas sides, making them flap. It starts to rain. Jo ties the leaky canvas closed as the children huddle together, trying to keep warm and dry. Some begin to cry, complaining about being hungry.

Ma pulls out bread and salami from one of our sacks and shares the food between us and the other children. Several other women do the same. We eat in silence.

"Bless you! We have no food for the journey," says a woman, her hair tied back with a tattered scarf.

She stifles a sob. "My children are starving and there is nothing I can do! We hid in a ditch outside our fence when we heard the planes, and I had no time to collect anything at all."

She begins to cry, wiping her cheeks with her grimy hands

and takes in a quivering breath. "Our house was the first in our street to be bombed! There was nothing left! Nothing!"

"I know how you feel," Ma murmurs, patting her back, "but we must have strength to get through this no matter what the Germans throw at us. We must be strong for our children."

The woman nods, smiling weakly, then wipes her little girl's face with a rag pulled out of her pocket.

Ma and the girls doze, their heads nodding with the sway of the truck. I try to stay awake. But now and then my head falls back against someone's legs, waking me with a start. I'm woken up for the umpteenth time by Jo shaking me. He has peeled the canvas back once again and is looking through the gap.

"I wonder where they are all going?"

Bleary eyed, I look at the people on the road.

"I don't know Jo, maybe they have family to go to like us."

I close my eyes once more, but sleep escapes me. I become absorbed in my own thoughts. I wonder about Auntie. Is she's okay? I'm sure she is. She's a tough woman. My thoughts drift to the warm summer days, we've spent on her little farm, fishing and swimming in the river.

A white picket fence needing a coat of paint surrounds her house, enclosing the sparse front garden. Overgrown bushes grow along the sides of the house. Lanky, unpruned rose bushes, a long-ago gift from Ma, struggle to survive on either side of the narrow pathway leading to the chipped and scratched front door.

I suppose the rambling two-storey building is still dull and grey, the window frames unvarnished. The gabled roof, covered in green moss, most probably has missing shingles and the windows are sure to still be grimy with dust.

I smile. Auntie's house is the most drab, ugly and unkempt building I've ever known. But her farm has always been productive, feeding her and her close neighbour, Pan Tolinski, for years.

I've never known anyone as self-sufficient as Auntie. She raises chickens, grows vegetables and tends a small orchard that grows sweet apples. I wonder if she still has the six nanny goats she milks every morning, or the grumpy old billy goat, and if she kept the horse she bought at the markets.

We had turns riding the mare around the paddock the day Auntie bought it, until she dug in her hooves and refused to budge. Auntie told us she was too old to be ridden and needed her strength to pull a cart. She was the only one who rode in the cart, venturing out every Saturday to sell her goat cheese to local grocery stores.

She would tell us stories about her first husband. The love of her life, he was killed in the First World War.

Three years later she married an older man who owned the farm. She said he was more like a brother to her than a husband. He died a few years ago from tuberculosis. I overheard her telling Ma she missed having a man around the house, but we knew she really didn't mind being on her own with her cats and farm animals.

Jo is gazing outside with his back towards me. He doesn't like Auntie's cats. Two summers ago, he fell down the stairs in her house, nearly breaking his leg. He'd lost his balance when he stood on an old tabby cat sleeping on the top step. Tumbling to the bottom, he banged his head and twisted his ankle. The cat flew into one of the bedrooms and wasn't seen for hours.

There was a lot of yelling that day with Auntie blaming Jo for being so clumsy and nearly killing old Tom, and Jo cursing the bloody thing. It didn't seem to matter to Auntie if Jo was injured, so long as Old Tom was alright. Jo had bruises for weeks.

It was the same summer I had a run-in with her old billy goat.

Whenever we walked past Old Billy's paddock, he charged, straining his rope almost to breaking point. Bleating loudly, he would paw the ground, his head bent low, threatening us with his huge horns.

The mean bastard took a special dislike to me.

Perhaps because I teased him mercilessly.

Thinking back, it was one of the most embarrassing days of my life when I had my ill-fated encounter with Old Billy.

One sunny afternoon I took the fishing rod and basket from the barn, determined to catch some pike for dinner.

I head for the river. Jo decided to stay back at the house to help Auntie make goat's cheese and paczki.

I passed Billy's paddock, the old goat, as usual, tugging on his rope, head down to charge. I picked up a stick, waving it about. This made the brute even more angry. He tossed his head, pawing the ground. Laughing, I banged the stick against the fence post, then continued my way.

Casting out a line, I settled into the long grass on the riverbank, and quietly watched the reflections of the willow trees on the still water as a swallow darted after insects.

Before long, there was a hard tug on the line. I stood, reeling it in, anticipating a big fish on the other end. But the next moment I was flying through the air. Dropping the rod, I landed on my face. The rod slid along the bank then went slack as the fish got away.

The goat trotted along the river, the broken rope trailing behind him, ready for another go. He snorted loudly, lowered his head and charged again. Dodging his huge horns and throwing myself sideways, I landed in oozing, foul-smelling mud near the edge of the water, my face half buried in the slimy muck.

This seemed to satisfy the old coot. He ran up the embankment, back to his paddock.

Rising unsteadily to my feet, I wiped my face with my shirt sleeve and swore, then picked up my fishing gear and headed back to the house.

Feeling foolish, I stood at the kitchen doorway covered in mud. Everyone went into hysterics. Ma had tears running down her face and Auntie rushed outside to the toilet. Jo and the girls fell against each other in fits of laughter.

Auntie returned, wiping her hands and face with her apron.

"What happened, Rys?" she asked between gasps.

"Old Billy broke his rope and butted me in the ass!" I whimpered.

"I fell in the mud, near the bulrushes!"

Jo guffawed.

The girls pulled their aprons over their heads and giggled.

Ma tried to suppress her laughter but failed.

"I'll get a new rope and re-tie Billy," Auntie chuckled.

"Go and have a bath, Rys," Ma tittered. "You're a bit on the nose!"

This made everyone scream with laughter once again.

That night I decided to get even with the old bastard.

The following afternoon I headed back to the river, with Jo in tow.

On the riverbank I waved my arms about, hooting and hollering, until the beast lowered his head and pounded the earth with his hooves. Jo, as instructed, untied the rope from the post.

Old Billy, feeling the rope slacken, charged towards me, determined to cause mortal harm.

At the last minute I swivelled like a Spanish matador as he bolted past. His horns brushed the side of my leg, tearing my pants. Billy went head-first into the river, the rope trailing behind him.

Only I didn't take his momentum into account. He ended up in the middle of the river where there was a fast-flowing current.

Bleating frantically, he was swept away in the turbulence, his head emerging and submerging as the water swirled around him. I remember yelling, encouraging him to keep afloat and Jo running up, cursing our stupidity.

In a panic we ran along the riverbank.

"Oh my God! … Oh my God Jo!" I screamed, "Old Billy is Auntie's prize goat! She's going to kill me!"

"I know! … I know, Rys! She'll have both our guts for garters!"

We ran harder.

The goat struggled to the other side of the river, finding his footing on hard ground. Bedraggled, he slowly pulled himself up the bank and shook his coat. The water sprayed in a wide arc as the wet rope flicked from side to side.

He staggered along to a bridge a hundred metres upstream,

where we met him trotting along on stiff, unsteady legs, bleating mournfully. Jo picked up the rope and walked him back to his paddock. Where the poor beast lay exhausted, willing to be tied up.

Cautiously, I went up to him, knelt and patted his neck.

I will never forget the way he lifted his head to gaze into my eyes, totally defeated.

By way of guilty apology, I fed him a carrot or an apple every time I passed. It was a stupid prank. He could have died.

Thinking back, I caught a lot of fish that summer with Old Billy nearby in his paddock. By the end of the holiday, he became quite friendly. Old Billy bleated a welcome whenever I approached his post and handed him something to eat, letting me stroke his large, majestic horns. I told him they are the most awesome horns I'd ever seen. He would toss them around when he'd had enough petting, then nuzzle my hand.

From that day, I had no more trouble from the old coot. In fact, I grew to like him.

Now that I think about it, making Billy my friend was easy. All I had to do was show some respect and give a little praise.

#####

I'm jolted out of my reverie as the truck hits a pothole. It throws me back, hitting Angelika's legs. She pushes me off with a grunt.

"That hurt, Rys!

"Sorry!" I say, looking up to her.

I look out over the tailgate.

The truck slows down because of the heavy traffic, arriving

at the outskirts of Tomaszów Mazowiecki a while later. The driver slams on the brakes a few times, waking Ma and Angelika. They sit up, bleary-eyed, then doze off again.

Jo and I keep watch outside. It's twilight. A chill wind blows into our faces, making us shiver.

Farmlands full of crops, ready for the Autumn harvest, fan out towards the distant horizon. The moon is large and full as it slowly rises in the evening sky, above the flat plains.

Ma bangs on the back window and asks the driver to stop at an intersection where one of the roads leads to Auntie's farm. Jo and I jump down, stretch out our arms to help Ma and the girls off, then drag out the sacks from under the bench.

Thanking the driver and bidding farewell to the other passengers, who yell encouragement, wishing us good luck, we watch the truck pull away. Jo and I heft the heavy sacks onto our shoulders while Ma shuffles along the road, moaning in agony.

Once more the girls support her, gripping her arms. We walk slowly. Ma stops every few minutes, panting, then continues on.

"I've had enough," she states as she shuffles to a stop once more. "These shoes are killing me. I'm taking them off!"

Carefully, she peels each shoe off her bleeding feet and tucks them into her bag, then hobbles barefoot along the tarmac.

"Ah, that's better," she sighs and wiggles her toes.

"But I'm still finding it hard to walk," she grumbles. "Girls, you have to help me."

The girls grab her elbows and lead her along the verge of the road where the ground is a lot softer.

We finally come to a gravel lane, leading down to the river where an old farmhouse is perched on a small rise. We spot Auntie standing outside her rickety old gate, squinting at us in the evening gloom.

Recognising us, her face lights up. She quickly waddles to Ma, engulfing her in her large fleshy arms and kissing her on the cheeks.

Jo and I drop the sacks with a sigh as the girls slump against the fence. Zaneta peels Ma's bag off her shoulder and dumps it at her feet.

Auntie releases Ma and in turn squashes us to her ample bosom, until we can't breathe.

Anxiously, she turns to Ma.

"What happened Antoniya?"

Tears stream down Ma's face as she recounts the last two days.

"Oh, my lord! Your lovely home! I can't believe it!" Auntie cries.

"Well not to worry. You are all welcome to stay here for as long as you like."

She swings open the gate and holds it open as we pass her.

"I'll get your bedrooms ready," she says briskly in her high squeaky voice. "Jo and Rys, you two will be in the attic. Girls, you can sleep in your mother's bedroom. I'll make coffee, hot milk and how about some paczki, aye?"

Auntie gasps, as she notices blood dripping from Ma's bare feet.

"Oh my God! Why are you barefoot? What is wrong with your feet? Ah ... Don't worry! Don't worry! I'll get some cool water from the outside pump, and you can soak them."

Ma nods wearily and slowly climbs the porch steps. Auntie

scurries to the front door, leading her into the house. We follow behind, our sacks dragging behind us on the ground.

I look back at Auntie in the doorway. She's a plump woman, her large stomach pushing against her apron. Her kind round face and sparkling brown eyes shrewdly consider us all as we pass into her warm kitchen. She wears her dark hair in braids twirled around her head, the same style as Ma's. The sisters look alike. They are both short, with olive complexions, and straight, shiny, dark hair.

However, Auntie is far more talkative. I don't think she takes many breaths between words.

Ma relaxes as Auntie chatters non-stop. The girls sit, listening to every word. Jo and I get stuck into the paczki she's made. I love Auntie, in spite of the cats. She always greets us with hugs, a plate of paczki and hot milk, and treats us as if we are her own children.

A few days after our arrival we have settled into a routine. We all have chores to do.

The girl's job is to feed the chooks and keep their room tidy. Ma and Auntie tend the vegetable garden and milk the goats. Jo and I clean out the horse's stall, feed and rub down the horse and check on Old Billy. When everything is done, Jo and I play with the soccer ball in the next field, away from

Billy, while the girls play hopscotch on a concrete slab where a milking shed once stood.

At the end of the week Ma announces that on Monday we will be attending new schools in Tomaszów Mazowiecki.

4

On our first day of school, we're late catching the bus.

Yelling like idiots, we chase the old banger down the road with the kids in the back window, yelling and waving. The driver slows to change gears. Jo thumps the side of the bus for him to stop. Catching our breaths. we climb on board with everyone cheering. Jo salutes the crowd. Our sisters go red. I give a deep bow. Despite this warm welcome, the driver curses under his breath and grinds the gears.

"Don't be so bloody late next time," he snarls as he turns the bus onto the road.

Jo back-answers him. I spit out a crude word and our sisters poke out their tongues behind his back.

The journey takes an hour as the bus twists and turns into numerous side streets picking up students. It finally pulls into a parking lane in front of a pair of iron gates.

I sit up straight and peer through the grimy window at our new school. Built side by side, both the primary school and high school are made of the same dark brown brick.

Concrete paths connect the two main entrances which look identical, except for the kindergarten artwork displayed inside a large window.

Kids of all ages play on the asphalt in front of the school.

The older kids, about my age and over, gather in groups or sit on benches while the younger ones play skip and ball games.

Both schools are surrounded by a tall brick wall, curving at the street corners. Beyond it, I can just see playing fields at the back of the High School. One with a soccer net and another with a running track. I see boys running on both fields, chasing a ball. Smiling, I think this school might suit me.

Stepping off the bus, I flatten myself against the brick wall, making room for two women to rush past. The paths are narrow on both sides of the street, only allowing two people to walk abreast.

Horse drawn carts piled high with farm produce mount the gutter now and then, to avoid the speeding black cars, all flying swastikas.

German army trucks honk their horns as they make their way through the throng of pedestrians. Small shops line the street with people bustling in and out of doorways.

A grocery shop, opposite the school, catches my eye and I decide to check it out later.

School is boring. Pan Nowak, my home teacher, is boring.

I sit at the back of the class and listen to him prattle on for what seems hours as I peer through the window. A soccer game is in progress. My interest peaks. There seem to be some good players.

When the bell rings for lunch I race to the field where I meet a couple of lads my age already kicking the ball around.

"Care to play?" one asks.

"You bet!" I reply.

Jo joins us in a game.

Sport follows lunch, so the afternoon isn't as bad as the morning.

The grocery store across the road is where everyone hangs out to buy sweets and milkshakes after school.

The store is packed with everything you could ever need - fruit, vegetables, pickles, cans of beef, bread, sweets and homemade ice cream.

We saunter into the shop where a plump, jovial man greets us with a smile and a comment on the weather. He studies us over the rim of small spectacles perched on the end of his long nose and stands behind the counter near a group of young girls examining glass jars full of sweets. The shop is packed with students either drinking soda, thumbing through magazines or generally chatting as they share their candy.

Leaving the younger girls to make their choices, he moves along the counter towards us, wiping his hands on his pristine white apron.

"Good afternoon boys. You are new, I think? Can I help you?"

"We are," I reply. "We were bombed out and came to live with our Auntie. Could we have some candy canes, please?"

"Certainly. How many?" he asks.

"Oh, two sticks will do and a bag of jellybeans for our sisters, please."

The grocer nods and measures the sweets into a bag.

Jo pays, politely thanking the man.

"Welcome to Tomaszów Mazowiecki, boys."

The grocer holds out his hand. Jo shakes it.

"My name is Benjamin Loftmann and I'm pleased to meet you."

"Jo and Rys Muszyński," says Jo, pointing at himself and nodding at me.

Smiling, I shake his hand, too. He smiles back.

Later, Auntie tells us she knows the shopkeeper, Pan Loftmann, well. She once asked him for currants and with great difficulty he purchased some from the middle east. Because of the lengthy delay, he also gave her a bag of ground almonds. She was thrilled and praised him to all her friends and to anyone else she met in his shop. Sometimes, he would deliver her groceries to the farm in his old, red van, taking payment in the goat cheese and pickles she made.

On his deliveries, we watch him crank the handle of his van to get it started.

It is rare to see vans in Poland as most people have horses and carts. Only the very rich have cars. But I think Pan Loftmann might have bought this van from the old Jewish man who once owned the shop, years ago. The old van sputters and coughs then roars into life, making Pan Loftmann break into a smile. Pleased with himself he pats the red painted sides then squeezes into the driver's seat, honking the horn as he drives away.

#####

As the weeks pass, there is progressively less stock in his shop. Gone are the candy canes and ice cream bins.

The cans on the shelves are spread out and the bags of flour and sugar are smaller in size.

The piles of vegetables are now reduced to only a dozen cane baskets. Supplies are low due to the Germans taking most of Poland's food for their troops.

At lunch time, or on the weekends, we use the school's sports fields to play soccer. Jo and I join the school's soccer team and we both play wing on sports day. On the weekends, we bike ride to the field and play any position, then hang out with our new friends.

#####

Except for playing Soccer, I don't like school very much. I misbehave in class a lot.

One afternoon, Pan Nowak orders me to sit in the front row next to the girl I threw a paper aeroplane at, hitting the back of her head.

Scowling, I glare at her.

She turns and looks at me for a fleeting moment.

My heart skips a beat.

She is beautiful. Her hair glows with golden streaks from the light shining through the window, and curls around her head like a halo. Her skin is tanned by the summer sun which has sprinkled tiny freckles across her cheeks. Luminous brown eyes, framed with dark eyelashes, look up at me in puzzlement. She frowns, but then smiles. It is the most heavenly smile I've ever seen, and I automatically smile back, my heart pounding in my chest.

I can't take my eyes off her lovely face. Then I remember the paper plane and grimace.

"Oh, I'm so sorry about the paper plane! Did I hurt you?"

"I'm fine," she giggles. "You have a good aim."

"What is your name?" I whisper, leaning into her. I smell a

wonderful scent of roses.

"Helena." She smiles sweetly. "What's your name?"

"Ryszard. But everybody calls me Rys."

She moves closer to me, "I think I'll call you Ryszard. I like it better than Rys."

I grin back, lost in her enchanting eyes.

She leans forward, speaking in hushed tones.

"I've seen you and your brother on the soccer field when I ride my bike around with my friends."

"Oh! I remember you! You ride a yellow bicycle," I recall. "You have a lot of friends!"

Helena smiles and dips her head in a nod. I think she even blushes a little.

Ah, I am in love.

Smiling, mesmerised by her loveliness, I don't realise Pan Nowak is quietly standing at my desk.

Startled, I peer up at him as he glowers down at me. *Ah shit!*

His red moustache twitches as his beady, green eyes drill into mine.

"Are you quite finished chatting with Helena?"

I slowly nod. "Sorry sir!"

He takes a deep breath and exhales slowly. "I put you here for a reason, Ryszard. Helena can be a good influence on you. You've been giving me a lot of trouble lately. Sitting at the front next to Helena is the best option for me and for you!"

Ahh! He has no idea what 'trouble' I can be, It's my middle name.

\#\#\#\#\#

Over the winter months, Helena and I become firm friends. She lends me her books to copy and in return I sharpen all her pencils before the start of the school day. She has the sharpest pencils in the whole school, which makes her girlfriends quite envious.

From that day onwards, I get lots of praise from Pan Nowak, for 'having up to date book work'. I think he is surprised by my scholarly efforts and seems pleased he sat me with Helena.

But I still give him trouble.

Sometimes, I launch the occasional paper spit ball propelled by an elastic band I stole from his desk. I have a good range from where I sit. Helena giggles when my aim is true and my missile hits Pan Nowak on the back of the head, making him turn from the blackboard, scowling. Glaring around the room he glowers at me, knowing full well I am the culprit.

I sit up straight, my eyes wide with angelic innocence, looking completely guilt-free. I had lots of practice at my old school. Helena pretends to pick up a pencil from the floor, smothering her giggles. Pan Nowak growls and gives me the evil eye, then goes back to writing on the board.

One day he catches me. For once my aim is off. The spit ball hits the blackboard and slides down the maths question, leaving a slimy trail of saliva over the chalk.

I'm too busy loading up another one to realise Pan Nowak is standing next to me. He growls, "Got ya.", grabs my collar and yanks me up, marching me to his desk.

Snatching his cane from the blackboard he lifts my outstretched hand and gives me three whacks across my palm. I cry out with each strike and grip my stinging hand under my armpit.

Grimacing, I slowly return to my desk. Helena looks at me, pity reflected in her eyes, and searches for my stinging hand, holding it for the rest of the lesson.

My behaviour finally improves when Pan Nowak becomes our soccer coach giving us good pointers on passing and defending the ball. He trains us after school, and occasionally, at lunchtime, joins us on the soccer field for a short game.

Over time I come to like him.

#####

Helena is a Jew, and her father is Pan Loftmann, the grocery store owner.

It is shortly after we meet Pan Loftmann that Jo and I come into the store and see Helena stacking shelves. She smiles and stands behind the counter, looking very efficient and sweet in her white apron. I introduce her to Jo. He grins and shakes her hand, then kisses it. Helena goes pink. I scowl.

In the school playground, Jo and his mates always make a beeline for Helena and her friends, recounting their stupid pranks and pulling silly faces. I am Helena's boyfriend, so I drift over and grab her hand. Jo smirks, drawing her attention back to him with one of his lame jokes.

I stand there like a dumb idiot clinging to her hand, not saying a word.

Helena and I have our lunch together, holding hands and sharing our food. But Jo finds any excuse to sit with us, telling Helena he must tell her a funny story. He always squashes close to her, making sure his leg touches hers.

"Piss off," I growl under my breath.

Smirking, he places his arm around her shoulders and gives me a triumphant smile.

He knows exactly what he is doing. He's making me jealous. The prick!

One night, Jo tells me he really likes Helena.

I'm stretched out on my bed, reading a magazine when he comes into the room and sits on the floor. As he leans on the bed frame, he begins to boast about his feelings for Helena.

Swearing, I throw the magazine at him and leap from the bed. I haul him to his feet and take a swing at his head. He ducks and pushes me off. Backing away he puts his hands up in surrender and grins mischievously, knowing full well how I feel about her.

"You bastard!" I curse, bristling with anger.

Laughing, he backs out the door and runs down the stairs. Fuming, I'm left standing in the middle of the room.

Over the following weeks Jo's feelings for Helena grow stronger.

I can see it in his eyes every time he looks at her, and I hate it. From best friends Jo and I have become fierce rivals.

But Helena likes us both.

She never treats us differently. She laughs at Jo's jokes and smiles sweetly at me when I give her a love note or share my paczki with her. Sometimes she even holds hands with both of us at the same time, as if it's the most natural thing to do.

Occasionally, she brings poppy seed cake to school and shares it at lunchtime. We relish every mouthful making appreciative noises and exaggeratedly licking our fingers, making her laugh.

Yet at night, I lie awake wondering about this strange

relationship between the three of us. It's very confusing. Jo and I used to rarely fight, but now we fight a lot over Helena.

One afternoon, while we're both in the kitchen, I decide to thrash it out with him.

"Why do you need to sit so close to my girlfriend at lunchtime?" I growl at him.

"Why do you think she is your girlfriend?" he snarls.

"You know she is my girlfriend!" I yell at him. "I saw her first! You are interfering with my love life!"

Jo scoffs, "You have no love life. Besides, she's not your girlfriend. It's all in your head."

I scowl at him.

"You're so wrong!" I burst out. "She likes me! Only me!"

"She likes me a lot more!" Jo chuckles.

"Bullshit!" I bellow, pushing him.

Jo swings a punch, and we topple over a couple of chairs.

Ma bustles through the back door, breaking up the fight by slapping us around the head, telling us to shut up and stop fighting.

I swear at Jo, getting another slap from Ma. Stomping out to the backyard, I smash the soccer ball against the fence for a long time.

I ask Helena on a date the next day to see the latest American Western at the picture theatre. But I meet her there with her friends. Her parents are very strict, not allowing her to go out alone with a boy.

Jo finds out and makes a date to take her to a birthday party the following weekend. He is not allowed to pick her up at her house, either. Her father drops her off and picks her up at her friend's door.

On the very same weekend, I'm sick in bed with a bad cold. Sitting up now and then to cough into a rag and wipe my streaming eyes, I seethe for hours, thinking about what they are doing.

Later that night, Jo comes into the room and turns the kerosene lantern up. Smirking, he sits on his bed pulling off his shoes then glances at me with a smug look on his face.

I sit up in bed too quickly. Dizzy, I clutch the iron bedhead. Jo grins, lies on his bed fully clothed and reaches over, turning the light down low. He links his hands behind his head and stares at the ceiling, humming a tune.

"I was with Helena all evening," he gloats. "And kissed her before her father picked her up. It was a long kiss."

I see red!

Gathering my puny strength, I spring out of bed. I reef him up by his shirt front and take a swing. My first connects weakly with his chin. Spittle flies from my cracked lips as I hurl every foul word, I know, at him.

He falls back as I jump on top of him, throwing punches. When he throws me off, I land on the floor, knocking the small table between our beds.

The lamp flares then go out, throwing the room into semi-darkness. I get up on wobbly legs, my head pounding, and pounce on him again. He laughs as I pummel him with my fists. His laughter makes me yell with rage. I lay into him harder, landing a good one on the side of his head.

His face hardens and he lands a solid punch on my face, making me stagger back.

He grabs the front of my pyjamas, pushing me onto my bed where we start to wrestle. He wrenches me upright and squeezes me in a bear hug as I press my forearm against his throat. Facing each other we grunt and pant, spitting obscenities at one another.

Ma stomps up to the attic, shouting at us both to stop the thumping around.

Holding her lantern high, she rushes in and smacks us both hard across the back of our heads with her slipper.

Jo loosens his grip. I reluctantly release my grip on his throat. We sit on our beds, chests heaving and gasping for air.

Ma is livid.

"Both of you are to stop this fighting over Helena now! Do you hear? Now! Enough is enough! You are both acting like idiots over this girl!"

She scowls down at us, pointing her finger, "Ryszard, you will be cleaning pots for a week. And Jo, you will be cleaning the horse stall for two weeks!"

"How come Rys gets a week and I've got two weeks!" Jo whines.

Ma glares at him. "Because Jo, I'm certain you started this fight with your constant taunting! I'm sick of it! Your Auntie is sick of it! In fact, everyone is sick of it! You both need to get over her!"

I stare at her in disbelief as she marches out the door slamming it behind her.

"The girls must have told her," I mutter.

Jo scoffs. "Oh, they didn't need to. You go gooey-eyed whenever you see Helena. I overheard Ma telling the girls that you're like a love-sick puppy every time you're near her!"

He rubs his chin. I suspect a bruise is forming. I'm pleased. It is rare for me to land a good punch on Jo.

"Ma would never call me a love-sick puppy!" I gasp, coughing into my sleeve.

Jo rolls his eyes and starts to get undressed in the dark. I get back into bed and blow my nose into a rag.

I face the wall. I wipe my streaming eyes and breathe hard, causing me to cough more. I try to relax.

Christ! What are we going to do!

Why does Helena have to like us both?

I'll make her like me more!

The following week I decide to take Helena on a date and show her how I feel.

Our date is to the picture theatre to watch a Tarzan movie, starring Johnny Weissmuller. I put my arm around the back of her chair and lightly caress her shoulder. She turns, smiles at me then continues to watch the movie.

I keep glancing at her beautiful profile. Her hair is thick and long, cascading down her back over her yellow, summer dress. I long to stroke her silky locks, but instead I put my arm down and take her hand. It is small and delicate. Her fingers are long and tapered. I glance down at our clasped hands and gently squeeze her fingers, then kiss them.

I look at her lovely face again. She looks at me, smiles, then faces the screen. I just sigh and try to watch the movie, but I have no idea what it's about.

Her friends leave us at the theatre entrance and for once her father lets me walk her home. The Summer evening is warm and balmy with a scent of jasmine.

I hold her hand as she talks about the movie. At her gate I lift her hand and kiss it. She leans towards me so I can kiss her lips. It is a soft kiss. Our lips lightly press together, and we fall into an embrace. Her head rests on my shoulder. I stroke her long blonde hair and think about the softness of her lips. It is the first time I have kissed a girl and it is the most memorable event in my life!

Helena must like me more than Jo! She just has to!

I finally leave her at her door and walk backwards along the path. We blow kisses to each other. Then I vault over the small white fence and walk slowly up the street.

I don't remember walking home, but I do remember Jo abruptly opening the front door.

"Had a good time, Ryszard?" he sneers.

I look at him in a daze, then push past him to climb up the stairs, oblivious to everyone and everything, I'm so happy! Helena kissed me!

#####

As the months pass Jo and I get to know Helena's family and she gets to know ours. They invite us to Izaak's, Helena's younger brother's, bar mitzvah.

It's a small affair in their family's home as Jews aren't allowed to hold functions in their synagogues anymore. Jo and I know Izaak well. He plays soccer with us at school. He is a tall, thin lad who can dribble the ball with speed and skill.

Helena also attends my fourteenth birthday party.

#####

The day is cold and there is deep snow. It's two days before Christmas Day. Auntie agrees I can have a few friends over for a small party, but I think they are coming just for Auntie's alcoholic ginger beer.

During my party, Jo is constantly at Helena's side, trying to steer her away from me at every opportunity. All I can hear is: "Come to the barn, Helena, and see Auntie's chickens ...Come and help me feed the horse... We'll give him an apple!" When we are at the table, he fawns all over her. "Would you like another piece of poppy seed cake Helena, or some ginger beer? Can I get you something else?"

Blah ... blah ... blah.

It's impossible to talk to her privately, let alone have her to myself for a few minutes. Jo never leaves her side.

The party ends and Helena waits on the porch for her father to pick her up. She wears a red woollen coat, buttoned to her neck, and today I notice a yellow star sewn on the front with 'Jude' written in the centre. This is new.

"Why are you wearing the star?" I ask.

Helena wrinkles her nose in disgust, looks down and pokes it with her gloved hand.

"It was ordered by the Germans that all Jews have to wear one."

This is a new rule. Why the Germans need to do this? What is their reasoning behind it?

I glance at her white woollen hat pulled down over her ears and meet her bright, shining eyes. I love Helena. It doesn't matter to me that she's Jewish. I grab her gloved hand and tuck it under my arm. We are both silent, watching the snowflakes fall amongst Auntie's pot plants.

Jo loudly slams the front door as he walks onto the porch. He pulls down his cap over his ears and grabs Helena's other hand and talks non-stop about the latest Western movie. I bristle with anger but am determined not to start a fight in front of Helena. I stand there, allowing him to prattle on. Feeling stupid.

Helena gives us both a quick hug when her father arrives and climbs into the front seat of his van. She waves through the window. Jo blows kisses towards her. I just stand stiffly, slowly waving my hand.

When the van disappears at the top of the lane I stomp through the front door, slamming it shut, narrowly missing Jo's smug face.

#####

Winter freezes the ponds. The largest is big enough to skate on. We strap wooden skates onto our winter boots and skate all day. Sometimes Ma joins us, turning into a young woman again as she skates gracefully around and around. Her face flushed with excitement; she laughs joyously.

I'm glad Ma is having fun. She's been stressed about the food situation lately, and Pa going to war. Ice skating helps her to forget for a while.

Helena and I decided to go skating again on Saturday afternoon. She is at the park with her friends and I'm with some of my soccer buddies. Helena grabs my hand, and we skate to the opposite side, then around the pond smiling at each other.

Jo arrives with his mates and notices us skating past.

Quickly he straps on his skates and charges towards us. Grabbing Helena's other hand, he pulls us apart, then waltzes her across the ice. She looks up in surprise and laughs. Her face glowing with delight. I stand there clenching my fists in frustration and slump down heavily on the nearest bench.

"Oh Jozef … Jo stop! I'm dizzy!" Helena laughs.

Jo swings her into his arms. She pulls away, realising I've gone and looks around the rink. She is surprised to see me on the bench and skates towards me.

I notice Jo following her with his eyes, then skating back to his friends.

"What's wrong, Ryszard?" She asks as she sits next to me.

"Oh nothing." I say wretchedly.

She grabs my hand, "I can see you are upset, Ryszard. Please, tell me what's wrong?"

"Jo is always around when I'm with you," I say bitterly. "And he's always messing-up our dates!"

"I'm on this date with you Ryszard and only you. Come now, hold my hand and we'll skate with my friends!"

She offers me her hand. Pulling me up, she looks into my eyes, making me believe Jo doesn't exist.

CHAPTER

5

The situation in Poland grows increasingly dangerous for Jewish people.

They are made to wear an armband, like Helena's, with a yellow star that identifies them as Jews. Some are murdered in the streets by the SS, the Gestapo, or the regular German army. Even by the Polish Resistance. Most have their businesses, bank accounts and valuable possessions confiscated by the German authorities, making them very poor. Many Jews disappear from the city.

"What has our country come to," Auntie wails. "The Jews are our neighbours. Our friends! I wish we could help them!"

Ma comforts her. And warns the four of us to be careful. "We don't know who might be next," she says. "These are dangerous days for all of us, not just the Jews."

Late one Saturday afternoon, Pan Tolinski gives Jo and I a lift to the grocery shop on an important errand. We arrive as Pan Loftmann is about to close for the evening.

Jo and I stand outside the shop for a long moment.

'Jude' has been daubed on the shop front in white paint.

"Christ! What is the world coming to?" snarls Jo.

He climbs the steps and opens the door.

The discordant clang of the doorbell sounds dull and sad as

I trail in behind him.

The shop looks forlorn and bare.

I remember our first visit, straight after our first day at school. Then, the room was packed with all kinds of produce; barrels of apples, large hessian bags of potatoes, cabbages piled in a corner, and paper bags of flour and sugar piled together on a wide shelf.

The back wall, behind the counter, was jammed with cans of fruit and pickled cucumbers. Lollipops, boiled lollies, liquorice sticks squeezed in large glass canisters covered the corner of the counter.

Pan Loftmann even had a milkshake machine on the back bench. I only saw it working once, when a rich kid and his mother were in the shop on a Saturday afternoon. They ordered a vanilla milkshake topped with ice cream. I think they were from Warsaw. Anyway, it must have cost a lot as ice cream was already getting scarce.

Now most of the fresh produce is gone and only cans of meat and cabbage line the shelves with small sacks of flour and sugar on another. They are all spread out to make the shelves look fuller. From such a thriving business, it's a shame to see the shop now.

"Hello Pan Loftmann. Can we speak to you?" Jo asks.

Pan Loftmann is carefully stacking the shelves with cans, moving each one apart.

"Is Helena here? We would like to have this discussion with her as well." I add.

He moves around the counter and looks at his watch.

"Certainly boys, come through to the back."

He locks the shop's front door and turns the 'OPEN' sign

over to 'CLOSED'. We follow him through to the storeroom out the back, where Pani Loftmann is sitting at a desk writing in a ledger. Helena is in the corner, unpacking a box. We smile at her and her mother as Pan Loftmann stands next to his wife.

Glancing at Helena I clear my throat. "Jo and I would like to talk about the German threat, and how we can help you. We've discussed this with our mother and Auntie, and we want Helena to live with us, as part of our family."

Jo chimes in, "Her hair is fair. She can pass as a Catholic girl and be safe with us!"

Helena gives him a shy smile.

"No, no, no!" Pan Loftmann exclaims, taking off his glasses and rubbing them vigorously with his handkerchief. "Helena is my darling angel, and I will not be parted from her. I will not break up my family. She stays with us!"

Looking determined, he places his glasses back on his large nose and tucks his handkerchief into his pocket.

"Please Pan Loftmann!" I plead; my hands outstretched. "You may all die. You know what the Germans are doing to Jews. Please reconsider our offer. Ma will look after Helena! We all will! She'll be safe with us!"

Pani Loftmann looks up at her husband in anguish. Helena looks so much like her, except Pani Loftmann has a white streak of hair pulled back from her forehead and fine lines at the corners of her eyes.

"Please Benjamin!" she begs.

Pan Loftmann stands erect with his hands behind his back.

"No! No! No! Helena will stay with us!"

"But Benjamin, please think about what you are saying!" Pani Loftmann implores. "This is a chance for Helena to be hidden from the Germans. It could save her life!"

"I will not hear of it!" Pan Loftmann yells, slamming his fist on the desk as he glares down at his wife. "We are a family and will not be separated at any cost. I will keep my daughter safe! I will keep all my family safe!"

He glares at us pugnaciously. "Is that clear to both of you!"

"You're going to be her death, Pan Loftmann!" Jo shouts, clenching his fists at his sides.

My eyes brim with tears, "Please...Please, I beg you. Please let her come home with us!"

"I will not let her go; do you hear! Never!" Pan Loftmann roars, his face twisting with rage. "That is final!"

Helena reaches over the desk and clasps his arm. "It's okay, Papa. I will stay with you and Mama!"

He gives Helena's hand a squeeze, then walks briskly towards the door of the storeroom and opens it.

"You need to leave. Now! Now! Now!" Pan Loftmann's voice rises on each repeated 'Now!' until he is shouting at us. "Go! I do not want you in my shop again!"

"Papa! No!" Helena cries out, bursting into tears.

Her mother sobs into her hands.

Pan Loftmann stomps through the shop. After one last, agonised, glance back at Helena, we follow him. He unlocks the shop's front door and swings it wide, giving us a shove.

We stumble outside onto the pavement. Pan Loftmann locks the door and disappears into the back of the shop.

A few moments later, Helena hurriedly unlocks the door and quietly closes it behind her.

"I'm so sorry about Papa!" she cries as she runs down the steps. "He's acting so strangely these days, and he seems so confused. That's the first time I have seen him so angry." She grips both our arms. "Please forgive him! I think what is happening to our people is affecting his mind! He sees people shot and hanged every day. A lot of his close friends have died."

I take her hand. "That's why we came, Helena. We can't save everyone, but we can save you. It's not too late. Helena, please come home with us. Come now!"

"I can't Ryszard, I just can't!" she sobs. "They are my family. I can't leave them, especially with Papa being like this. Mama needs me, and so does Izaak. If anything happens to my parents, I need to look after him."

Taking both our hands into hers, she pauses and draws an unsteady breath. "I love you both! I really do! I can't decide between the two of you! You are the best thing that has ever happened to me! I love you both so much!"

A racking sob escapes her throat as she fiercely hugs us in turn. Helena wraps her arms around our necks, kissing our lips, not caring about scandalous stares from people walking past. I taste the salt of her tears.

Responding to her grief, tears run down our cheeks, also, as the three of us embrace. I stroke her long, silky hair. Jo kisses her forehead. We part, with both of us stroking her arms.

Wretchedness lingers on Helena's face as she turns and walks slowly back into the shop. She closes the door, looks out through the glass partition with tears streaking down her face, and slowly turns away.

Jo and I look through the shop window, the glass reflecting the anguish written on our faces. Never to see Helena again! The thought is unbearable. Taking a couple of backward steps onto the road, I'm stunned by what just happened. What Helena has just said.

She loves us both. Is that even possible?

Have we really lost her?

Jo peels his gaze away from the shop front and looks at me.

"That didn't go down very well with Pan Loftmann."

"You think!" I bite back, still staring at the shop front.

Jo thumps his fist against the window of the shop.

"Her father is a bloody stupid fool! He's not right in the head. You heard what Helena said about him. He is going insane!" He thumps the window again.

I nod, then look back at him, taking a deep audible breath.

"I'm so worried about them. All of them, not just Helena."

Jo looks back through the window.

"Me too Rys!" he whispers.

We stand silently for a full minute, our hands deep in our pockets, glaring at our reflections.

"I'm sorry for the fights we had over Helena," Jo murmurs. "Especially the one in the attic."

"Me too Jo," I say, my voice cracking.

Jo sniffs back tears.

"I love her, Rys!"

"I know," I sigh.

CHAPTER

6

Life goes on.

We see Helena at school, but it's not the same. Jo and I still sit with her at lunch time but gone are Jo's silly jokes and Helena's poppy seed cakes. Helena is quiet and seldom smiles. At times she stares into space, sad and worried. There is nothing Jo and I can do!

We take out our grief and frustration on the soccer field, playing fiercely and more competitively than ever. With unexpected results.

We reach the semi-finals!

Pan Nowak has us practising every afternoon as this is an important game. He tells us our school has never come this far in the school soccer league before. It's not just Jo and I helping to improve the team performance, but Adam and Piotr as well.

They came from a high school in Warsaw, known for its good players. We're playing against a neighbouring high school with some excellent players, but some dirty ones as well. They won the finals last season.

The game is rough with a lot of injuries. Abel, our striker, is carted to the change room with a torn ligament from a savage tackle. The big idiot who tackled him ended up receiving a red card and was sent off the field.

Their goalie is our main concern as he has saved at least four goals without much effort. Looking at least sixteen, he is unnaturally tall with his hands reaching the top of the goal posts.

At half time we discuss the tactics of the other team. We believe they are cheating. It seems to us they have placed older players in important positions, like the goalie and the striker. Pan Nowak thinks so too.

He tells us there is nothing we can do about it at this late hour, so we have no other choice than to fight back with everything we have.

It is a tough battle with a lot of fouls, but a minute before the final whistle Piotr sets up the winning goal and Adam, our striker, taps it in, winning the game three to two.

The crowd goes ballistic.

We run around the field, waving our team shirts over our heads and jumping in the air. With a big grin on his face, Pan Nowak claps everyone on the back, giving Piotr and Adam a vigorous handshake.

I'm disappointed Helena isn't in the crowd. It's unusual for her to miss the game, especially as she knows how important this match is to us. Helena *always* attends our school soccer matches. I begin to worry.

On Monday, Helena is not at her desk.

I look around anxiously, but she is not in the classroom. I ask Amelia, one of her friends, if she's seen her but she shakes her head.

Deep down, I feel something is wrong.

At lunchtime I tell Jo Helena is absent from school.

Anxiously Jo tells me, "Helena's family may have been sent to the ghetto. I've overheard Ma talking to Auntie about an area.

A restricted area for the Jews. They said it's made to keep them all in one place. The fencing is all barbed wire and high wooden palings, and there are guards stationed everywhere."

Agitated, Jo runs his fingers through his hair. "They also said the Jews are slave labourers for the SS, who have been killing the Jews ever since they got here. But a slave ghetto could be a lot worse. It could mean a slow death for all of them!"

I pat his shoulder, not knowing how else to comfort him. Or myself. I've heard the stories too.

"I think after school we should go to her father's store," I suggest. "So, we can find out what really happened."

From the outside, the grocery store looks the same. But, looking up we see the sign 'Klaus Grocery Store' in bold red letters above the shop front window. We peer through the glass and find the inside totally changed. No more empty shelves or spread-out items. The shelves are full and neatly stacked, like before the war. A large man is wiping down the counter.

"What the hell!" I hissed. "What happened to Pan Loftmann?"

"I've got a bad feeling about this." Jo hisses back. "Let's see what this fat bastard has to say."

We saunter in. Through small watery eyes, set in a fleshy face, the man glances up at us suspiciously.

"What do voo want?" he asks in broken Polish as he keeps moving his cloth in slow circles.

"Could you tell us where the previous owners are?" I ask.

"Nein!" he grunts. "I do not know!"

He begins to take down some cans and replace them with small bags of sugar.

"Do you own this store now?" Jo asks.

The man turns to face us. I notice a name embroidered on his white dust coat. 'Erik Klaus.' *So that's your name, you big bastard.*

"Ja, Ja I own this shop now!" He beams.

"When are you getting the sign that says, 'Jews and Dogs are Forbidden to Enter' like the rest of the shops around here?" I ask sarcastically.

"Soon, soon. Tomorrow it may come!" Klaus replies loudly, smiling a toothy grin. "I had to ask two dirty Jews to leave already today!"

I sense Jo seething.

"Do you find the shop to your liking?" Jo asks acidly.

Not recognising the sarcasm, Klaus exclaims, "Ja! It is good! I find it is very central to the city and a very good position. Lots of customers."

Jo becomes angry, "I bloody hope so, you German bastard, you stole it from our friends!"

Klaus's thick black eyebrows pinch together in a frown.

His fleshy jowls quiver as his small mouth opens and closes like a goldfish.

"Get out!... Raus! ... Raus!" he bellows.

Grabbing a couple of apples from a basket we bolt through the doorway, then stop in front of the shop window, giving him the one finger salute.

We take off running. The Klaus bursts out of the shop, chest heaving.

He lumbers up the street after us, sweating and snorting like a bull. We keep running, hooting with glee, stopping now and then to see how far away he is.

Laughing, we scoot around a corner and run into Danuta, Helena's best friend. She stumbles. Jo grabs her arm to steady her and pulls her into the alley.

Flattening ourselves against the wall, we stifle our laughter as the puffing Kraut stumbles past.

When he is gone, Danuta turns to us, eyebrows lifted.

"What are you two doing? You will get shot if you are not careful!"

I look into her eyes and my smile disappears as I recognise the grief reflected there.

"Do you know what happened to Helena and her family?" I ask.

"I saw what happened! I was there on Saturday after the soccer game. I was on my way to find out why she didn't go, and as I came around the corner, I saw an army truck filled with people. Jews, I think. I saw some of those nasty yellow stars." Her face screwed up in a distasteful grimace.

"Helena and her family were pushed out their front door with only a few suitcases. Then the rest of their belongings were thrown onto the street. I think all their valuables were taken by the SS. I tried to help them collect a few things off the road, but Pani Loftmann told me to go, in case I got into trouble. I ran when I saw a German soldier coming towards me! I feel so bad for leaving Helena, but I was so scared!"

She starts to cry and wipes her eyes with the palm of her hand.

"I couldn't go to school today. I was to upset!"

I pat her shoulder. "There is nothing you could have done, Danuta."

Through her tears she continues, "I found out yesterday

from their neighbour, Panni Polinska. They were sent to the ghetto and will be working in a leather factory which makes rucksacks, belts and boots for the German army. The factory is on the south side of the ghetto, near the boundary."

Jo and I silently stare at Danuta in disbelief.

Helena is so smart. She could have been a doctor or a teacher. She told me once she would like to go to university, and now she makes German boots! I can't believe it.

"Bloody hell!" hisses Jo.

#####

Slinking around the fence surrounding the ghetto, we discover the leather factory by chance. Around six that evening, a group of factory workers emerge from a large brick building, all heading for a block of apartments.

Helena and her family are amongst them. She is walking slightly ahead, holding a boy of about six or seven by the hand.

Staring in silence, I grip Jo's arm. He nods. "I see her," he whispers.

We continue to stare in silence. It's too dangerous to call out to Helena, so instead, we hide, and surreptitiously study the surrounding area. The factory is built just inside a tall wire fence which runs alongside a gravel lane. The fence joins an ancient brick wall about three metres high and fifteen metres long. It curves slightly in the centre, causing a blind spot.

Thick bushes grow against the wall, making a perfect hiding place.

Every ten minutes, a German guard patrols along the length of the fence to the edge of the brick wall and back again. Now and then he walks up the lane but doesn't inspect the bushes growing against the wall. Instead, out of sight from the guard house, he smokes a cigarette then strolls casually to the end and back again.

Opposite the wall, two large brick buildings face the lane with a dark, narrow alleyway separating them. It's here we bob down low behind a couple of overflowing garbage cans, with a good view of the guard stationed at his sentry box and the full length of his patrol route.

Jo and I wait until he is walking back to his box to dash across the road and dive behind the bushes. We discover a small space, big enough to crouch in. Squatting down, we examine the bricks.

They seem intact, but on a closer inspection some of the old mortar is crumbling. Jo scrapes it out with his penknife, removing a brick. We both move closer and peer through the hole into the ghetto. There is a clear view to the factory's entrance.

"I think this will do," whispers Jo, picking up the brick and jamming it back into place.

From the alleyway, the next day, we see the same young boy, who walked with Helena, leaving the factory alone.

He heads towards the gravel lane.

When the guard has his back turned, we sprint quickly across the road, and casually saunter along the wire fence line, gesturing to the boy to follow.

Ducking through the bushes, Jo pulls out the loose brick, calls him over, and asks if he knows Helena Loftmann. The boy bobs down smiling and nods enthusiastically. I pass him a note addressed to Helena and pay him with a small bag of sweets.

The following day we see Danuta entering **'Klaus Grocery Store'**. We wait on the other side of the road until she emerges, holding a grocery bag. We scurry over and steer her into an alleyway. I ask her if she'll be our lookout for the meeting with Helena. She grabs my arm, her eyes brimming with tears.

"Of course ... Of course. I'm more than willing to help!"

She breathes in a ragged breath.

A sob escapes her lips.

I grip her hand.

"Don't worry Danuta. We'll keep Helena and her family alive." I promise.

We work out a signal if there is any danger of the guard finding us. Danuta will cross the road from the alleyway and walk past the bushes near the wall. Fumbling through her bag she will complain about misplacing her lighter and take out a cigarette pack from her bag.

Detaining the guard, she'll ask for a light. We, in turn, will be able to slip out from the bushes and return to the alleyway.

It's very dangerous, but Danuta is courageous enough to do it for her friend. For Helena.

Jo tells her the meeting with Helena is late this afternoon, just before dark.

"I'll wear my sister's clothes and her lipstick," she tells us eagerly. "I'll meet you at the bus stop near the school gate."

Jo lightly grips her arm and whispers hoarsely. "Don't let her find out!"

She pats his hand, "I won't. My parents and my sister will still be at work."

I like Danuta. Not only is she a very good friend to Helena

but is also an attractive girl with shiny auburn hair and bright blue eyes.

She is tall for her age and looks older than fourteen. Which is good for our plan.

Later, we wait at the gate and watch Danuta walk towards us. Jo wolf whistles, making her smile. Her hair is up, and she wears a green dress under a stylish grey coat. The high-heeled white sandals on her feet click on the pavement as she walks. Pink lipstick makes her lips full and luscious. As she comes closer, I smell her perfume. She smells of lilacs.

We catch the bus and get off near the ghetto where I place her arm into the crook of my elbow, as if we are on a date. Jo lingers behind, hands in his pockets, looking at the ground. As we approach the buildings we duck into the alleyway. Helena and the boy are already walking alongside the gravel road.

Jo and I move quickly, zipping across the road and walk parallel to them on our side of the fence, then dive behind the bushes.

The boy walks further on and hides near the back of the factory.

Danuta stays behind in the alleyway, watching the guard.

We sense Helena behind the wall. She starts to scrape around the mortar with her fingers, looking for the loose brick.

"Don't worry Helena, we'll get the brick out from our side," Jo whispers, pulling it out.

Kneeling, she peers through the gap, exclaiming in an excited whisper.

"Oh! Jozef and Ryszard, I'm so glad to see both!"

Eagerly, we gaze at her face. It's drawn with fatigue and there are grey smudges under her lovely eyes, but she is still beautiful. Jo and I inhale ragged breaths. My heart aches.

"How are you, Helena?" I ask in a whisper.

She smiles weakly. "I'm okay, but it's very bad here. We don't have enough food, or fuel for our stove."

"There is little or no medicine in case we get sick," she adds. "Papa is very worried about Izaak. He's coughing a lot."

"Don't worry, we'll help you," Jo whispers back. "We'll come to the wall every week, but on a different day so it won't be too obvious to anyone, especially the Krauts. We will be here tomorrow at about the same time. Give us a note of what you need, and we'll tell you what day to expect us. Don't forget to tap the wall in reply when we tap.

That's to tell you it is safe to talk. Oh, by the way, Danuta is our lookout."

Helena's face beams.

"How is she?" she asks. "She was so upset when the SS came."

"She's okay. She misses you though. We all do," I reply.

Helena sighs, "Oh, I miss everyone too!" I'll be here tomorrow."

She hesitates and adds, "I love you both!"

She puts a hand through the gap. We both hold onto it stroking her fingers. Jo bows his head as tears spill down his cheeks. She finally pulls her hand away, stands up and quickly walks away.

The boy follows.

Jo puts the brick back.

That night, Ma and Auntie package items of food for us, even though our own supplies are getting low.

Auntie wraps goat cheese and salami in wax paper and fills

small cloth bags with sugar and flour. Jo and I hide them in the secret pockets in our jackets and school satchels, which Zaneta and Angelika have sewn in.

We wait in the alleyway the following day, as the sun sets behind the buildings in the ghetto, and watch the workers spill out from the factory. Jo and I cross the road and dive into the bushes, while Danuta stays behind.

Helena and the boy keep to the back of a group of workers. She slows to a stop when everyone has disappeared around a corner, then runs to the wall and taps the bricks when it's safe.

The boy keeps walking and slips into a gap between the factory and a timber building. He is Helena's lookout, watching the guards without being noticed.

Jo carefully removes the brick, and we gaze at Helena and take turns touching her hand. We pass her the small parcels and she quickly stuffs them into her coat. It is all done within seconds.

Helena looks through the gap and whispers, "Thank you so much for the food."

Jo passes her a small note to tell her the next rendezvous.

Helena takes it and passes one back.

"This is what we need. If you can't get it all we'll understand. I can't stay long. The guard could be here any minute, so I thought I would write letters to tell you both what's happening here."

Two neatly folded pieces of paper, with our names written in her neat handwriting, are passed through the gap. Mine has a small paper aeroplane drawn on it, which brings back memories of the day I met her.

"I would love it if you could write back to me," she murmurs softly. "And if I can't come to our meetings, Levi will come and pick up the parcels. He is the boy you gave the sweets to. He lives with us now." She smiles. "Just give him candy and you'll have his devotion forever."

Helena looks into my eyes, making my heart skip a beat.

She smiles. Her face radiates so much love for the two of us. I thread my hand through the gap. She grasps it tightly. I release her grip as she stands.

Jo peers up at her.

"We love you Helena," he whispers.

Before she can reply, Levi walks past, a signal that someone is coming.

We quickly put the brick back and squat down lower. It's not a German guard on Helena's side but a ghetto policeman. Jo and I hold our breath, listening through the bricks.

Danuta emerges from the alleyway, crosses the road and walks towards the wall. She signals loudly, taking a cigarette out from her purse.

Ah shit! The guard is coming on this side as well.

But instead of crawling out and running for the alleyway, we stay hidden behind the bushes and try to hear the conversation between Helena and the policeman.

"What the hell are you doing out here?" The policeman demands.

"I... I lost my... my key for my apartment," Helena stammers, "I was searching for it. Look! Here it is!"

She must have pretended to pick it up and show him.

He growls. "Just get going. It's past curfew. No one is to be outside. If I see you again, I'll take you in for questioning!"

He must have shoved Helena because we heard her cry out.

Jo snarls and tries to stand. I grab his arm and pull him back down.

We hear Helena run towards her apartment. The policeman pauses for a moment. He taps the wall. Jo and I hold our breaths, both of us staring at the loose brick, waiting for him to find it. But he loses interest and walks away, gravel crunching beneath his boots.

When it's clear, I carefully crawl under the bush and look for the guard on our side. He is nowhere to be seen.

We dash across the street into the alleyway and notice Danuta smoking a cigarette with the German guard only metres away. Fortunately, he has his back turned towards us.

Smoking in a flamboyant fashion, as if he is a bloody movie star, he waves his cigarette about.

He draws the smoke in deeply and squints his eyes as if the acrid smoke is burning his throat.

He tilts his head and breaths the smoke out then leans towards Danuta and whispers something. She plays her part well and doesn't step back but lets him move closer.

Glancing our way briefly, then back at him, Danuta makes him laugh and touches his arm. Lecherously, he places his hand on her shoulder. She holds him back with the palm of her hand and smiles, making him shrug and drop his hand. He steps back. Danuta says goodbye.

Not waiting any longer, Jo and I dash out of the alleyway and around the building to the main street.

The guard calls out to Danuta.

She turns, giving him a wave, but keeps walking.

Leaning against the wall, we wait for Danuta to pass, and casually fall in behind her. We all stop when we are a safe distance away.

Danuta turns to us, exasperated.

"Oh my God that was close! I hate smoking cigarettes, and that idiot was a complete moron!"

I pat her arm. "Thank you, Danuta! You saved us! I'll buy you a packet of gum to take the taste from your mouth."

I start to move away, but she grabs the back of my jacket and pulls me back, her green eyes blazing.

"I can buy my own stupid bubble gum! You've got to be a lot more careful, the both of you." She looks from me to my brother. "This is not a game. You both need to take notice of my signals. You can get shot!"

She shoves me. Her face is furious. I stumble back in surprise, nearly losing my balance.

"We could all get shot! Including Helena and her family!" Danuta snarls while adjusting the strap of her bag.

Tossing her auburn hair over her shoulder, she marches in front of us, her shoes clicking loudly on the pavement.

Jo quickly catches up to her and grabs her arm.

"I'm sorry Danuta! You are right. We should have left as soon as you warned us." Jo says apologetically.

She shoves his hand off and sniffs, holding her head up high.

Jo walks beside her, trying to make amends as I meekly follow behind, my hands in my pockets.

It's dark by the time we get back to the high school gates, so we walk Danuta home.

By the time she's at her house she has calmed down. She gives us both a kiss on the cheek, thanking us for helping Helena and her family. I kiss her hand.

"Thank you, Danuta, for being our lookout," I whisper.

"Without your help Jo and I could have ended up in a cell somewhere."

She nods grimly and goes inside.

CHAPTER

7

A month after Helena and her family are sent to the ghetto, the schools close and most of the teachers leave. We never did play in the school soccer finals.

Leaving school is a sad day. At the end of the day, we file out through the classroom door. Pan Nowak pats each of us on the shoulder and wishes us good luck. I take all of Helena's coloured pencils and hide them in my pockets, although the sharp tips pierce the fabric. Pan Nowak notices, and smiles.

"I wish you all the best sir," I say, looking up at him.

He pats my shoulder again.

"You too Rys… You too."

In the corridor he says goodbye to the rest of the class, then turns and slowly walks back into his classroom, shutting the door.

With leaden steps I pass through the school entrance for the last time. I meet up with Jo and we both sit at the back of the bus, waiting for our sisters.

Five minutes later, the girls clamber aboard, their faces wet with tears, and sit at the front. They swivel around to see if we are there and give us a sad, disheartened wave, then turn back to speak to their friends. The trip home is a sad and sober one.

Our world changes.

Gone are the days playing soccer after school, meeting up

with friends and going to the movies. We now live in a country governed by the Nazis' harsh rules. Every day we hear of people being arrested, murdered or forced to relocate.

No-one is free to leave. But there is also a secret world. A hidden world of the Polish Resistance, the Armia Krajowa. It fights to weaken the German forces by clandestine means. Fighting back so the Polish people will one day live in freedom again.

I find out it is not just the Armia Krajowa causing disruption among the Germans by blowing up trains, roads and bridges, but also the civilian branches of the Resistance. They have created secret schools to educate young people. A counter-intelligence branch distributes leaflets exposing falsehoods in German Propaganda, and there is a bureau for forging documents, mainly ID papers.

I join the small sabotage branch where young people distribute anti-German propaganda, attack cinemas that are playing German movies with stink bombs and paint the anchor symbol on walls. This symbol is made of a P and W crossed together which means 'Fighting Poland' and is the symbol for the Polish Underground. These small sabotages are enough to be a bloody nuisance for the Germans.

Being older, Jo is drafted into another group that performs more daring escapades, like putting dirt in fuel tanks, slashing tires and stealing supplies out of German warehouses.

We meet at secret locations where the leaders in our groups, attached to a bigger Resistance organization, give us our orders.

During these meetings, we also buy stolen goods from the men who sabotage the German trains and steal the cargo on-board. These supplies help us a great deal, especially in feeding our families.

Jo and I decide not to tell Helena about our escapades with the Resistance. It will only worry her. It's dangerous for us and our family as well as her family if she mentions it to anyone. Not that she would. But after our meetings with her, Jo and I sometimes go our separate ways and join our respective gangs to wreak havoc on the Germans.

#####

Another month passes. Helena lacks her usual vitality. Her naturally pale skin has turned sallow, and she is pitifully thin. She wears a dull, brown head scarf with small tufts of hair poking out around her face. Her badly cut hair is unfashionably short. Her clothing is worn and dirty. Her dress, modified to hide the parcels we give her, looks too big and bulky for her slender frame.

After reading Helena's letters on the way home we share them with Danuta and discuss the Loftmann's dire circumstances.

We are worried about them.

Helena writes,

16th of June 1941

Dear Ryszard and Jozef,
I can only write one letter so please share this between you both, as I don't have the paper to write two. Thank you for your parcels, we are all so grateful.

At our last meeting I saw you both looking at my scarf, exchanging worried looks. I had to sell my hair to a wig maker so I could buy more food for my family. Don't worry. It will grow back.

My family is only allowed small portions of meat, coffee substitute, barley, brown sugar, butter and vegetables per month. One loaf of bread needs to last three days! We go to a soup kitchen at midday, but the soup is dreadful. We are all starving and get a lot of stomach cramps. It's very painful, so we don't sleep well at night.

Could you get some flour or potatoes for me please? Anything you can spare will do, and Papa asks if you could get him some pain killers. He is suffering from dreadful headaches lately.

My family sends their love and thank you again for the food.

Let me tell you about the ghetto. The ghetto fence is guarded by the Schupo. They are stationed every 50 metres except for our brick wall where guards are stationed further apart. You were so lucky to find that wall! The ghetto is totally sealed from the city, so we are cut off from the rest of the world and have no idea of what is happening in Poland.

The gates are opened and shut by Jewish police, who in turn are supervised by German police. Some of the German guards kill people for no reason. I saw a guard shoot a man while he was asking a question. I was quite close, and it really scared me.

I ran all the way home and told Mama. She told Izaak and I that we are to avoid the guards at all costs. One of the Jewish Elders, Pan Kozlowski, has been appointed as our Mayor by the Germans. He gives us orders that come from the German authorities. Pan Kozlowski is hated by most Jews. People believe he is a traitor. He has a lot of henchmen to do his bidding and Papa said he is controlled by the Gestapo. My Papa says he is a fool and a criminal.

Before the war, he was known within the Jewish community for stealing from his factory workers and not paying them their right wages.

He was also involved with a mob of gangsters.

He hand-picks the men to become policemen. Being Jewish, we thought they would be more lenient than the Germans, but they're not. They have pulled up our floorboards and smashed our walls looking for valuables for Pan Kozlowski and the Gestapo. They found nothing in our apartment, so they beat my father instead. My poor Papa now has a broken nose.

Pan Kozlowski gives speeches every week and were made to line up outside his office and listen. All he talks about is the authority given to him by the Germans, and how he has helped us with suitable food rations and medicines. I look at our people and see only starved faces. But he and his men do not look starved at all. He has a fat stomach while my Papa has lost his tummy and looks ill. I will say this only to you two. Pan Kozlowski is full of shite and his speeches are full of deceitful lies.

His police are called the Soderkommando, and they are the elite unit of the ghetto police force. On the surface they have innocent duties like guarding the food stores, sentry duty and keeping law and order.

But behind this facade they work for the Gestapo,

who order them to make arrests and round up people for deportation.

A lot of people are beaten and robbed by these policemen. The policeman who caught me at the wall was one of them.

I was so lucky he didn't search me. I don't think I would be alive today if he did!

They all look well fed and well dressed. I know they have special privileges and security for their families because my cousin has become one of them. We don't receive any of his privileges as Papa has refused his handouts. He said, "It's all stolen goods that have been taken from the Jewish people!

It's absolutely immoral and against everything I believe in. Abraham is a bloody traitor!"

I haven't heard my Papa swear before, so we have nothing to do with my cousin Abraham's family now.

I am so angry about what is happening here! I'll tell you more in the next letter.

I love you both, my boyfriends,

Helena

xxxxx

P.S Please, a little more coal if you can and we love your jokes, Jo.

My letters always include a poem. I try to make it as corny as possible. I used to share my poems with Helena at school and it became a competition between us. We tried to write the corniest poem possible. I never shared them with my family as it was something special between Helena and myself.

The poems are about the animals at the farm or my family

and sometimes the Germans.

Helena never comments in her letters about my poems. She knows it's between us, but I know in my heart she loves them.

I also write about playing soccer with Jo and the mischief we get up to. But never our Resistance mischief. Also, about bartering with the neighbours for extra food and fuel using Auntie's homemade vodka. She has made a distillery in the barn and sacrificed one of her potato patches.

I tell Helena about the everyday life of my family, the antics of Auntie's cats and how much I miss her and my friends, and finally, how much I love her.

Jo and I write separate letters and I know he includes jokes in his. Sometimes he reads them aloud, making us all laugh.

Our parcels contain anything we can spare. Ma buys food on the black market and we buy contraband from the raided trains. Together she and Auntie pack food packages and a small amount of coal.

The rest of the items are packed by the rest of us. I always give Helena writing paper folded in small squares.

24th of June 1941

Dear Jozef and Ryszard,

Thank you so much for the coal, food and the oranges. How did you find the two oranges? No, don't tell me. I can only guess it was taken from some local grocery store near the high school. The oranges were delicious, and Mama roasted the peel with a little sugar, and it was like candy.

I was wondering if you could get us some medicine for Izaak. He is very sick. Our doctor, Dr Janssen, said it's tuberculosis.

He asks if you can get calcium injections. It will help him. Also, if you can spare a few potatoes, we will make him soup as well.

Papa is asking for a favour. At the back of our store there is a loose brick under the windowsill where he hid a package containing valuable jewellery belonging to Mama. Could you retrieve it for him? It will help us to buy more food. Our money is nearly gone, and Papa has no bank account here as the Germans took all our money.

We must use Jewish money and if we are found with Polish Zlotys we will be shot. So don't ever give us any money. Anyway, we can't eat money.

More about the Ghetto. We have a hospital, schools and a public kitchen, which I mentioned in my last letter. The soup is still terrible, but we dare not complain just in case we don't get any. The food queues here go on for at least half a kilometre and sometimes Mama can't get any food. There isn't enough for all the people here, so it goes quickly. I have seen starving people with swollen feet and faces walking around the streets. Some fall over and never get up. They are just left where they lie.

There is a terrible man here. He is the commander of the Kripo, the German Criminal police, and he has been known to murder people. I was told by a friend, who works in the factory, that those who are taken to a red brick building near his headquarters are never seen again. We are all very frightened of him.

My family relies so much on your parcels, and we are so grateful to you all. Please thank your sisters for their beautiful drawings and thank you for the writing paper. I always burn all your letters. I hate to do this, but they could get us shot if they are ever discovered. Anyway, they're good to start our fire with.

I cry at night missing you both. I miss Jo's silly stories and your smile, Ryszard. I miss my life.

All my love, my boyfriends,

Helena. xxxxx

Jo and I sneak around the back fence of her father's grocery store the following night, careful not to make any noise. We peer over the railings and notice a large Alsatian dog tied up near the back of the shop. It snarls, baring its long fangs, straining at its rope and barking wildly.

We jump the fence into the yard just as the Klaus, the grocer, lumbers out the back door, hefting a shotgun. We duck behind a shed, holding our breaths.

The German unties the rope and uses it as a lead. The dog's hackles are up, the fur bristling along its back. It lunges forward and pulls the rope out of the Kraut's hand. He falls, landing on his knees. He yells at the dog.

"Raus Rex!"

The maddened animal races up to the shed, barking madly. Strings of slobber drool from its snarling lips. As Rex rounds the shed's corner, Jo tries to hit him with a stick he picked up.

The dog grabs the stick in its teeth and begins to tug it from side to side. Jo hangs on for dear life, shouting over his shoulder.

"Run! For Christ's sake, Rys! Run!"

I scale the back fence. Jo drops the stick and runs after me. He shins up the palings.

The mongrel bounds up, sinking his fangs into Jo's leg, making him cry out in pain.

Cursing the animal, he tries to shake him off, but he can't. Rex has latched on.

The Kraut fires his shotgun. The dog lets go. Pellets pepper the wooden palings as Jo throws himself over the fence. He yelps when he lands on his injured leg. I grab him around the waist, and we move as fast as we can, until we're two blocks away.

"That was close," Jo gasps, bending down to catch his breath and inspect his calf.

Blood runs down his leg and he tries to stifle the flow with his hand. There are puncture wounds where the dog's teeth have penetrated his skin, but luckily it wasn't too deep. Jo's trousers stopped the bite going in any further. Sitting in an alleyway, with Jo inspecting his leg every few seconds, swiping the blood away, I take off my sock and wrap it around the wound to stifle the flow.

"Thanks, Rys," murmurs Jo.

I pat his knee.

"Let's get home. Maybe we can hitch a ride," I suggest as I lace up my boot.

Jo limps along the lane, until we come to a main road where we get a ride from a truck driver.

He drops us off at the start of the gravel lane near the farm.

Ma is worried about the dog bite. She bathes Jo's leg with vinegar, sprinkles on a small amount of sulphur powder, and wraps a tight bandage around it.

We check out the shopkeeper's yard the following night by climbing a tree in the back lane, but there is still no way in due to the dog prowling along the fence. It looks like he has been left off his rope this time. Growling and snapping, the dog madly scratches the palings, barking his head off again.

We clamber down the tree. Jo grunts as he lands on his feet, and we hastily make our way back to the road. There, Pan Tolinski sits in his old truck, smoking his pipe and gestures for us to get in.

He is an old man, maybe around sixty, rather thin and always wearing a dirty green beret pulled over his ears. Two days ago, Auntie arranged with him to pick us up when we're in the city, paying him with home-made vodka. After giving him the place and time, he heads into the city and waits patiently until we arrive.

On the third night, the dog is nowhere to be seen. We wait for an hour just in case it's inside the house.

Climbing over the fence, we creep along the back of the shop and Jo quickly retrieves the small pouch from behind the brick, tucking it carefully into his jacket pocket.

I hear a strange whimpering. I creep to the sound, and through the filtered light coming from the window, I see the dog lying on his side with a roll of wire tightly wound around his back legs. Blood trickles down from deep cuts along his flank. He tries to get up, but the wire stops him.

Whining he flops down. I put out my hand. He snaps at it. I pull it back quickly and sit on my haunches.

"It's okay boy," I whisper. "I won't touch you. Try not to struggle."

Jo scurries over.

"Ah Christ, he's in a mess," he hisses.

"Poor mate, it doesn't look good," I whisper to the dog.

"What do you mean 'poor mate'?" snarls Jo. "He nearly took my leg off!"

"He was only doing his job guarding the shop," I mutter then look up at Jo. "Now, get going. I'll knock on the door."

"Are you sure Rys? It could be dangerous. That Kraut was mad as hell last time."

"I'll take my chances Jo," I whisper hoarsely. "I can't just leave the dog here to die."

Jo grunts and quickly moves through the dark. I hear him vault the fence. I sidle to the door and knock loudly, then step into the shadows. I hear heavy footsteps, then the door is reefed open.

"Who's there?" Klaus bellows.

Rex yelps, then whimpers. Klaus bounds down the steps.

"Rex! Rex! Vere are you!"

I call out. "He's injured... He's tangled in wire... Over near the side fence."

"You hurt him? I kill you if you hurt him!"

"Nein, nein I found him that way!" I hiss back. He lumbers over to where the dog is lying and crouches down, forgetting me.

"My poor Rex. I help you boy," he says softly.

I take this as my cue and bolt for the fence, scaling it quickly and jumping to the other side, then run like hell towards the main road.

It's dangerous to be out at night as the Germans are frequently on patrol, so I scurry through the shadows and head out of town.

Pan Tolinski once again picks us up in his truck several blocks away from the grocery store. I greet him with a nod. Jo is already sitting in the cab.

"What happened to the dog?" asks Jo when I settle into the seat.

"The Kraut came out, saw the dog and totally forgot about me."

"I've tasted dog in the great war and it's not bad tasting meat!" says Pan Tolinski out of the blue. Jo snorts and I gaze back at the old man in shock.

Glancing at us he retorts, "Don't mock me Jo and don't be so shocked Rys! Dog meat makes a good stew!

He grins, "I bet you've eaten it already. The meat your aunt gave me yesterday was dog. Well, it smelled like dog meat."

Aghast, I look at Jo. Laughing, he stares back.

"Come to think of it, the stew we had last night did smell and taste strange," Jo chuckles.

"I got the meat from a lad in my gang."

Grimacing at the thought of us all eating dog meat, I fall silent for the rest of the trip with Jo occasionally snickering.

When we get home, everyone gathers in the kitchen and Jo spills out the pouch's contents onto the table. An expensive looking ruby ring, and a beautiful emerald bracelet tumble onto the tablecloth. The girls pick up the jewels with reverence, putting them on and admiring their hand and wrist.

Ma just huffs, holding out her hand as the girls reluctantly take them off, giving her a petulant look.

The jewellery is placed in the next parcels. The ring is nestled amongst our letters, along with a pencil sharpener I stole from a girl in my class ages ago. The bracelet is wrapped in writing paper and the calcium injections that Auntie was able to get from a doctor, who deals with the black-market.

The last parcel is wrapped carefully by Jo. It's a sculpture of a squirrel, curled in sleep no bigger than an egg. Jo carved it from wood, using a penknife.

He takes the small parcels upstairs for us to deliver later in the week.

CHAPTER

8

For two weeks Helena hasn't appeared at the wall. Levi meets us there with a note which only contains what they need. No letters, and Levi doesn't talk, so it's no use questioning him.

When we ask a question, he only nods or shakes his head. Helena told us once that he hasn't spoken since witnessing his parents being killed by the SS. She thought the shock of seeing the murders had caused his muteness.

We don't know what is happening to Helena and her family. We're worried sick.

Near the middle of July, on a cloudy and wet afternoon, we watch Helena walk slowly to the wall, head down and despondent. A light rain falls on her tattered head scarf and grimy raincoat as she kneels near the gap. Tears, mingling with rain droplets, trickle down her face and onto her collar.

"I'm so sorry I couldn't come to our meetings," she whispers.

She muffles a sob.

"My... my... my brother... Izaak has died!"

Jo grasps her hand which is resting on the bricks. "Oh Helena, I'm so sorry!" he whispers.

I lower my head as Jo gently squeezes Helena's hand. Faced

with her terrible grief, words fail me.

She sighs deeply and grips Jo's hand tightly.

"But that's not the worst," she whispers bitterly through her tears. Taking a deep breath, she looks up at us through reddened eyes reflecting a terrible anguish.

"My Papa went crazy and took his own life!"

Jo and I gasp.

My heart breaks to see such misery etched in her beautiful face.

Helena draws in a ragged breath. "He became worse when we were put in here. He lost his mind completely when Izaak died! His grief drove him to the brink. I raced after him when he ran out of the apartment, but I didn't know where he was going. I lost him. Then I saw him running towards the gate. It was locked and barred, but he threw himself on the wire and tried to climb. I never thought he had such strength. It was suicide."

Squeezing Jo's hand, she sobs.

"The guards shot Papa over and over again. ... They laughed and called out rude names. ... I remember falling to my knees, screaming ... and screaming," her voice trailing into a whisper.

She pauses and takes in a gulp of air "Papa went limp and fell to the ground. He didn't move! I couldn't go to him! I watched from behind a building as a guard dragged him away and left him in the gutter."

The rain begins to ease. Helena breathes out another shuddering breath, wiping her face with her free hand. "Levi and I managed to get him home, with the help of our neighbour, Pan Hoffman. We carried Papa using an old blanket. Mama cried all night and the next day I helped her to wash

Papa and dress him in his best suit. We were allowed to bury him at the back of the ghetto where a deep pit is dug for dead bodies. We tried to lower Papa into the pit, using the old blanket, but he rolled out and landed on his stomach, his face hidden in the mud. Mama screamed. We stood on the edge of the pit. There was nothing we could do. Pan Hoffman found a shovel and covered Papa's body with dirt."

She bows her head and whispers through tears. "Just like Izaak, he has no gravestone. No marker to tell me where he is buried."

Quietly weeping, Helena leans her forehead against the wall. We bow our heads while Jo still holds her hand. I look up and meet her eyes.

"What can we do for you, sweetheart?" I ask.

She takes a slow breath. "Nothing … Nothing … just keep us alive with your parcels. The jewels only bought enough extra food for Izaak. The ring bought a loaf of bread."

She releases Jo's hand, and with trembling fingers, takes out her damp letter, passing it through the gap. Exchanging it for parcels, we quickly shove in the brick, whisper our farewells and scurry away.

Danuta moves cautiously from the alleyway and runs to meet us as we trot across the street.

"What took you so long? What has happened?" she asks in a harsh whisper. Her eyes wide with fear "You were lucky the guard stayed in the sentry box. But if he came out, he would have found you for sure… I was so scared! I don't understand. What's going on?"

"For god's sake Danuta, not know!" I say callously, overcome by the bitter reality of what Helena is going through.

Indignant at my outburst, she lifts her chin and sniffs while adjusting her damp scarf around her head.

Jo gently takes her arm and threads it between his.

"Let's get back to the bus stop before it starts to rain again." He suggests, sensing the tension between us.

We walk briskly back to the bus shelter and sit on the bench in silence.

I look at her pretty profile. Her lips pouting.

"I apologise Danuta," I say softly, taking her hand. "I didn't mean to speak to you in that way."

She turns her head and looks into my eyes.

"Okay, apology accepted but tell me the truth. Is Helena, okay?"

"Yes, yes. She's okay," I ensure her. "We'll tell you what's happened on the bus."

She bites her lower lip, looking worried, and grips my hand tightly. I pat it reassuringly as the bus rounds the corner and the three of us climb on board.

Because Helena's family has become smaller, another family, the Pillarmanns, have moved in with them.

They have the bigger bedroom and take their meals with the rest of Helena's family.

22nd of July 1941.

Dear Ryszard and Jozef,

Our grieving over Papa and Izaak has become more bearable with Pan and Pani Pillarmann and their two boys living with us. They are very entertaining people. Pani Pillarmann has a beautiful singing voice and Pan Pillarmann plays a button accordion. The boys, Noah and Jacob, are always making up silly games, like who can pull the most stupid or ugliest face. Levi always wins this game.

The boys are constantly squabbling and squealing like piglets. If it turns into a real fight, Panni Pillarmann tries to break it up by smacking them around the head with their father's sock. Their father hides outside in the corridor and smokes a cigarette, shouting at them now and then through the closed door to all behave. Mama, Levi and I get the giggles.

It is all over in a very short time with their mother apologising and making us all coffee and something nice to eat from what little we have. Noah and Jacob shake our hands, apologising as well, while their father sneaks back in. He pulls out his accordion from under the bed and plays a tune to cheer everyone up. I must admit, I do like their silliness.

At teatime we share some of your food parcels with them and they never ask for more. Pani Pillarmann makes a tasty meal out of our meagre rations. The Pillarmanns work at the leather factory too. They told us they are leaving and moving to the countryside to work on farms. Pani Pillarmann said there was better food in the country, and a better life for her boys. Mama tried to warn them about Mayor Kozlowski's speeches 'of a better life'. That they are full of lies.

She even warned them of the rumours that people are taken away in these 'deportations' and killed by the Germans.

That there was no resettlement at all. But Pan Pillarmann just laughed and said they were false rumours and not to worry. But we do. We sang silly *songs last night. Levi clapped instead. I told them some of your jokes, Jo, and we all laughed. Pani Pillarmann snorts when she laughs, and this makes us laugh even harder.*

It's so nice to have fun again. I have no special requests this time so please, just send us what you can.

All my love, my boyfriends,

Helena xxxxx

On a separate piece of paper Helena has drawn a robin redbreast using coloured pencils. It is perched on a holly branch with a blue background. She must have seen one close enough to draw as she put in a lot of detail. Helena is a very good artist.

When Jo goes to work the following day. I look at her picture in the privacy of our bedroom. Noticing some writing on the back, I turn the page over.

'I drew this red robin for you to treasure,
My soccer stars, my clowns, who bring me joy forever.
A symbol of love and hope, this little bird will be,
As you both mean so much to me.'

It is so corny I have to chuckle. I kiss the drawing and stick the page on the wall with the robin redbreast facing out.

Every day I study Helena's drawing, admiring her skill.

At the next meeting we ask about the Pillarmanns. Helena says they have already left on the cattle wagons.

Her mother tried one last time to persuade them not to go,

but they were adamant the deportation is safe, and they are leaving for a better life. Helena's eyes brim with tears so we change the subject and ask about her mother instead.

We swap our letters, packages and move away.

One afternoon, Jo tells us he has decided to search for a job. He looks around the city for days until one of his friends mentions to him that his uncle is looking for an apprentice chef. So just like that, Jo scores an apprenticeship at one of the city's most popular restaurants, *Przyjemność, Pleasure*, which is now owned by Germans. I'm not too surprised. Jo has always been interested in cooking. Discussing recipes with Ma and helping Auntie with the cheese making.

I prefer to bang on the old piano and make up silly songs.

Jo mentions to his boss that he needs to leave early one day a week to help his sick mother. A lie of course. It's the time we meet Helena at the wall.

On the first week of his job, Jo makes sure he is early at our rendezvous with Helena. He hides in the shadows of the alleyway waiting for Danuta and I to creep around the corner. When we do Jo and I run to the wall.

Helena's letter is delivered by Levi. We ask if Helena is alright. He nods, but I see in his eyes something is very wrong. Without questioning him further, we hand him our packages and make our way home.

That night we read Helena's letter.

10th of August 1941

Dear Jozef and Ryszard,
I'm sorry I can't make it. Don't worry. I am fine but my Mama is very sick.

Doctor Janssen told me she has typhoid. I must be very careful nursing her or I'll get it too. She woke up one morning and was running a fever and complained of a terrible headache, so I gave her some boiled water to drink and bathed her forehead. She was running a high temperature and I'm worried about her.

I've told the factory manager that Mama is feeling unwell and will be back soon. This is so they won't get too suspicious. Doctor Janssen has ordered me not to tell anyone that it is typhoid, because the authorities will take her away. He explained the symptoms and how to look after her. As well as her high fevers she frequently vomits. Dr Janssen told me to wash her face and arms with cold water when she has a fever and wash the bucket and floors in diluted bleach. I'm not allowed to eat from her plate, and I need to keep her plate and spoon separate from mine and Levi's. He emphasised that I need to wash my hands after nursing her. I have decided to wear a mask made from one of my scarves when I am around her. Doctor thinks it's a good idea.

Mama has recovered a little now but is still very weak. Doctor Janssen has asked me to find painkillers for her as he has only a few. Could you possibly do this for me?

Love Helena xxx

A few days later, Jo and I manage to get a lift to the city with Mr Tolinski and pick up Danuta.

Hiding in the alleyway, we see two guards near the ghetto fence, idly talking and sharing a flask.

We spot Levi walking along the gravel lane and motion him to go to the brick wall.

There I give him food packages that contain painkillers and gifts for Helena, as it's her birthday in a couple of days. Ma has given her sugar-coated almonds that were bartered for with goat's cheese and Jo carved a robin red breast out of a piece of soft wood. The girls knitted a red wool hat with a matching scarf, and I gifted Helena the sharpened coloured pencils I took from her desk. We also put in a bag of sweets and a knitted beanie for Levi.

Levi meets us at the wall wearing an oversized jacket. He hides the packages quickly inside secret pockets. He looks bulky and I hope he doesn't look too suspicious. I tell him to be careful.

His jacket looks familiar. I think it's Izaak's as I remember him wearing it at school. Helena must have altered it for Levi.

Quickly, Levi scurries away while Jo replaces the brick. We crawl out from under the bushes and run across the road to meet up with Danuta.

"Didn't you see Helena?" she queries as we run towards her.

"No, only Levi." I reply, panting.

I glance back at the ghetto and watch the Jews leaving the factory.

"Christ! They look like the walking dead," I mutter.

I shake my head, looking down at my shoes as I wipe the tears from my face.

Jo pats my back.

Danuta strokes my arm and whispers.

"I know Rys…. I feel the same."

We slip out of the alley and walk to the bus stop in silence. As soon as Danuta gets on the bus, Jo and I go our separate ways to meet up with the sabotage gangs.

It's a successful night, painting slogans under a bridge, knowing full well the German transport trains pass through it during the day. Their officers will be mad as hell! Helena returns the following week, but our meeting is very short as the guard is walking our way. We quickly exchange a few words and grasp her hands. They're nearly skeletal and her face is now even more pale and drawn.

She quickly thanks us for the birthday presents, stands up and walks briskly back to the road behind the factory. Levi comes out of his small alcove and takes her hand.

17th of August 1941

Dear Ryszard and Jozef,
Thank you so much for the beautiful birthday presents. I will cherish them forever. I cried when I opened the parcels. It was such a surprise to receive them as I had forgotten my own birthday this year. Please thank your family for me. I recognized my coloured pencils Rys, thank you for saving them.
The painkillers have helped Mama so much. It is a miracle that you could deliver them so soon.
I'm sorry I couldn't collect them. Levi wrote everything down when he got home. He is such a good boy to remember it all.
Thank you for all the food, especially the sugar almonds. Levi, Mama and I eat one every night, sucking all the sugar off then slowly chewing the nut. Mama wept when she saw them. I managed to make

make Mama some soup with the potatoes you gave me and she's feeling a little better.

We have another family living with us now, but they are nasty and mean. They call us dirty names.

We keep away from them as much as possible. Levi and I share a small bedroom and I put Mama in a small separate room near us, it's more like a closet. These people don't bother us as they know Mama is sick. I worry, as I do not trust them.

They have robbed us once. They found the bread you gave us, so now I hide our stores under mama's bed. I'm sure they will not go anywhere near Mama.

I'm glad you both like my drawing. The little robin redbreast used to sit on the kitchen windowsill at home.

Love Helena xxx

Helena's letters are becoming briefer, and we worry about Pani Loftmann. The next note is also delivered by Levi. We hand him more painkillers and supplies.

25th of August 1942

Dear Ryszard and Jozef,

The people who live with us told the authorities about Mama. She was put into a hospital two days ago. I've cried and cried. I don't know what to do.

I've tried to see her, but I'm always turned away. Yesterday, when I arrived at the hospital, I saw German guards putting Mama into an ambulance. She looked very sick.

I ran up to them and asked where they were taking

her, but they just laughed and said it was to a better hospital. I tried to speak to her, but they shoved me away. When the back doors were slammed shut, I noticed it had no windows.

Which seemed wrong. As they got into the cab one of them yelled back at me that the ambulance was a Spezialwagen. I've heard rumours these vans gas people to death.

I screamed and ran up to the back doors. I banged on them, calling out to Mama. I couldn't make out what the people inside were yelling. Then I heard her voice. She was shouting through the gap in the door. She told me she loved me.

As the van began to move away, I ran along the side until I reached the soldier driving and pleaded for him to stop, but he ignored me and sped away.

My poor Mama! She has gone from me forever! I don't know what to do! Levi and I are so alone!

Helena.

As I re-read the letter in our bedroom I turn to Jo.

"I'm so worried about Helena! I'm afraid she has lost all hope!"

Jo sits on the bed and stares at me.

"Don't say that Rys."

His expression changes from absolute despair to anger.

"Don't ever say that!" he yells. "Helena will *not* give up! I know she won't! I... I... I won't allow it! She will go on living, whatever it takes! I will never give up on her!"

I stare at him. "What do you mean 'you won't allow it'? What the hell can you or I do? It's bloody hopeless, Jo!

And another thing, I won't give up on her either!"

He swears. Jumps up and storms out of the room, then bolts down the stairs. I look out the small window and see him running across the field towards the river. Jo is out all night. I don't see him again until the next day when he returns drunk and bleary eyed.

Levi collects the parcels the following week but there is no letter. We ask him about Helena, but he only shakes his head.

Now, we are very worried.

The following week a man walks towards the brick wall gesturing for us to join him. Wary of a trap, we run across the road and squat behind the bushes. He stops near our loose brick and taps the wall.

We remove the brick, gazing up at him apprehensively.

He squats down and peers through the gap. He has kind brown eyes, fuzzy short black hair and the typical look of the ghetto Jews, pale and starving.

"Hello Helena's friends, I am Doctor Janssen," he whispers in a thick Dutch accent. "Helena has asked me to give you these two letters. She asks if you can read this one now."

He taps a folded piece of paper.

"But do it quickly," he adds, furtively looking over his shoulder.

We take the letters from his hand, unfold the note, and begin to read.

I've decided to take Levi and myself to the train station and board a cattle wagon to the camps. Please give Dr Janssen the packages. He will distribute the contents to people in need. Love Helena

We each let out a quivering breath. Jo screws up the note and shoves it in his pocket.

We dig around in our coats, empty the satchel and hand Dr Janssen the packages.

He puts them in a medical bag.

"Are you going to these camps, too, Doctor?" I inquire as I pass the last item, a small bottle of aspirin. "What about your family?"

"My wife died years ago in the Netherlands," he murmurs, closing the lock on his bag. "We had no children, and I can't get back to Holland. So maybe I can help at the camps."

He stares through the gap at our grief-stricken faces.

"Helena is a strong girl," he whispers. "At the moment she is grieving for the loss of her family, but I believe she will get through the grief, find some hope and survive this war."

"I hope so too Doctor," I whisper.

Jo puts the bricks back and we both sit there for a long moment, staring at the brick wall.

Riding back on the bus we read the second letter.

8th of September 1941

My Darling Boys,
I'm finding it too hard to meet you both one last time.

It has become unbearable without my family. I miss them so much. I am so miserable that I cry every night. I find every day so very hard and at times I'm so sad I couldn't be bothered to collect our rations, so Levi has taken on this job.

The people I live with are terrible. They steal the

104

food you give me all the time, so I hide it outside in the rubbish behind the building. It sometimes spoils but we eat it anyway. I think they spied on me two nights ago as the food you had given me has disappeared.

Dr Janssen has suggested we get on the next train to the camps. The ghetto is going to close soon, and all the Jews will be transported in the next few weeks.

He heard this from one of the guards. He hopes to be put in a camp where he can still practise medicine.

I know the train could possibly lead us to our deaths, but I must take the chance. We could just as easily die here. Hopefully, Levi and I will survive and see you both again. Thank you so much for helping us, and please thank your family for their parcels and their friendship.

I will miss your letters. I have always cherished your devotion to me and my family.

I love you both dearly. Helena xxxxx

Stoically dry-eyed, Jo slowly refolds the letter as I use my sleeve to wipe tears from my cheeks. Danuta cries bitterly over the loss of her best friend. Jo and I cry over the loss of our beloved Helena.

Telling our family is hard. The girls run upstairs in tears. Ma and Auntie sit at the kitchen table. Silent. Staring into space.

With heavy hearts, Jo and I trudge up the stairs and lie on our beds. Staring at the ceiling, we talk late into the night, recalling our time with Helena. Sharing how much we love her.

As dawn breaks over the roof of the barn, we finally fall asleep, only to be woken soon after by a soft tapping at our door. Ma stands beside our beds with a tray bearing hot, sweet tea and two slices of bread.

"Get up, boys," she says gently. "Come and help around the farm. It will take your minds off Helena."

Less than a week later Jo and I try to find Danuta. We knocked on the door and went around the back of her house.

Her neighbour pops her head over the fence. An old woman, her head covered in a black scarf. She squints at us through rheumy eyes.

"Are you looking for Danuta?" she asks in a raspy voice, a rollup hanging from her thin bottom lip, "she and her family have left. Her Ma told me they are heading for Switzerland. She told me to help myself to her furniture. So, I did. And got a nice rocking chair to go near my fire as well as a set of silver spoons. Fancy leaving those behind... I wouldn't have left silver spoons behind."

Her eyes glaze over as if she lost her train of thought.

She looks at us confused. Her whole demeanour changes into an angry old crone.

"What do you want?"

"Nothing lady. Just looking for our friend," says Jo then under his breath, growls, "crazy baba yaga".

Muttering, she and makes her way to her backdoor, slamming it behind her.

CHAPTER

9

Jo becomes withdrawn. Quiet and morose. He hardly speaks to anyone.

I, on the other hand, get on with life, accepting the reasoning behind Helena's decision. I still love her and miss her with all my heart, but I know there is nothing I can do to change her situation. I accept it. Jo doesn't. I hear him whispering her name late at night through muffled sobs.

His grief is a deeper than mine.

He improves as the weeks pass, grooming the horse, raking out the stable or fishing in the river, but he still isn't his normal self. For long periods he gazes into space, deep in thought. Gone are his silly jokes and stupid antics. He is a different person altogether. He seems years older than me. An adult.

One quiet Sunday afternoon, with the rain beating against the attic window, Jo and I sit on our beds playing checkers on our small table. The atmosphere is oppressive.

I move my black chip diagonally across the board.

Jo moves his red chip, blocking my black and glances up at me.

I meet his eyes, sensing something isn't right. Jo hesitates then draws in a breath as if he is about to say something unpleasant, but instead looks down and studies the board. He picks up a captured piece, twiddling it through his fingers.

I frown.

He looks nervous. He keeps biting his lower lip.

"Out with it, Jo!" I say with a sigh.

"I'm going to join the Armia Krajowa tomorrow." Jo meets my eyes, his words tumbling out. "I need to fight the Krauts, Rys. Every day they take more from us. Today at the butchers there was a new owner. Another bloody fat German!"

He stands and paces the room. "I've been thinking about joining for months. This week I asked around and a couple of men I know at work told me about the Polish Resistance. A man approached me yesterday when I was outside having a smoke. He gave me a note."

Pulling it from his back pocket, he hands it to me. The note simply states a time and place for him to meet someone.

Jo takes the note back, strikes a match and burns it, crushing the ash into a dish.

"If you join, I'm joining as well!" I insist as Jo cracks open a window, allowing the smoke to escape.

"Not straight away Rys," Jo sighs. "How about joining later? Ma isn't going to like it if both of us join. Give it a few months."

"I don't want to, Jo! I want to fight the German bastards too. Right now!"

Jo glances my way. "I know, but please, Rys. Don't join just yet. Think how Ma will feel."

"Shit! … Shit! Okay, Jo. But I still don't like it!" I grumble loudly.

All the fight leaves me as he pats my shoulder. I stand and walk slowly to the attic window, watching the rain hitting the glass. Rivulets of water track grimy patterns across the surface.

I trace one then turn to face him.

"What about your job?"

Jo sits down and leans back on his bed, "I'll still work at the restaurant. I'll work around my job and the Resistance."

Jo has been the rock we have all depended on for the last twelve months. If he gets caught by the Germans, he will most probably be shot, then all the responsibility of the family will lie on my shoulders. *I shy away from that idea.*

The next morning, I roll over from the wall I'm snoring into. Jo is gone. His bed is empty. His rucksack is missing.

Ma quizzes me about Jo's early start. After a few attempts at lying, I tell her the truth.

Her face darkens. The porridge pot bounces off the stove, spraying the bench top with small, grey clots of oats.

Auntie, who had been glancing at her with a worried expression, moves to her side, putting an arm around her shoulders.

"Antoniya! I believe what Jo is doing is his way of fighting the Germans. I know it's dangerous, but he's not leaving us completely. He's growing into a man. Let him do what he feels he must.

He was so upset when Helena left, and being involved in the Armia Krajowa may be his way of moving on. You know the older men will keep an eye on him."

Ma huffs, she picks up the pot, adds more water and some salt, scoops the spilled oats back in, then places it back on the stove. Scowling, she vigorously stirs the porridge. Everyone is silent. I sit at the table and fiddle with my spoon and bowl.

"Rys! Stop that!" Ma snaps at me and spoons grey mush into my bowl. My appetite wanes at the sight of thick lumps clinging to the side of the bowl, but I splash goat's milk on it and eat it anyway. I'm always hungry. And I know there's nothing else.

Jo returns late that night, telling me the Commanding Officer, who he cockily calls the CO, is pleased he works at a posh restaurant. Jo's job is to take notice of who dines there, especially if they are German officials, and if possible, recall their conversations. After his shifts, he will be trained in sabotaging trains, rail lines, bridges and setting explosives.

I'm sick with envy but bury the feeling deep, putting on a false smile.

"It sounds great Jo. When do you start?"

"Tomorrow night," Jo exclaims excitedly as he prepares for bed. I turn to face the wall faking sleep. I don't want to hear any more.

"The man I met a few days ago is a lieutenant," Jo continues, pulling off his socks, "he's going to help me out, you know, train me. I can't wait!"

Two days later Jo pulls me upstairs to the attic and shuts the door.

"I saw SS at the restaurant last night and later reported it to the CO," whispers Jo, so Ma and the girls can't overhear. "Something big is going down. But I couldn't understand all that was said, even though we seated them near the kitchen doors. I need to learn German fast. One of the men at headquarters is going to teach me, and I'll ask Ma to help me as well."

I nod with approval, though the envy has still not left me. I leave the attic, allowing Jo to catch up on some sleep, and bolt through the kitchen to the back yard, savagely taking out my frustration on the soccer ball.

Over the coming week Jo practises German with Ma, speaking it all the time.

By the end of the week, he's learned enough of the language to understand the SS officers at the restaurant. He reports his findings to his CO that a large shipment of ammunition is to arrive soon by train.

"When the cognac flows, so do their tongues," chuckles Jo as he sits on his bed in the morning light and takes off his shirt. He's been gone all night.

He grins as I sit up to face him. "The CO was so impressed with me," he gloats. "He said I can go up a rank and have my own team."

"Great! Now I can join!" I say beaming with pleasure.

"No Rys. No. I told you before, it's too soon. Like I said, give it a couple of months," Jo pleads.

"Come on Jo, why do I need to wait?" I whine, feeling deflated.

But Jo doesn't reply. Instead, he turns his back towards me, feigning sleep. I sniff and get up, noisily putting on my pants then my socks. I stomp downstairs and meet Ma on the landing.

"Is everything alright with Jo?" Ma asks in a worried voice.

"Yep! He's hunky dory!" I say in an American accent, something I heard in a western movie.

Ma frowns as I roughly pull open the back door and run outside into the crisp morning air.

#####

Jo's spying continues for three months. I hardly see him. He gets up early and arrives home late at night. Sometimes he never returns at all. He told me once that he wouldn't finish his assignments until two in the morning and then he had to start work in a couple of hours. So those nights he sleeps on a straw mattress at headquarters.

He doesn't tell me much about his work or the underground, but I can see it is taking a toll on him. He seems anxious. Stressed. His face gaunt, his eyes bloodshot. We hardly talk anymore, and when we do it's the same old arguments. Usually about me joining up.

Jo doesn't return home for two days.

Ma goes to the restaurant to inquire about him, only to find Jo has not reported for work, either.

She learns that an Armia Krajowa headquarter was raided two nights ago. A lot of men were shot, but many were put on trains. Nobody knows where they were sent.

Ma returns home very worried and upset. She sits at the kitchen table, sobbing, unable to stop.

Through gasping breaths, Ma tells Auntie about the raid and the transport train. Auntie stands behind her, gripping her shoulders, reassuring her that Jo could still be alive, but Ma is too upset to listen.

Their cheeks wet with tears; the girls quietly stare from Ma to Auntie as the story unfolds. Auntie finally puts Ma to bed where she stays several days, nursed with cups of tea and comforting chatter. The girls remain with her day and night. I keep out of her way.

It's hard to sleep. I lie on my bed for hours, staring at Helena's drawing pinned to the wall. Closing my eyes, I pray for

Jo and Helena to still be alive. I pray for Pa to be safe.

I don't know if God heard my prayers that night, but I believe he did, because a week later, when we learned the names of the men shot by the SS. Jo's isn't among them. He was put on the train and transported to God knows where.

Losing Jo makes me feel broken inside. I'm lost without him.

I stay out most nights with my mates, causing havoc.

I paint the Resistance's slogan everywhere, including the town hall where the Nazis are based. This is very dangerous, but I've lost all sense of caution.

I know Ma is upset about my skulduggery and getting in at all hours in the morning, but I don't care.

Something has died within me.

CHAPTER

10

Two weeks after Jo goes missing, I join the Polish Resistance.

I talk about joining every time I meet up with my sabotage gang, until one night, one of the lad's brothers, a private in the Armia Krajowa unit near our area, arrives at our hideout. He pulls me to the side where we have a lengthy discussion about the Polish underground.

"Each city has different levels of commanding officers overseeing their units in specific areas" explains Marcin. "Our nearest one is two kilometres away. We change our location regularly."

He pulls out a cigarette from a packet and lights it. Exhaling the smoke he adds, "The Polish Resistance is a mix of armed forces, strictly military with levels of hierarchical order. It's governed by the Polish Underground State which acts in accord with the Polish Government in Exile, and it was first led by General Stefan 'Grot' Rowecki but now by General Tadeusz 'Bor' Komorowski."

He looks into my eyes. "I can see you are keen. I'll tell my CO and he'll send someone to meet you."

Two days later, as I'm queuing for bread, I see a man across the street, lighting a cigarette. He gestures with his hand as he places the cigarette to his lips, using a signal I learnt from the gang, where we put the thumb up while dragging on the fag.

He leans against a brick wall, waiting for me to cross the street.

He is tall, lean and looks to be in his twenties. His cloth cap is pulled down low on his brow allowing only the bottom half of his unshaved face to show.

I casually stroll towards him with the loaf tucked under my arm. He drops the cigarette on the footpath, squashes it with his boot and secretly passes me a small slip of paper, as I walk by. I slide it furtively into my pants pocket.

I fly upstairs to the attic bedroom and quietly close the door. Sitting on my bed I pull out the note. My heart races. Excitement mounting, I scan the scribbled handwriting.

Bombed church near Legnica Kunice Plaza at 1700.

Legnica Kunice Plaza? I think I know where that is. But to be sure I'll ask Auntie, she'll know.

I place the note on the side table. My chest constricts with fear but my heart thumps excitedly. I'm finally in it! The Resistance. Elated, I jump from the bed and dance around the room, kissing Helena's drawing. Oh yeah! I am interested alright!

Picking up the note, I set a match to it, remembering the day Jo did the same and watch as the paper turns to ash. I crush the embers on Jo's ashtray.

I flop on my bed and stare at Helena's drawing, daydreaming about sabotaging German trains and blowing up bridges. Being a hero.

Arriving early at the meeting place, I make my way to a nearby wall and watch and wait. I look around.

The ruins are silent, dark and cold.

An avalanche of snow clings to the inside walls, covering the charred pews and overturned altar.

The steeple has withstood the explosion, but the huge bell that once hung in the tower has fallen to the ground amongst the charred roof timbers. Failing light from the moon penetrates a cracked stained-glass window between two upright stone pillars. The place feels eerie as the muted colours dance along the snow. On edge, I jump when a piece of timber crashes to the ground. Even with the cold, a trickle of sweat runs down my back and my hands start to tremble. I snort at my fear, gripping my hands under my arms to keep them from shaking.

Startled by a loud thump coming from the back of the church, I turn to see the same man I met yesterday, ploughing through the deep snow towards me. I drop my arms and stand very still, watching his every move. He stops at my side and looks furtively around.

"How are you, Ryszard?" he whispers.

"Fine," I murmur. "How do you know my name?"

"Private Wozniak told me. He was the one who recommended you. I am Corporal Jan Michalski."

He turns and grips my shoulder.

"What do you think? Do you want to join us?"

"Bloody oath I do!" I hoarsely whisper. "When do I start?"

"Good. Good. I like to see new recruits being keen," he chuckles as he shakes my hand.

He looks me in the eye, "You need to be at 12 Crotz Street at 16:00, tomorrow. Don't be late. Knock on the door and when it opens say 'bears in the forest hut'."

#####

I can't sleep. The night drags on. I toss and turn for hours waiting for the sun to peep over Auntie's barn. As the feeble rays hit the wall above my head, I jump out of bed already dressed, and run downstairs to the kitchen.

Sawing through a stale loaf, I madly chew the slice as I pour goat's milk into a glass. Gulping it down between bites of bread, I pull down a rag from the rack above the stove, wet it at the sink and scrub my face. I rinse my mouth with water and pat my hair down.

Tiptoeing through the house, I close the front door softly behind me, put on my boots and run up the path. Bolting over the gate, I race to the main road and hitch a ride to the city to meet up with the gang. In our hideout we plan our day. I don't mention the meeting with Corporal Michalski.

I'm not paying attention when the leader of our group is giving us instructions. Something to do with a train station. Anxiously, I keep looking at an old clock hanging on the wall. The leader notices so I finally tell him and the gang that I'm joining the Armia Krajowa later in the afternoon. They clap me on the back and congratulate me. I beam back at them with pride.

Walking briskly along the pavement to 12 Crotz street, my heart is pounding with every step, my hair feels damp under my cap, even though it is minus 20 degrees.

I arrive at a rundown hovel. I check the house number. Yep, it's the right address, but it looks deserted. The windows are boarded up and paint is peeling from the front door. It looks like it hasn't been lived in for years. There is no knocker, so I rap on the door, then blow into my hands and rub them together. I stamp my feet, thrusting my hands into my pockets.

I'm cold but it's not just from the freezing weather.

The door creaks open.

An old man, like an old wizard out of a fairy-tale, sniffs loudly and wipes his nose with his filthy sleeve. His long white hair hangs limply around his shoulders, matching his long scruffy beard. He scowls around the edge of the door. His rheumy eyes, cold and belligerent, pierce into mine.

"What do you want?" he snarls at me in a phlegmy voice.

I stand there like an idiot. My mind goes blank. I start to panic.

For Christ's sake what is the password?

He grunts, shutting the door in my face. I grab the door handle, push it back and blurt out the code. Sniffing in annoyance, he pulls the door wider, its hinges screeching disapproval, and dramatically gestures to me to come in. As I slide past him, I smell the reek of alcohol on his breath mixing unpleasantly with the rank odour of his unwashed body.

Closing the front door with a bang, he leads me through a dingy corridor to the back of the house and leaves me facing yet another closed door. I can hear muffled noises behind it. Cautiously, I open it and creep down the creaky stairs into a basement.

A single bulb lights the scene. The room is hazy with cigarette smoke. A small window, along the top wall is ajar, letting in cold winter air while allowing some of the smoke to escape.

I stand on the bottom step, mesmerised. A group of men is pouring over maps on a desk, a man is talking into a radio transmitter in the corner. Another group is cleaning rifles. Yet others sit at a table talking in hushed tones. All are wearing a white and red armband with the Armia Krajowa insignia.

Corporal Michalski notices me and calls me over.

"Good to see you, Rys," he whispers.

"Men," he says in a louder voice, "this is Ryszard."

I nod a greeting.

They murmur back, then return to their tasks.

A man approaches and shakes my hand.

He looks tough. He's around thirty years old with a barrel chest, strong, large hands, fair skin and light brown hair receding at the temples.

I recognise him.

We met at a soccer game four years ago where he barracked for the opposing team. Jo and I stood next to him, yelling at the referee about a decision he made. This man looked down at us, amused. I jumped up and down in frustration, banging into him and stepping on his feet.

I remember him bending down to me and yelling. "You're a little pest, just like a Mala Mucha, a little fly!"

I glared at him and blurted out that our team was going to thrash his team. As soon as the words left my mouth his team scored a goal. He just laughed and ruffled my hair.

My thoughts return to the room as one of the men comes up to him and relays a message. The man nods his head then turns back to me, smiling.

"I know you. You're that pesky kid at a soccer match I went to years ago. That's right we won two to one. I remember you weren't too pleased about that score. What did I call you? Ah yes, Mala Mucha."

He smiles again, displaying a gold incisor. I just grin back, totally in awe.

"Instead of Ryszard I'll call you 'Mucha'. Is that okay?" he asks.

I stand taller. "That's okay with me sir!"

"Good! I'm your commanding officer," he affirms, "but everyone calls me CO or Major."

He smiles at me and pats me on the shoulder. I beam back at him.

His blue eyes crinkle as he peers into mine.

I feel so proud to be one of his men.

The Major nods towards a tall lanky youth about my age, who is seated on a wooden bench. I watch him slowly lean forward, with his elbows resting on his knees, and study the men at the table, intent on what they are saying.

"The lad over there is your training partner and you'll both be put into a team as soon as possible," says the Major.

He pats my shoulder again, then turns and walks back to his maps. I move to the corner of the room and sit down next to my new partner. He straightens and introduces himself as Franz Polanski. I introduce myself and offer my hand.

He takes it with a firm grip and looks me straight in the eye.

An indication he is a decent chap.

Tall and wiry, Franz's skin and hair are darker than mine, similar to my mother's olive complexion. He has strong, bony features from which hazel eyes, greener than brown, peer from beneath dark brows. Except for a chipped incisor, his lips curl in a guarded smile over straight white teeth.

"Have you been here long?" I ask.

Franz bends over and ties up his boot lace. "Nah just started today."

"Do you know the CO's name?" I ask.

"He's Major Leon Zielinski. I asked one of the men when I got here. He told me the Major worked as a railway engineer before the war. He knows the railway system well.

"When were you recruited?" I ask.

I'm curious about Franz since he's going to be my training partner.

He casually fiddles with his satchel's strap, adjusting the buckle, then looks up.

"Today. I was inquiring about the Resistance a week ago. Yesterday a man came to the garage where I work and slipped me a note as I was checking the oil in his truck. I was to meet him at this address."

I point to the Corporal. "I was approached yesterday as well by the man over there."

"I had a different recruiter," comments Franz and leans against the wall, stretching out his long legs. I notice he's still wearing his garage overalls with the insignia 'Mazek Motors' above his left pocket.

Taking off his cap, he sweeps his dark hair back with his hand, then pulls his grimy cap back over his forehead.

He watches the men moving around the room.

We sit in silence, watching the activities in the room. It's really crowded but surprisingly quiet. The only noise is the murmuring at the map table and the static of the radio transmitter.

Corporal Michalski walks up to us. We stand but he waves us back onto our bench.

He squats in front of us, his knee resting on the floor.

"Your job is to be 'sniffers' which means you carefully observe the Germans around the railyard and discover the cargo on the trains. It's important to the Resistance to know what they bring in. Observing is your first objective, scavenging the second. Dress yourselves in old clothes. Pick up any coal dropped by the trains, but most importantly, spy on the Germans."

#####

Franz and I become efficient railway spies and scavengers, quickly learning to work together as a team. Scurrying stealthily towards the unguarded wagons, Franz and I slide the door open as one of us climbs in and scouts around. We are very careful. And quick. It's a dangerous job. If we get caught, we'll be shot on the spot, or hauled off to the Gestapo to be interrogated.

After a month at this job, the Major promotes Franz and I to a crew who trains us in using explosives.

Until we know what we're doing, it's too dangerous to use the real thing. Using four-gallon drums, Corporal Michalski shows us how to set detonators and place dummy explosives.

We practise and practise until we're perfect, then Corporal Michalski checks our work with a critical eye, looking for mistakes.

A week later, he allows us to help the more experienced men blow up railway carriages using real explosives. We learn new techniques, such as the best place to stick the explosives on train carriages and how long to make the fuse.

After this training, Corporal Michalski informs us we're to organise our own crew of six young boys to scrounge around the rail yards. They'll be lookouts when Franz and I blow up

railway carriages or tracks.
     We've become saboteurs.

11

Franz has to leave his daytime job. The new German owner replaced him and his boss with his own mechanics. He has no other job to go to, so we both become full time members of the Armia Krajowa.

Apart from Jo, Franz is the best friend I've ever had, and is also the toughest guy I know. Except for his temper, he rarely shows his true feelings. I've seen him knock a grown man down with only a couple of good punches, just for teasing him on the length of his hair. If he is hit hard in a fight, he staggers around until he gets his breath, then dives in, delivering blows. His opponent, or opponents never stand a chance. I rarely see him take a fall.

As sabotage partners, Franz and I do everything together. We plan and execute missions and organise our small crew on scavenger hunts while spying on the Germans.

Three months after our recruitment, we are given our first important mission.

We are to blow up a train parked in the shunting yards.

The dark railyard appears deserted. Thick fog shrouds stationary trains, spilling out along the tracks. Except for a dull light shining through a grimy window in the station masters office, from where I can hear faint laughter and music, the night is quiet. We creep towards the trains and crouch behind a wall.

Raucous laughter suddenly disturbs the night.

Holding my breath, I peek around the corner.

"Can you see anything, Rys," Franz whispers. He moves closer, peering through the darkness.

"I see five Krauts about ten metres away," I mutter. "They're moving towards the last carriage."

"Well then, we'll blow up the first two wagons!" Franz sniggers.

I grin back at him.

"Let's give the Krauts a friendly welcome to our beloved homeland."

We ease around the wall and scuttle towards the string of carriages, at times crawling like flattened lizards. Peering through the slats of the wagons as we creep past, we see wooden crates labelled with the word 'Uniforms'.

"The Nazi bastards are going to miss those," I murmur under my breath.

Through the fog, we can just make out three guards sharing a flask as they smoke, their backs turned, about two hundred metres away.

Silently, we creep between the first and second wagons. Crouching low we dig through our satchels and pull out our gear, laying each item carefully on the sleeper beneath the coupling. Hearing the crunching sound of someone walking on gravel, we freeze, not making a sound. Stealthily, we crawl under the wagon to wait.

Beyond the train wheels I see a pair of boots marching past, heading for the guards further up the line. I wait a long, long moment before I slide out to check what the Germans are up to now. The newcomer is greeted with more laughter. It sounds as if they're telling smutty jokes. Anyway, they're making enough noise to cover any we make.

Squatting between the wagons, I motion to Franz to join me. He slithers forward, his body inadvertently crunching the gravel. We stop to listen before he cautiously lifts himself up.

"Let's do this job quickly before the bastard comes back," he hisses.

Working quickly, we attach explosives and detonators to the undercarriage of the first two wagons. We light the fuses, then run like hell across the tracks towards safety.

The train disintegrates with an earth-shaking explosion. Glancing back, I see a hellish inferno. Flames and roiling plumes of smoke fill the midnight sky. Deadly shrapnel falls around our heads. Small splinters of wood smack into our bodies, like burning arrows. The blast hits us, knocking us to the ground. I take a couple of panting breaths then bounce back up.

Heaving and spitting, I take off running.

My heart pounds in my chest.

Franz gallops past, a feral grin stretching from ear to ear.

I catch up with him, racing him back to the truck parked on the street. Gulping in air, we fling ourselves over the tailgate into the back. Our crew reach out to pull us further in. The truck jerks into motion then speeds back to headquarters.

Still breathing heavily, we report to Corporal Michalski,

Some of the younger boys chiming in with added details. It takes us some time to settle down before the Corporal commands us to head for home.

Exhausted, I fall into bed and sleep till midday.

#####

Franz habitually sweeps his overlong brown hair out of his eyes, tucking it under his cap. He told me once he couldn't afford to go to the barber as most of his money was spent on food.

I suppose he might be seen as handsome by the ladies. I don't really know. I just see him as Franz.

So, it is very strange, one cold wintery day, that Franz walks into headquarters sporting a black eye. His head shorn, cuts marking his scalp.

"Christ, Franz! Did you get caught by a mad sheep shearer?"

He glares at me, then relents. "Na, Rys. It was the old man. He pinned me down and used the clippers on my hair. I gave him a shiner for it, though."

Looking pointedly at his black eye, I stifle a laugh, fearing I'll also be sporting a shiner if I'm not careful.

"Yeah, well," he mutters, avoiding my eye, "the old man belted me right back."

"Why aren't you wearing your cap?" I ask.

Rubbing his scalp with his hands Franz grunts, "Dad took it after I gave him the black eye."

The poor bloke looks like a hardened criminal who just escaped from gaol. *Not a good look!*

I see how uncomfortable he is, pulling up his collar and looking around. A few of the men glance his way, smirking.

Taking off my cap, I hand it to Franz.

"Here, have mine," I say, "I have a spare one at home."

"Thanks, Rys," Franz murmurs as he takes hold of it, tugging it tight over his ears. "You're a good mate!"

Sometime later, the CO allows us to work with an older crew from a different section. They blow up larger structures like bridges, roads and buildings.

They call us 'Goffers' - go for this, go for that, hold this, hold that - but we don't mind. It helps us gain experience and become better at our own job.

One night we're given our most important assignment to date. It's to blow up a munitions train hidden behind a disused railway station on the outskirts of the city.

But first, two extra crews and ourselves are to remove as much ammunition, guns and explosives from the carriages as we can carry. A few of the toughest older men take care of the guards.

Heaving and grunting we work two to a crate, scurrying with backs bent to the waiting trucks. They take off, leaving our crew to set the explosives. Our boys stand sentry, well hidden behind a fence. Franz and I jog towards the wagons just as three drunken German soldiers stagger into the yard.

We hide behind a boarded-up building.

"Can we get any closer without the Krauts seeing us?" Franz whispers.

"Not without a distraction," I murmur, thinking hard till inspiration strikes. "Let's get Alek to do something useful for a change." Alek is the CO's nephew, and a real whiner.

"The Sniveller," snarls Franz. "He always starts sniffing and snivelling when the pressure is on! But I suppose we can trust him to do as he's told."

"Christ Franz! You have a name for everyone!"

"I haven't got one for you, you little runt!" he smirks.

"That's enough, you bastard." I thump his shoulder, then

get back to business. "How about we get Alek and the boys to start yelling and throwing stones at the Germans?" I suggest. "They'll have to keep their distance, then run like hell."

Franz agrees. He creeps along the track to the back of the yard, relays the order to Alek and the lads, then moves back to me.

Our boys are very impressive. The swearing is like hearing Pan Kalinski on one of his vodka benders.

The Germans can't resist chasing our lads. As they return the abuse and fire their guns wildly, we scoot to the first and then the middle wagon, and tape the explosives, ironically stolen from an earlier German train to the undercarriage.

The detonators set, we light the fuse, making sure it's long enough for us to get behind the dilapidated carriages further down the line. We've learnt by experience how to judge this better than on our first job.

Then we run like hell, sprinting over the tracks.

The explosion is massive.

Huge.

We used too much dynamite.

As I run back to the waiting truck my face stings painfully, my eyebrows are singed and the back of my neck burns. The back of my jacket is smouldering and there is a deafening ringing in my ears. My cap is scorched, with a line of blackened holes along the brim.

Our CO is not too pleased with the waste of explosives, but seeing our red faces and burnt hair, he bursts out laughing.

Franz scowls. With his brittle singed eyebrows and soot-smudged face he looks like a puzzled owl. It makes the CO laugh even louder. He slaps us on the back, telling all of us to be more careful next time.

A week later, The Polish Resistance learn that a large consignment of German ammunition and supplies are arriving that night.

While, once again, the tougher men take care of the guards, the rest of us set about unloading the carriages filled with ammunition, food and medical supplies.

Our top priority is to remove all the ammunition and medical supplies first, then the food. This is one of our biggest hauls yet. Crews from several other districts are involved in this heist. The amount of stuff we steal is staggering, filling our convoy of trucks to overflowing. It's a blessing for all of us, and I'm finally able to get some decent food my family and friends.

We're almost finished when Franz hands me a pair of boots someone has dropped.

"They're too small for me. You take them Rys. You never know when you might need them."

Boots are valuable, so I tie the laces together and sling them round my neck. "Thanks. They will be handy on the farm."

We move on to the next crate.

I prise open the lid and pull out a rifle.

"Good find. Let's get some others in here so we can unload these quickly," says Franz.

The Germans are losing so much from their supply trains, they re-enforce the guards with more SS soldiers and deploy extra patrols, making it very dangerous for us to rob trains in the rail yards.

The Resistance must find another way.

The Commanding Officers from a couple of units devise a bold plan to steal German army trucks, hide them in vacant warehouses and barns and use them to transport men to railway lines, kilometres outside the city. With their German markings, the trucks blend in with other convoys, allowing us to transport the stolen goods to our hidden depots.

Franz is recruited into the 'auto crew' for a short time and tells me all about it when we meet up.

"We lifted three trucks last night. It was a good haul. I worked on them when we got back. Just minor stuff like cleaning spark plugs and checking the points."

In this new operation, loading crews hide in the forest, watching and waiting. As the train approaches, a demolition team blows up the railway lines, derailing the engine. The older men quickly board the disabled train, killing the guards, so it is safe for us to plunder the wagons.

We fill the trucks with ammunition, guns and fuel. Whatever is useful.

The trucks then drive to the outskirts of the city, to a safe house or abandoned warehouse, for us to off-load.

On our way back to headquarters, the drivers dodge the German night patrols roaming the city, parking the trucks in deserted warehouses along the riverbank where we hide until it's light, then make our way home.

I always arrive home exhausted, sleeping in my clothes until noon, then making my way back to headquarters to await further orders and another eventful night with Franz and our crew.

CHAPTER

12

Late one afternoon, a couple of months after the big heist, we sort out the boys for a mundane coal scavenging job. Our team has grown to eight with three younger lads joining last week.

The lads are scrounging around the railway yard picking up bits of coal, while Franz and I have a quiet discussion behind a carriage. I hear a noise, and glance to my side. A big policeman unexpectedly steps in front of us. I almost laugh. His gut, overhanging his belt, stretches his uniform jacket almost beyond its limit. I look beyond him and lose all inclination to laugh. More police officers emerge from hiding.

"What are you two doing here?" he wheezes, thrusting out his fat hand.

"Show me your papers!"

We produce our documents. Snatching them from our hands, he studies them up close as if he has poor eyesight, then hands them back. To our surprise he produces a gun. Franz and I slowly raise our hands. When he shouts to his men to round up the boys, our lads scatter.

The police fire their weapons into the air, sending the boys diving for cover.

However, one of the lads flees, disappearing into the evening gloom, a policeman giving chase.

The fat policeman orders us out from the shelter of the two carriages. He grabs my collar, shaking me forcefully. Heavy-handedly, he pushes me to my knees. Trembling, I place my hands behind my head as another policeman grabs Franz, who fights back.

They scuffle. Franz punches the man in the stomach, winding him. His knees buckle, and he falls to the ground. But Franz is soon overpowered by two other officers and pinned down. He is jerked to his feet, his arms wrenched behind his back.

The police gather the rest of the crew at gunpoint and push us into awaiting truck, ordering us to sit on the floor. I look around me to see if everyone is okay. Unhurt, the younger boys are terrified, their eyes wide with fear.

"These traitorous bastards must have been bribed by the Nazis," whispers Franz.

"I hate them," I whisper back.

Ten minutes later the police throw us into a holding cell, a dingy room at the back of the police station, where we squat against grimy walls covered with graffiti. We stare at each other in silence, with only the occasional sniffle from Alek, who wedges himself tightly between Franz and me. I try to calm him by holding onto his arm.

He's only just turned thirteen and I don't blame him this time for whimpering. Even Franz refrains from snarling at him.

The Police taunt us through the bars of the cell. Shoving their guns between the gaps, they pretend to shoot.

The fat one jeers at us, telling us we are all going to die.

With a guttural laugh, he points his finger in a gun gesture to his fleshy temple and grabs his crotch.

Franz and I give him the one finger salute, changing his glee to rage. He slams his hands against the bars, his fat, wobbling cheeks livid, as he snarls obscene curses. He takes off his jacket and flings it at a chair in the corner, missing it totally. His fat stomach, too big for his shirt, a white, mottled roll overhanging his belt which disappears into the flab. His stomach presses against the bars, indenting ribbed channels into the flabby skin. We laugh.

Becoming apoplectic, he reaches for his gun, but it snags on the holster flap. Furiously, he pulls and tugs to free it. Suddenly the gun fires into the concrete floor, the ricocheting bullet making everyone duck. The idiot jumps up and down, squealing like a pig, making us laugh even louder. He's shot himself in the foot!

An exasperated Police Sergeant storms in, putting a stop to his constables' antics.

"Out!" he orders. Back to your duties! I'll see you in my office, Constable Balik!"

The constables slink out. Still muttering curses and clutching his gun, the fat bastard, Balik, limps out after his mates.

Narrow-eyed, the sergeant scowls us, then huffs, straightens his belt, and walks back to his office, slamming the door behind him. But it's a flimsy bit of rubbish. We can hear every word he shouts.

"Those swine are SS property, Balik! They pay us to catch them for interrogation! If we shoot their playthings, **we get nothing!**"

There is a mumble from Balik which further incenses the sergeant.

"**Nothing! Do. You. Hear. Me. Constable. Balik!**" He bellows, then moderates his voice, but not by much. We still hear every word. We're laughing fit to burst at our captor's comeuppance.

"You stupid git! And for god's sake stop waving that bloody gun around before you put a bullet through your other foot! Damn it all, Balik! You're bleeding all over the floor. **Out! And get that foot seen too!**"

We hear a mumbled "Yes sir.", then silence.

#####

Hours pass. Alek and the younger lads are miserable. Some cry. The rest of us lean against the prison walls, silently reading the graffiti left by former inmates. Above Franz is the Polish Underground symbol. Hopelessly, I bow my head.

How little we have achieved fighting the enemy is as sad as the actual thought of dying.

Wearily, I peer at the clock on the wall outside the holding cell. It's midnight. An hour ago, we heard the police officers departing at the end of their shift.

Only one man remains on duty, the sergeant informing him he'll be back in the morning to meet with the SS.

There's a scuffle in the office.

The guard swears. There's a grunt, followed by a loud thump. Startled, we scramble to our feet to see a man standing in the open doorway, holding a hessian bag in his hand.

"Come now," he chuckles as he leans on the doorframe, "You didn't think we would leave you here?"

"It's the CO!"

"The Major's come for us!"

We whoop with joy.

"Quiet! Quiet!" he hisses. "You'll have the whole German army down on us." He shakes his free hand showing us a bunch of keys. "Let's get out of here so I can blow this traitor's nest to smithereens." He swears under his breath.

We rush to the bars as our CO unlocks the bolt. Running out of the cell, through the adjacent room, we pass the still form of the police guard, the man Franz winded, and bolt into the still night. Major Zielinski tosses the limp body of the policeman into the truck with us, slams the tailgate, and pulls down the canvas flap to hide us. He jumps into the passenger seat and shouts at the driver.

"Take off you stupid Polak!"

An explosion erupts behind us as the truck speeds away. Debris rains onto the truck's canopy. We cheer and slap each other's backs.

The truck stops five minutes later beside a park.

The Major and the driver jog to the back and pull down the tailgate.

"Is the policeman dead, Uncle?" asks Alek.

"No boy, he's just knocked out," the Major answers softly. He lifts the body by the shoulders, the driver grabbing the legs.

"Why didn't you kill him?"

"Well Alek," his uncle pants as they carry the still form.

"There are enough people... being murdered... every day... I don't need to add this misguided fool to the Nazis' tally!"

They dump the policeman on a park bench, then jump back into the truck. We start singing the Polish National Anthem as we drive off.

"For God's sake, shut up you lot or we'll all be caught!" the Major hisses through the cab's back window, then turns to the driver. "What are you waiting for? Christmas! Get going!"

The driver crunches the gears, jerking the truck, then drives us back to headquarters.

CHAPTER

13

We must carry our ID papers, the Kennkarte, with us at all times.

False documents cost five hundred zlotys and are made for people who are trying to escape the authorities

Our unit has a very good forger, Berlinski, who is a civil servant working for the town council. He supplies the Resistance with these documents to help smuggle people out of the country or change the ID of the Polish Resistance personnel.

This Kennkarte consists of a thin sheet of grey cardboard measuring 30 cm by 14 cm with two parallel folds and writing on both sides to make a six-page document.

Each page measures 10 by 14 cm. The letter P is stamped near the name to mark nationality. A fingerprint goes in one corner and a photograph is stapled to the appropriate square.

But my Kennkarte is the real deal.

I applied for one when I reached fifteen. Mother supplied my birth certificate and made a formal declaration that I was Polish and belonged to the Aryan race.

Six months have passed.

During the day Franz and I deliver coded messages to other Resistance HQs in the city.

Each morning we study the city map, making sure we know the quickest route through the streets. HQs aren't marked, as it's too dangerous if it falls into the wrong hands, so we memorise the streets instead.

On our routes we keep our eyes peeled for snitches, German collaborators, Poles who sell their souls to be in bed with the Germans. These bastards betray their people for an extra loaf of bread. Just like the police.

A month ago, one of our men, Private Malinski, was captured by the Gestapo, when a snitch reported to them, he had seen Malinski carrying a weapon. Pure fabrication. But it is making us all nervous.

Major Zielinski moved headquarters three times in one week until one of his lieutenants found the snitch and handed him to 'The Polish Resistance Assassination Unit' that deals with these collaborators, most of them ending up in a ditch. Dead.

#####

One chilly morning in the middle of spring, Franz and I walk casually around the streets, scouting the area.

A lot of German patrols are checking papers. Further up is a roadblock stopping civilian traffic. The roads, cleared and swept, are busier than usual. Jeeps and black military cars full of dignitaries are madly driving in all directions, scattering pedestrians.

Huge red flags with black swastikas hang from the buildings with smaller flags outside apartment and office windows. Something big is happening. Maybe an important German dignitary is arriving soon.

We rush back to report to the Major.

"I'll find out what's going on!" he says.

That afternoon, he sends us out with important coded messages.

Before we leave, Major Zielinski tells us Heinrich Himmler, one of Hitler's top men, is visiting the city tomorrow and it is important to get these messages to six of the Resistance strongholds north of the city. He hints of an assassination but refuses to go into detail.

Placing the city map on the wooden table, he points his finger to certain streets, and I memorise the areas.

"Be bloody careful and don't get caught! These messages are of utmost importance," the Major repeats.

He orders other runners to go in the opposite direction and deliver messages to the southern part of the city.

"Have you got your messages safe?" whispers Franz, rifling through his satchel.

It looks like we're going to work, and the satchels are our lunch bags.

"Yes," I patted the side of the bag. "I hid them in a secret pocket covered by old lunch paper!"

Franz climbs the basement steps, calling over his shoulder "Let's get going before the German patrols come around. I'll meet you later outside the library."

"Okay, I'll see you then," I whisper, as he opens the door.

I follow him, adjusting the satchel on my back.

We creep behind a kitchen wall, carefully scanning the area.

I hiss under my breath, "Look! There's that fat bastard, Balik. He's out of uniform, leaning on a door frame across the street."

Franz smirks. "Let's give him the run-around."

Slipping around the wall, we casually walk along the road. Balik eases out of the doorway and follows us.

We split up and zigzag our way through crowds of people, dodging into quiet lanes that connect to major roads, making our way north.

I stop now and again to see if he is behind me.

I see him near a shop front, a confused expression on his pig-like features. His eyes dart to and fro, his fat stomach heaving. I snigger and duck behind a building.

After a while I trot along a recently bombed street. People are picking through the debris, mostly for tin and iron which they can sell on the black market. I look back, spotting him coming around the corner. Melting in the crowd, I pick up a tin pot as I check him out.

He waddles down the road, scrutinising the ruins. I scurry behind a brick wall, watch him pass, and wait for five minutes, then scramble over the rubble, throwing the pot into an old woman's basket. I dart up the street, glancing up the alleyways, but he's nowhere to be seen.

I trot, zig-zagging an extra kilometre through the streets, finally rounding a corner where I signal to a lookout. He signals back that all is clear, and I bolt down the basement steps, two at a time. Pumping with adrenaline I race into the room and deliver my first message to a man sitting at a desk.

Between gasps I tell him it's important and before he can reply I race out again.

All afternoon I duck and dodge, delivering the rest of my messages, constantly on the watch for the fat bastard, but he seems to have disappeared.

Jogging up to the library, I notice Franz sitting quietly on a bench reading a book. I slow to a walk and pass him without looking. He casually gets up, follows me a few paces behind, tucking his book into his satchel.

He has so much more stamina than me. Sometimes I'm bewildered how he gets around so fast. We head back to HQ.

Laughing about our escapade with Balik, we bolt down the stairs. I knock on the door and whisper the password. The door quickly opens, and I step through.

Straight into a tall man wearing an immaculate SS uniform.

My heart stops!

Looking up from the shiny black boots and grey tricot breeches, belted with a silver buckle embossed with the Nazi emblem. I stare at his grey jacket with its many insignias, a medallion of the iron-cross is pinned to his chest, and three silver diamonds stitched to his black collar. Terrified, my eyes come to rest on neatly parted blond hair plastered to his skull and a long, narrow, scar running down his close shaven cheek.

I flinch. My stomach clenching, I meet icy pale blue eyes. Merciless, cruel eyes.

His cologne is so strong my eyes water. A shiver goes down my spine and the blood drains from my face. I look down. Surprised, I notice my pants are wet. I've pissed myself.

With a malevolent smile he looks down at the stain between my legs, twirling his grey military cap in his hand. Placing it back on his head, he tugs the brim down then thrusts out his hand, snapping his fingers.

"Papers."

We hand him our Kennkartes then take a step back. He

scrutinises them for a minute, then hands them back. Drawing his swagger stick from under his arm, he taps it gently against his thigh.

"You cabbage heads," he smirks in Polish. "I do like Polish boys. They are such fun!"

His terrifying smile returns. I begin to shake. Franz growls obscenities under his breath.

"What were you delivering?" The officer asks, rubbing the stick against Franz's shoulder.

"Nothing," says Franz, glancing at the stick rubbing back and forth. "We've just come back from work."

"Liar!" The kraut bellows. He hits Franz hard, forcing him to one knee.

Fire in his eyes, Franz slowly rises to his feet.

I quickly intervene.

"We were delivering propaganda leaflets. Umm ... to people on the street!"

The officer's eyes narrow, studying my face, not believing a word of it.

I start to panic. "Please Sir, it's the truth. I swear on my mother's grave."

Pursing his lips, he taps the swagger stick softly against his palm. A minute passes. I fiddle with my satchel strap, turning my eyes towards the ground.

Franz stands completely still as does the Major and our crew lined up against a wall with rifles pointed at their chests. I feel I'll start blubbering like a baby any minute. Finally, the officer, a lieutenant I think from his uniform, gestures to his men and they haul us further inside the room and shut the door.

Our satchels are ripped off our backs and emptied. Old apple cores and lunch papers fall to the floor, and Franz's book. The SS officer moves the garbage around with the toe of his boot then picks up the book. He shakes the pages, thumbs through it and reads the title, *Moby Dick*, then places it very deliberately on the table.

"Take off your caps! Slowly! Place them at your feet," orders the lieutenant.

"What the hell," mumbles Franz as he drops his cap to the floor.

Puzzled I do the same, peering curiously at the officer.

Two SS soldiers do a body search, examine our caps then our bags for any secret compartments. I hold my breath, but fortunately their cursory search misses the well-disguised false bottoms. They shake their heads.

The lieutenant taps his thigh again. One of his eyes twitches. Angry, red blotches stain his pale cheeks.

"Put them with the others!" he growls, waving his stick towards the wall, where a body lies in a corner.

"Chin up, Mucha," the Major murmurs to me as we're lined up with him and the men.

"Get them all out of here!" The SS officer shouts, angrily smacking his stick harder against his leg.

We're forced outside at gunpoint and dragged to a waiting truck. Out of the corner of my eye I see Balik talking to our captor. Franz's book is tucked under the lieutenant's arm.

"Hey, you Balik! You fat bastard! You're a shit eating Nazi dog that licks German feet!" Franz yells, aiming a hacking spit in his direction.

"You're a bloody traitor! You've got shit for brains!" I shout.

"I hope you shoot your other foot off!"

Balik squints and tries to make out who we are.

The idiot needs glasses.

Revealing his rotten teeth, he smiles scornfully as he finally recognises our faces.

We give him a one finger salute, but this time he just laughs with his mouth wide. His fat jowls wobble as he points in our direction. The officer glances our way and smiles, handing over a wad of money to Constable Balik. The price of our betrayal.

The fat moron tucks the money in his pants pocket and watches, snickering to himself, as we're thumped on the back with rifles and pushed into the back of the waiting truck.

My mind whirls.

Is our capture my fault?

I should have warned the men! I should have gone back and told the Major about Balik when I saw him in the doorway.

I feel sick!

I hate the bastard!

I hope he's caught by the Armia Krajowa assassins!

We sit in silence in the truck. The Major tries to speak to us, but he's smashed in the mouth with a rifle, splitting his lip. Blood spurts from his nose and he wipes it away with his sleeve.

I hear a young voice cry out. That's when I notice Alek sitting with the older men.

Oh God no! He was supposed to be with his aunt. What is he doing here?

I look around the truck again, relief sweeping over me as I realise the rest of our young crew aren't among us.

I lean back wearily and peer through the canvas flaps, to see

Constable Bloody Balik lumbering off up the road as we slowly pull away.

The army truck belches smoke.

The city disappears from view.

Part 2

1943

CHAPTER

14

The Krauts drive us to an old mansion surrounded by farmlands. Its grey, lichen-covered stone walls, surround a once neatly manicured garden. Now the flower beds are withered and dry, the lawn overgrown and dotted with weeds.

The truck slows on the gravel driveway, coming to a halt at an imposing portico. We sit in silence as our SS guards jump from the tailgate and aim their rifles at our heads.

"Schnell! Get off now!" The taller one shouts.

They order us to line up facing the old building. A black staff car pulls up. The blond lieutenant gets out, straightens his jacket and walks briskly to the entrance of the house.

I study the old building. It would have been magnificent in its day.

A portico, supported by Roman columns, shelters wide front doors now chipped and scratched. Broad steps descend to where we stand, weeds growing through the cracks. Tall bay windows are open to let in the cool spring air. Lace curtains billow out softly in the breeze. White roses climb up one side of the building, spreading out above the top windows.

The house belongs to a bygone era. I wonder who really owned it. Maybe a banker or a rich merchant. Most probably a Jew.

But the pleasant scene is marred by a huge red and black Nazi banner draped from the top window and lounging SS soldiers smoking on the steps. They idly glance our way, then hastily stand to salute the lieutenant.

Our CO is dragged off to a small brick building and shoved inside. A guard follows him in, slamming the door.

Our guards march us to the rear of the house. We're ordered inside a dingy barn where about thirty men sit along the walls or lean on posts. A couple of the men have been badly beaten, blood still oozing from their battered faces. Near the rafters, grimy windows leak afternoon light onto the filthy, straw covered floor. Dark and dank, the barn reeks of human shit and animal dung.

There are men from Resistance HQs throughout the city, but many others are strangers to me. With the addition of our group there are now about forty-five bodies in this airless prison.

Two German officers appear at a small door, their silhouettes ominously black against the outside light. They stride into the barn. Six guards carrying rifles spread out behind them. I recognise one of the officers as the bastard who captured us. The other paunchy, shorter man wears the grey-green uniform of a German kommandant.

They stand in the faint light from a high window. Staring at us. The older man rocks on the balls of his feet, a cruel smile on his thin lips as his dark eyes dart around the room, taking us all in. My mouth goes dry. Fear creeps into my stomach at the thought of the horror to come. I don't know if I'll be able to withstand torture.

"Schnell! … Schnell!" the lieutenant bellows. "Get up, Polish scum!"

The prisoners against the walls stumble to their feet, stiff-legged from sitting so long.

The SS guards raise their rifles, and we quickly shuffle into four lines.

The kommandant paces around the room with his hands behind his back. He stops now and then to pin a man with his unblinking stare.

He doesn't say a word.

We stand to attention.

Silent.

Still.

He returns to stand in the light from the window, rocking back and forth as I study him. His uniform is pristine, every silver badge gleaming in the pale light. Each lapel of his jacket is decorated with a silver laurel wreath against a black background. The collar of his white shirt is stiffly starched. His black tie is knotted tightly under his receding chin.

A dark brown strap diagonally crossing his chest carries a gun holstered at his hip. Brown hair, shaved around his ears, can be seen under a military cap decorated with a silver cord wrapped above the black brim. A silver eagle, its wings spread wide, is pinned to the centre of the band.

He also sports a 'Hitler' moustache, in fact he could pass as Adolf Hitler's brother.

He sniffs, then looks at us contemptuously.

"You are all enemy agents of Germany," he screeches in Polish, in a surprisingly high voice, "I have been commanded by our beloved Fuhrer to deal harshly with you all! Tomorrow will be the day..."

He falls silent as if he's contemplating his next words. The blond lieutenant stands slightly behind him, his expression one of utter boredom. The kommandant turns to him and whispers, as he removes a monocle from his left eye, polishing it with a freshly laundered handkerchief. The lieutenant nods, an evil smile spreading across his Aryan features and gently taps his swagger stick against his leg.

The kommandant paces the room. Turning his back on us, he screws the monocle back into his eye and carefully folds the handkerchief, replacing it in his pocket. Huffing, he turns to face us, once more clasping his hands behind his back, making his paunch stick out.

Staring at us, he rocks on his heels.

Long minutes tick by.

Sweat drips off our faces.

We wait for the rest of his speech.

But to our surprise he turns and goose-steps out of the barn, the lieutenant close on his heels.

We are ordered to fall out, and shuffle back to our vacated spots. The guards file out, locking the door.

"Has anyone tried to find a way out?" Private Wozniak whispers as he sits on a pile of straw.

"We've already looked," growls a man of around forty. Dried blood streaks his neck from a deep gash on his left cheek.

"The barn has been reinforced, the windows and doors are barred from the outside. There're no gaps anywhere and the ground is hard as stone. The Krauts have cleared out anything we could use, even old nails in the walls. There are two armed guards always stationed at the door, so if we tried to break it down, we would have no chance."

Wozniak rubs his face. "Ah shit! Okay! What was that all about with the kommandant?" he asks.

"Kommandant von Becker!" The man turns his head and spits. "The man is crazy!"

Another man adds in a hoarse whisper, his thick moustache quivering in fury. "Bloody von Becker never finishes a sentence. I'll tell you what, Hitler can pick 'em! That's for bloody sure!"

He runs his fingers through his hair and scowls. "And I tell you what else. His offsider, that blond bastard, Lieutenant Ludwig, is a bloody lunatic. When we were captured, he shot one of our boys in the head. All because he took his cap off! The bastard ordered one of his men to inspect the cap. I thought, what the hell? What's he doing? Then it dawned on me, he was looking for a secret weapon. A secret weapon! Where the hell can you hide a secret weapon in a cap for Christ's sake?" He spits on the floor. "They're bloody 'nutters', both of them."

"I wondered why he ordered us to take off our caps back at headquarters," replies Wozniak, chewing his lip.

"It could be something to do with the scar on the bastard's face," he adds. "I've seen a similar scare done by a razor blade. A blade that small could be easily hidden in a cap, I suppose."

The man with the bleeding face tentatively touches his cheek

Timon, a lad from our crew pipes up. "It could! I know of a gang who used blades." His eyes grow wide as the memory comes to him. "They did hide them in their caps. Just under the brim."

A hushed, but heated discussion starts between the men,

all voicing different opinions.

"Like I said!" the moustached man snarls in a hoarse whisper, reclaiming our attention. "Those two are bloody psychos, especially that bastard Ludwig!"

He slouches against the wall, his moustache twitching with annoyance, ending the discussion.

Throughout the day we hear snippets of conversation from the guards and with my limited German, I translate for the others.

"I think they are talking about the Reichsfuhrer" I whisper back. "Something about Himmler... he's in the city... von Becker is going to a reception in his honour... the city is in lockdown." I listen intently, my ear to the wall. "The Gestapo discovered an assassination plot... the Poles in the barn are to be... Ah! I can't hear any more, I think the guards have moved away."

Without food, with only a bucket of water between us all, we're left alone overnight.

Alek, Franz and I scoop water with our hands and gulp it down fast, aware of the men behind us, waiting their turn. Two empty buckets are used as a latrine.

I'm hungry. I haven't eaten since breakfast and that was only a stale piece of bread and a slice of salami. My stomach groans as I lean against the wall.

"I'm bloody starving!" I moan softly.

"Me too!" groans Alek, clasping his stomach.

"I doubt we'll be fed," whispers Franz. "Try to get some sleep."

The night turns cold. I sit on the hard floor, my head resting on my knees. Tears spill silently down my face. I pull my jumper up around my ears and hunker down, wiping my eyes. I am not going to behave like a baby, crying for his mother.

We huddle together for warmth.

Alek keeps close to me and Franz, wedging himself between us.

"We're in trouble," grunts an old man, sitting opposite, padding his jacket with dirty straw for extra warmth.

Franz laughs.

"Bloody hell! Of course, we're in trouble, old man!" Franz snorts sarcastically. "We'll all be meeting our maker soon and I know for bloody sure mine is not residing in heaven!"

Alek whimpers. I pat his arm and give Franz a withering glance.

"No more uplifting speeches Franz!"

Silent now, Franz rests his head against the wall, peering up to the ceiling.

Alek wipes his eyes with his sleeve.

"I'm too young to die!" he sniffs. "I don't want to die!"

"I know. I know Alek." I whisper.

I grip his shoulder, making him turn to face me.

"Why were you at headquarters?"

He looks at me, with tears streaking his grimy face, and whimpers.

"I was delivering a message for Auntie," he whispers. "She was warning Uncle about all the SS soldiers milling around the area. I ran as fast as I could and had just told Uncle when the SS burst in through the door.

Corporal Michalski pulled out his gun and there was shooting. He was killed. The SS officer told us to line up against the wall and that's when you and Franz came down the stairs."

"Where were the lookouts?" I ask.

"I don't know, Rys."

I frown at that, smelling a rat. I am quiet. Thinking. I glance at Franz. His expression grim, he stares into the darkening gloom. I think he is thinking the same as me.

"Try to get some sleep Alek," I sigh.

Still sniffing, he leans his head on my shoulder as Franz and I secretly discuss the betrayal and who might be the traitor. We lapse into silence as exhaustion takes hold and we drift into sleep. Restless, I wake during the night. I'm worried about the Major. Worried about what tomorrow will bring. Worried about dying.

#####

At dawn, the guards drive us outside and line us up against the courtyard wall. It's peppered with bullet holes. The vine that once grew there is tattered and torn, probably by the spraying bullets. A fine layer of frost covers the grass. We stamp our feet and blow into our hands, shivering in the freezing air.

Hours pass.

It's Sunday, church bells toll in the distance, calling the faithful to mass. The place is practically deserted. A handful of SS privates are standing around. Last night must have been a big night. I wonder if the Reichsfuhrer is recovering from a hangover. I hope he has a massive headache, the bastard! My mind wanders, Pa suffered from headaches when he and Uncle Thomasz drank too much. Ma wasn't that pleased when Pa got drunk. He was always loud and swore a lot.

I'm brought back to reality by an uncomfortable pain in my

bladder. It's no good asking for the toilet. The last man who tried that got belted round the ears with a rifle butt. Disgusted, I piss where I stand. It flows down my trouser legs into my boots, spilling out onto the ground. My pants reek with the smell.

I'm thirsty. My tongue is like thick leather, clinging to the top of my mouth. I can hardly swallow.

Men start to wobble, staggering forwards or leaning back onto the wall. We sweat as the unrelenting midday sun belts down onto our heads.

It seems unreal that we were so cold in the morning but now we're sweltering. It's turned out to be an unusually hot spring day.

I look towards the sky and see a large flock of birds flying towards the forest beyond a freshly tilled field. Nothing else moves.

I'm hot.

Time passes slowly.

Men slump to the ground, exhausted by the heat, only to be mercilessly beaten by the guards. Their comrades roughly pull them up and hold them upright.

I glance at Franz. His face glistens and sweat drips from his chin. Alek has gone very pale and starts to slowly topple forward. Franz grabs him, firmly holding the back of his jacket, and pulls him up. He keeps his hand there to keep Alek from falling.

My head spins as if I'm going to pass out as well.

Wozniak grabs my collar and keeps me upright. When I think I won't last another minute, one of the guards places a bucket filled with water at the end of the line and we take turns ladling it with a tin mug, gulping it down fast and passing it along. Another guard empties out a wheelbarrow near our feet. Picks and shovels tumble out in a heap.

"Pick them up and form two lines!" He orders in German, then gestures with his hands.

There are only six shovels and two picks. Franz and I and six other men pick them up as the guards chivvy us into two lines and march us down a path and through a wrought iron gate.

We stand on the edge of a freshly ploughed field.

"Start digging a trench!" a guard yells. He demonstrates the action with his arms.

"Why?" utters Franz under his breath.

I shrug and start digging.

I glance up to see Kommandant von Becker and Lieutenant Ludwig, who is carrying a bag, walking briskly down the path and through the open gate. They have a quiet conversation with the guards.

Ludwig picks up a stick, drags it along the dirt the full length of our line and orders us to start dig along it. The ploughed ground is boggy. The thick loamy soil makes a sucking noise as we turn over the sods.

It's strenuous work and every shovelful of the slippery mud feels like I'm lifting twenty kilos.

My muscles spasm and burn.

The intense afternoon heat burns our backs. The men take off their jackets, I pull off my jumper and we throw them into a pile.

An ornate wooden chair with a matching table is brought down from the mansion and placed under a shady tree off to the side.

Fine china cups and a silver tea service are laid on the small table by a young officer. He arranges dainty sandwiches on a plate. Von Becker takes off his jacket and drapes it over the back of the chair, then loosens his tie. He sits down waiting for his cup to be filled and takes a sandwich, delicately biting a corner. Crossing his legs in a feminine fashion, he observes our progress.

Lieutenant Ludwig stands, as utterly bored as before, behind his superior's chair, bending at times, to hear his words.

Kommandant von Becker inspects our work off and on during the afternoon, occasionally ordering us to make the trench wider or deeper. He orders one of the prisoners to stand in the trench while he squats at the edge and measures the height and width with a stick. Satisfied, he struggles to his feet and goes back to his chair under the tree, sitting down heavily as his cup is re-filled from a fresh pot of tea.

They let us drink again from the tin bucket, near the edge of the field.

The Nazis piss along the fence as time stretches on. We have no toilet break. So, we piss where we stand.

We swap tools regularly when we become exhausted. But in the end, we're all spent.

It takes three hours to dig a trench three metres wide and two metres deep and about twenty metres long.

"Stop!" Lieutenant Ludwig commands.

We throw our tools onto the ground and clamber out of the trench.

The kommandant carefully sets his cup down in its saucer, then stands, placing his hands on his hips. He stretches his back. If I wasn't so exhausted, I'd laugh at the way his round stomach sticks out. Removing his military cap and tie, he places them on the chair, then rolls up his shirt sleeves.

Ludwig also removes his jacket, folds it neatly, and places it next to the tea service.

He reaches into the bag near his feet and pulls out two leather aprons, handing one to von Becker. Still wearing his cap, he speaks to the two guards as he ties the apron straps around his back.

The guards disappear back to the mansion and come back dragging Major Zielinski between them.

His face is swollen, unrecognisable. Blood trickles from a deep cut above his eye. He grunts and spits blood. Unable to support himself, his feet trail uselessly behind him. His hands are mutilated. One finger is cut off, dripping blood. Another is distorted, the knuckles shattered. One of his ears has been slashed, hanging by the earlobe and jiggles as he's hauled towards the trench.

My heart thuds in my chest as I stare at his hands and face. He was once a strong, robust man who wreaked havoc on the Germans. We admired him. His patriotism influenced us all. Now he is reduced to a bloody mess, his torn shirt revealing oozing burns across his chest.

Tears spill down my cheeks as the guards push him onto his knees near the edge of the trench. The Kommandant picks up his Luger and walks towards him.

It becomes obvious what the trench is for.

I look at the length of it. The same length as the row in which we are standing. I shiver runs down my spine. A terrible dread tightening my chest. This is no hole to stand in as a form of torture, but something even more sinister. A grave.

Bile fills my mouth.

I spit.

Alek vomits.

A few men shout obscenities at the Germans while some cry out in alarm. Most keep silent. Enraged, the Kommandant bellows at their insubordination. Ludwig takes control of the situation, ordering his men to beat us with their rifles.

I'm belted in the back and go down on my knees. I look up at von Becker. He is livid, his cheeks a blotchy pink and his small moustache quivering. The bastard looks like he's going to have a seizure. I wish.

The guards shoot four men in the back. Wozniak is one of them. We all fall to the ground, our hands covering our heads, our foreheads pressing into the loamy soil. We lie still, waiting for the next round of bullets.

I hear von Becker draw in a heaving breath. In his high-pitched voice, he screams at us.

"Get up at once and watch this piece of shite, your beloved major, take his last breath!"

We slowly get to our feet. Our CO lifts his head, gazing at us, his motley team, and smiles as he recognises our faces.

The German bastard shoots him through the temple.

Blood and brains blow out the other side of his skull.

He pitches slowly forward, his body tumbling into the ditch.

We cry out.

Alek lets out a piercing scream.

I gasp, clutching his arm.

Franz curses, clenching his fists.

The rest of the men hang their heads in grief.

Von Becker orders the guards to separate the younger men

from the older men. They shove us around until we are arranged from the oldest to the youngest. It's as if they have a ritual procedure for executions.

Such a German thing to do.

Ludwig orders us to kneel beside the trench. Our legs trembling, we drop to our knees. I grab Alek's arm, supporting him. He pisses himself.

Beginning the executions with the older men, von Becker and Ludwig simultaneously fire their lugers, then reload, moving steadily down the line towards the younger men.

Us.

I turn my head and watch dead men topple into the muddy ditch like a surreally choreographed dance of falling bodies. It reminds me of a movie I saw with Helena where beautiful ladies dived in sequence into the depths of a pool. They swam around waving their arms in unison.

I let go of Alek's arm and for some unfathomable reason I look down at my knees anchored in the mud. I am fascinated by a trail of ants scurrying towards the trench then disappearing over the edge. I'm mesmerised by these little creatures. Momentarily forgetting about the shots ringing in the air, the spray of blood floating in the breeze, Alek praying beside me and Franz breathing heavily.

Once again, I look towards the shooting.

Everything appears to be happening in slow motion but is all so very clear. The bodies fall languidly into the trench as if a rope is holding them back, slowing their momentum.

Bullets that penetrate the men's skulls drift through a red mist. The German executioners' movements are slow. Unhurried. Methodical and precise. Their guns gradually kick back as they take their time, then move to the next man. They both sport cruel smiles. Clearly enjoying themselves. The SS guards slouch against the tree smoking their cigarettes. The ends burn brightly with the smoke drifting aimlessly away.

My breathing is calm and even. Relaxed.

My rapid heartbeat has slowed to a dull measured thudding in my chest.

There's a kind of ringing in my ears. Not the same as the ringing from the sabotage explosions. This is more of a soft tinkling sound.

I look past the trench to see a strange man standing on the other side. He's dressed in an old-fashioned army uniform, with a pointed cap, maybe from the first world war. Perched on his shoulder is a robin red breast.

He smiles at me.

A radiant glow emanates from his body. I smile back, utterly calm. Somehow relieved that my time on this earth has come to an end.

He salutes as he and the bird slowly fade away.

I shake my head.

I must be seeing things.

Remembering silly things.

I inhale a ragged breath and gradually return to reality. My heartbeat accelerates and the ringing stops.

The two sadists have paused once more to reload. Their arms and faces are speckled with blood, their leather aprons dripping with gore.

Everything is as it was before.

Except that most of us now lie sprawled and bleeding in the bottom of the pit. Dead.

I look up as a shadow spread over me. Storm clouds blot out the sun. A large drop splashes on my head. Then another.

Even the Heavens weep.

"Shyster!" the kommandant mutters under his breath. He is very close to me. I notice his brown boots covered in blood. I keep my head down and only look up when he walks briskly back to the table followed by his fellow executioner. They carefully re-holster their weapons and wipe their faces with dampened cloths.

Hurrying as lightning flashes and thunder rumbles across the sky, the two bastards remove their aprons, toss them to the ground and put on their jackets.

There is a slow communal intake of breath as the remaining men turn their heads to watch.

Von Becker stands erect at the end of the trench, his hands behind his back, disregarding the slow splatter of rain on his pristine uniform.

"You will all be executed at dawn tomorrow!" he yells as heavier raindrops drum on his cap. "We will be rid of your menace once and for all, and our Fuhrer's plans will be fulfilled in this God-forsaken country." He waves his hand dismissively. "Go! Enjoy your last sleep on this earth!"

He takes out his monocle and wipes it vigorously with a fresh handkerchief.

Abruptly he turns and jogs through the gate, the back of his jacket streaked with raindrops. Lieutenant Ludwig follows close behind. The young officer, who arranged the tea service, runs down the path with an open umbrella and meets them halfway. Von Becker yanks it from his hands and walks briskly onwards, leaving his junior officers in his wake.

The guards roll the four bodies they shot into the trench as the rain becomes heavier. On quivering legs, we stare at each other, wiping the streams of water from our faces. I can't believe our reprieve. I look at Franz, then Alek. Both are still staring at the retreating backs of the Germans.

Storm clouds cover the sky from horizon to horizon. Shimmering sunbeams peep through a tiny rift, spreading fingers of soft light over us like something from a religious painting.

I think of the soldier and the small bird perched on his shoulder, wondering about their true meaning.

Could the rain be their doing? Is there hope after all?

We collect our sodden clothes from a jumbled pile and line up at the gate.

I grab hold of Aleks arm and give it a gentle squeeze. He glances back, still afraid. The poor kid.

I pat his back reassuringly as the guards lead us up the wet path and back to the barn.

Our prison for one more night.

Our last.

15

We slump against the walls, exhausted, as the storm rages outside. Flashbacks of the major tumbling into the pit; the blood spraying over the kommandant's leather apron; the evil bastard's smile as he pulls the trigger and the blond lunatic reloading his gun, swirl through my brain. I grip my head with trembling fingers, trying to erase the grotesque scene of bodies lying in the pit, a tangle of limbs, the metallic smell of blood lingering in my nostrils.

I shudder. Lightning flashes through the windows, bathing everything in a silvery light. Rain beats down on the roof. Water leaks onto the rafters and puddles on the floor. We huddle against the walls away from the constant drips.

A lad softly sings a Polish folk song, giving me a little comfort. I look at Alek trembling in the gloom then at Franz, his head bent, twirling straw between his fingers. I lean my head against the wall dwelling on what tomorrow will bring.

#####

The barn door swings open with a bang. We jump to our feet.

A guard, silhouetted in the morning light, aims his rifle through the doorway, his finger on the trigger in case we get any crazy ideas of escape.

"Raus jetzt! ... Raus jetzt!" he yells "Out now, out now!"

"I supposed this is it!" Franz murmurs as he shakes my hand. I grip his hand tightly. His clear penetrating eyes, utterly fearless, look into mine.

A brotherly love fills my heart. Giving me courage to face what's to come.

"I suppose it is Franz," I say, smiling. "It's been nice knowing you for the last two years."

Franz pats my shoulder affectionately and grins.

"Likewise, Rys."

We follow the men stumbling through the doorway into bright sunlight. My mood lifts slightly at the sight of swallows diving in the rain puddles, frolicking in the water. It reminds me of swimming in the Bzura River at home, splashing water at Jo.

My heart aches at the beauty of the scene around me. This is my last day to see rain bringing colours to a garden. Wild red poppies, vibrant against a brick wall, shimmer in different shades of red and orange. Here I am looking at a beautiful garden, knowing my death lies behind the wrought iron gate we are passing through.

I feel sick to the core. Drained of my momentary burst of courage.

Standing along the trench, from where a putrid smell of blood and shit rises, making us gag, I avert my eyes from our dead comrades lying in oozing sludge with a haze of black flies swarming over their bodies.

I heave and spit.

Alek stifles a sob.

Franz grabs his shoulder.

"Be brave Alek," Franz whispers. "It will be over soon."

Again, a guard bellows orders to kneel in the mud. They lift their rifles, aiming at our backs. Lieutenant Ludwig, already dressed in his apron, loads his pistol.

I look towards the sun, almost enjoying its paltry warmth. A totally different day than yesterday. I smile ever so slightly. Maybe I will meet the strange soldier and the little robin red breast. Maybe God will forgive me for all the worry I put my mother through.

I bend my head, waiting to be shot.

I hear shouting from outside the gate. "Wait! Wait Lieutenant Ludwig! Please sir, wait!"

The old iron gate opens, its rusty hinges screeching a protest, then slams shut.

The blond officer's gun is pressed against the back of my head. He slowly lifts it away, cursing in German.

I look up to see a young SS soldier, wearing thick glasses, sprinting towards the trench, waving a piece of paper.

"There is a new directive from Berlin, sir," he says apologetically cowering under the dark scowl on the SS officer's face.

"You mustn't execute these prisoners!"

The gate screeches open again. I glance up. Kommandant von Becker's face is red from exertion. He gasps for breath. He gestures for us to stand.

Staggering to our feet, we face him.

"All of you ... will be ... will be transported to the Fatherland!" he splutters.

I bow my head to hide my smirk. The short bastard pronounces Fatherland, Farterland. He's the 'farter', the big bag of wind.

"Our Fuhrer has plans!" Panting, he continues. "Plans for able-bodied young men to work hard ... and build up our German war effort. You will be transported ... as soon as possible ... to the appropriate camps ... where you will suffer unbelievable ..."

Confused, he pauses, unsure what to say next. He glances back at Lieutenant Ludwig who is looking straight ahead, a blank expression on his face. There's no help there. Falling back on the standard German response, the kommandant inhales deeply, abruptly shoots out his arm and shouts "Heil Hitler!"

He turns, marches through the open gate in long strides, slamming it shut behind him and goose-steps back to the mansion with his clerk close on his heels.

We look at each other in stunned disbelief.

Ludwig grunts in disgust, holsters his gun, then angrily peels his apron away, violently throwing it to the ground.

A guard gingerly pick it up as the officer grabs his jacket from another. He swings it over his shoulder and storms up the path, cursing all the way to the house.

We watch the bastard stride away as the guards again throw the shovels at our feet, ordering us to fill in the trench. Franz and I, with a few of the lads, slowly pick them up, our eyes still following the kraut's retreating back.

Distracted, I shovel the dirt into the pit. The major's arm is amongst the tangle of bodies, I haphazardly aim the soil to cover it, until it disappears from view.

What just happened? I should be dead! I can't believe I'm not! Ah! But it was so satisfying to see that crazy bastard so mad. His day hasn't started so great, but mine has. I'm still alive and kicking!

Grinning, I shovel in more dirt.

Alek stares at my face, puzzled.

I pat his shoulder.

"We're still alive, Alek!" I chuckle under my breath. "We're still alive!"

Grinning now, he digs into a pile of dirt and spreads it over the bodies.

When I'm exhausted, I hand the shovel to a lad behind me and walk to the same tree the kommandant sat under yesterday. I slouch against the trunk, closing my eyes. Franz and Alek join me and watch the others fill in the trench.

Leaning their rifles against the fence posts, the guards light up cigarettes and chat, unconcerned if we make a run for it since there is nowhere to go.

The boggy field is surrounded by wire fencing. A prisoner would only get half-way across before they took a pot-shot at him.

Later that afternoon, the guards move us back to the barn and feed us a watery potato soup and a slice of stale bread. As the reality of what's to come sinks in, we eat in silence, not daring to speculate. Whatever's to come at the hands of the Germans won't be good! That's for sure!

After the meal, I sit leaning against the wall. Alek, sitting cross legged next to Franz, is wide-eyed and scared, jumping at every sound. Franz, cap over his eyes, is slouched against a pole, his face creased in a frown.

My mind is racing.

I don't trust the Germans. Will these work camps just be a slower form of death? What did the bastard mean '... you will suffer ...'? I wish he'd finished his speech. Are we going to be thrown from the frying pan into the fire?

Maybe tomorrow, we'll find out.

CHAPTER

16

Thumping our backs with their rifles, pushing and shoving us along the railway tracks, the German guards drive us into position alongside a row of cattle wagons. They order us to stop. One of the guards slides open a large wooden door, pushing a lad towards the opening.

"Schnell! Schnell! Komm nun rein! … Quick! Quick! Get in now!"

He shoves him in with the butt of his rifle.

We clamber after him, scraping our knees on the filthy floor. The dimly lit wagon is filled with young men.

Worming my way into a corner, my eyes soon adjust to the gloom. Franz and Alek follow close behind.

With so many bodies in a cramped area the fetid air is hard to breathe. I slump onto the wood floor, panting, sweat dripping from my brow. Alek coughs, his eyes watering from the stench. Franz swipes his hair back and unbuttons his shirt. I peel off my jumper, tie it around my waist and wipe my face with my sleeve.

The sliding door slams shut with a bang, making us jump. In semi-darkness, we sway to the jerky motion as the train slowly picks up speed.

There is just enough light to see the boys sitting next to us.

The one closest hang his head, his arms gripping his knees. Franz leans towards him.

"Where are we going?" he whispers.

The lad looks up and straightens, pushing his sandy blond hair back.

"I have no idea," he says, "it could be somewhere in Germany. I heard there are lots of slave labour camps in Germany."

Alek grabs my arm and murmurs, "I'm scared."

"We all are Alek, but we mustn't give up. Your uncle wouldn't have wanted that."

Alek is quiet for a moment then whispers back, "I'll never forget him and for what he stood for. I will try to be strong and live up to him."

I put my arm around his shoulders.

"We'll keep his memory alive; I promise you!"

Franz nods, agreeing.

The train stops an hour later, and more men are shoved aboard.

Now the wagon is so packed we're made to stand. We shuffle to make room, pressing our bodies close to one another, breathing each other's air as we yell for water and the need to piss.

Ignoring our demands, a Nazi guard bellows, "Das schweigen, be silent!" And slams the wagon door shut after the last man climbs in.

"Ah Christ. Your breath stinks, Rys!" complains Franz as the train starts to move.

"No worse than yours, Franz!" I sneer, pinching my nose, trying to keep my balance.

Alek covers the bottom of his face with his elbow, coughing. "Who farted?" he gasps.

"Stop hitting me in the back!" A lad snarls at Alek, as more boys yell protests

"Shut up! The whole lot of you!" Franz growls. "Everyone! Keep yourself upright and try to stay still. Link arms with each other if you need to. We'll take turns sitting down! You at the back and front, sit down now! We'll rotate and let everyone have a rest. I'll get Alek here to tell us when fifteen minutes are up."

Alek looks at him incredulously, then mumbles to himself as he counts down the minutes. He's good at timing, especially when measuring fuse rope.

We all move around when the time is up, dripping sweat and pissing through a hole in a corner. When we come close to the gaps in the planks that make up the walls, we gulp in fresh air and have a glimpse of the outside. It changes from the city to Poland's flat farmlands.

Rocking with the motion of the train, we stumble back and forth. Some lads become angry, especially when feet are trodden on, or stomachs elbowed. Fights break out. Fists connect with jaws and the side of heads.

"Everybody settle down!" yells the lad Franz was talking to. "Do as the guy here say! Hold onto the person next to you and try to stop stumbling around!"

Everyone seems to quieten as we clutch arms and hold onto jackets.

I peek through a gap. The sun is setting. Its brilliant colour paints the sky in shades of pink and mauve. Gilding clouds, streaked with a silver light, hover above the horizon.

This could be my last glimpse of Poland.

Franz pats my shoulder as tears spill down my face. He is usually cold and aloof, showing little emotion, but when I look up at him, his eyes are moist too.

We both sit on the floor, with Alek squashing between us and the lad we just met, sitting next to us.

"My name is Tomek Wisniewski," he says, shaking our hands. I study his face. He looks about the same age as us with blue eyes and curly blond hair.

He smiles and reveals slightly overlapping front teeth. He's tall and bunches his legs in front of him.

I'm curious, so I ask him about his past.

"I've been an apprentice chef at my father's restaurant for two years," he says. "I worked for the Resistance in my spare time and was really lucky the Nazis didn't put me into the German army. I heard the Polish recruits do all the menial work like guard duty, digging ditches and even cleaning the officers' boots. You see, my mother is German, and many lads of German descent are put to work in the armed forces."

It reminds me of Lieutenant Ludwig's boots. I wonder if their blood-spattered boots were cleaned by some unfortunate Pole.

Ma told us never to tell anyone about her German side of the family and to deny it if asked.

She isn't embarrassed about her family, in fact she is immensely proud of her heritage, but she must have known about the Nazi policy.

I refocus on what Tomek is saying.

"Being able to speak German, I became an interpreter for my unit. I handled the radio transmitter and listened to the

Nazis' conversations."

Tomek smiles a crooked smile. We're impressed. Working as a radio transmitter is a responsible job, usually done by a senior recruit.

"My crew and I were caught as we were leaving headquarters. Some bastard betrayed us. I think I know who he was. Bloody Wojcik! A guy I used to play soccer with. Most of my unit were lined up and shot by the SS, but surprisingly, the younger lads, like me, were spared and put on this train."

Just like us!

Tomek turns to Franz, "What's your story?"

Franz speaks for all of us and recalls the last couple of days, but his conversation soon dies away as night settles in. Alek calls time, reminding us we need to move. Franz frowns and demands everyone's attention.

"Form lines, face each other's backs and sit in between each other's legs."

We all squat down, shuffle around and sit on the floor then I make sure Alek is in front of me, facing the wall.

Franz is able to prop himself up against the wall with Tomek between his legs. They're the same height so Tomek's head is just below Franz's chin.

This arrangement seems to work for everybody. I am grateful for Franz's sleeping plan. Sometimes he is a genius.

I doze fitfully throughout the night but wake before dawn.

I peer through a gap above Alek's head and notice we're passing through a city.

The landscape has changed to warehouses and canals with long barges moored along concrete walls.

The railway stations have German names. Some as long as

my arm.
    My chest tightens.
    My heart aches.
    We have left Poland.

CHAPTER

17

I doze again till I'm jolted awake by the screeching of brakes as the train slows to a juddering halt. Voices outside yell orders. Dogs bark ferociously.

Alek lifts his head. Bewildered, he sits up, rubbing his eyes. I rub my chest, feeling the imprint of his head becoming a permanent dent there.

Everyone stirs.

"Where are we?" mumbles Alek, half asleep.

"No idea," I say.

"I can hear dogs barking," mutters Alek.

"I think we're here. Wherever 'here' is?" grunts Franz, pushing Tomek.

Tomek grumbles and tries to lie back but Franz pushes him harder. He quickly sits up, gripping Franz's arm. They glare at each other for a tense moment.

Christ, the last thing we need is a fight between these two!

After much hissing and shunting, the train finally judders to a stop, then stills. Fully awake, fear gripping my chest, I stare at the sliding door.

Alek seizes my arm, his eyes wide with panic. The door is wrenched open, slamming against the wagon's side and a lantern held high is thrust into the wagon. We stagger to our feet. I stumble, grabbing Alek's shoulder to steady myself. I take in a quick breath. My legs are numb, with pins and needles shooting up my thighs.

"Alle raus! Alle raus! Everybody out!" shouts a guard.

It is still dark. No stars or moon. The lantern provides the only light. Heavy fog swirls around us as we jump to the ground. Gravel crunches underfoot.

More lanterns sway in the eerie light as SS guards drag snarling dogs back on their leads. The Alsatians, ears pinned back and saliva dripping from their jaws, lunge at us, savagely snapping at the backs of our legs. We tuck our hands under our arms and gather into tight groups.

The guards bark out orders, shoving and pushing us into lines, then march us to waiting trucks, open to the elements.

Planks of timber form a makeshift barrier along the sides and two seats along its length. We are forced to jam in tight.

Grabbing Alek's elbow, I keep him beside me. He shakes uncontrollably and I try to calm him down. I'm fearful for his safety, since he has no ID papers and is too young to be here.

The trucks drive along the road. The rising sun streaks a yellow haze across the sky, burning the fog away from deep shadows. I smell a horrible stench. A burning smell. It doesn't smell like wood or coal burning, but something alien and strange.

The stench grows stronger as we approach a long, narrow building, two storeys high.

From the front it looks like pictures I have seen of a Spanish hotel. Small vertical windows are set side by side on the top storey. Two doors on the lower level are flanked by more windows. The centre of the building is much higher than the rest with wrought iron gates set back to make a short tunnel. The whole building is painted a pristine white, its gabled roof covered in red clay tiles. Flowers grow in neat beds along its walls.

But the pleasant look of the building is marred by towering concrete walls on either side, topped with razor wire.

I peer up as the truck turns into the wide opening. A couple of soldiers look down from the windows above us. I crane my neck to look at the clock tower at the very top but can't make out the time.

The truck stops at the gates, waiting for two guards to open them.

As we pass through, I see words shaped in the metal.

Arbeit Macht Frei.

Tom whispers to me, "It says, 'Work Makes You Free'."

I frown at him.

What the hell! What does that mean?

Tom shrugs as if he reads my thoughts.

We're ordered out of the trucks to stand in a small courtyard. Waiting, we watch other trucks, full of prisoners, leave through the gates. The prisoners stare down as they pass.

I shudder. They look half dead.

I tear my gaze away and look over my shoulder at a modern house with large windows. It faces a small garden of bright flowers.

A guard stationed on the porch stands at attention, his back ramrod straight and his rifle at port arms across his chest. He grounds his rifle and salutes, his arm outstretched, as an SS officer enters the house.

Marched through another set of gates, we halt in a larger

semi-circular courtyard. Mounted on a concrete platform under the clock tower, a manned machine gun points down. At us.

A guard shouts in my ear. I stare back at him, not quite understanding his unfamiliar German accent. He hits me across the back with his truncheon. I stumble forward, falling into line. My pulse quickens and sweat runs down my spine.

The man in front of me shuffles to face the guards. I do the same. Standing still and erect, we are ordered to empty our pockets into a bucket being passed from man to man, but to keep our papers. I have no money, only a piece of string and a dirty rag, but I throw them in the bucket anyway. However, Franz has a few zlotys. Disgruntled, he tosses them in.

Furtively, I look around. The compound is huge. Hundreds of long huts, barracks, face each other, radiating out from the roll-call area. At the back of the courtyard is a set of empty gallows. The strange stench is much stronger here. It seems to be coming from a brick building to my left.

What are they burning?

My attention is drawn towards an SS officer, young enough to still have pimples dotting his cheeks, emerging from the administration building carrying a chair and a small collapsible table. He sets them up at the head of our line and asks in Polish for our papers. As we shuffle down the line past his table, he scans our papers, filling in new identity cards.

Alek is in front of me and when it's his turn, I hold my breath, dreading the worst.

Stuttering, Alek explains that his papers were taken by the Polish police and never returned. He was trying to get them back on the day he was captured. The SS officer inspects him closely, asks his name and other particulars, fills in a card, then waves him on.

Relief washes over me. I touch his arm. He glances back and gives me a weak smile.

Another SS officer moves us, one by one, in front of a white board and takes our photos. As I move along in the line, I see an SS Kommandant walking towards the spotty clerk.

Glancing up, the young officer quickly rises to his feet and salutes. The Kommandant salutes back, gesturing for him to complete his task.

The Kommandant studies us, and we him.

Wearing black rimmed glasses, he is a tall, thin man with stooped shoulders. He rocks lightly on the balls of his feet with his hands clasped behind his back, like a school master, ready to address an assembly.

Except that in his grey-green SS uniform he looks like a rat peeking from beneath a military cap.

Finishing his reports, the clerk once again stands and waits. The Kommandant turns towards him, speaking quietly.

The clerk stands very erect, his lean body taut as a bowstring, then yells at us in Polish.

"When your photo has been taken you are to strip. All clothing and valuables are to be placed in the baskets provided and if anything of value is found on you, then you will be shot! Is that understood?"

He finishes in German, "Schnell!" "Schnell!"

We quickly strip off our clothes and throw them in a pile.

Totally naked we shiver in the freezing air. Some men cover their private parts. Others are less modest. I don't care, nor does Franz, however Alek looks embarrassed and cups his hands around his privates.

Looking down at my discarded jumper, I remember the day my sisters gave it to me as a birthday present. I hated the colour, the soft yellow of freshly churned butter. It was alright for a boy around six but not for me at my age. Nevertheless, I wore it every day as it's made of wool and keeps out the cold. Today its cheerful colour is muted with dirt and grime. I wish I'd been more appreciative when the girls gave it to me. Creamy yellow is not such a bad colour after all.

Sighing, I look up, remembering where I am. The guards are swearing at the prisoners, shoving them into new lines. Hastily, I take my place beside Franz, not wanting to be clubbed again.

A man, his hands in the pockets of his white coat, strolls towards us A black stethoscope draped around his thick neck, informs us he is a doctor. Bending his head to the side, he scrutinises us through small pig-like eyes behind wire-rimmed spectacles.

A brown moustache droops over thick lips and his coat gapes where the buttons fail to meet across his stomach.

The Kommandant walks up to the doctor and speaks to him in a lowered voice before walking back to a building.

Striding pompously towards us, the doctor pulls the stethoscope from his neck with an exaggerated flourish while the clerk runs beside him with a clipboard and pencil.

The Doctor examines each of us, listening to our backs and chests. Gesturing and ordering us in German to open our mouths, he examines teeth and tongues. As he finishes with each man, the clerk asks our names again, writing them on cards pinned to the clipboard and filing them in order.

The fat quack orders us to run around in a circle, observing our strides and breathing. Nodding his head in approval, he sends us into a bathhouse. Taps and washing troughs surround the walls. The next room has a deeper trough running its full length. I see prisoners in striped uniforms standing with razors poised, silently staring ahead. I glance around. The concrete floor and walls are spattered with blood.

We're forced to stand in front of these 'pyjama men' who dispassionately and carelessly shave our heads, our bodies and our private parts. No water or soap is provided so the razor rasps across my skin, causing it to sting. I wince at every stroke.

Many men, including ourselves, bleed from numerous nicks and cuts. I look over to Franz who is staring straight ahead, twitching slightly as the razor scrapes his scalp. I feel self-conscious, standing there, moving my balls to the side so my groin can be shaved. trying not to get nicked.

As each man is finished, he is ordered by the guards to run through the trough in the next room. Standing on either side are two SS guards, hosing everyone with disinfectant.

The room smells like a hospital. Droplets of the spray cling to our eyelids and drip off our ears. Our cuts burn, making us all yell, curse and jump around. The guards howl with laughter, twisting the jet to its maximum. Even the doctor smiles and jokes.

Christ, are they all evil sadists?

Back in the courtyard, large trestle tables are stacked with striped blue and white cotton shirts, matching pants, caps and wooden clogs. The clothes are all old and worn, just like those the 'pyjama men' are wearing. Our own have disappeared.

The guards yell in German and point to the piles of clothing. We hurry over, take a pile and dress quickly, but the mismatched sizes make us look ridiculous. We laugh at our new fashion until a guard shout at us to be silent, then hits a couple of men to reinforce his order. Silently we swap with each other. Buttoning up a shirt and pulling up a pair of pants, which are too long, I slip on the clogs and place the cap on my shorn head.

We look like clowns.

For hours we stand in the middle of the courtyard, the sun beating down on our heads. There is no food or water. Those who sit on the ground are beaten, then dragged upright again.

Two disgruntled guards walk back to the shade of a building, where they slump in chairs and light cigarettes.

I sway in the heat, struggling to stay on my feet.

It's late in the afternoon by the time our new documents are issued. Each one with a set of badges with numbers and a red triangle with a 'P'. *I suppose 'P' means Polish.* I study my card. My photo is stapled in the right-hand corner with a circular imprint stamped over it, showing an eagle gripping a swastika. A number is written below it. The same stamp is in the bottom left-hand corner as well.

A red 'Pole' stamp is next to the word 'Auslander' 'Foreigner', also stamped upside down.

On the other page is stamped 'Seventh of May 1943' and the place I was captured, 'Tomaschow-Maz', with a signature alongside. The doctor's report is also there. I read the document again. I must keep it safe if I'm to survive, so I tuck it into my pocket.

To our surprise, we are marched out of the camp and ordered to climb back onto the same trucks we arrived on.

Bewildered and uneasy, we wait as the drivers have a last

fag before climbing into the cab.

I stare at the wrought iron gate as the trucks pull away, wondering where they are taking us now.

Instead of heading back the way we came, they turn towards a nearby town, built on a low hilltop.

CHAPTER

18

It is late afternoon. Deepening shadows creep between the buildings facing the town square. Shafts of light dance across shop windows and sparkle on drops of cascading water jetting up from a fountain, on the very top of which is an angel, wings held high, watching the pedestrians below. A castle, old and grey, nestles on a hill, just above the skyline.

Spotting a shop front bearing the words '*Oranienburg Bakery*' in faded letters, I learn the name of the city we're passing through. Oranienburg? I vaguely remember Pan Nowak talking about Oranienburg when he was teaching us German history. He said it was known for its thirteenth century castle. It must be the one I glimpsed a moment ago.

We drive through a neat, tidy suburb where front doors are painted in assorted colour. Bright spring flowers bloom in window boxes and ceramic pots placed on doorsteps.

The truck detours around the back streets and over a wide river, then through an industrial area. It pulls up at a Prisoner of War camp, outside the city limits.

This camp is much smaller than the one we left twenty minutes ago. Instead of thick concrete walls and guard towers manned with machine guns, it has a high, barbed wire fence and an old iron gate at the main entrance. Twin timber guard towers, each manned by a single guard holding a rifle, stand at each end.

The rusty gates are pushed open as we drive through, then padlocked shut behind us.

Thumping men in the back with their rifles while ordering us out of the trucks, our guards hustle us into two lines and march us into a courtyard. I stare at the rows of wooden barracks, already aged to a slate grey, with the front doors facing an assembly area. Gravel roads separate each block.

At the end of the courtyard a row of skeletally thin prisoners, their necks twisted at an obscene angle and their swollen, blackened faces unrecognisable, hang from gallows. Dried blood streaks their uniforms, staining the white stripes red.

I've seen Jews hung on lamp posts in the city and I always found it sickening, but also morbidly fascinating. Sometimes I stood there, watching the bodies swing in the breeze.

But not today.

Swallowing hard, I turn my eyes away from the gruesome sight.

"Don't look at them Alek," I whisper hoarsely.

He puts his head down, gagging. Spit slides off his chin and he swipes it off with the back of his hand.

The guards march us to an open-sided red brick building further down the road. Men sit on benches at long wooden tables, using wooden spoons to eat from tin bowls.

At the entrance to the kitchen, three huge cast iron pots on gas stoves are manned by prisoners. About fifty men line up at each pot as the cook ladles soup into bowls.

One of the cooks suddenly swears at a prisoner, flinging boiling soup at him. The man screams in agony, clutching his face and falling to the ground. Another prisoner dives for the cook, smashing his face with his fist. They topple over a table, where men sit eating their meal.

All hell breaks loose.

Prisoners swear at the fighting men. Two of them give the cook a couple of swift kicks to the head. Meanwhile, other prisoners brandishing canes, unmercifully flog anyone within their reach. Men are yelling, crying out with pain or hiding under the tables.

We fall back and huddle together, trying to avoid the vicious maniacs with the canes.

Completely disinterested in the fighting or the flogging, the guards push us forward regardless, and order us to line up for the meal.

Just as suddenly as the fight and beatings began, it stops.

Men go back to line up in front of the cooking pots or sit once more at the tables.

The cook is dragged away and replaced by another prisoner.

The poor man who had the soup thrown on him, is semi-unconscious. He is roughly pulled out of the way and dumped against the kitchen wall.

Our lines shuffle closer to the huge cooking pots. I keep glancing at the man, wondering if he's dead. His legs have stopped twitching.

A brawny bald man, his hands covered in scars, is handing out small loaves of bread from a hessian bag.

"The bread has to last a week!" he yells at us at the top of his voice.

Pointing, he orders us to pick up a 'kit', consisting of a tin bowl, wooden spoon and a tin mug from those stacked on a table nearby. We pick up a set as we pass, and he hands us the bread.

It's stale, hard as a rock and mixed with sawdust. I break mine open to find mildew inside. It looks disgusting.

It's then I do something really stupid.

I go back up the line to the man handing out the bread, showing him my split loaf.

"Excuse me," I say politely. "But my bread has mildew in the centre."

"Let me see," the man sneers.

He grabs the bread. His pockmarked face peers closely at the mildew, as if he is nearsighted, then sighs exaggeratedly.

"So, it has. I'll see what I can do!"

I knew then I was in trouble.

Without warning, he smashes the loaf into my face. My eyes fill with tears. Blood spurts from my nose, spilling onto my shirt and pants.

"You bloody bastard!" I hiss, spitting blood, swiping more blood off my face.

"Piss off!" He jeers and hands a loaf to the next man.

I clench my fists, about to throw a punch into his ugly smug face, when Franz kicks my leg from behind. I twist around, glowering at him.

"Don't fight back!" He murmurs, flicking his head towards the 'heavies' with the canes.

Reluctantly, I move back into the soup line wiping the blood and snot from my nose.

"Hey! Polak! Come back here, and I'll give you a nice fresh loaf!" the bastard yells sarcastically.

"Eat shit, you moron!" I yell back and spit a glob of blood in his direction.

His pale eyes narrow into slits. He shakes with fury and moves towards me, ready to throw a punch.

"Get back to work, you stupid bastard!" A guard bellows, stopping him in his tracks.

Unwillingly, he walks back to the bread line, his eyes smouldering.

The cooks ladle what looks like pig slop into our bowls. Potato peelings, cabbage, and carrot tops float in a grey watery broth. There is no meat and no fat. It smells terrible. Ma's soups were thick with meat and vegetables and always had tiny balls of fat floating on the top. She said this is what gave the soup its flavour.

I later found out there was barley at the bottom of the pots, but this went to the bosses.

We walk around the tables, until we see six men sitting near a water trough at the far end of the canteen. I recognise them as Polish because of the 'P' on their jackets. They eat in silence, occasionally grunting and slurping.

One looks up and moves along the bench to make room, then mumbles to the others to do the same.

Between slurps the man points to a concrete trough.

"You can wash your kit there when you're finished," he says, swallowing a carrot top.

We sit down slowly and stare at them.

They look starved. Dirt clings to their shaven heads and pale grey faces. Their eyes are dim and sunken. They concentrate on their meal. Bony hands shake as they grip their bowls and spoons, bringing the broth to their quivering lips.

They remind me of the Jews in the Tomaszow-Mazowiecki ghetto.

The walking dead.

Gulping and chewing madly, they eat the foul broth as if it's their last meal.

Maybe it is.

My stomach lurches.

Oh my God! Is this going to happen to us?

Scared, I turn uncertainly to Franz. He grimaces back.

A man turns to face us, his cheeks covered in bruises.

"Don't dally boys!" he croaks through split lips. "The guards don't wait for anyone. You could miss out altogether and the next meal is a long way off."

I dip my spoon, take a tentative sip and make a face. Yep! It tastes as bad as it looks, but I take the man's advice and eat it as fast as I can. Trying not to let the foul taste linger too long in my mouth.

I'm rinsing my bowl in the trough, when a 'heavy' shouts an order, swishing his cane through the air.

"Into lines now! Now! You stupid Polaks!" He bellows, smacking a man over his shoulders. The man yelps and scrambles along the aisle between tables, then stands to attention. Hastily, we move into line behind him.

The 'heavy', dressed in the same uniform as us but wearing a grey military jacket, leads us to Barrack 31. The sun has set, leaving the camp in darkness, except for the gravel roads which are lit by glaring electric lights.

The men from our table trudge behind us, then wander into

the neighbouring hut.

This must be the Polish section of the camp.

We approach a long wooden building. A metal pipe pokes out from the middle of the timber roof, and another is attached to the side of a lean-to shed, joined to the side of the main hut.

We're ordered inside and stand at attention in a recreation room. To my left I see a concrete bathroom leading to a room full of wooden bunk beds. The rec-room has benches and trestle tables around a small combustion stove. About forty young men sit on the benches or on the floor as four older men, with truncheons strapped to their hips, pace around them.

I do a quick head count. Our group brings the count to sixty-five. There isn't much room for us. Alek is by far the youngest one here.

Thank God he is as tall as me and lied about his age. He is just turned fourteen and not fifteen as he told the spotty clerk. I don't think he would be here otherwise, but on a train to another camp. Or dead.

A large man, his face red and sweaty, strides into the centre of the room. Placing his feet wide, he clasps his hands behind his back. At least six feet tall and completely bald, his thick neck folding over his collar, he wearily studies our faces.

"Pay attention!" he hollers in Polish.

"Get yourselves into lines!" yells a 'heavy'. "And face the Boss!"

In two uneven lines we scramble to attention, arms straight as boards at our sides. The other lads fall quiet. Some sidling into the bunkroom.

The big man wipes his nose with a snotty rag.

"The Kommandant and guards are in control of everything in this camp!" he bellows. "They decide all our fates. If we live or die. However, basic discipline in this camp is handed out by other prisoners.

"Bevauer is the Camp Elder. He is German and is my boss. We are all called Bosses, so you will always refer to me as 'Boss'. I am in charge of your hut, and I'm called the Blockaltesten. Below me is the Stubendienstan. Call him Kapo. Below him are his lieutenants. They maintain discipline in this hut!" He nods towards one of the 'heavies.'

He draws in a laboured breath.

"We all carry batons and canes, and we can flog anyone at any time.

"I will now tell you the camp and barrack rules!

"You are to sleep three or four to a bunk and if we get crowded you will sleep six to a bunk.

You are to be ready at five am sharp every morning. Breakfast is ersatz coffee and a piece of sausage.

You may eat your bread at this time. How much you eat is up to you but remember, you need to ration it to last a full week. The main meal is at six pm and there is no lunch. The meal is soup and your bread."

He hacks and spits on the floor.

"Do not try to escape. If you do, you will be beaten and hanged. You saw the hanged men outside. They tried to escape yesterday."

He takes another wheezy breath.

"You are to keep your bodies and bedding clean of lice. You are to keep all possessions, including your papers and bread, on your person at all times. If you steal from anyone, you will be harshly dealt with."

He wipes his lips with his sleeve and speaks in hushed tones. "You are lucky to be Poles as the Russians here are much worse off than us. They are not given as much food, and many have starved to death."

Raising his voice once more he roars, "The SS will shoot you on the spot if you can't produce your papers. If possible, avoid the SS guards.

You only speak to the SS when spoken too and you must call them 'Herr' at all times. Be aware you can be killed for no reason. As I said before, they control who lives and who dies."

Speaking has made him breathless. He coughs, sounding like a saw rasping over rough bark. His head glistens with sweat and he wipes his mouth with the rag.

We stand in stunned silence.

Then he gestures towards the room at the far end.

"Go! Find a bunk. And no fighting, or you will be flogged!"

We don't see much of the Blockaltesten after his speech. He leaves the running of the barracks to Kapo and his five henchmen, only appearing when the Block Fuhrer, an SS officer, occasionally inspects the huts after roll call.

We find out later that the Blockaltesten has his own room attached to the hut with a clean bunk, a stove, and privileges. He is the one who gets the barley from the bottom of the soup pot, before we are served. Kapo tells us that in his former life the Blockaltesten was a hardened criminal belonging to a notorious mob of gangsters who had committed many murders.

We scurry through the washroom towards a lieutenant

directing us to the spare bunks, which are simply wide wooden shelves nailed to the walls. There are eight bunks on each side, a narrow corridor separating them. The two bunks towards the back have blankets and wooden boxes stashed in corners. This is where the lieutenants sleep.

Franz selects a bunk on a lower level, nearer to the back. There are no blankets, pillows, mattress, or sheets, only the rough wooden planks to sleep on.

Tomek joins us and we discuss how we should sleep, deciding head to toe is the best option since it's nearly summer.

Alek lies down squashing himself into the corner against the wall. Franz and Tomek wander into the rec room. I amble towards a doorway near the back wall and peek around the door frame.

A stretcher bed is against one wall with a blanket and dirty striped pillow. A shelf made of planking is nailed on the opposite wall, holding jars of nuts and bolts, a couple of old books, and an old thermometer, propped against a lantern. A battered kitchen chair sits under a small table near the doorway.

A large hand grips my shoulder.

"I wouldn't be getting any ideas, boy!" a voice snarls. "That's the Kapos quarters. You could be thrashed to death if you enter his quarters."

I'm yanked backwards and turned around. Glaring down at me is a tall man, wearing a deep scowl. His face is lean and gaunt, with a high forehead and a long nose. He wears a grey jacket and holds a baton, which he twirls in his hand.

His dark eyes bore into mine.

"What's your name?" he asks.

"Rys, sir," I squeak.

"Well, Rys, if I were you, I'd get back to your bunk and stay there."

He shoves me hard, whacking me with his baton.

I stumble and nearly fall.

Scrambling back to the bunk, I dive along the planks panting with fear.

My heart is pounding in my chest. The soup I had an hour ago rises in my throat. I struggle to it down.

The 'heavy' turns as he hears a voice from the rec-room. "Hey Wapasha, you're needed here!"

The tall man strides through the doorway, disappearing from view.

I wipe the sweat off my hands down my shirt.

Christ Rys, stop nosing around. You're going to get yourself killed.

I stay close to the sleeping Alek and watch the doorway, waiting for the others to return.

Lying down fully clothed, too exhausted to care, we try to sleep. I'm woken during the night by lads crying out in terror-filled dreams, the bunks creaking as they writhe in their sleep.

"Christ Rys," Franz murmurs, as we're both woken by a shout, coming from one of the sleeping lads. "It's like trying to sleep in a hen house, with all the squawking and moving around."

I turn to face him.

"How are we going to survive this?" I whisper.

"Shit! I don't know!" he hisses. "But I know one thing, we better keep our heads down."

He shuffles onto his side, and using his arm as a pillow, closes his eyes.

But I can't sleep. I stare at the planks above my head, worried about what's to come.

CHAPTER

19

"**A**ufstehen, aufstehen los!"

"Get up, get up!"

"Get out, schnell!"

A cane lashes against the bunks above our heads.

I wake with a start. Alek cries out. Franz curses, while Tomek grumbles under his breath.

Kapo's lieutenants bellow out orders.

"To the washroom! Now!"

"Everyone to the washroom! Now!"

A constant, loud metallic ringing is coming from the roll call area. It sounds like someone striking a metal pole with a hammer.

We clamber out of the bunk and scramble around, looking for our shoes. Running to the washroom, clogs slipping and sliding along the floor, we find everyone jostling for position to piss into four toilet bowls. There are no cubicles or urinal troughs. Six to seven lads try to piss in each toilet at the same time. Those behind them shove with their elbows in their backs, trying to aim for the overflowing bowl.

We join them, grabbing shirts and jostling for a place, but end up pissing on the floor like the rest of them.

Pushing through the throng, we vigorously wash our faces at the taps in the centre of the room and rub them dry on our grimy shirts.

Wapasha storms in.

"Get to the rec room! Get to the rec room!"

Boys push their way to the lockers to collect their kits. We do the same. We hold out our mugs to the four lieutenants pouring ersatz coffee. Not real coffee. This muck tastes more like burnt grain, but it's all there is. Chewing on a piece of bread and a thin slice of sausage, we gulp the warm, brown liquid to wash it down.

We are allowed ten minutes, starting from the banging on the pipe in the courtyard, until we line up outside for roll call, to piss, have a wash and eat our meagre meal.

All the Kapos are yelling at the same time as we shuffle into line.

"Hats off! Hats off! Fall into line! ... Fall into line!"

Striding up and down the lines, bellowing orders, they shove us into rows, whacking our shoulders and the back of our legs with their canes to hurry us up.

We stand to attention, avoiding the switch as it swings from one man to another. Franz winces as a bamboo rod lands on his back. He grits his teeth and stands his ground.

The Block Fuhrer starts counting heads. We look straight ahead, knowing if we glance his way, he will order us to be flogged. A man coughs and a Kapo is onto him like a shot, caning him savagely.

Unperturbed, the officer keeps counting. When he's finished, he clicks his heels, and arm high, salutes a more senior officer, yelling his report in German.

"Heil Hitler! The prisoners have been counted and verified and the number is correct!"

After roll call, we're given another ten minutes to clean the barracks.

Supervised by 'heavies' swinging their canes, we dash around sweeping floors, wiping down tables, stacking firewood and scrubbing out the bathroom. No-one wants that filthy job, but we get no option if it's our turn.

Dividing us into work parties, the lieutenants line us up and march us to the main gate.

The Kapos order us to turn our heads to the left, as we march past the kommandant's office. A man in kommandant's uniform stands on a dais, stiffly erect, his hands clasped behind his back while two subordinate officers stand to attention beside him.

They observe us prisoners filing past.

The Kommandant's uniform is flawless. The grey overcoat is tailored to make allowances for his protruding stomach and his black boots gleam in the morning sunlight.

He is a big man with close-set, beady eyes and bulldog features. Heavy jowls hang low on his florid cheeks. Against these heavy features his nose looks comically small compared to his thick sausage-like lips. A deeply ceased brow and downturned mouth indicate a chancy temper.

I get the impression he could order us shot with a flick of his stick if we offend him.

We march past, keeping in step, our footsteps the only sound breaking the silence, until we reach the trucks parked outside the gates. We climb aboard and sit amongst a load of shovels and spades.

The driver steers the truck down the middle of the road, dodging potholes. A big burly guard smokes a cigarette in the passenger seat. Two more guards brace themselves against the tail gate, their rifles cocked and ready.

On the outskirts of the town, the trucks stop alongside a major road pockmarked with huge potholes, some half a metre deep. The guards jump off and order us down. Anyone too slow is hauled off roughly and flogged with batons.

We stand back on the verge as a convoy of heavy, armoured vehicles rumbles past, barely missing us. One hits a pothole, breaking the road up even more.

Two more trucks pull up, one carrying hot tar, the other loose gravel and extra tools. We are assigned shovels, spades, picks and wheelbarrows. Two prisoners are allocated to each barrow, mixing hot tar and gravel together. Taking turns shovelling the road-mix into the potholes, we tamp it down with our shovels or spades.

As the hours pass, my shirt becomes wringing wet. My hands blister and my shoulders ache.

Stinging sweat drips from my brow into my eyes.

It's the most strenuous work I have ever done.

My mouth is parched. Dry. My tongue sticks to the roof of my mouth. I crave water. I glance sideways when a man staggers and sits down.

A guard pounces on him, hitting him with his rifle until he is unconscious. He orders a prisoner to drag him off the road. The SS guards, carrying whips and rifles, keep a close eye on us as we work. They hit and kick us mercilessly, flogging us repeatedly with their canes if we slacken off.

The big bastard who was the passenger in the truck, kicks me up the ass. He seems to think I'm too slow pushing the heavy wheelbarrow full of road-mix, but my back is breaking.

I can't work any harder.

"Raus! Raus! You stupid Polak!" he bellows, kicking me again. This time finding the back of my legs. I stumble, stagger, and grip the barrow's handles harder, determined to push it faster.

Wincing with pain I stop in front of the men. They quickly shovel the steaming, black mix into the holes. Furtively looking back to see where the guard is, I rub my ass before picking up the shovel, knowing full well the steel cap on his boot will have left a large purple bruise.

It's midday before we are given water.

We stand around the bucket, passing the ladle to one another, drinking in big gulps, just in case the guards force us back to work early. Luckily, they talk amongst themselves, smoking cigarettes and eating wedges of cheese and salami. Inwardly I groan. My mouth begins to water. My stomach cramps. I'm so bloody hungry.

Later in the afternoon we're taken back to the camp where Kapo orders us out to evening roll call.

Standing for an hour, we wait to be counted once again.

I'm desperate for a piss. So is the rest of the crew. When we are dismissed, we dash to the toilets and once more jostle for position.

"Hurry! Hurry!" A lieutenant bellows, striding into the washroom. "Collect your kits and get into two lines!"

Bellowing orders, he shoves us towards the door.

"Schnell! Schnell!"

We line up near the steaming pots to receive the foul soup. The horrible smell lingers at the back of my throat. I swallow, my empty stomach churning.

The 'heavies' prowl around, striking anyone in their way. Sitting down at a table and tearing pieces off our loaves, we dip the bread into the soup to soften it up and eat in silence. I glance up at Franz. He looks dead beat. Dark smudges circle his eyes. He glances back, grimacing, shaking his head. Alek seems exhausted, his head nodding over his bowl.

Back in our hut we peel off our shirts, wash our faces and upper body as best we can. The tar sticks to our hair and is ingrained in our skin. I rub again, bathing my arms under the tap. But the black oil only smears, making it worse. There's no soap to break down the grease. Giving up, I quickly dress in the same filthy clothes.

There is very little talk among us as we stagger to our bunks and collapse on the wooden planks. I turn to look at my friends. Alek is quietly sobbing. Franz stares into space. Tomek faces the wall. I close my eyes, thinking of home and the life I've left behind. The farm, fishing for pike, swimming in the river, and playing soccer with my mates. I bury my face into my arm and cry. I've lost so much.

I've passed through the gates of hell.

CHAPTER

20

I can't do this. My back is breaking.

The cement bags weigh thirty kilos. I know because it's written on the side. Straining, I pull one up and balance it on my shoulder, then grab a bucket of gravel in my other hand. Staggering, I follow Franz up the stairs, watching him as he drags himself up the metal steps, his neck bent, his legs quivering under the strain.

I hear Tomek's heavy, uneven breathing behind me, the clanging of the steps as he ascends. There is no railing to cling to. Not that we have a spare hand to do so, anyway. We totter and sway with each laborious step.

My thoughts drift to Alek. Smaller and younger, he would never withstand this heavy work. Thank God he's back at the camp, helping Kapo with another job.

Today, we were sent to the industrial area on the outskirts of town, to fill cement trucks. The stairs reach up to the opening of the mixing bowl where the concrete moves slowly around and around. One of the bosses is stationed at the top of the stairs and slashes open the cement bags.

We tip the cement and gravel into the turning drum, as he adds water from a hose, to make a concrete slurry. Barking orders, he sends us down again to collect another load. When the mix is ready, the truck moves away, and another takes its place.

Cement dust enters my lungs with every breath. It gets into my clothes, rubbing my skin raw. By the time I return to camp, I'm hacking up globs of grey phlegm, along with the rest of the crew.

We all look the same. Exhausted. Near to collapse. And covered in a grey film.

When the job changes back to road work, we wash our clothes and dry them near the stove in our barracks or outside on the road. We can never fully remove the cement. Our shirts and pants feel like cardboard and can stand on their own as they dry. Careful not to laugh out loud, we move them in a variety of positions, especially sexy ones.

"Look at this one!" sniggers Tomek as he bends his trousers at the knees and makes them kneel on the floor. He wanders over to Franz's creation, his trousers copulating with his shirt.

"That's a good one," Tomek smirks as the other lads drift over to watch our silly stunts.

Wapasha strolls through the doorway. We grab the clothes in a hurry, laying them flat near the stove. The other lads scatter. He eyes us warily, knowing we're up to no good, but doesn't say a word. He moves towards the washroom, his eyes darting from us to our clothes, lying stiff on the floor.

We avoid his stare and wander outside to sit in the shade.

#####

The weather cools into autumn, making the nights more bearable, the days shorter. The bosses carry lanterns, the light swaying around the tables. We're ordered to eat fast and head back to our barracks in a shorter time than before.

Cool autumn leads into freezing winter. The temperature often falls to twenty degrees below zero.

We sleep huddled together, taking turns to sleep in the middle to conserve our body warmth. We're given coats, but they're not enough to keep out the freezing cold. Before climbing into the bunks, we wrap our coats tightly around ourselves and sleep with our clogs on.

Scavenging for extra clothing is crucial in or outside the camp. When the opportunity arises, we steal from the dead who are usually left outside the barracks in the morning. When a body is found we quickly strip it bare, shoving the items under our jackets to examine later. But we must be careful, some pilfered items can cause trouble. I heard a man committed murder over a tea towel and was later strangled by it.

Just before morning roll call, Kapo reads out the temperature from his thermometer letting us know what we will be battling outside. Even in the daytime it can go as low as minus fifteen degrees. In this bitter weather, men keel over during roll call, like felled trees. Frozen to death.

Franz and I share a locker with six others. Each kit is identified by its owner by a set of initials. It stops us from catching any diseases. But we must be quick grabbing them. Some lads take anyone's, causing a lot of fights.

Jurek, a big boned lad about Franz's height, decides he likes Franz's kit better than his own, and grabs it whenever he can, which pisses Franz off big time.

Late one afternoon, Franz finds his kit taken again. Jurek

makes his way to the door with Franz's kit under his arm, leaving his battered bowl and split spoon in the locker.

Franz bounds after him and spins him around, jabbing his fist into his guts. Jurek doubles up winded, dropping the bowl and spoon, but still holding the tin mug. Franz rips the mug out of his hands and whacks him on the head with it. He picks up the rest of his kit from the floor, wiping it with his hand.

"Do that again you bastard, and I'll beat you bloody!" Franz snarls at the writhing form.

Jurek, groaning with pain, stays down, not daring to look up.

"So much for keeping *your* head down!" I snigger in Franz's ear.

Franz swivels around, anger still flaring in his eyes. But seeing it's me, heaves out a pent-up breath and follows me out, clutching his kit in his hands.

"I'm not sharing my kit with anyone," Franz mumbles under his breath, "especially that dirty bastard. You don't know what diseases he's carrying."

Kapo sees the whole incident but doesn't say or do anything.

It doesn't stop Jurak. At every opportunity he throws a jab in Franz's back or trips him up, always apologising with a smirk on his face.

But Franz is no angel. He does the same. He deliberately grabs the back of Jurak's neck and squeezes hard, or spits at his back as he walks past, or thumps him in the ribs at roll call. Anything to get back at him.

The aggravation escalates when Jurek is shoved from behind banging his head against the wall. He sees Franz, heading for the washroom. Knowing he is the culprit, he runs after him, punching him in the kidneys. Franz staggers, gasping. He turns and ploughs into Jurek, gripping him in a headlock, punching him on the nose. Blood sprays everywhere, pouring down Jurak's face and Franz's arm.

Jurek pulls his head free, pushing Franz away. They face each other, circling and snarling. Jurek lunges and punches fly in all directions. The fight ends up outside. Franz gives Jurek an uppercut, making him stumble back. Jurek throws himself at Franz again and wrestles him to the ground. Franz tosses Jurek off at the same time as men are running out of the barracks, yelling, and jeering, egging them on.

Franz jumps to his feet and pulls Jurek into another headlock, careening him around and around. Until Jurek's face turns purple with spit drooling from his lips.

Kapo barges between them, ripping them apart and belting both with his baton. His lieutenants join him, flogging the bystanders.

Everyone scatters.

Jurek falls on the icy ground, panting, clutching his throat. Kapo still lays into him, making him curl into a ball.

Franz takes a beating from one of the lieutenants, his arms protecting his face.

"You both are stupid bastards!" Kapo bellows as he straightens, tucking his baton in his belt. "You're going to stop this bloody fighting right now and if you start again, I'll kill you both! And it won't be quick! You're bloody lucky the SS aren't around, or you'd be shot!"

The beating stops. Franz draws in a deep breath and slowly lowers his arms. He rubs his ribs, knowing full well he'll be black and blue the next day.

Jurek rises unsteadily to his feet and hobbles back inside the hut, blood dripping from his nose, his jaw red and swollen. Franz has bruises for weeks and Jurek's nose looks broken. But Kapo's warning seems to have sunk in. The stupidity between Franz and Jurek finally stops.

If Kapo thinks it is necessary, and especially if we fight amongst ourselves, he'll have us flogged. In saying that, he's not a sadistic pig like most of the Bosses in the camp. Some are homicidal maniacs who think nothing of committing murder. One is notorious for killing the men in his hut. He once killed a man in roll call by kicking him to death.

But that doesn't mean Kapo, and his henchmen don't put on a performance for the Blockaelsten and the SS officers, if it means keeping their jobs.

Yelling at the top of their voices, they lash out with the canes, making us all flinch and cringe in pain. Some days are worse than others, depending on the mood of the Kommandant. If it's a bad day for him, it's a bad day for us. A lot of men are flogged on those days.

Spring brings heavy rain, creating thick, sludgy mud and pools of stagnant water around the barracks. It also brings disease and flies. Millions of flies. They buzz around the huts, attacking our bodies and invading the washroom.

The washroom pipes, frozen in Winter, have burst with the expanding ice. Blocked toilets, overflow with crap. Now the frozen muck is defrosting in the heat, burying the washroom in shit. We clamber in and out quickly, not wanting to be there any length of time.

We're put on work duty to clean up the mess. Given buckets and scrubbing brushes, we push the muck through the floorboards or out the door, sloshing the floor with fresh buckets of water. The pipes are finally repaired. But it doesn't stop the miasma and sickness that follow.

Men become dangerously ill. Many die. Typhus and Cholera spreads rapidly. Bodies are dumped daily into freshly dug pits out the back of the camp and covered in lime.

There is little relief as the warmer weather becomes a sweltering summer. Under the burning sun, we're rife with body odour, lice and sores. The lice bite into the soft tissues around our groins and under our arms creating cankers and boils.

Kapo barters with the medics at the hospital for a carton of little packets of sulphur. He distributes it around the hut, ordering us to treat each other. We inspect each other's bodies and sprinkle small amounts of the precious yellow powder into the seeping craters. Sometimes we lance a boil and pack it with the powder. I dry-heave every time.

We try to give ourselves a good wash at least twice a week in the sweltering weather, using our shirts as washcloths. I scrub Franz's back and he does mine. Alek scrubs Tomek's and he in turn scrubs Alek's. But the dirt is entrenched in our skin, and without soap, no amount of scrubbing can get rid of it.

Our rib cages and back bones poke out through our mottled skin. Our stomachs are caved in. Our shoulders hunched. We are scrawny, starved and half dead, like the men we sat with on our first day.

After washing, we drape our wet, grimy shirts around our necks and sit in the shade to catch a cool breeze.

At night we use pieces of coal we steal from the kitchen in place of toothbrushes. We rub it over our teeth, dislodging bits of food and scrubbing away the yellow plaque. Kapo gave us this advice the second day at the camp. He lined us up to instruct us on hygiene practices. One was to keep our teeth clean; another was to keep our pricks from getting infected.

"I once knew a man who had a massive infection under his foreskin!" Kapo lectured that night. "Within a month he was dead!" He rubs his face at the memory, "It was the most painful death I've ever seen. I urge you boys to keep your peckers clean.

Even though the rest of your body is not."

We all take his advice.

Hangings, ill-treatment, thrashings, executions by the SS and men wasting away from malnutrition or diseases are common occurrences in the camp.

Nearly every day, men are tied to a pole and lashed with a cane. For the most trivial things. Smoking, getting in a guard's way, glancing at an SS officer, being slow to answer. Minor things. The thrashings can be so severe, some men die.

Younger men like us in barrack 31, are not so badly treated. We are warned every day not to go near the SS. It isn't to say we aren't harassed by the 'heavies' every day. More than once, I've been kicked up the ass.

But the hangings are the worst. For days we're forced to march past the gallows to view the bodies left swinging there as a warning. Sometimes, the bodies are left to rot for over a week, the reek of decaying flesh overpowering us as we line up for roll call. The brutality of the beatings and executions is taking a toll on me.

At night I'm having disturbing dreams and nightmares.

One recurring dream is, I'm standing at the gallows with the noose around my neck, ready to be hung. But the rope is a large snake that keeps wrapping itself around my head.

I cling to its thick body and try to pull it away, but it tightens its coils. I begin to scream, choking as it squeezes.

I wake everyone in my bunk. I blink away the sweat, gazing into Alek's hovering face. He wipes my forehead with his hand.

As I try to sit up, he holds me down, whispering "Everything is alright, Rys." Tomek and Franz grumble under their breath and roll away. I move to the edge of the bunk, trying to forget the large snake squeezing the life out of me.

But I'm not the only one. Everyone is having bad dreams. Kapo informs us one night our nightmares are a result of months of starvation.

"I believe starving us is a form of torture by the SS, I can see them sitting around a table drinking cognac, discussing the best way to torture the prisoners with starvation being top of the list and freezing to death being the next."

We nod in agreement.

As far as food is concerned, working on the roads can be beneficial. Sometimes the townsfolk sneak us food.

It could be a small piece of salami, a potato or an onion, slipped into our hands as we march past or dropped at our feet where we're digging.

But most of the time we scavenge in abandoned or bombed houses, hiding the treasures in our pockets when the guards are looking elsewhere.

At the end of the day, we give whatever food we find to Kapo. He makes soup for us in his old tin pot on the wood stove, in addition to what we are served in the canteen.

We look forward to this extra, though still meagre meal.

Finding food for the soup is important to all of us. If anyone holds back, Franz deals with them behind the hut.

Now and then, Kapo adds a bit more soup to our plates.

Tomek questions him one evening as we sit along the table, eating our small portion.

"Why do you feed us more soup, Kapo?" He asks, as he scrapes his bowl with a bit of his bread.

"It's important you young ones survive the camp," Kapo mumbles as he chews a bit of cabbage. "You're our next generation. It'll be up to you to put things right."

I smile as I savour a sliver of onion. Kapo has made a good point.

After the meal, we chatter about the food we like best. Christmas tortes, the smell of paczki, and fresh bread baking.

An argument over the recipes for placki (a potato pancake) and kapusta (cabbage cooked with bacon) is thrashed out between Tomek and Filip. One of them asks Kapo's opinion.

"I don't know boys!" says Kapo as he holds up his hands in surrender. "It all sounds delicious to me!"

Tomek tells us about his father's restaurant and the food they served, the most popular dish and who frequented the restaurant.

In silence, we stare into space, wondering if such a place still exists.

Food governs our thoughts every waking moment. There's not a day we don't think about food.

However, every day, Franz and I also plan our escape.

Knowing the machine guns and barbed wire fence are a problem, we start to plan escapes for when we're outside the camp. One idea is to slip away when the guards take a break.

Tomek tries to discourage us.

"Where will you go?" He whispers hoarsely when we're lying in the bunk.

He grips my shoulder, "You have no civilian clothes, you'll stand out! The German people will inform the authorities. You will be recaptured and hanged! I'm telling you; you can't trust the Germans and there is nowhere to hide! The whole of Europe is a prison!"

He's probably right, but it doesn't stop us planning. Only now we also consider the problems he's listed.

Making plans gives us hope we'll live for another day. I've seen men lying in the snow, wishing to die or running at the gates to be shot by the guards. I prefer to plan an escape, knowing full well if we're caught, we'll be swinging from the gallows. You never know, we *might* escape this cesspit one day.

Kapo encourages us to learn German.

"It's a matter of life or death if you need to communicate with the Krauts," he says. "I will help now and then."

But it's Tomek with his excellent German who becomes our teacher.

Smiling at our silly pronunciations, Tomek repeats the words slowly as we repeat them back to him.

At night as we lie huddled in the bunk, we have a final practice. Tomek corrects us until we can pronounce the German words perfectly, keeping a score on the wooden plank above our heads.

It becomes a game. Franz is winning and Alek is coming last. I had a head start, already knowing some words, but now Franz's score is way ahead of mine. He's smarter than he looks.

"Take it seriously! This is not just a game," Tomek whispers gravely when Alek and I giggle at my mistakes. "It's very important you speak the language well. One day it could save your life."

I lie there, staring at the bunk above me, considering what he said. He's right. Speaking German could save our lives, especially if Franz and I find a way for all of us to escape. And we plan to.

21

Kapo could have been a teacher. If it wasn't for the war.

In the evenings, those who are not too exhausted, sit along the wood benches and tables and talk about our pasts.

Kapo, weary of the older men's company, occasionally sits with us. Speaking in Polish he tells us how the war is progressing and what life is like in Sachsenhausen.

One of his frequent contacts is another German prisoner in the big camp, who keeps him informed about what's going on. He also deals in contraband, especially cigarettes, a form of currency here and in the big camp. He barters with anything we can find. It's amazing what can be made from a spent cartridge or a small piece of leather.

With his height and receding hairline, he reminds me of Pan Nowak, except Kapo has black hair and piercing brown eyes. His undernourished body, once muscular, is now gaunt and underweight.

He crosses his legs and leans back in a chair which is one of his privileges and begins to speak.

"I'm a civil engineer.

My beautiful wife, Eva, is a nurse, and we have a boy called Lucas, who would be five years old now. He's a smart boy, reading and counting to a hundred at the age of three!"

Kapo rarely smiles, but he beams as he talks about his family.

"Is your family okay Kapo?" Filip asks.

"Yes! Yes! They managed to get out of Germany. A friend got them papers when he heard I was captured. They now live in Switzerland with Eva's sister and her husband."

He changes the subject to his favourite topic, history, and current political affairs. We are allowed to ask him questions.

"You're German. How come you're not a Nazi or in the German Army?" inquires Tomek.

"I'm a German Communist and I have different philosophical beliefs," Kapo replies.

"Kapo why were you not executed?" another boy asks.

"Engineers are too valuable to the SS and the Todt Construction Company. I've been a civil engineer most of my life and in this case, it saved my life. Otherwise, I would have been shot like the rest of the communists in Germany. A new directive by Albert Speers was enforced, to keep men like me alive. The Nazis force us to work on the roads, in factories and on construction sites, making huge profits for the SS."

"How were you caught?" I question.

"Oh, the usual way. I was picked up while I was lining up for bread. The SS asked for my papers then took me to a holding station. From there I was transported to Sachsenhausen. That was in 1941."

"Could you tell us about Sachsenhausen?" Franz asks, leaning forward.

Kapo begins to sing a song of promise and liberty. When the song fades away, Kapo heaves a deep sigh.

"This song belonged to Mikhail, a young man, who was

instructed to compose a camp song by an SS camp leader. He was a Ukrainian and he created this song to keep alive the hope of freedom. It was very popular with the prisoners, and we sang it often, but it was soon banned by the camp authorities. So now we only sing it in secret."

Kapo rubs his eyes, "Mikhail was killed a few months later." He straightens, sniffs and peers into our faces. "You all saw the big camp on the first day? Well, you only saw a small section. Sachsenhausen goes on for kilometres. It's a formidable prison. There is no escape. There's only one way in and two ways out, either through those double gates with machine guns trained on your back, or in death."

My mind drifts. I look outside at the darkening sky and the smoke haze from the barracks' chimneys, remembering the day we arrived. The foul stench and the machine guns aiming at us from the concrete towers. A shiver runs down my spine as I look back at Kapo, catching up with what he's saying.

"... the wire fence that encircles the inside of the concrete wall is electrified. I've seen guards making sport with the prisoners. Ordering them to try and escape so they can shoot them in the back or wait until they are electrocuted on the fence. You see, they get a bonus if they kill an escapee."

We gasp.

"The food is the same as ours. Soup and bread and this foul coffee." Grimacing, he lifts his mug. "Their canteen is similar to ours but bigger. It has murals of animated vegetables painted on the walls to brighten the place up a bit. I think a prisoner painted them.

It doesn't make the soup taste any better though."

We chuckle.

Kapo smiles but then turns serious.

"The Jews have their own section in the camp. When they arrive in Sachsenhausen they're left to starve for three days. Certain Jews are picked on by the SS because they're either too tall or too short, wear glasses, or have gold teeth. You see, the gold is extracted from the teeth when they die. So, these poor bastards are bashed by the SS every day until they're dead. After three days the rest are sent to Death Camps like Auschwitz."

Balint pipes up. "My neighbours were rounded up like cattle and forced into the back of a truck. I never saw them again, but later I heard they were sent to Auschwitz!"

Kapo glares at him for interrupting. Balint fidgets in his place, nervously looking at Kapo then the floor.

Kapo huffs and continues. "I recall Jews standing for hours in the courtyard, morning to night, many dying from the cold. But later on, Albert Speers arranged with Hitler and the Todt company to put the Jews to work in the factories. By then labour was in short supply in Germany due to all the German men going to war. In a way Speers may have saved a few thousand Jews. Not a very Nazi thing to do."

Tomek sniggers, covering his mouth with his hand. I realise this is why we were released at the mansion. The Krauts must have got a message to send us here. I glance at Franz who glances back, mirroring my understanding.

Kapo takes a slow sip from his mug and sets it down on the table. "When I arrived in February in 1941, we had to stand for a morning roll call for five hours in the same quadrangle you were standing in when you got your new papers. The SS commander had the roll called three times because one of the prisoners went missing. It was minus 12 degrees centigrade They left us out there in the freezing snow. Some of us died and a lot of us got frostbite. I have a couple of toes missing from that day.

He takes another sip from his mug. "They eventually found the man dead underneath a hut. He looked like he had been bashed to death."

Kapo peers down at his striped shirt under his grey-green camouflage jacket. He takes his jacket off.

"As you can see, my clothing is striped pyjamas, just like yours. We were given a tattoo on our forearm." He rolls his sleeve up, displaying a series of numbers in blue ink. "This number is to dehumanise us, so we have no name," he says through a sigh. "I don't know why you weren't given a tattoo. Maybe being shoved straight into a labour camp, they thought it unnecessary."

He pauses in thought, then continues.

"We were also given a winter coat, boots, and a beret. There are insignias and badges we had to sew on all our clothing, identifying us by another number."

We look down at our shirts as he points to his. "I also know that the number 31, that you all wear, means Polish political prisoner. Mine is different because I'm a communist. The letters and numbers are to identify you as a Jew, a Pole, or a homosexual etcetera.

The homosexuals are badly treated, both here and at the big camp. Most work in the brick factory in Oranienburg and are constructing a dock at the river. It's a terrible job. Bloody dangerous. Its without adequate shoring. When the wall collapses, which it frequently does, it buries the prisoners underneath. The SS won't allow them to be retrieved until the end of the day. A lot of men have died under that rubble and dirt. Their bodies are brought back in wheelbarrows and dumped in a pit at the back of the camp." He is silent for a while, staring at the floor, then asks, "Did you see the gravel road surrounding the barracks in Sachsenhausen?"

We all nod.

"Well, that's where the SS make the prisoners test out German Army boots. The poor buggers are made to march forty kilometres a day in boots, some too tight or too loose, carrying heavy packs. It's to find out how long the boots will last for the average German soldier. It sounds like an easy job, but you must understand these poor bastards are sick from starvation, and this type of treatment kills them in a day. Most just lie down and die, either on the road or later, in their barracks. Some are taken to the infirmary, never to be seen again."

Kapo sighs deeply.

"That hospital is a very bad place. It's where SS doctors experiment on children sent from Auschwitz. I heard they are injected with terrible diseases so those quacks can observe the results. Most of the children die.

The staff who work there are usually prisoners with only limited medical knowledge, like a first aid officer or an ambulance driver. There is maybe one doctor on call for hundreds of patients. The Russians are never sent there. They are left to die in their barracks. The Nazis see them as subhuman, just like the Jews, and many are shot or hanged as soon as they arrive.

In the year I came to the camp, the kommandant, Hans

Loritz, a bloody corrupt bastard, mass murdered thousands of Russian prisoners. The SS even ordered incinerators to be built to cremate the bodies as there were too many to bury. That's the stench you can smell at times. It drifts this far, depending on the direction of the wind."

Ah! So that's the yellow haze I saw as we arrived at Sachsenhausen. The lingering rancid smoke was human flesh being cremated! I can smell it now. Bile rises to my mouth. Christ! How inhuman are these Nazi bastards?

"Once, when I was loading bricks on the back of a truck," Kapo recalls, "a small boy came up to me and asked if we were burning bodies today because of the stench in the air. I can't believe the German people tolerated the smell but did nothing about it. I even bet you the majority of Germans don't even know what's happening in the concentration camps."

He reaches in his pocket for a cigarette but realising its not there pats the tattered fabric instead. "They know the incinerators are in there for the dead. But I doubt they know that hundreds if not thousands of people are being murdered by the SS every day, then fed into the ovens."

One of Kapo's men interrupts.

"Kapo it's curfew," he whispers.

Kapo stands. "Into your bunks," he says urgently. We leave our seats and scurry to our bunks, shuffling along the planks. Alek is quite chatty, discussing what Kapo said, unaware of hostile stares from the others.

"For Christ's sake, shut up Alek!" Franz hisses. "You'll get us all in trouble!"

Alek sniffs indignantly and faces the wall.

I pat his shoulder.

"It's okay Alek, I'm also amazed by the story!"

#####

The next evening the lads discuss the ovens in Sachsenhausen and the terrible smell when they arrived. Some talk about the murals in the canteen, others about the type of work the prisoners are made to do.

Kapo places his chair near the stove, putting his mug on the table. We fall silent and look his way.

"Did you work on the roads like us, Kapo?" Filip asks.

"I'll tell you about the work I did. I made bricks, ammunition, and German uniforms, among other jobs.

In 1942 Hans Loritz was replaced by Anton Kaindi, who was more of an administrator than a soldier. He organised building the sub camps and the factories."

He takes a sip from his steaming mug, "Sachsenhausen is growing all the time. It even has a dog handling unit. All kinds of factories have been built and extended. A bigger ammunition factory and vehicle depot was built last year alone. A brickwork factory outside the camp has been there since 1938 and is still the largest and most productive of all the factories. It supplies bricks for a new Reich Capital to be named Germania, planned by Adolf Hitler and Albert Speer. Their vision includes the construction of huge ostentatious buildings, all looking like Roman temples and palaces. The Reich Chancellery has already been built with a domed roof, looking like a Roman Basilica.

Hitler and Speers want to show the world how great and powerful Nazi Germany has become."

"What does ostentatious mean Kapo?" asks Alek, his ignorance reminding me how much younger he is than the rest of us.

"It means over the top," Kapo answers. "Over done or made to impress."

"Kapo, what do you think of the Nazis?" Tomek chimes in.

"You must understand the Nazis are like a separate race," explains Kapo. "Like an evil offshoot of the German people. The SS are groomed by an evil bastard called Heinrich Himmler. He is the leader of the Nazi party and orchestrated the creation of the SS. He also arranged for the mass murder of Jews by special SS forces.

When the regular German army conquered a country, like France, these SS forces would follow behind and commit terrible atrocities against the local people. They murdered tens of thousands. And it was Himmler who instigated and planned the construction of huge gas chambers in the camps, big enough to kill hundreds of people in just twenty minutes."

Pausing, Kapo shakes his head.

"You see, Hitler and Himmler have the same beliefs. They believe humanity must be of pure Aryan race and everyone else should be put to death or made into slaves. Their ideals have brought about illogical passions and irrational behaviours in others, resulting in the killing of thousands of innocent people."

He rubs his chin.

"Himmler groomed the Nazis and especially the SS, to adopt all his philosophies. Especially about political prisoners like the Communists, socialists, liberal democrats, trade unionists, members of the university, Christians, pacifists, or fanatics.

They are all viewed as malevolent opponents of the Nazi party and are seen as criminals in the Nazis' eyes. To be totally eradicated from this earth. The Nazis also see the Jews as a plague of rats and the political prisoner as a criminal. The Jews are to suffer, and political prisoners are to be punished. Death for all of them. For all of us. The aim of the camps is a slow death of degradation. We're looking at human barbarism in its highest form. Committed by fanatical, psychopathic men and women."

Staring at Kapo, we shudder fearfully.

"However, now the SS have a different point of view. They believe it's in their best interest to use the prisoners as slaves for their own monetary gain. These bastards are getting very rich indeed. Some German companies are in partnership with them, all wanting to keep us alive, so we can work for them as long as possible, until we keel over and die.

But the larger concentration camps would see to it you are exterminated by any means possible. You can be easily replaced in a concentration camp, unless you are young like yourselves or have experience like me and the older men in this sub-camp. We're not so expendable. You see when Albert Speers made us slave labourers; we became part of the German war effort.

How ironic is this; Speers saved you from being shot, as most political prisoners were shot in the past, only to work you to death so he and the SS can make a lot of money. Mind you the SS still shoot us for any trivial reason."

I bow my head, remembering the men we left in the trench, their bodies twisted at odd angles, flies buzzing around them. That bastard Speers didn't save my friends or the major. He was too bloody late. I think back on that terrible day and wipe my eyes on my sleeve.

"This camp is owned by a construction company called Todt," I hear Kapo say. "A civil and military engineering group. Fritz Todt is high up in the Nazi regime. He is a close friend of Adolf Hitler and has made a lot of money by using us as slaves for his labour force. This camp mainly consists of 'quick-reaction squads' to quickly repair and clear roads. Other sub-camps construct bridges or buildings, like the factories in and around the town."

Kapo leans on the wooden table clasping his hands and peers into our faces.

"Time for bed!"

The next day, the Bevauer visits our hut with a couple of his men. They roughly search us, throwing our belongings into a pile, then sift through them, taking what they want. Next, they overturn the bunk room and rec-room, pulling everything out from the lockers. We stand on the sidelines, not daring to protest. Even Kapo and his men are frisked and robbed.

The Bevauer takes a compass from Kapo's pocket and five packets of cigarettes from his alcove.

That night Kapo talks about the Bevauers.

"Okay. What happened today is nothing new. The Bevauer are usually German nationalists. They are given a green triangle under their prison number bearing the insignia B.V which means professional criminals. They deal with contraband and steal from everyone in the camp. They are also informers for the SS. So, keep clear of them. Some can be real mean bastards. The SS allow them to organise the Kapos and the Blockaltesten in dealing out punishments.

They supervise the labour force or carry out administrative tasks which minimises costs. It allows the camps to function with fewer SS. The Bevauer has a lot more privileges, like much better food and accommodation. When I was in Sachsenhausen, there was a Bevauer who was a total psychopath."

Kapo moved his arms up and down, as if he had a skipping rope. "He would skip around as if he was in a playground, thrashing anyone with his cane, sometimes to death. He was totally insane. A real evil bastard.

He was finally demoted. I can't think why, maybe the SS guards wanted to see what would happen next. Anyway, he only lasted one night. He was found strangled in his bed the next day.

The Bevauer in charge of my barrack was a decent man. He was fair with the punishments and generous with the distribution of food. Contraband like cigarettes was tolerated and he managed to bargain with the Norwegians in the camp. They were believed to be a more superior race by the Nazis, because most had blond hair and blue eyes."

He pulls out a small red tin, the paint scratched off, and peels the lid open. Inside was a needle, threads and one button.

"They were given Red Cross parcels, which held a lot of precious items, usually soap, combs, and sewing kits, just like this one. We would trade with the Norwegians using cigarettes, handmade cigarette cases and lighters. We had a very clever man in our barrack, called Mikolaj, who made lighters out of cartridge cases."

"What happened to him, Kapo?" I ask.

"He was finally found out and shot," he answers with a grunt.

We all fall silent.

Kapo carries on with his lecture.

"The punishments are terrible in the big camp. A sloping table called a Trestle is used for beatings. It has belts that fasten on the prisoner's shoulders and behind his legs. Their feet are encased in blocks to keep them from bucking."

He describes the trestle using his hands. "These beatings are administered on the back or ass by one of the Bosses using a cane. The poor bastard is strapped on this contraption and made to count the number of strokes, usually twenty-five. If he loses count the beating will start all over again. Most men die from their injuries."

He sighs and lowers his voice to a whisper. We lean forward.

"In May 1942 we witnessed a public hanging. It was Whitsunday when a man called Hans Trobel was hanged for trying to escape the previous day. He had fled the brickworks and was caught by the guards, here in Oranienburg.

The SS forced another prisoner, who later went insane, to carry out the hanging. Trobel died a horrible death by strangulation as the noose was poorly made.

Heinrich Himmler was visiting at the time, so at the execution, he proclaimed that this poor man had stolen food and clothing from the camp to supply his escape. Which we all knew was bullshit," he hisses. "Trobel, the poor bastard, was then dragged into the courtyard and hung. He swung for days."

Some of us swallow hard, others rub their face.

"At roll call, we had to march past with our caps off," Kapo adds. "The SS thought it would be a deterrent against further escapes. But we all felt the greatest respect for Hans Trobel, and in some way, it had an effect on all of us."

He looks into our faces. "It does something to the human spirit when you see someone executed.

It can either harden you to the extent it's a normal occurrence in everyday life, making you glad it wasn't you on the end of the rope, or it can make you respectfully mourn the loss of a comrade."

He strokes his forehead and sighs.

"Torture, of any kind, is well known in Sachsenhausen. There's a T-shaped cell block in the middle of the camp separated by a concrete wall where they intern special high-profile prisoners, like British and French airmen. I know it is governed by the Gestapo and what happens there I won't tell you. But I know it's a place where torture and murder take place. It's a very bad place indeed, where prisoners die by very cruel means."

Kapo falls silent.

We stare at him, our faces more ashen than usual.

"The barracks in Sachsenhausen are overcrowded with prisoners. There are times when there is no room at the tables, so you sit on the wooden floor. Whenever you move around, you're either thumped or pushed. Most sleep six to eight men in one bunk. Like here, there are three tiers of bunks built along the walls, leaving very narrow aisles. If you can't get a bed you sleep on the ground.

The whole place is teeming with bugs and disease is rife, especially Typhus. It's just like here in winter, bloody freezing. Plenty of men died of hypothermia."

"What's hypo...hypothermia?" inquires Alek.

"It means you die from the cold," Kapo answers patiently.

"Like I said before, the Russians are worse off than any of us. Especially in Sachsenhausen. We'd secretly organise food supplies for them which we code named 'Rote Kuhle'. It's usually a slice of bread the men gave from their meagre rations. However, some of the Russians didn't trust us, thinking we were poisoning them. These men never lasted long.

Even today, the majority are murdered by a bullet fired at their necks. They are told to stand behind a slotted wall to be measured but are shot instead. There are Russians in this camp as well and we feed them whatever we can. The kitchen staff mostly help them out with slops."

He sighs, looking at our bewildered faces.

We try to absorb what he is telling us.

"Lads don't lose hope or faith in mankind. More importantly, don't lose your own humanity. If you do, the Nazis have won. It's important to believe in goodness in others, just like the townsfolk in Oranienburg, who have no need to supply us with food, but they do. Treat everyone with respect, even if they don't deserve it.

Remember, you were given a name by your parents, not a number. You are all human beings and it's okay to feel hate or even love in this hell hole. If used properly, hate can be a very powerful tool and love can save a life. Both can keep you alive. So, remember you are human! Even if you are treated below the rank of animals."

He studies us for a few moments.

"Now it's time for you to hit the sack. Or in your case the planks!" he chuckles.

We crawl along our bunks, whispering about the main camp

... Sachsenhausen.

"I'm grateful I'm not in the big camp," murmurs Alek, nestling beside me. "And I'm so glad to be with you, Franz and Tomek. I know if ever I got sick you would look after me."

I frown and look closely at his face, looking for signs of illness.

I settle in for the night, staring at the panelled wall on the side of the bunk. For a long moment I think of all Kapo said.

Especially, his philosophy on human nature. I wrap my arms tightly around my chest.

I believe hate is the way to go.

I can survive on hate.

As I fill in a pothole the following day, I think back on Kapo's lecture and it dawns on me that friendship and brotherhood is the key to survival in this camp, not hate. It's going to be hard.

I love to hate.

Especially the Nazis.

22

It's hard to keep our spirits up with so much misery and fear around us. Every day a prisoner like us is beaten, hung by the neck, or disappears, either in the camp or working outside. We live in dread.

Alek is especially low. He's listless, finding it hard to make conversation. He cries every night. So, we decide to cheer him, and ourselves, by whispering stories to each other. We limit them to one story per week.

We're all too exhausted to do any more. Our chosen day is Sunday, which we know by the ringing of the church bells and the Germans allowing us to be off work detail outside the camp. Instead, we're ordered to clean our barracks, bathe, wash our clothes and if needed, get our heads shaved.

Huddling together on the bunk, one Sunday evening, I begin whispering my story.

#####

I was about eight years old and in a gang at school. We were always in trouble, daring each other to do stupid things and getting up to mischief. My mates and I got the cane a fair bit.

One of the dares involved a tree and the fire brigade.

One day, egged on by my mates I climbed a large fir tree in the school playground. It was a huge tree which no one had ever climbed before. Naturally, it was against the school rules to climb it.

Ahh! I didn't give a damn! I was going to show my mates I wasn't scared of anything!

At lunch break, the gang gathered around the tree, and hoisted me up to the first branch. I began to climb.

I went up and up while everyone cheered. At last, I came to the top and sat on one of the branches, looking at my beloved city. Sochaczew.

It shone brilliantly in the sunlight. The Bzura River gleamed and shimmered. I saw the department store my Pa worked at, the railyard with trains going back and forth, and green farmlands in the distance. I saw the forest on the outskirts of the city where my family would pick mushrooms and picnic amongst the pine needles in spring.

A church spire peeked over the rooftops, and I knew it was the one Ma worshipped at every Sunday. It was next to a statue of Frederic Chopin mounted on a tall plinth. I remember Jo and I peering up at the famous composer, amazed at the fine carving of Chopin's coat and breeches, and how his wavy hair was swept off his face as he gazed into the distance.

I'm lost, deep in memories for a moment. I swipe away a tear running down my face.

I sniff and return to my story.

I must have sat there for ages until my bum started to burn. It was time to get down. I peered down through the branches, seeing these tiny people below.

They were no bigger than my tin soldiers.

Everyone was yelling, but I couldn't make out what they

we're saying. It was a long, long way down.

Suddenly, I felt dizzy. I started to panic.

Sweat ran down my back. My hands felt clammy, and I started to shake. Fear clutched my belly. I thought I might throw up!

I stop my story and with two hands hold my stomach, pretending to gag, then settle back down onto the bunk and continue. My friends grin at my playacting.

I was so scared I froze with fear.

"I can't get down!" I shouted. Tears rolling down my face.

Using a megaphone, a teacher yelled back at me.

"What do you mean? You can't get down?"

"I just can't! I'm too scared!" I screamed back.

By this time, the headmaster had arrived, grabbed the megaphone, and yelled up at me.

"If you got up there, Ryszard, you can easily get down!"

But I kept yelling back that I was truly stuck.

After at least an hour trapped on the branch, with my bum becoming really sore, I saw a fire engine drive through the school gates and park below the tree. A newspaper man followed in a car. He jumped out and started to take photos.

As I looked down, I saw a fireman's ladder swing into the air and extend to its full length. It leaned against the tree and a big fireman climbed up. He looked like a real hero with his fireman's helmet and red uniform, and I thought I would like to be a fireman when I got older. He told me to slide along the branch by scooting my ass along it. So, I did.

I edged towards him, and he grabbed my arm. It hurt a bit, but I didn't say anything. He put me between himself and the ladder rungs, telling me all the while that I was an idiot.

Well, I knew that already!

He gripped the back of my shirt as we climbed down the ladder and carefully stood me on the ground. My legs wobbled and I found myself kneeling at the feet Pan Labriski, the headmaster. He pulled me up by the collar as everyone cheered. Well, except for Pan Labriski, the teachers, and the firemen.

The headmaster took me by the ear and marched me off to his office where I got a couple of whacks with the cane on my numb bum.

When I got up the next morning, Pa was reading the newspaper at the kitchen table. He looked up, frowning over the top of the paper. He lowered it and stabbed his finger at

the photo on the front page. It was of me coming down the ladder with the fireman.

The paper read 'Lad Stuck in Schoolyard Tree.'

Pa stood up with his hands behind his back and gave me a very stern look. He began to lecture me about the reputation of the family and 'how was he to explain this to the staff at the store.'

I thought I was in for another belting, but do you know what, he just burst out laughing and ruffled my hair. I was stunned. I thought I was going to cop it big time!

But I did cop it with Ma.

I chuckled.

She grounded me for the rest of the week. I couldn't play soccer with my friends, and I had to wash the dishes every day. Well, until I broke too many."

We muffled our laughter so as not to attract Kapo and his lieutenants.

#####

The following Sunday is Franz's story.

When I was little, about eight years old, I roamed the city streets a lot, Franz began. *Dad didn't really care where I went, so long as I came home before dark. He had his radio, vodka, and cigarettes to keep him company.*

You see, I had no mum. She died when I was little.

Anyway, one day I saw this snotty-nose kid, a Jew kid I think, eating a long yellow fruit with its skin peeled away. The peel was half-way down. It was like it had a handle with these skin things hanging and I thought what the hell was that? You see, I'd never seen a banana before.

I walked past him, waited a moment, turned, and walked behind him, grabbed the fruit and bit into it, snot, and all. It tasted amazing.

We all groaned at that image.

I was only halfway into it before the kid's father gave chase, yelling that I was a thief.

"I've always been a thief," he shrugs, looking from one of us to the others. "So, what was new?"

I ran like hell, dodging and swerving through the streets.

At this point Franz waves his hands around.

I thought I lost him. But I didn't lose the banana!

His voice lowers even further.

I crept into a quiet alley and was about to stuff the rest into my mouth, when," Franz becomes more animated, *"I was reefed up by the collar by the kid's father. I tried to swallow the banana, but the man shook the bejesus out of me and made me drop the banana skin. The rest of the banana stuck out of my mouth like a big yellow tongue, wobbling up and down.*

The man, not watching where he was going, suddenly slipped on the banana skin, taking me with him.

I landed between his legs and banged my head into his balls, making him screech like a monkey. He squealed and squealed really loud.

I managed to swallow the rest of the banana before I started to laugh. I couldn't stop laughing. I rolled on the ground in hysterics. He sounded like a monkey screeching its head off. That man was angry. His face turned a purple colour. He tried to get up, but he kept slipping and sliding, landing in dog shit. He screamed at me, but I didn't wait around. I got up in a flash and ran like hell, all the way home.

Franz folded his arms behind his head, "That banana was delicious, snot and all, and from that day on I've always liked bananas. I would steal one whenever I got the chance!"

Next Sunday is Tomek's story.
I was about thirteen and my brother worked at my father's restaurant. He is much older than me and a bit on the girlie side!

Tomek cocks his wrist.

We interrupt him to ask what type of restaurant it was? What did it serve? What was the most popular dish? We are obsessed with every detail.

After patiently answering our questions Tomek begins again.

Anyway, we went into the forest to find mushrooms for the restaurant.

We interrupt again, discussing in hushed tones how to cook mushrooms.

Tomek sighs, rubbing his face.

"Come on, give me a break!" he mutters.

Anyway, we found quite a lot of mushrooms and filled our sacks. When we were heading home, I spotted a beehive up a tree. I climbed up, to see if I could get some honey.

We all groan.

Tomek rolls his eyes.

I stuck my hand in the hive and made the bees very angry. They began to swarm around me. I scrambled down the tree pretty fast, yelling at my brother to run. He, being on the fat side, couldn't run fast, so they stung the shit out of him. He literally, shat his pants!

We snicker.

I ran home. Flew into the kitchen and slammed the back door shut. I didn't realise at the time it had locked itself. It always had a dodgy lock.

Meanwhile, my mother and brother are still outside.

Ma was hanging out the washing but stopped when she saw me run into the house. My brother, Bartosz, was yelling at her about the swarm.

They began screaming and banging on the door. I frantically fiddled with the lock. But it wouldn't open. So, I told them to run to the front of the house and get in that way.

They both barged into the kitchen, Mother giving me a tongue lashing, followed by my brother slapping me around the head and shrieking at the top of his voice. I wrapped my arms around my head, trying to defend myself.

Tomek demonstrated, wrapping his arms around his head.

Anyway, after a while he gave up and began to hit my shoulders instead. Anyone else would have picked up a stick and given me a thrashing, but I don't think he even thought about that. His method of fighting was to squeal like a piglet and smack like a girl.

Ma and Bartosz kept hollering at me, 'How dare I lock the door!' and, 'What got into your stupid head to lock the door?' I kept telling them it locked itself, but they didn't believe me!

I didn't know I was allergic to bee stings until I got stung that day. My face blew up like a balloon, making me look like Quasimodo, the hunchback of Notre-Dame.

We laugh.

Tomek looks over his shoulder.

"Shush. Be quiet," he breaths in a hoarse whisper. "That bastard, Bogdan, is looking our way!"

We furtively peep over Tomek.

Seeing the mongrel glaring at us from his bunk. we quickly lie back, becoming very still, ready for him to pounce on us.

Minutes pass.

Nothing happens.

Tomek resumes his story in a low whisper.

Father was furious. My brother was one of his chefs, and being a wuss and a girl, he complained all night about the strings on his face.

Tomek mimics Bartosz in a girly voice, *"I can't possibly go to work looking so ugly. What will everyone say? I need to heal. Don't I Mother? And to stay in bed as my nerves are frazzled! You need to punish Tomek more severely, Mother."*

Tomek is so funny, we burst out laughing, but quickly shut up as Bogdan looks up from his bunk, slamming his tattered magazine onto the mattress. Snarling, he swings a leg over, then thinks better of it and lies back down. He picks up his soot-stained magazine and continues pretending to read while straining his ears, trying to hear what we're laughing about.

Tomek takes a deep breath and turns to face us.

So, after school, he murmurs, *I washed the dishes at the restaurant for a month and only broke one plate in all that time!*

He glances at me and smiles.

"But you know what, if it wasn't for that misadventure, I would never have been working in the restaurant, and never been taught the art of creating fine cuisine."

He emits a long sigh. "The next year the chef made me his apprentice and it was the best time in my life!"

Franz and I give him the thumbs up. His story was great.

Alek is unusually quiet. He's usually quite chatty and always asks lots of questions, especially if it's about food.

"Don't forget, Alek, it's your turn next Sunday." whispers Tomek, as he turns to look at him.

Alek just nods and turns to face the wall without saying a word. We look at each other uneasily.

Tomek quietly asks Alek if he's okay.

But Alek is silent. He drifts into a restless sleep.

CHAPTER

23

Alek struggles to stand the next day. Hot and clammy, his drawn hollow face has a feverish sheen. We wedge him between us at roll call and stand at the back of the lines, trying not to be seen.

With his legs wobbling, Alek's head rolls forward.

"The light hurts my eyes," Alek murmurs as Tomek clamps his hand under his arm to keep him upright. Franz does the same on his other side. The men around us make sure we are well hidden.

"Shut your eyes Alek," whispers Tomek in his ear. "But keep standing until roll call is finished, then we'll get you back inside."

Without incident, we drag Alek back to the hut, hiding him on the top bunk. Franz places a mug of water near his head, hoping he drinks it during the day.

For two days, before boarding the work trucks, we follow this routine. By the end of the second day Alek's condition is a lot worse. He is unable to get up on his own, or eat, or drink. We must drag him to the toilet before he shits himself.

He thrashes around through the night, keeping us all awake.

He complains of stomach pain, headaches, and body pain. His chest and arms are covered in a red rash.

Collecting his soup from the canteen and dipping his bread

into it, one of us would place it into his mouth and encourage him to chew. But he finds it too difficult to swallow.

He hallucinates. Shouting out to his family whom he believes are hovering at the end of the bunk, he tries to sit up, reaching out with his hand to touch them. In a croaky voice, he calls out their names until exhaustion claims him once more, and he falls back onto the hard bed.

We soothe and reassure him, taking turns throughout the night to nurse him, giving him sips of water and bathing his face. Nonetheless, we all fall asleep, clutching the damp cloth, only to wake through the night with him moaning in pain.

There is nothing more we can do.

We are terrified he will die.

Kapo needs to know.

We approach his cubicle and stand in silence at the opening. He peers up from a book he's reading. Seeing our expressions, he levers himself up from his chair.

Kapo listens to Tomek describe Alek's illness, then asks a couple of questions to confirm what he fears.

"I knew he was sick, but this is Typhus. He needs to go to the infirmary."

Carefully, we remove Alek from the bunk and place him on a make-shift stretcher we made by tying our shirts together. Wapasha helps us to carry him to the hospital at the back of the camp. It is like the rest of the barracks, but instead of a number painted on the side, there is a blue cross.

Slowly, we climb the concrete steps and gently heft Alek up to the door. Wapasha opens it with his free hand and leads us down a dim corridor to a vacant desk. We lay Alek down on the ground and stand half naked, grimacing at the terrible moaning and woeful cries in the adjacent rooms. I gag at the stench of shit and vomit. I hold my breath and finally breathe through my mouth.

After some time, a harried doctor, tall and thin with black framed spectacles, bustles through the door near his desk.

He shakes his head when Wapasha describes Alek's illness and tells us he'll do what he can, but explains he has hardly any medicine, just a few painkillers. He leads us into a room packed with the dying. Men are stretched out on canvas stretchers or lying on filthy straw pallets. Some with little clothing as their fevers ravish their bodies.

The doctor points to a vacant bed in a quiet corner of the room where we gently place Alek. Franz retrieves our shirts from beneath him.

Untying them, I wipe his face with mine.

Tomek holds his hand as we all say our goodbyes, but Alek is non-responsive.

"Body lice cause this disease. They bite an infected person then pass on the disease to the next. Try to clean your clothing regularly, as well as any bedding. Delouse each other every day."

He waves his arm towards the open doorway.

"Now go back and wash your clothing immediately and watch for signs of the disease, like a headache or a rash."

Tomek, Franz and I return to the hospital the following evening and wait in the corridor for a long time. Eventually the doctor sees us standing near his desk and walks toward us.

His face is grim as he whispers, "I'm sorry, but your friend died in the night."

I stand there in shock. I don't know why but I'm openly

weeping, the tears running down my face. I knew all along Alek was dying. But to know I'll never see him again leaves me numb. Tomek covers his face with his hands, and a sob escapes his lips, but Franz, dried eyed and stoically erect, only draws in a quivering breath.

"I'll go back and tell Kapo," he croaks.

#####

Although Timon and other lads catch the disease and never recover, as the week passes there is no further sign of the illness among us three, which is a miracle.

I don't know where Alek or those other lads are buried, but I guess there's a big pit somewhere out the back where bodies are dumped. There's no memorial or headstones for the dead, only numbers recorded in a ledger somewhere. Like Kapo said in his lecture. We're nothing to the Bosses and SS.

We all miss Alek. Our skinny, whimpering, pain-in-the-arse friend. Silently, at night I speak to him, telling him I will never forget his kindness, especially when a real bastard a couple of months caned me during roll call.

It was Alek who found a cloth and gently bathed my back with water, spreading the cold rag over my skin to reduce the swelling.

In the last twelve months, I've noticed how kind-hearted Alek really was. He'd comfort anyone depressed or upset, not just us. He'd be the first to fetch water and borrow a rag to wash blood of a back or a fevered brow.

Tomek loved him as his little brother. Alek would snuggle up to his foot, clutching it, just before he fell asleep.

One evening, I told Tomek about the days in the Resistance when Alek was in our crew and the antics we got up to. But Franz didn't say much. He just sat quietly on the bench, staring into space.

Even though Alek whimpered at any provocation, making Franz's hackles rise, he was surprisingly very protective of him. If anyone threatened Alek in any way, Franz stood in front of him, fists at the ready. Alek would defuse the situation, either by speaking calmly to Franz or the lad he was about to punch, pulling Franz away.

Wapasha had also taken Alek under his wing. He told us once; Alek reminded him of his youngest son. He would stay the hand of anyone about to hit him. I noticed he spoke to Alek whenever he had the chance and at one time, put his arm around his shoulder when Alek was upset.

Kapo realised, when we first arrived, that Alek was lying about his age and was a lot younger than he looked. So, he arranged for him to work in the kitchens, which was a lot easier than working on the roads. Alek didn't mind the work. He smuggled out vegetables, and occasionally barley for the barracks' soup, always gossiping about the cooks.

He always had a potato or turnip in his pockets.

Apart from his caring manner, Alek had a beautiful singing voice and sang on Sunday mornings, after roll call. This is the best time Most of the guards weren't around. Maybe too busy sleeping off the booze or in rare cases being with their families.

I remember we'd form a circle around Alek, most of us sitting on the floor and Kapo, his lieutenants, and the Bevauer standing behind us, their canes and batons forgotten by their sides. For a full ten minutes we listened to this thin, frail boy with wonder and admiration as he sang the most beautiful hymns.

Trying not to break the serenity of the moment, we'd fall silent and still, closing our eyes to enjoy his heavenly voice. We felt absolute peace. A rarity in this god-forsaken hole.

Occasionally, I'd glance around the room and notice men from other huts wandering in. They'd stand along the walls, some gazing towards the ceiling, with tears running down their faces, seemingly transported to a better place and time.

Alek would slowly bow at the end of the last hymn. Hushed for a long moment, we would savour the last of his ringing notes, then soundlessly bow back. It was our way of applauding him.

But before long, the bosses would bark orders for us to get back to our Sunday tasks and return to our pitiful lives.

I will never forget Alek. My dear snivelling friend.

CHAPTER

24

Separated from us by a wire fence, the Russians in the camp look like human skeletons covered in thin grey parchment. Their eyes are empty, as if their souls have already departed.

Through feverish, sunken eyes, dull and vacant, they stare through the wire as we pass by. Having little energy, most sit on the ground with their hands extended through the wire, begging for food. They are dying. Disease is rampant among them. Even more so than on our side. Their living conditions are utterly barbaric. They have no stoves, running water or any proper toilets, just buckets. They collect what rainwater they can.

The SS treat them as sub-human and let them starve. Just as they do the Jews.

We feel sorry for the poor bastards and try to help them when we can.

The men in the camp try to feed the Russians with the meagre scraps from the kitchen. They pass the bucket over their fence into outstretched hands, receiving a desperate.

'Spasibo' thank you.

We would watch the Russians crowd around the buckets and scoop the raw vegetable scraps into their mouths not bothering to cook it.

I score kitchen duty for a whole week in the last weeks of summer.

Ripping a pocket and buttons from a dead man's shirt, before someone else claims it, I barter with three of the buttons for a needle and thread. I sew the pocket inside my pants, near my balls.

Every day I steal a potato or onion and hide them in the secret pocket, adjusting it so it doesn't bulge. Every morsel contributes towards Kapo's barracks soup. Tomek is in charge now, being designated 'soup maker' after Kapo found out he could cook.

After working in the kitchen for a couple of hours, I'm sent by one of the cooks to deliver the slop bucket to the Russians.

As I'm ambling up the road a severe pain jabs into my back. I gasp, my knees buckling. I go down in a heap, spilling the slops all over the ground. I scramble up fast to face the bastard who kicked me, only to see a young SS officer, no older than myself, standing at arm's length. He is pointing a gun at my head. His eyes narrow as he squints down the length of his gun.

I put my hands on my head.

"Aye Cabbage Head! What are you up to?" he sneers in a nasal voice, aiming his weapon behind my ear.

I keep my mouth shut.

"Oh, you're going to feed the Ruskies are you? I don't think so, you filthy Polak!" he snarls through clenched teeth.

I stand stock-still. Everyone gives us a wide berth. No one looks my way.

I see Franz coming up the road towards us. He catches sight of the scene and stands motionless, a look of horror on his face.

I avert my eyes, not daring to look at him or the SS officer. Keeping my eyes straight ahead, I see the Russians shuffling up to the fence, peering through the wire. I see real concern on their faces.

"I think I will kill you, you dirty Pole," the bastard hisses, pressing the gun harder into my skull.

I start to sweat. Rivulets of perspiration run down my cheeks and between my shoulder blades. I close my eyes. I imagine diving into the river near Auntie's farm and sitting on the bottom holding my breath.

I hold my breath now, waiting to die.

Laughing, the officer slowly lowers his gun and kicks me in the arse, making me fall to the ground again. I scrape my face on the gravel but still link my hands behind my head, pushing my forehead into the sharp stones.

He squats down, pushing his Luger into the back of my neck.

"I'll shoot you if I ever see you giving food to the Ruskies again," he growls, loudly enough for everyone nearby to hear. "I'll shoot you dead, Cabbage Head! Believe me, I will!"

I sense him standing. He kicks me again. A searing pain explodes along my ribs.

After a long moment, I swivel my head to see him striding back towards the SS quarters, shoving his gun back in its holster.

Scrambling up fast and fleeing back to the canteen, I run past a cook stirring a pot.

He grabs my arm, making me stop.

"Are you okay?"

I jerkily nod, wiping the sweat from my eyes, breathing rapidly.

"I thought I was going to die!" I gasp.

The cook studies my pale face.

"Don't worry. I'll do the slop bucket from now on," he growls as he looks towards the SS barracks. "That bastard looks younger than my nephew. The Krauts must be getting desperate if they're recruiting kids that age!"

He returns to his pot, stirring the grey water with angry strokes and mumbling under his breath.

I'm reeling, rattled by what could have happened. I need to be more careful. What if the bastard seeks me out to finish the job?

I touch my crotch, feeling a third lump. I can't remember if I stole a potato or an onion. If he'd found it, he really would have shot me!

I race into the barrack, after my shift. Franz is waiting by the door. He grabs my shoulder, swinging me around to face him.

"Are you okay?" he asks.

I gaze into his face, comforted by his concern.

"We need to escape Franz. We need to do it soon," I state in a hoarse whisper.

He pats my shoulder, reassuringly.

"I know... I know Rys."

I sense him following me as I slowly walk to our bunk. I crawl in, facing the wall. Franz lies behind me.

"I promise you, Rys, we will find a way to get out of here! I promise!" he whispers.

I stare at the wall for a long time, wondering if he really can keep such a promise.

25

Kapo scores Tomek a job in the camp kitchens.

Hoping to improve the terrible soup, he recommends Tomek to the cooks. Unfortunately, there is nothing much even Tomek can do with cabbage, carrot tops, potato peelings and barley, except to add some salt, which he manages to do. Although he soon has the bread tasting a lot better.

Word of Tomek's abilities as a chef soon reaches the Camp's Kommandant nicknamed 'Bulldog' due to his saggy jowls and squashed nose. He recruits Tomek to become his personal servant, cook and cleaner. Also, his ability to speak perfect German and limited English allows him to translate when needed.

Tomek told us months ago he could speak a spattering of English due to the British patrons from the embassy who frequented his father's restaurant. But mainly he learnt English from a family friend, who visited their house regularly and taught him and his brother some English phrases like 'please pass me the salt and pepper' or 'how do you do.'

Tomek has no other choice than to leave the barracks. And us. His job is to run errands, prepare meals, clean the kommandant's apartment, press his uniform and shine his boots. In return he's given his own room with a decent bed, clean sheets, pillows and blankets. Even a bedside table with a lamp. He also has clean clothes to wear and better food to eat.

Franz and I can't believe Tomek's good luck. We feel he has a chance to survive this war, even though for now he is a slave to Bulldog's every whim.

Tomek doesn't forget his friends. In the evenings, whenever he has the opportunity, he quickly delivers his messages to the SS officers, then visits our hut.

Clambering up the steps and standing at the open doorway, with a wide grin on his face, he softly whistles. We turn from what we're doing and run to him. We're all pleased to see him, greeting him with handshakes and slaps on the back.

As the evening shadows spread throughout the camp, the three of us discreetly slip behind the hut for a quiet, private conversation. There, Tomek slips us sugar cubes taken from 'Bulldog's' tea service.

Closing our eyes in ecstasy, we dissolve them in our mouths. I think of home and the paczki Auntie would make in her old tin pan.

Tomek's hair and skin is scrubbed clean, and he has gained weight. He has lost the cadaver look we have and looks healthy once more.

Secretly, he hands us whatever he has pilfered. We quickly hide the 'treasures' under our shirts, tucking them in our pants.

They mainly consist of small pots of jam, cubes of butter, or pocket-sized bags of salt and sugar. Occasionally, he even manages to steal packets of cigarettes and matches. These are valuable currency in the camp.

We all miss him. Kapo often mentions Tomek's 'barrack' soup, and the other lads speak of his recipes, but Franz and I miss him the most, especially his funny stories.

Late one afternoon, we meet him behind the hut as usual. After delivering the 'treasures', he leans up against the wall with his hands in his pockets.

"An English officer was brought to Bulldog's office this morning. I was called to interpret for both of them and was surprised the man was in the camp," he says in a low whisper, "as most English POWs are sent to Sachsenhausen. But apparently, this man is a civil engineer."

Later, as we're handing Kapo the food, we tell him about the Englishman. He looks astonished. I grin. I've never seen Kapo look surprised before. Grabbing his cap, he briskly walks out of the barracks and is gone for the rest of the night.

As the weeks pass, Kapo becomes friends with the English officer and several other British prisoners.

Sometimes they visit Kapo in his alcove. Four, tall, pale men wearing tattered British air force uniforms, squash inside the tiny space, drinking coffee. They speak English, a strange language, which I'm surprised to hear Kapo speak. We hear laughter and an occasional splatter of German, as if the Brits are trying to speak the language. I expect it's important for them too.

#####

As the months pass, Tomek's visits become less frequent, until they stop altogether.

We worry, imagining the worst.

Then one evening, we see him trot up the steps and enter the rec room. Franz and I ran up to him, smiling and patting his shoulder in greeting, excited to see him at last.

"Let's go behind the hut for a quiet word," whispers Tomek.

We follow him outside and hide in the shadows as Tomek digs into the pockets of his grey wool jacket and pulls out four sugar cubes. Taking them with reverence, each putting one in our mouth, we suck it with relish as we study Tomek.

He looks so well. I admire his new clothes. He's wearing grey flannel pants and a wool jumper with a clean white shirt collar pulled over the neckline. I hesitantly touch his sleeves and the front of his jacket. It feels soft and clean. Realising what I'm doing I pull away, tucking my hands into my pockets.

I glance up, embarrassed, and am about to apologise, only to see Tomek is too downcast to notice.

"Are you okay Tomek?" I ask.

He smiles his crooked smile and sighs.

"I'm okay. I'm sorry for not seeing you for a while but Bulldog has his nephew running his messages. The little twat is stupid as well as being a right bastard!"

"Is he about the same age as us and carries a luger?" I ask.

"He's never without it," Tomek replies.

"I know that bastard. I thought he was going to kill me," I say, rubbing the back of my ear.

I quickly recount the incident. Franz and Tomek listen in silence.

Tomek rubs his forehead, his mouth a tight grimace.

"You were lucky, Rys. I've seen him shoot a Russian. He died a few hours later with a shot to the stomach. I've seen things that really go against my grain and that's one of them."

"What other things?" Franz asks, his eyes narrowing.

Tomek tenses and bends his head to whisper, "I've seen the

kommandant take young men into his bedroom after the evening roll call and shut the door. I have to clean up the mess in the morning. Sometimes, I usher the lad out of Bulldog's bed and tell him to get back to his barrack!"

I grab his arm.

Bulldog is a bloody pervert!

"Shit Tomek!"

Tom shudders, fear written over his handsome features.

"He hasn't touched me yet, but it's only a matter of time!"

His expression then turns to anger. "I'll kill the mongrel if he tries!"

Franz grips his shoulder.

"Christ! Be careful, for God's sake! If you must kill him, do it in a way that you won't be caught."

We're all silent for a full minute. Franz and I are both worried.

"I'll be okay," Tomek murmurs, patting our shoulders. "Anyway, I'm leaving the camp!"

"When?" I ask.

"Tomorrow. I'm going to live with Bulldog's family and be their chef."

"They already have a cook," he adds, "but they want a chef as well. They entertain a lot and I'll probably be shown off to their Nazi friends.

Anyway, I might be able to listen to their conversations and somehow report information to the Resistance."

"Shit! Don't do that! You are on to a good thing! If you spy, you could be caught. Please think about it ... please!" I beg.

Chuckling, Tomek rubs my scalp. "Okay...okay. I'll get settled first and then I'll see about spying."

Franz suddenly grabs his shoulders and spins him around.

"You need to be serious Tomek, don't become a spy for the sake of it. It could cost you your life. It's not worth it!"

Tomek's face becomes serious, "I'll be careful Franz. I promise you!"

There is a quiet pause and I break the silence with a question. "Where does Bulldog's family live?"

"In Berlin," Tomek answers as he leans on the wall. "They live in a big house, most probably taken from Jews. I've been there a couple of times. When I was scrounging around in the kitchen cupboards, I found photos of another family amongst the cookbooks. They were standing on the front steps, all of them smiling."

His voice lowers as he looks at the ground. "There was a man and his wife with three children, the youngest just a baby."

He swallows and peers up at us.

"Anyway," he says brightly as he straightens. "The house is huge, more like a mansion, with antique furniture in every room. I've never seen so many paintings hanging on walls and there is a crystal chandelier swinging from the ceiling in the dining room."

We gape at him.

"How did you manage to score this job?" I ask in wonder.

He shrugs, looking sheepish and smiles his crooked smile. "I can cook, and I look Aryan. I guess I'm lucky."

He certainly is. He looks exactly the way Hitler wants his master race to look. Tall, good looking, blonde and blue eyed. What irony, that Hitler is short with dark hair and can be mistaken for a Jew.

We stare at Tomek for a long moment as he reaches into his pockets and takes out a bag of tea leaves, small cubes of butter and jars of jam. He carefully passes them to us as we whisper our thanks and hide the items in our torn jackets.

"This will be the last time I'll see you both," he murmurs and touches our sleeves.

Franz and I wish him good luck. Tomek gives us both a hug and wishes us all the best. He grabs our hands in both of his, shaking them vigorously. Softly, he laughs through his tears.

"I suggest it would be a good idea if you devise a plan to escape this hellhole."

Franz grins back at him.

"We're always making plans my friend," he chuckles.

Tomek lets go of Franz's hand and turns to leave.

I lift my fists into a boxing position.

"Don't let Bulldog get you down. Keep your guard up!" I whisper hoarsely, punching the air.

"I'm always on my guard," claims Tomek, feigning a punch towards me.

Franz and I slowly walk to the front of our barracks and watch him amble back to Bulldog's apartment, shoulders slumped, and his hands thrust into his pockets.

Slowly, he climbs the steps, and, stopping on the threshold, glances back, smiling.

He lifts his hand in a final farewell, then disappears inside.

We never see Tomek again. I often wonder, as we chat about food around the table, if he's okay.

I imagine him owning a posh restaurant after the war, where he'd order his chefs about and walk around the tables gossiping with his patrons.

Now that he is fitter and stronger, he has a good chance. He might possibly make it through.

CHAPTER

26

The Allied bombing intensifies in the autumn of 1944. Germany is bombarded by French, British and American planes every night, causing havoc and destruction in cities and towns.

Now our job is to dig people out of bombed buildings. We clear away the rubble using shovels, picks, or our bare hands, listening for noises under the debris. The forward crew pass concrete and bricks down a line of men who deposit it on a truck. Sometimes we find bodies under fallen timbers and mounds of bricks, or people trapped alive.

One morning, a woman and a young boy are trapped inside a cellar, their house blown to bits. An old man, pain etched in his weathered face, frantically calls their names as he scrambles over the rubble.

A metallic twang rings out from metal pipes, protruding from broken bricks, then shouts are heard. We become a disciplined machine, quick in our actions, passing the bricks and slabs of concrete efficiently, determined to get this family out.

Finally, a small boy is lifted through a gap in the floor, followed by a young woman.

The old man cries with relief, grabbing them both and planting kisses on their foreheads as he hugs them fiercely. He thank us profusely, telling us that the young boy is his grandson and the woman his daughter. They seem uninjured except for a few scratches and bruises. All of us stare at the woman. We haven't seen a pretty girl for a very long time. Some of the men smile at her. She smiles back as she crosses the rubble, hugging us in turn, thanking us for saving her life and the life of her son. Startled, the men stand like statues, their arms straight as boards at their sides. I worry about how bad I smell, but it doesn't seem to worry the nice smelling lady, so I hug her back. It's wonderful to feel a soft feminine body once more.

Meanwhile, the old man, a shopkeeper, holds his grandson's hand and stands under a sign nailed above his shopfront. The sign reads 'Juden Und Hunde Eintritt Streng Verboten' which means 'Entry Strictly Forbidden for Jews and Dogs'. Franz asks him the meaning of the sign although most of us knew the answer. But his reaction to the question is surprising for a German.

He lets go of his grandson's hand and runs into the shop, emerging a moment later dragging a chair. Climbing on it with wobbly legs, he pulls down the sign and gingerly steps down with the help of his daughter. Determined, he marches next door to the bombed house and flings the sign wide. It crashes onto the top of the smouldering timber.

"How stupid are we?" he yells, looking back at us. "We are supposed to be the superior race, but we're not, instead we're all bloody fools. How could we let it get to this? I have no home. My business is up the shyster, and my Ingrid and Hans were nearly killed. For what? To be better than everyone else! I think we're all bloody crazy! We should have stopped this madness sooner and got rid of the bloody Nazis!"

The young woman tries to hush her father as he waves his arms about, shouting profanities. He storms into his shop. The woman quickly apologies to the guards and grabs the boy's hand, hurriedly following the old man inside.

We're enjoying the antics a little too much and start to laugh. The guards are really ticked off, roughly pushing us back to the waiting trucks, thumping us with their batons. We climb aboard still grinning.

So now, the German people are sick of the Nazis and the havoc they've caused. Too bloody bad! The Allies, of late, are giving them a taste of their own medicine.

What a good start to the day!

After the shopkeeper's entertaining speech, we're driven to a wealthy district on the outskirts of Berlin, stopping in front of a large, partially demolished house. I look up, noting the second storey is still standing. It's like a doll house with its front lifted away to reveal the rooms. Like one I saw in a store window a long time ago. One room looks intact even though most of the roof is missing.

I gaze higher and can just see the tops of bedroom furniture, and a poster of Adolf Hitler stuck on a wall.

Disembarking from the trucks, we shovel bricks and broken bits of concrete from the road. I look up to the bedroom again, wondering what is really up there. I have a weird feeling there is something important to find.

Kapo orders a break. Franz and I scrounge around for food in what was once a kitchen.

"I have a feeling Franz. We need to go scavenging in the upstairs bedrooms," I whisper.

We climb up to the second storey and investigate the nearest bedroom. Identical twin beds, unmade and covered in a light snowfall, are near a desk strewn with schoolbooks. The poster of Hitler, his face tilted to the heavens is taped to the wall above the desk. Franz thumbs through a book as I scamper towards a wardrobe.

I look inside, then slowly back away.

The day just became better.

Hanging amongst four or five plaid shirts are two Hitlerjungen uniforms. A brown rucksack is wedged in a corner. Military caps and brown shoes, stuffed with socks, sit neatly on a shelf.

"Franz! Franz! Come here!" I whisper hoarsely, pointing to the interior of the wardrobe.

Noting my expression, he tiptoes to my side and peeps inside.

"Go back and see what the guards are doing," he whispers urgently, inspecting the uniforms. I creep along the floor and peer over the ledge. The guards are leaning against a brick wall, chatting.

They're recent recruits. Old, slack and lazy.

They smoke their cigarettes as the Kapos pass around a water bucket. The crews lean on their shovels drinking from the ladle.

I creep back to Franz and touch his arm.

"It's okay. They haven't noticed anything. What do we do now?"

Franz reaches into the wardrobe.

"We'll put the uniforms in the rucksack and hide them in the rubble and hope to God they're still there when we really need them."

Hastily, we pull out the two Hitlerjungen uniforms, each with a belt, and stuff them in the rucksack, followed by the caps, shoes and socks. Hiding the bag under a fallen beam in the next room, we jam bricks around the beam, sweeping up dirt and ash to conceal the bag.

"Franz, this could be it! It's our way to escape!" I whisper excitedly, pushing more dirt into the gap.

"I know Rys!" Franz grins back at me. "Now let's get the blankets off the beds and some books and throw them down with the plaid shirts, just in case others come up. We'll tell the Bosses there is nothing else up here worth saving."

The Bosses let the men gather the loot we hurl over the edge, noting every piece. I suspect it will all go into the bartering pool back at the camp.

Franz and I quickly climb down, using a beam as a ramp.

"That was a good find!" says Kapo as we reached the ground.

"Yeah, it was!" says Franz.

We re-join our group. Kapo offers us a drink and we're soon back at work. Franz and I furtively glance up at the second storey now and then. I smile secretly at him. He grins back. What a find!

When we arrive back my heart is leaping in my chest.

I can't contain my excitement. I jump and skip around grinning from ear to ear. Men give me strange looks. Franz grabs my arms and gives me a shake.

"Settle down Rys. You look suspicious. Men are looking!" he says furtively, peering around.

Trying to contain my joy, I take two deep breaths to steady

myself. He smiles at me, patting my head.

"Just settle down before you get noticed. It can be very dangerous if someone starts asking questions!"

We're both restless during the night. Tossing and turning until the others in our bunk tell us to quit moving about.

Finally, we drift off to sleep around midnight when Kapo does his rounds. He doesn't sleep much, wandering around the barracks at all hours.

Bleary eyed but exulted, I wolf down my coffee and bread. Franz whispers to me to act normal or we could be in trouble, so I keep a subdued look on my face as we line up for roll call.

I look around, noting most of the SS are missing and in their place are older men, in different army uniforms.

Back in the barracks, I whisper to Franz about the new guards. He agrees something is amiss.

Something which could be beneficial towards our escape.

27

"**W**apasha, guard the door." orders Kapo, waving us after him into his alcove.

"Sure boss," Wapasha answers, standing outside the door while Kapo pulls the tattered curtain down, closing the gap.

Franz and I fidget nervously. I scratch my scalp and my neck while Franz runs his hands up and down his thighs. He crosses his arms and shoves his hands under his armpits, then stares at the floorboards. I look fixedly at Kapo's back as he takes a loaf of bread down from his shelf, slices a piece and smears a little jam, a 'Tomek Treasure,' with a kitchen knife.

He offers us the bread cut in two. I take it gingerly, wondering what this meeting is all about. Kapo only distributes these treasures on special occasions, so he must think this is one of them. We eat in small deliberate bites, savouring every mouthful. Food, always scarce, is becoming scarcer in the camp since the guards have changed.

Kapo sits at his desk, facing us. He picks up his mug, filled with strong liquor.

"What's this I hear about uniforms? He asks, sipping from the mug "Are you two planning to escape?"

I choke! Bits of bread lodge in my throat.

Ah shit! Is he a mind reader?

Franz glares at him with a sudden flash of anger as he madly chews the piece of bread.

I defuse the moment by answering the questions between coughs.

"We found Hitler Youth uniforms in the big house, Boss," I gasp. "And ...And we plan to get them when we breakout from the... the camp."

"Christ, Rys!" Franz snarls, turning to face me.

"It's okay Franz," Kapo chuckles, lighting a cigarette and drawing in the smoke. "Not many know your secrets. I have boys coming up to me all the time divulging snippets of gossip for an extra slice of bread. Most of the time I oblige them when I need to know what's going on. All I can say is you both need to be damned careful planning your escape."

He flicks ash off his cigarette, "Anyway, this information came to me only recently."

Franz seems to deflate a little. His shoulders slump as he stares at the back wall.

Who knew? How? We never told anyone else. Someone must have overheard us late last night when I murmured softly to Franz, "I'm worried about the uniforms. Somebody might have found them."

He shushed me quickly, but we must have been overheard.

As if they are on fire, I shuffle from one foot to the other, staring at Kapo's grinning face.

"Come on boys, your secret is safe with me!" he whispers.

He rocks back on his chair, drawing deeply on the cigarette, letting the tip flicker into a glow. He blows a thin stream of smoke towards the ceiling.

"You've seen the new German guards?" he says, changing the subject.

Franz looks at him, confused.

"Yes. But what's that got to do with anything?"

"Well, they are the German Home Guard," Kapo explains. "Old men who were left out of the war. They haven't got the Nazi mindset like the SS and are lenient on the rules, especially contraband."

He waves his cigarette towards the alcohol on one of his shelves.

"Anyway, the camp is not as well guarded as it should be. Mind you, Sachsenhausen is still well guarded by the SS. There is a lot of important information the Allies can find in that camp. Anyway, my advice is, if an opportunity arises to get out of here, take it!"

"What happened to Bulldog and the SS?" questions Franz.

"They left!" Kapo snaps with derision. "More likely left the bloody country. Bloody cowards, the whole lot of them! The new kommandant is some old bastard the Nazis have dug up somewhere ... Anyway, if I were you two, I wouldn't waste time putting your escape plan into action."

"We won't Kapo," Franz murmurs. "We won't."

Kapo rises from his chair and pulls the curtain to the side. Wapasha glances our way as we pass under the small opening.

We don't look at him, but scamper back to our bunk.

"Who the hell told him?" I hiss, as I move against the back wall.

"Ah, some bloody snitch," Franz mutters as we lie head to toe.

"We don't discuss anything here. It's too dangerous! Too many ears!"

A week passes and we watch the guards. Kapo is right, they are idle and lax.

We even manage to pour dirt into an unattended rifle left against the canteen wall.

One good thing from the change of guards is, the Bosses stopped beating the men. In fact, some of the mean bastards disappeared altogether. One of them was found outside looking like he had been drowned in a toilet bowl, shit smeared all over his face.

Throughout the next few weeks, we hear the nightly sound of the Allies bombing Berlin in the distance. A faint red glow reddens the horizon most evenings.

The night Oranienburg is bombed, snow falls steadily around the camp, piling high against the barbed wire fences. Shivering with cold, we huddle around the little stove, blowing into our hands.

The hut shakes as a massive explosion rocks its foundations. We run outside to find the camp gates are a tangle of barbed wire and wooden poles. Smoke rises from the rubble covering what was once a road. As we stand there, an unmanned watch tower slowly topples to the ground.

There is a lot of shouting. The guards run to take shelter in the canteen bunker, leaving us to fend for ourselves.

Kapo grabs our shoulders and shoves us towards the gaping hole, hollering above the noise.

"Go! Go now!" he shouts.

Instead, Franz and I dart the other way, towards the canteen, and find two loaves of bread, stuffing them under our jackets.

We dash back.

Running through the gateway, we are mobbed by prisoners running out. Kapo and Wapasha, both wearing civilian shirts and carrying firearms, are running alongside four men...the Englishmen. In that split second, I realised Kapo's intention in befriending the English. He was making sure he is rescued by the Allies, possibly escaping Germany. I take my hat off to him. He is bloody cunning.

He must have brought Wapasha into the deal. I remember seeing him standing guard at the alcove when Kapo had his meetings with the Britts.

Kapo, Wapasha and the British airmen disappear into the dark as Franz and I crouch beside a brick building just outside the camp, waiting for the bombardment to stop. I look at the camp wishing the British would bomb it again, but it doesn't happen. Instead, the planes trail away with their engines becoming a distant hum in the cold night air. The air-raid sirens ease to a faint whine as smoke, ash and a flurry of snow swirl around us.

Coming unsteadily to our feet, Franz peers around the corner and gestures with his hand to hurry. Warily, we jog along the street, ready to duck under cover at any moment.

We plunge into a dark alleyway, leading to the main street of Oranienburg. An old army truck slowly drives up the road, with its headlights turned off.

We run behind the tailgate and silently jump into the back. I crouch in a corner while Franz keeps a lookout on the road as well as the driver.

The night sky is lit with glowing pockets of red and orange. The trip takes us through German towns, all burning in the aftermath of the air raid. As we approach Berlin, the truck slows to a stop in front of an office building displaying the Nazi flag. Jumping off, we kick off our ungainly wooden clogs and run barefoot through the deserted streets, frequently stopping to catch our breath.

I gasp and heave, spitting on the ground. Franz pants, his hands on his knees. A result of being starved for so long is that both of us lack stamina.

Franz has a good sense of direction and soon finds the bombed house with its perilous walls still standing upright. It looks untouched since we were last here. We cautiously climb to the second storey, using the ramp, and scramble into the bedroom. The whole room is now covered in layers of snow. The rest of the roof has caved in. Climbing over the rubble, we make our way into the next room and frantically push the snow and debris away from the hiding spot. Franz pulls the bag from under the beam and empties it onto the floor. We grin at each other when the Hitler youth uniforms tumble out. Working quickly, we put our ID papers and the two loaves of bread into the knapsack.

Shivering with cold, I wonder just for a brief moment about the boy who owns these uniforms. Or maybe it was twin boys seeing there were two uniforms. I wonder why they never claimed them. Maybe they are buried in the rubble below us.

I shrug. Thought no more of it and peel away my filthy rags. I'm about to put on a shirt then stop, smelling my armpit and cringe.

"I really stink bad, Franz!"

Franz pulls a face as he smells himself. "I think I saw a toilet in the next room," and picks up the tattered shirts as we scramble into a small bathroom.

Franz examines the toilet bowl and using a brick smashes the ice, lying across the surface, into shards. He dips his camp shirt into the freezing water and gives himself a quick wash. He rinses the shirt in the bowl and hands it to me. Using my camp shirt as a towel he rubs his face and body vigorously.

The dirt and lice can't be removed so easily, but by the moonlight, I notice Franz looks a little cleaner. Hurrying back to the bedroom we put on the uniforms.

I pick up the long sleeve brown shirt with its insignias and the black swastika printed on a red and white arm band pinned on the sleeve, and hastily pull it on. I wrap a black neckerchief around my neck, adjusting the leather woggle and flicking over the shirt collar. Scrambling out of the striped prison pants. I step into the shorts made from black woollen cloth, tuck in the shirt and fasten the belt buckle, adjust the shoulder strap and fastened it to the belt.

Sitting on the floor I roll the brown socks to my knees, finishing it all off by placing the light brown campaign cap on my shorn head, I stand up to face Franz.

"So far so good," breathes Franz as he tucks in his shirt." Don't forget we need to speak German."

The uniform pants are a bit short for Franz and a bit long for me. We're so skinny the uniforms swim on us, so we both pull the black leather belts tighter to keep our pants up. Franz sits on a fallen roof beam and wriggles a shoe onto his foot.

"Let's get these shoes on. My feet are freezing!"

They fit Franz but are too big on me as I place each foot into the brown shoes and freely wiggle my toes. I feel the heels slipping up and down as I walk around.

"These are going to give me blisters!" I hiss under my breath.

"We'll find some paper to fill them," Franz whispers.

"But not now, let's get out of here. We'll head for the railway station. Without coats, we're going to freeze in these uniforms. We'll stay in the station's waiting room to keep warm. We'll have to sneak on board the train, seeing we haven't got any money."

We slide down the ramp and briskly march along the street, until we see a railway sign. We trot up to a low brick building and in the darkness, I see a dim light under the blackout curtains. Peeping through the crack, we see a station master sitting at his desk, writing in a book. This must be the ticket office.

Chilled to the bone, we creep into the dark waiting room and feel our way around.

My knee hits the side of a bench. I stifle a grunt as Franz's hand grips my arm. Slowly we feel the wooden benches, and then warm water pipes along a wall. Slumping down, not saying a word, we lie there, spent.

I sit up with a start.

It's morning.

I've been woken by the screeching of brakes and hissing of steam as a train pulls up to the platform.

Franz is already standing behind the door listening intently.

He turns to face me. Tense. On edge.

"Shit," he whispers hoarsely, "we could be in trouble."

He opens the door a slight crack and peeks out. Stealthily, I tiptoe behind him and peer around his shoulder. A gasp escapes my lips as the scene unfolds before me.

Marcia Wakeman

Part 3

1944

CHAPTER

28

Fifty to a hundred boys, dressed in Hitler Youth uniforms, spill out of the train onto the platform.

It's dark, and hard to see. Smoke and steam billow from the train engine blanketing the milling crowd.

Through the smog, cadets noisily call to each other over the bellowing of the SS officers who are trying to get the boys into some kind of order.

We stand in a daze just outside the door of the waiting room, deafened by the noise.

Anxiously, we stare at the unimaginable scene. My heart hammers in my chest, my hands are clammy, and my mouth dry as old wood.

We're swept up in a surge of brown uniformed bodies.

I try to grab the back of Franz's shirt but the boys swarm around us, pushing us along the platform and through the station gate, towards the road.

An officer shouts, "Los Schnell! Quickly, on the trucks!"

Franz and I are pulled apart in the chaos.

He's led to a big truck, and I'm pushed onto a smaller one.

I'm crammed in, my legs jammed against another boy's back. Around me boys laugh and shout excitedly, some singing the German national anthem. I'm tempted to cover my ears as the noise is unbearable, but instead I wedge my hands under my knees and look around in horror and disbelief.

Peering desperately over the boys' heads to the larger truck behind, I try to locate Franz. I can't see him anywhere We haven't been apart since the Resistance days.

Fear builds in my chest. I feel sick.

My truck takes off, bouncing and swaying, making me even more nauseous. I manage to stand, wedge myself near the tail gate and spit on the road, then look up to see the larger truck following us.

I pray to God in heaven that Franz is on it.

The trucks pull up in front of a German army garrison. Impressive iron gates, hinged to large brick pillars, stand ajar. We spill out, line up and march into the parade ground. The whole place is already filled with hundreds of Hitler youth, each carrying a rifle slung over their shoulder. They mill around excitedly in large groups.

SS officers and senior cadets shout to be heard above the mayhem as boys shuffle and push themselves into lines. The officers try to get us newcomers into some kind of order by dividing us into smaller groups and marching us inside a brick building.

Lined up against a wall are racks of firearms, beside which two senior cadets stand at attention. They pass rifles across a wooden bench. The officer bellows at us to hurry.

Lining up once more, I copy the boy next to me. Facing the front, I stand at attention, clutching a rifle across my chest.

Music screeches through loudspeakers.

"Left! Right! March! Eyes to the front! Left! Right!" shouts a senior cadet, an older boy. Lean and extremely tall, he seems to be in charge. He keeps in time with the marching unit, bellowing orders every few minutes.

Goose-stepping to the German national anthem, we march around the quadrangle, in time with the music. I follow the boy in front of me and try to mimic his pounding feet, but my goose stepping is erratic and clumsy. The lad next to me keeps glancing my way with a questioning look. He frowns as I once more miss a step. Panic rises in my chest, and I gulp in air.

Keep calm, I order myself. *Look normal. And keep in time!*

Furtively, I look around, to see if I can spot Franz.

The senior cadet bellows in my ear. "Eyes front!"

I snap my head round and stare at the boy in front of me.

I finally pick out Franz about ten metres away. He is marching along in another line. For a long moment I simply gaze at the back of his head, breathing out a sigh of relief.

After parading around and around in circles, we are led into a large brick building where rows and rows of long trestle tables are set up, filling the room. The rest of the units file in. Dropping their rifles on the tables, the cadets pick up white rags piled in buckets, and wait for instructions.

My unit does the same. I follow suit. A lieutenant lays down his rifle and begins to dismantle it, lining up each component. He starts to clean each part with a large white cloth, instructing us all the while, on the art of cleaning the weapon. He then orders us to do the same.

The lads confidently pull apart their rifles, laying each part neatly on the table and proceed to clean them.

I carefully watch the boy in front of me and mimic his every move. The instant he finishes, he reassembles his rifle.

This is the moment I come unstuck. I fiddle around with a

piece of the trigger mechanism for a while. The lieutenant, seeing me struggle, wanders over and takes the rifle then slots in the part, handing it back to me.

He studies my face. I avert my gaze, looking instead at the rifle in my hands. He stands for a long moment and sniffs. I'm edgy, maybe he can smell my bad body odour. He is about to place his hand on my shoulder when there is a shrill whistle from the front of the room. His attention is diverted to the senior cadet who faces us, standing stiffly at attention.

"Fall in! Fall in!" he shouts.

Moving quickly and mingling with the crowd, I glance over my shoulder. The lieutenant is busy talking to another group of boys.

Christ! I hope he doesn't come looking for me!

We're led to the armoury, returning the rifles into the hands of the waiting cadets and line up for a meal inside the canteen.

I look around for Franz and even more urgently for the lieutenant. Seeing neither, I face the boy behind a big cooking pot as he piles up a plate and hands it to me. I gaze at it and inhale. My mouth waters. It's a stew. Chunks of meat swimming in gravy, on top of a pile of mashed potatoes. I haven't seen such food for years. I pick up the cutlery and look around, baffled, trying to find a place to sit.

Franz is sitting at another table eating his stew. Between mouthfuls he looks my way and shakes his head. A signal which means to sit somewhere else.

I decide to sit next to a small boy, who turns to me with a beaming smile. He looks like he's a healthy twelve years old.

I suddenly wonder if I look out of place with my sallow skin and skinny frame.

The boy is very friendly. I answer his questions carefully, trying not to gulp my food down, and ask him some questions in return.

He tells me a lot about his family, saying his mother is at home looking after his little sister. His father is in the army and was sent to the front to protect Germany from the invading enemy. My ears prick up at this news. He said the invasion is coming from the Russians in the north-east, and the Americans and British from the west. As the boy is talking, I slide the bread roll into my pocket and eat the stew with gusto, nodding now and then to his constant chatter.

My stomach churns. I belch. I think I ate too fast, or maybe the food was too rich. I stand abruptly, run around the back of the canteen, holding back the regurgitating meal in my throat, then vomit in a shallow ditch. My stomach cramps. I buckle over with the spasms, bringing up more food. Feeling giddy, I peer down at the vomit. A sob escapes my lips. I can't believe it. The first decent meal I've had for years and now it's a disgusting mess on the ground.

I stand there for a dispirited moment, wiping my face. On shaky legs, I walk up the steps to the latrines to wash my face and rinse out my mouth.

I sit on the concrete step, breathing in gasps. I still feel nauseated.

Slinking back to the canteen I notice Franz is missing. I almost panic, then wonder if he is also vomiting somewhere behind a building. I decide to wait a few minutes before looking for him. So, I sit with the young cadet once more, thinking I'll strike up a friendship and find out the layout of the land.

But before I can say a word, I look up to see the lieutenant coming my way. He studies me intently, a scowl on his face. I suck in an uneasy breath.

"Lieutenant Schneider!" another cadet calls out. "You are wanted at the administration building!"

Still frowning, Lieutenant Schneider studies me for a long moment but turns on his heels and follows the cadet to a low brick building.

I bow my head, breathing hard. But In spite of my situation, Lady Luck has once again shown her pretty face.

Another officer shouts through a megaphone ordering us back to the parade ground.

When he is satisfied our ranks are perfectly straight, he snaps his arm diagonally to the sky, his officers and lieutenants doing the same.

"Heil Hitler!"

"Heil Hitler!" we return the salute. *I'm amazed I keep in time with the rest of the boys.*

One of the officers, very senior by his profusion of gold braid, stands on a podium. He adjusts the tilt of his cap and tugs down the sleeves of his jacket, making us wait.

"You should all be proud to fight for Germany, and for our beloved Fuhrer!" He proclaims in a loud voice, ignoring the offered megaphone.

Generating greater fervour, he exhorts, "You should be honoured to take up arms and fight against the invading enemy at our borders! You will be fighting next to our brave, courageous, German soldiers to free the fatherland from this unlawful invasion! Now, go home to prepare and say goodbye to your families. Return to the barracks tomorrow at 0700. If you can't go home, you may stay at the barracks for the night."

Almost as an afterthought, he adds, "Those returning home must report to Lieutenant Brugg."

He points at a short, pale officer standing beside the podium.

Ah! This is our opportunity to escape.

We're dismissed and the boys chat excitedly, some moving to the barracks and some lining up in front of the officer.

I scout around for Franz and see him at the back. He looks my way, signalling with a quick nod.

When it's my turn, I salute and in perfect German tell Brugg I need to go home and would certainly be back at 0700. He stares at me with his brow furrowing. He nods slowly and looks at the boy behind me. But I feel his eyes on my back as I walk away.

Calmly sauntering to the gate, but inwardly terrified, I keep my back straight, hold my head high and mingle with the crowd.

Breathlessly, I wait behind the gate pillar, only to see Schneider and Brugg running through the open gate, searching amongst the crowd of boys walking up the road.

I back in further, squashing myself against the bricks.

In an instant, Franz is beside me breathing hard and adjusting the rucksack. I pull him back into the shadows and whisper in his ear. He peeps around the pillar at the officers and ducks back.

We wait for both to return to the garrison and after five minutes take off at a run, dodging the boys still spilling through the gates, only slowing down when the garrison has disappeared from sight.

Realising our original train station is too far, Franz asks an old man where the nearest one is located.

He points down the road saying it's two kilometres away. We take off in a jog then slow down to a walk, breathing hard. Finding the station isn't difficult. We can hear the shunting of the trains and the piercing shriek of a whistle before we see the station.

Franz notes the directions of the trains as one pulls away from the platform.

"We're on the right platform to go South," he confirms.

I nod, too weary to discuss the possibility he could be wrong. Anyway, Franz is rarely wrong.

In the vacant waiting room, I slump onto a wooden bench and rub my face. Franz follows and faces me as he slouches against the wall and takes off his cap. He rests his head against the bricks.

I look over at him.

"I was in deep shit, Franz. I think that Schneider bastard was onto me! He was suspicious, that's for sure!"

Franz grimaces, running his fingers along his scalp then pulling his cap over his forehead.

"How did you get away?" I ask.

He grins, peeking under the brim. "Well, I spoke in perfect German to Lieutenant Brugg, telling him I need to pack my army kit and say goodbye to my mother and twelve brothers and sisters!"

Kapo told us it was the Nazi policy that all German women were to have as many children as possible for the war effort and in doing so collected gold, silver or bronze medals. This make-believe mother must have collected a gold medallion called 'The Cross of Honour for German Motherhood' for her fine breeding effort.

I burst out laughing, an unintentional reaction as if a pressure valve is being released. Franz looks astonished by my outburst then joins in, his laughter loud and raucous.

"Were you sick when you ate the stew?" I croak as I wipe my eyes.

"Like a dog!" he barks with laughter again.

"Me too!" I chortle and between gasping breaths splutter, "I thought I was going to die there and then!"

We can't stop laughing and I take a couple of deep breaths to steady myself. It really isn't that funny. We could have died. But it was the absurdity of the moment or the stress we were under in the German garrison that made us crack up. There we were, dreaming of food all the time in the camp, but when we're well fed for once we couldn't hold the food down and nearly died.

"I think we need to be careful what we eat and more importantly, we need to find the Allies. Soon. Before we get caught where there's no escape." I shudder, imagining being hauled in front of a firing squad.

Franz composes himself and wipes his eyes.

"Good idea Rys. Kapo told me a couple of days ago that he heard they are advancing through Belgium. Maybe we should try to head there."

I relay the conversation I had with the young cadet, and we both agree our destination should be the south-eastern part of Germany adjoining Belgium.

A train pulls up at the station and people disembark while others wait to board. We venture outside only to see papers being checked by German soldiers.

I clench my teeth and hiss. "Shit … Shit!"

"Ah Christ! Now we are in real trouble!" mutters Franz under his breath.

29

We mingle with the crowd, keeping close together. Determined not to be parted again.

Noticing a woman in her late twenties, struggling with a suitcase and shopping bags, I pull Franz's arm, nodding towards her. He looks through the crowd seeing her balancing the bags on one arm and trying to pull the suitcase up into the train. He grabs my sleeve as we plough our way through the throng, dodging the soldiers and finally stopping behind her.

"Can we help you Madam?" Franz asks, giving her his best smile as she turns her head.

In response she smiles back, still struggling with her suitcase.

"Why thank you, young man!"

She slides it towards him.

Seeing her noticing me, I smile at her too.

"Oh, there are two of you!" She smiles and hands me her grocery bags.

We follow her down the train corridor leading to individual compartments, finally stopping at the entrance to a vacant one. The lady steps inside and removes her gloves and her navy-blue coat, laying them on the seat.

We store her bags on the top racks. Smoothing down her skirt, she sits on the forward-facing seat. We sit across from her, giving her our best smiles again.

She's a very pretty lady, with brown wavy hair and green eyes. She wears a dark green jacket over a cream blouse tucked into a matching straight skirt. Her smartly tailored clothes fit snugly to her lovely figure. A stylish green hat, with a cluster of white and brown feathers tucked in the band, holds her shoulder length hair behind her ears.

A glint of sunlight, coming through the carriage window, dances off a brooch on her lapel. I peer closer and can't believe it. The small bird sitting on a golden branch is like an omen. A happy one.

Quizzically, she looks at me, then follows my gaze to the brooch on her jacket.

"It's a robin redbreast," she says, stroking the brooch with her finger. "It once belonged to my grandmother. I always wear it as it reminds me of her."

"Madam, may I look at it?" I ask a little breathlessly.

For a slight second she hesitates, then smiles a beautiful smile.

"Of course! Of course!"

Unpinning it she places the exquisite piece into my grimy hand.

I turn it over, noting the hall mark. It's made of gold. I flip it back to the front. The bird itself, facing in a three-quarter view, is enamelled in beautiful colours. A striking orange for its breast with bright silver for its head. A coppery-brown enamel, encased in gold, is crafted for its wings and tail feathers.

A small black stone is set as an eye above its small silver beak. Perching on a narrow branch, made of twisted gold wire, it looks towards the viewer. I touch the wings, admiring the workmanship. Helena would have loved it. The thought of her makes me smile.

I carefully hand it back.

"It's beautiful," I say, wistfully. "I've always liked robin redbreasts."

"So have I," she says, pinning it back on her jacket.

Standing, she takes out two apples from one of the shopping bags we put on the rack above our heads and offers us one each. We thank her politely and take restrained bites, trying not to look too desperately hungry, although we are.

"Where are you going Madam?" I ask as I put the core in my pocket to suck on later.

She takes off her hat and smooths back her hair, allowing it to once more fall along her shoulders. Her hair gimmers with coppery tones in the sunlight and is curly along its tips. I've never seen anything so beautiful for a long time.

"To Hannover," she answers as she takes a handkerchief out of her handbag and dabs her nose. "Where are you two going?"

"Hannover as well Madam," Franz replies.

"Your families live there?" she queries, while placing her handkerchief back in the bag.

"Oh no Madam," I say, beaming back at her. "We're heading south from there to our army barracks."

"Why don't you two help me with my bags to my house and I'll give you a meal before you continue with your journey," she suggests.

We both hesitate, finding it hard to trust anyone.

"Oh!" she adds. "We've not been introduced. I am Frau Klara Schmidt." She smiles again leaning forward and holding out her hand. We shake it in turn. I'm aware of the softness of her fingers and the velvet texture of her skin. Just like Helena's. I hesitate for a moment deciding if I should tell her our real names and decide not to."

"My name is Helmut, and this is Karl," I reply, nodding towards Franz. Hoping she hasn't seen through the lie.

She looks me straight in the eye for a long moment. I hold her gaze, but I feel my cheeks burning.

"I promise you; it will be quite alright to come to my home," she says, patting my hand.

Remembering the robin redbreast omen, I take the initiative. She seems trustworthy.

"That would be wonderful Frau Schmidt!"

I avert my gaze and glance at Franz. He's frowning but relaxes when he reads my thoughts. *If anything happens there are two of us against one of her.*

The train rolls forward and starts to pick up speed. We settle back into our seats and look out the windows at the countryside flashing by.

Hearing a clicking sound, I look up to see a conductor at our compartment door, swaying with the train's momentum. He eyes Franz and I suspiciously.

"Tickets please!" he asks in a gravelly voice, holding out his hand.

We both freeze. Staring straight ahead, with my heart pounding in my chest I pretend to fumble in my pockets.

Frau Schmidt, noticing something is wrong, opens her handbag.

"How silly of me," she apologises as she fumbles through the contents, "My nephews and I were running late, and it was so overcrowded at the station I didn't get the chance to purchase tickets before the train left. I'm so sorry for the inconvenience." She takes out her purse and beams up at the conductor. "Could I buy them now?"

He smiles down at her, bobbing his head and punches three tickets. Smiling graciously, she takes out a couple of notes and thanks him as he gives her the tickets with change. He stares at Franz and I for a few seconds before turning on his heel and leaving for the next compartment.

I take my cap off, wiping the sweat off my face with my sleeve.

"Thank you, Frau Schmidt."

She dips her head and, quietly looks out the window.

After a while I close my eyes.

I feel a hand on my shoulder, gently shaking me. Bewildered, I stare around, forgetting where I am. Franz is sitting next to me, his head lolling against the back of the seat.

"Wake up. We have arrived at Hannover," Frau Schmidt says gently to Franz. He wakes with a start, pulling up his fists as if to punch, making the lady back away in alarm.

He apologises profusely, not meeting her eye, but grabs his cap from the seat beside him and pulls it on his head.

He looks up at her. "I'm so sorry Madam. I didn't mean to startle you. Please forgive me."

She nods, picking up her coat and gloves, putting them on, and adjusting her hat with her reflection in the window.

I stare at Franz, saying nothing, hoping he hasn't given the game away.

We pull down her luggage and venture onto the station, seeing it's less crowded this time. Only a few families make their way through the station's gates. We struggle along the platform with Frau Schmidt's bags, looking out for any German soldiers checking papers. Seeing none, we hurry out into the street.

It's a short distance from the station to her home. We stop in front of a white granite apartment building. Carved scrolls swirl along the lintels. Four marble steps rise towards a glass door which is covered on the inside with brown paper.

"Very fancy digs! She must be rich!" Franz whispers to me.

I peer up at the building, nodding.

Frau Schmidt fumbles with her keys, unlocks the door and gestures for us to follow.

Franz and I stand in a long corridor with several identical doors along its length. Frau Schmidt unlocks a door to her left and ushers us in. It leads into a small foyer, tastefully decorated in embossed wallpaper. A large ornate mirror hangs above a narrow side table with bright coloured vase placed on top. Franz drops her suitcase at the foot of a flight of stairs. I still held onto the groceries.

Franz swings the rucksack off his shoulder and sets it on the floor. I put the groceries down and I peel my shoes off and suggest Franz do the same. He quickly pries his shoes off with his toes.

"I'll make tea," Frau Schmidt says, taking off her hat and coat, and hanging them on wooden hooks along the wall. Peeling off her gloves, she tucks them in her coat pocket.

She turns to face me.

"Could you carry the grocery bags into the kitchen, Helmut?" she asks.

"Certainly madam" I say, picking up the bags.

She leads us through to the parlour where Christmas cards are carefully placed along a mantelpiece and a small, decorated fir tree fills one corner of the room. I look around. A bookcase full of old books stands against one of the walls next to a large painting of a Dutch landscape. All the walls are papered with the same embossed print, matching the crimson curtains. The room exudes a modest opulence.

Frau Schmidt ushers us into the kitchen. I drop the groceries on the kitchen counter.

She pulls out a chair from under a wooden table. "Come, sit down. I'll make that tea."

The afternoon tea of bread and jam is delicious. It reminds me of when Mother would set the table in the parlour for her church friends. Frau Schmidt is very hospitable and offers us extra slices of bread. Franz and I eat with gusto. It's been over a year since I ate white bread. As I'm consuming my second slice, I gaze up at her pretty face, suddenly aware of her intense gaze. She leans back in her chair.

"Your German is quite good!" she muses.

Slowly, I put the bread down on my plate, my appetite deserting me.

Franz abruptly stands.

I push back my chair and stand defensively at his side.

"Sit down, sit down," Frau Schmidt commands in a soft voice. "Please. Please sit," she adds, waving her hand.

We hesitate but remain standing.

"I will not go to the authorities! I promise you!" She gestures again for us to sit, then adds, "I guessed who you both are by your malnourished bodies and shorn heads." She looks at Franz, "Also by the way you reacted, Karl, when I woke you."

She looks at our clothes and asks. "Did you steal those uniforms?"

We both ease back into the chairs, looking at her in astonishment.

"No …" Franz answers hesitantly. "We found them in a bombed house while we were clearing out the rubble."

We start to fidget, anxiously glancing around for a back door.

She calmly looks at us and grasps our hands with her own. "Like I said, I won't alert the authorities. I know about the atrocities in the camps. I have seen the women where I work. They're from the camps. They have your same grey skin and a haunted look in their eyes, as if they have lost all hope. But you two don't have that haunted look!"

A smile dimples her cheek. "I can see it in your eyes. You are both determined to get through this war."

She releases our hands and leans back in her chair.

"I'm a member of the Nazi Party."

Franz and I gasp, half rising from our chairs.

"It's okay … really. Please don't be afraid. You are both safe. I promise you. Let me explain. I joined in 1938. I thought Hitler was going to liberate Germany and make it a wonderful country. You know he could have if he wasn't such a psychopath!" Her eyes turn to look at a photograph on the wall. "It was at one of the party meetings where I met my husband, Stefan."

We follow her gaze to see a picture of a slender man wearing an SS uniform, his military cap under his arm, a slight smile on his chiselled face and dark hair swept back from his high forehead.

"We were married for five years," she says in a sad whisper, "I couldn't have children. After a time, our marriage suffered. He was so involved in the party I didn't see much of him in the last three years. But I still loved him."

Her beautiful face hardens as she turns to face us.

"I started to doubt the Nazi's philosophy years ago. Especially the role of women in Germany. We're told that we're all to be homemakers, giving birth to lots of children, being dutiful wives. We are to question nothing and to have no opinions. A stupid, stupid rule! A woman having a profession is frowned upon by the Reich. One of my female friends, a professor at the university, had to give up her job to stay at home while her husband works."

Her eyes flash angrily. "The Nazi philosophy is to exterminate any human race they believe unworthy, like the Jews. It is abhorrent. What gives them the right to play God?"

She exhales a deep breath and pauses for a few seconds. "Nevertheless, I kept silent. Telling no one about my true feelings. Stefan was a high ranking-officer, and it would spoil any chance of promotion if the party knew my views. In fact, I think I would have been killed and maybe Stefan as well."

Crossing her arms, she leans on the table. "I had a good job at the same university as my friend. I was a researcher for an Art History professor. I loved the job. When the Nazis published a propaganda leaflet slandering the Jews, I became disillusioned with the Party. I find it hard, even today, to believe the German people could believe such lies. I discussed this with Stefan only for it to end in a terrible argument. He was furious that I had such thoughts."

Frau Schmidt stares vaguely out the kitchen window.

"I felt him distancing himself from me. Maybe he thought I was a Jewish sympathiser. I suppose I am, but I believe everyone should have equal rights and no one should live in slavery or be discriminated against because of their race, culture or beliefs."

Spreading her hands along the soft white tablecloth, she looks down and traces the pattern with her fingernails.

"Stefan would stay at the SS headquarters for longer and longer periods of time, finding any excuse not to be with me."

She twists her wedding ring around finger, her voice softening to a whisper. "It broke my heart."

She exhales a quivering breath and looks up. "But I'm still a member of the Nazi party. It's too dangerous for me to leave. It would be considered very suspicious if I did.

I think the Gestapo would welcome any excuse to question me, so I must be very careful."

I lower my head, resting it on my folded arms, not knowing why this lady is telling us all this or why she invited us back to her home.

"Why did you bring us here?" Franz asks in a hoarse whisper.

"Let's say I'm trying to make amends for what this Nazi Regime has done to its people and the people of Europe," she answers.

I slowly sit up to face her.

What now, beautiful lady?

The three of us sit in silence for a long moment. Frau Schmidt studies our uniforms. As if struck by inspiration, she claps her hands and beams.

"I know what to do! You both need warmer clothing for the

winter, so I'll alter Stefan's pants!"

Pushing her chair away, Frau Schmidt stands and rushes upstairs. She brings back two sets of black trousers. Franz and I looked at her in disbelief.

Noticing our worried expressions, she places the garments on the back of a chair and pats Franz's arm.

"It's alright. My husband won't be coming back," she says, tears welling in her eyes. "He was killed a few months ago. The allies bombed the SS headquarters, where he was stationed."

We're silent for a few minutes as Frau Schmidt wipes her tears with the back of her hand. Composing herself, she smiles.

"I'll alter his trousers to fit you both. Why don't you two go upstairs and have a bath?

Leave your clothes outside the door and I'll try to clean them. I'll put on supper and get out my sewing machine. Come here and I'll measure your waists and the length of your legs."

She pulls out a tape measure from a dresser drawer and we stand in front of her as she kneels and measures us. She shakes her head, frowning, and looks up, "I hope you find these pants too tight after you have been liberated by the Americans and fed big American meals!"

"Madam," I say seriously, looking down at her, "could you make us something simple to eat? We were very sick when we ate beef stew yesterday. I thought I was going to die. I think our stomachs can't hold down very much. A little soup would be very nice."

Understanding, she smiles at us and nods. We look at her pretty upturned face and smile back at her.

#####

It takes a long time for both of us to have a bath. To share the bath water is impossible. We're so filthy.

Franz gets in first, as he wins the toss of a coin left on the sink. I sit on the floor near the tub and watch him ease himself into the water. His ribs stick out above his concave stomach.

He looks down and frowns at his torso.

"I look like a Russian from the camp."

I chuckle, remembering the poor bastards behind the wire fence.

"I hope some of them got out of that hell hole!" I mutter.

Franz lathers his chest and looks up.

"I hope so too, Rys."

When it's my turn, I refill the bath and step over the side into the water.

It takes us an hour to bathe. We drain the water when it becomes a dark putrid colour with dead lice floating on the surface and refill it with fresh hot water. Scouring our shorn heads with soap, we scrub at the dirt with a white face cloth which soon blackens and needs to be rinsed out over and over.

Wiping his face with a clean towel, Franz sits down on the floor, a second towel wrapped around his waist.

"What do you think about Frau Schmidt?" he asks.

"I think she's okay." I reply, washing under my armpits. "I'm glad we took the chance to come back here, but it's very risky. We should leave straight after the meal."

"You're right," agrees Franz. "We can't stay too long. Someone could come to the house and find out what she is doing. It's too risky for her as well as us."

I sink further into the warm water and submerge my head, coming up for air while scrubbing my face. "I agree, but food first, Franz."

"Absolutely!"

Ten minutes later, we find neatly folded trousers, clean underwear, socks and two black wool jumpers as well as our newly pressed uniforms outside the bathroom door. We put on our old uniforms and notice the ironing has killed the lice. We add the new clothes on top, leaving the wool shorts underneath for extra warmth, but I notice the apple core and stale bread roll are missing. The jumpers are a bit long, reaching our thighs, so we roll up the sleeves.

We head downstairs to the kitchen.

The wood stove burns brightly, and Frau Schmidt has laid the table with napkins and silver cutlery. The kitchen is warm and cosy, with bright purple check curtains and cupboards painted a pale yellow.

We sit at the table as vegetable soup is ladled into bowls and placed in front of us. Our mouths water from the delicious smell.

I smooth my hands on the tablecloth feeling its fine woven texture. I bow my head and tears drop onto the napkin on my lap. Franz pats my back and Frau Schmidt comes around the table and gives me a hug.

She lifts my head, pressing it to her soft body and smooths my cropped hair. She smells like Jasmine on a summer's day, fragrant and sweet. It makes me sob even more. After a few minutes, I control my tears and she finally release me and pats my shoulder. I wipe my face on the napkin and look up at her. Frau Schmidt smiles through her tears and strokes my forehead. I haven't felt a motherly touch for so long. It seems like years. I smile back tentatively, as a pleasant warmth spreads throughout my body.

"Come. Let us eat before the soup gets cold," she suggests, wiping her cheeks and siting down.

I look at my bowl and it's piled high with vegetables in a thick chicken broth. It's the most amazing sight I've seen in four years. I regretfully pushed the bowl towards her.

"I'm sorry Madam, but I can't eat this much. I will be sick if I'm too full."

"Of course. Of course. I'll scoop a little back into the pot," she apologises, and proceeds to do so.

Franz gives a displeased grunt and pushes his bowl towards her as well.

We eat in silence, finishing with a cup of sweet black tea. Apart from the taste of the beef stew at the garrison, it's the most amazing meal I've ever had. Well, ever since Auntie's meals before the war, but that feels a lifetime ago.

I stand up, followed by Franz.

Frau Schmidt puts her hand out, grasping my arm.

There's a silent pause as I glance down at her.

"We need to leave now Madam."

"I thought so," she whispers through a sigh. "I know it will be dangerous for me and certainly for you two if we are discovered."

Scraping back her chair, she stands as well and reaches for her handbag on the kitchen counter.

"I'll give you some money to help with train tickets and food."

Rummaging through her purse, she hands me a small bundle of German Reichsmarks.

"Thank you so much Madam," I say, pocketing the money.

"I thank you as well, Madam," Franz adds with a nod of his head.

We walk to the front door and Frau Schmidt hands us back our rucksack.

"There are sandwiches, apples, two packets of matches and two tin mugs. I also hid your papers under the lining and sewed it up, so it can't be seen if anyone searches your bag."

"Please forgive me for going through your rucksack!" she adds as we put on our shoes.

"We have nothing to hide, so don't concern yourself," Franz says, looking up. "We appreciate everything you have done for us, Frau Schmidt."

I nod my agreement as we stand facing her. She smiles and grabs our hands.

"Ryszard, Franz I wish you both the best of luck!"

We look at her, startled, then realise she has read our papers, so of course she knows our real names.

She hugs us in turn, and I take her hand and kiss it. Franz places a kiss on her cheek.

She opens the door and peers into the corridor. It's empty. I can hear music behind the door across from us. Frau Schmidt creeps outside, gesturing for us to hurry.

"It's dark. Be careful," she whispers as she opens the glass door to the chilled night air.

We slip outside onto the pavement, and I turn to her as she stands in the doorway. A weak glow of light halos her from somewhere within the building. She looks like an angel, radiant and ethereal.

"Madam, what is the date?" I ask, thrusting my hands under my armpits. The snow is starting to cling to our jumpers and wool caps.

"It's the twenty-seventh of December.

"And the year?" I ask.

"1944... Why?"

"I believe it's my birthday. I'm eighteen."

She smiles, then whispers, "Happy birthday Ryszard". I watch her as she slips behind the door and silently closes it.

Running back along the deserted street towards the railway station, we dash to a bench near the ticket office and sit heavily, trying to catch our breath, blowing warmth into our hands. It's very cold and even with the warmer clothes Franz and I shiver. I look around and see the station is practically empty.

I make my way to the ticket office and buy tickets to Frankfurt. In moments, the train pulls into the station, billowing smoke and steam. It grinds to a halt as we climb aboard. We walk through the carriages to find an empty compartment where we slump on the seats facing each other.

After a while I ask.

"What was your impression of Klara Schmidt?"

"I think she was very beautiful, and if she asked me to share her bed I would have obliged," smirked Franz.

"Me too," I say with a chuckle.

"Rys, Rys," Franz utters with a sigh, crossing his arms and leaning against the seat. He extends his long thin legs and crosses his ankles. "After me she would have been too satisfied and too tired to even think about entertaining you!"

I guffaw then add. "I don't think I'd have the energy... or know what to do!"

"Ah Rys, Frau Schmidt would have taught us a few things. It

would have been a nice belated Christmas present, or in your case a birthday present, don't you think?"

I bob my head with a grin.

Wearily he exhales.

"But you're right. I wouldn't have the energy either."

He places his arms behind his head as he peers up at the ceiling.

"Although, I don't want to die a virgin," he adds.

"Me neither," I say with a huff and settle into the seat.

We look out the train window and notice the city of Hannover has disappeared, replaced with snow covered farmlands. We are silent for some time letting the sway of the carriage lull us to sleep with our heads propped up against the windowpane.

The conductor wakes us for our tickets and Franz asks for the time. It seems we only slept for half an hour, but it feels a lot longer. We fall back to sleep as soon as he leaves.

The train's whistle screams and its brakes screech. We're jolted awake, and peer through the window.

We're not in Frankfurt. Not any other town, either.

This is the middle of nowhere.

30

"Off the train! Everyone off the train!" announces the conductor, stumbling slightly as the train jerks to a complete stop. "The railway line has been blown up further down the track, either by the British or Americans, which one I don't know. All passengers for Frankfurt are to leave by those buses parked on the road outside this station."

"How far is Frankfurt?" I ask.

"About five kilometres south," he answers over his shoulder as he strides to the next carriage.

"Catching the bus could be dangerous," whispers Franz as we rise from our seats. "We should walk." He picks up the rucksack and leads the way.

Disembarking with the rest of the passengers, we weave through the crowd and onto the road, disappearing into the shadows. We peek around a brick wall, spotting German guards checking papers. Behind bushes, we crouch down low and wait for the buses to leave.

I hear someone pissing a metre from our hiding place. I hold my breath, bend my head, and press my knees close together as the steady stream is making me want to piss too.

Franz is coiled like a spring, ready to leap out at any

moment. He takes in a couple of deep, steadying breaths, making a fist.

The snow crunches as the man moves back to the station's entrance. Franz and I slowly crawl out from under the bushes and stand against the wall, which smells strongly of urine.

I relieve myself as the snow falls on my hunched shoulders. "Bloody hell!" Franz swears in a whisper, wiping his face with his sleeve. "That was too close, Rys."

I shake my head as my hands are preoccupied. "Ah, a bit of snow won't harm us Franz!" I quietly snicker as I pee a steady stream against the wall. I zip up my shorts then my trousers and pull down my jumper. I stand there looking at Franz.

"Well, what are you waiting for? The bloody Americans!" he snarls, shouldering the rucksack.

"Bloody oath I am!" I say with a grin.

We gingerly step onto the road and look around. Everything is quiet. The guards are gone. The station is dark, with only a flickering light behind the curtain in the station master's office.

Moving stealthily, we creep past the window. The snow changes to sleet.

Franz, his back bent against the wind, curses again. I snigger once again, then stuff my hands into my pockets to keep them from freezing.

We trudge up the road for what feels like hours. The weather begins to clear, the clouds parting to allow moonbeams to illuminate the farmland around us.

"What time is it?" I ask wearily, as I shiver uncontrollably and drag my feet through the snow.

"Maybe one in the morning," replies Franz, blowing warm air into his hands. "We need to find shelter. I'm bloody freezing!"

A barn comes into view. The fence posts are down, fencing wire pulled back and tracks leading to barred double doors. Trucks have recently driven through the snow to the barn. It must have been only a short time earlier, as patches of bare dirt still peek through the freshly fallen snow.

The farmhouse, next to the barn, is razed to the ground. Charred black timbers lie broken across crumbling stone walls. However, the barn looks intact.

Opening the door, we peer inside. Something huge, round and solid stands in the centre of the room. There is a musty smell, like wet wool, coming off the mound.

"It looks safe enough," says Franz, "but I have no idea what that mound is! I'll look for the matches."

He rummages through the rucksack.

"Thank you, Frau Schmidt!" he whispers under his breath when he finds a packet.

"Okay," I whisper. "Let's get inside."

Franz strikes the match as we step over the threshold, surprised to see piles of discarded clothing.

We fumble our way around, until my foot kicks something. I explore it with my fingers. It feels strange. I touch a patch of skin. It feels rough and cold. I jump back, gasping. The match, which gives out only a small amount of illumination, reveals an arm, then a leg. I back away in shock.

Franz throws down the match as it dies away. "Oh Christ Rys! I think they're bodies! I think they're dead soldiers!"

"Ah shit! ... Franz for Christ's sake, light another match!"

"Okay, okay!" he growls.

As the match ignites, we take a closer look at the mound.

Franz is right, bodies of dead German soldiers are piled carelessly on top of one another with arms and legs at weird angles.

"There's a lantern on the wall," says Franz, gesturing towards it.

I run over and retrieve it.

Franz waves out the second match, strikes another and lights the lantern. We look around, astonished as its glow lights up the gruesome scene.

Gagging, I spit on the ground.

"Why did they leave them here?" I ask wiping my mouth.

"I think the Germans ran out of trucks. They could possibly come back tomorrow to collect them," Franz says, distracted. "But it's bloody weird." He pauses. "Anyway, these men can't harm us. I say we make the best of it and shelter here for the night."

I grunt, wiping my hands down my jumper.

When I touched that dead skin, I felt a bit sick.

Franz looks at me apologetically, "I know. I know, it's not the best solution but we're going to die from the cold if we stay outside. Now, let's try to get warm."

He struggles to move a couple of bodies, their bones cracking as he does so.

He places them into a type of well, arranging stiff arms and legs in different positions to form a circle.

Removing two overcoats from bodies furthest from the mound he carries them to his well, settles down between the bodies and covers himself with the coats, leaning his head back onto a dead torso.

I stand there aghast, looking around helplessly at the scene in front of me. Then I shrug and do the same.

I've seen worse.

"I wonder why they don't smell?" I wonder aloud as I settle between two arms, three legs and a head with its blank eyes staring at me. I place his helmet over his face and cover my chest and legs with an overcoat.

"It's so bloody cold I think it's keeping the bodies refrigerated like in a morgue," Franz explains as he nestles down into his cocoon. "They could have died just yesterday, which makes them still fresh."

He changes the subject. "I'm warmer now … How about you?"

"Yes. Yes, I'm warmer."

Franz yawns. "Let's get some sleep."

I curl up in a ball and wrap the coats around my ears.

"Okay, but we keep the lantern burning low tonight, Franz."

Franz chuckles, "Righto, Rys. We'll keep the light on!"

The next morning, I wake abruptly, feeling a hand on my forehead and a foot on my crotch. Cringing, I push the dead limbs aside and leap to my feet, briskly brushing myself down, cursing all the while.

Franz slowly wakes and peers up at me. He has a hand resting on his head and an arm slung over his chest. I laugh at the sight as he looks down and quickly sits up.

He lifts the arm off his lap and lets the hand slip down his back.

"Well, that's the closest I'm ever going to be to sleeping with a Kraut." He shudders. "Well, except for Frau Schmidt of course!"

He grins at the thought of a dalliance with the lovely lady

and stands, stretching his arms above his head. He wanders around the bodies, searching for money, guns or anything of value and huffs disgruntledly.

"Looks like they've been stripped of anything worth keeping before being dumped here."

"It doesn't surprise me, Franz. Guns are valuable. However, we might find jackets, overcoats, and decent boots."

We try on the overcoats we had as a blanket, but they are far too big. Rummaging around the dead, we find two bodies about our size. We dig them out of the heap and roll them around on the floor. They are stiff with rigour mortis, just like shop dummies, as we try to peel the clothes off them. It's like peeling a huge onion.

At last, the coats and jackets are free. We try them on. Mine is still too big, but Franz's jacket and coat are a good fit. We both begin to feel warmer.

I button my overcoat up to the neck and pull the sleeves down over my hands. I'm not exactly a fashion statement.

"You look like the village idiot!" Franz smirks.

"The class buffoon, you mean." I say, bounding around like a monkey. "That's what Pan Zebrowski, the headmaster at my old high school used to say to me practically every day!"

I pretend to scratch under my armpits.

Franz laughs. "Sometimes you crack me up, Rys!"

We peel the boots and socks off the bodies and quickly remove our shoes. We roll the warmer socks up over our own, place our feet into the boots and buckle them up. My boots fit fine.

"No more newspapers for me," I grin.

Franz squirms and grimaces. "Ah! I'll need to find another

pair. These are too tight!"

He rummages around, finding a bigger pair on a taller Kraut and walks around as if he's in a shoe store, bobbing his head in satisfaction.

"My Dad may have been a drunkard, but since his toes were deformed from poor fitting shoes when he was a boy, he always insisted that I wore properly fitted shoes."

He picks up the rucksack and walks towards the door. "Now, let's get out of here."

We trudge towards a small village two kilometres down the road. There, we buy a small wedge of hard cheese and a piece of salami from a lady who's shovelling snow from her step. She doesn't agree to sell until I pull out the wad of money from my pocket.

Using our tin mugs, we drink freezing water at a pump, then hurriedly wash our faces and necks.

We move on, avoiding the German convoys heading North, by hiding behind trees or buildings, only emerging when the coast is clear.

It's midday when we come across a farm where an old man is repairing a wire fence.

Franz asks him where all the trucks are heading.

"To the Front, I heard. Prum or St Vith, at the Belgium border."

"How far is it?" I ask.

"I don't know, but you could get a lot more information if you go to Völklingen. Just keep following this road."

"Völklingen?" Franz queries. "Not Frankfurt?"

The farmer points to the road we had just walked. "You've missed Frankfurt. It's about ten kilometres north of here."

I turn to Franz in surprise.

"We must have passed a turn off last night or this morning."

"Shit!" He growls and kicks a mound of snow.

We thank the farmer and walk for two more hours, eating Fraulein Schmidt's sandwiches.

"I could do with some water." I say, my tongue, thick and dry.

"Let's find something we can fill up apart from our mugs," Franz suggests.

We come across a body tangled up in fence wire with his head down and his back bent as if he is bowing after a performance. He looks like he died a couple of days ago as the snow is piled up high around his thighs and upper arms.

Franz investigates the body.

"There is a water canteen, a gun and an army knife strapped to his waist," he says as he feels around his back. "He seems to be an officer, but why he was left strung up is a mystery."

He clears some of the snow away and unbuckles the belt, pulling it hard.

The corpse suddenly twitches, vibrating the fence wires, and lets out an all-mighty burp.

I nearly shit myself. I cry out, falling backwards onto the road with my bum sliding on the ice until I come to rest a couple of metres away. Startled, Franz stumbles back with the belt in his hand, the precious items dragging in the snow. He regains his footing.

"What... What the bloody hell was that!" I blurt out.

"He must have had air trapped in his belly when he died or maybe it was gases built up after his death," Franz explains as he calmly inspects the belt.

"Christ!... That was scary!" I splutter, pulling myself up from the road.

He threads the canteen and holster off the belt, takes the gun out of the holster, checks the safety is on, then places all the items on the ground.

"I'll wear the knife," Franz states matter-of-factly as he straps on the belt. "We'll fill up the canteen at the next village."

Leaving the holster, he casually picks up the gun and canteen, and stuffs them in the rucksack.

"Christ you're tough, Franz!" I exclaim. "I nearly shit myself and you just raise an eyebrow!"

"You and I have seen plenty of dead bodies, Rys. But I must admit that was a bit freaky."

"You think!" I gasp as I swipe my cap off the road and dust off the snow.

Franz shrugs and continues to walk along the road. I brush myself down and follow, looking back at the corpse, just in case it is still moving. I look back at Franz, walking casually as if nothing has happened.

As I trudge through the snow, I think back on how tough Franz is. Even in the camp dead bodies didn't faze him. I would throw-up at the sight of a decaying corpse. Whereas, Franz walked by the bloated body, calm and unfazed, as if it was normal. He appears undisturbed by death.

CHAPTER

31

The late afternoon sun does little to warm us as we trample the narrow snow ridges criss-crossing along the road. The traffic has eased the last couple of hours. Only a couple of army trucks have sped past us.

In a quiet moment we sit on a log beside a tree and divide an apple. Franz cuts it carefully using his newly acquired army knife and hands me half.

While taking a bite of his half, Franz asks out of the blue, "What is Jo like?"

"He's a good soccer player. A really funny guy, always telling jokes," I mumble with my mouth full. I only take a couple of bites to finish my half. Franz nibbles, making his apple last.

I put my part of the core in my pocket as I swallow the last piece.

"We both loved the same girl." I say pretending nonchalance, as I bend over and retie the laces on one of my boots.

Franz is so astonished he forgets to take the next bite of his apple. "You loved the same girl?"

"Yes. She's Jewish. Beautiful. We both fell in love with her." I say this quite matter-of-factly as I adjust the other boot.

I glance up, "Funnily enough, she loved Jo and myself equally."

Franz snorts in disbelief, "What! Now that's totally weird!"

"I know how it sounds, but it's the truth," I say, brushing snow from my trouser legs, surprised to realise I no longer mind.

"We were all very young then," I add with a sigh and straighten up.

I'm quiet for a few minutes, gazing into the distance, thinking back to the time Helena left for the camp and how badly Jo took it. He became a different person in those months, not my brother at all. I guess I knew, even then, that his feelings for Helena ran deep. Deeper than mine.

Getting up from the log, Franz picks up the rucksack and we continue to walk along the road. I kick a small rock between us as if it's a soccer ball. Franz finishes his apple and kicks the rock back.

"Helena ended up in a ghetto and was later transported to a concentration camp," I add after a long pause.

I tuck my hands in my coat pockets and exhale deeply. "I wonder every day if she is still alive. Jo was really upset when she left. Mind you, I was too, but Jo was *really* heartbroken. It was not long after, he joined Armia Krajowa and a couple of months later he was captured when the Germans raided their headquarters.

He wasn't in the body count, which meant he was on a train heading for a camp somewhere. I don't know if he is dead or still alive! Alive, I hope."

I pause, squinting into the wintry sun, chewing my lip. Thinking about the rest of my family.

"I think my father ended up in France," I add. "I overheard Ma telling my aunt that most of the Polish army, including Pa's regiment, fled to France. This was in the first few weeks of the war, when the Nazis annihilated Poland. But now that France is occupied by the Germans, I don't know where he is."

"What about your sisters?" Franz asks, kicking the rock out a couple of metres, aiming towards my side of the road.

I told him about my family when we were in the Resistance, but we'd rarely spoken of them since.

"Oh, I think they're probably okay." I answer. "They're very close to my mother and never get into any trouble, not like Jo and I. Knowing them, they would stay close to home. Safe."

As safe as anywhere, with the damned Nazis rampaging all over Europe. Which isn't safe at all.

I say a silent prayer for Zanita and Angelika.

"I remember them being very artistic and loving crafts. Always drawing pictures and knitting hats and scarves. They once gave Pa a striped beanie in pinks and purples that he wore with pride for a whole winter. He looked hilarious."

We both laugh.

"Jo is artistic too." I continued. "He carves animals from pieces of wood using a pen knife. His sculptures are very good."

I jog up to the rock and give it a couple of small kicks, passing it back to Franz.

"What about you, Rys, are you artistic too?" Franz asks sarcastically, tapping the rock back to me.

"Me? Well, I like to write poetry." I announce casually, shrugging my shoulders, I dribble the rock along the ruts in the road.

"What, like 'roses are red, violets are blue'?" Franz scoffs.

"Well, something like that," I reply. "Not many people knew I wrote poetry. The only people who did know were one of my high school teachers, Pan Nowak, Helena and now you.

When Helena was in the ghetto, I would sneak letters to her and always put in a silly poem. I asked her not to mention it in her letters back to me, as it was our little secret and I knew if Jo found out he would try to outdo me with something else. Jo was always competitive when it came to Helena."

I kick the rock harder in Franz's direction.

"Helena is the Jewish girl?" he asks as he stops the momentum of the rock, driving it into a rut in the road.

"Yeah," I sigh.

"I'd love you to recite one of your creations," Franz snickers.

"Okay," I say enthusiastically, ignoring his sarcasm. I launch into one of my favourites.

"Oh cat, oh cat,
As black as a bat,
Who's always in Auntie's way.
You meow for food, you meow at the door,
'Go away,' says Auntie who knows you're a stray.
'Squeak, squeak,' says the mouse. Whack! goes the paw.
And the little mouse is no more!

Oh cat, oh cat,
Who's black and quite fat,
Who governs the house all day.
You prowl and you flounce,
Reducing mice with a pounce,
Then crunch them without delay.

Oh cat, oh cat,

Who's black and a brat,
Who sleeps on the kitchen floor,
You bask in the sun,
Dreaming of mice and of fun,
As you roll on your back and snore!

Oh cat, oh cat,
Who's black as a bat,
You're the favourite there is no denial.
May your days be long,
As you meow your song,
And slumber in the warm kitchen aisle.

With a sideways glance, I add, "I don't know if I've finished it or not!"

Franz chokes with laughter.

"Oh! It sounds finished. It's certainly long enough. Still, what do I know?" he chuckles. "Although, I'll give you some advice."

I look at him expectantly.

"Don't give up your day job!"

I laugh.

"I'm determined to write them down one day and get them published." I declare, half seriously. "I'll call the book 'The Corniest Poems Ever Written'."

Franz laughs again, kicking the rock into a ditch, ending the game.

"What about you? Did you have a girlfriend?" I ask.

"Nah! I was too busy making a living and putting food in my belly. Mind you I do like girls, but I didn't find one I *really* liked.

I spent my weekends tinkering with an old motorbike in Dad's shed or playing soccer with the lads up the street. I lived in a poor section of town. We had no soccer fields, so we made do with a nearby road. A boy I knew, Albin was his name, always brought the soccer ball. It was an old thing he must have found in a garbage can. It would deflate half-way through a game, and he had to pump it up with an old bicycle pump for the next half. I remember thumping that stupid thing towards the goal, only to see it crawl towards the oil drums so slowly it gave the goalie enough time to finish a fag, casually pick it up and throw it back to Albin."

I laugh at the image then ask. "How about your family?"

"Well, you know my mother died when I was young and that dad was always drunk," he states. "I had no real family, but I did have an uncle on my mother's side.

He was a total sleaze. When I was little, about four years old, he kept tempting me with chocolates to sit on his lap. I could see he had a hard on, the dirty bastard. I never took the chocolates and I never, never sat on his lap!"

I spit on the ground in distaste.

"I hate paedophiles!" I snarl.

"I've seen that word somewhere, maybe in a book I've read. Does it mean adults who sexually molest children?"

I grimace before answering.

"Yeah. It does."

Franz suddenly stops and pulls my arm to face him, concern written on his face.

"Christ Rys, how do you know that?"

"Don't worry, I wasn't molested," I chuckle. "I overheard Pa saying to my Ma that he didn't want us children going to church as the priest was a paedophile. Ma didn't believe him, but later a choir boy was interfered with, and the priest was moved to another parish. She believed Pa then!"

"Shit! That's terrible. He could molest other boys!" Franz claims.

"Exactly!" I huff, striding down the road, kicking the snow.

Franz catches up and silently walks beside me, his hands in his pockets.

"Did the Nazis make you leave school like me?" I ask, looking his way, changing the subject again.

"Nah, I got out when I was fourteen. I had to make my own way. We had very little money, and I had to hide my wages from Dad, or he'd steal them to buy vodka.

You already know I worked in a garage. Well, I was an apprentice motor mechanic. The garage was owned by Jews. They owned a couple of garages and houses. The owner was okay. He always greeted Emil, the garage manager, and me, with a handshake. He treated us well enough. We had no complaints.

In fact, the owner gave me an old motor bike engine to work on at home and he let me practise on an old truck engine he left in the garage. I only worked on it an hour a day. Emil would spend most of the hour explaining the working parts of the engine to me. I really liked Emil. He was a decent guy."

"Ah! That's how you know so much about truck engines! I wondered how come you knew how to sabotage one!"

Franz nods then looks up at the trees around us.

"I joined a street gang once," he discloses. "We terrorised the Jews. I didn't like doing it, but when you're in a gang you need to fit in. I once hit an old man on the head with a stick, knocking him to the ground. I'm not proud of that!"

"Me too. I was also in a gang that threw rocks at old Jewish men," I admit. "I know how you feel. I also have regrets."

I glance sidelong at him with a questioning look. "But I've always wondered. How did you get around the city so quickly when we were delivering the coded messages?"

Franz smiles a sheepish grin.

"Ah… I stole a bike and hid it in an old shed. When I had to travel a long way, or deliver a lot of messages, I would use the bike. I didn't tell anyone, not even you Rys, as I knew it would be borrowed all the time, so I hid it away.

I knew it was selfish of me, but I never had a bike before and I wanted to keep it for my own, even though it was stolen."

Understanding, I bob my head as Franz scuffs a pile of snow with his boot. Our conversation comes to an end as we trudge towards a village, each lost in our own thoughts.

32

The village is silent. Eerie.

The air is still.

A strange greyness permeates everything, as if the dust will never settle.

Franz and I wander up the deserted road, glancing nervously from side to side. Cold dread sends shivers up and down my spine. The aura of old evil, the relic of ancient cruelty, permeates this place which feels as if it has experienced worse horrors than this war.

We manage to get water, not yet frozen, from a pump in the backyard of an old house. Not bothering with my mug, I drink thirstily as Franz pumps the handle. I do the same for him.

"Bloody creepy place," murmurs Franz, filling the canteen and putting it back in the rucksack. "I think we'll get out of here, pronto."

The hairs on the back of my neck are sticking up. "Someone, or something is watching us," I whisper, glancing over my shoulder.

"I feel it too!" mutters Franz. We scurry out of the backyard into the desolate street and trot to the edge of a steep slope. Franz and I slip and slide down to a road, heavy with traffic being directed by a policeman.

Marcia Wakeman

Leaving the sense of foreboding behind us, I am relieved to see trucks and horse drawn carts going about their normal business on the wide road. We reach the crossroad and walk briskly alongside a horse and cart, my heart pounding, as if we've had a lucky escape. I glance up the slope and wonder what really lurked in the shadows of the war-torn houses in that strange village.

Our relief makes us careless.

The police officer spots us and calls us over.

Reluctantly, we cross the busy road to stand facing him. He stands on a large wooden box, a lunch pail at his feet. Palm up, he stops the traffic on one side of the road. With his other, he directs the opposite side to move ahead. He pauses momentarily to inspect us.

"Where are you boys heading?" he asks as he starts to wave his hand to and fro.

"Völklingen," I answer, not meeting his eyes.

"You look like you've seen a ghost," he chuckles. "Been through the village up the hill, have you? Bad place, that village. No one goes there. It's said to have some strange folk lurking about."

"Yeah, we got the feeling something wasn't right," says Franz.

"I've heard people complain of weird sightings of an old woman, dressed in black, prowling around the ruins," claims the policeman as he waves on the traffic on his right.

"A lot of old women dress in black," Franz comments.

"This old woman is different," the policeman replies, "she wears a cloak made of human scalps!"

"What?" I cry out, rubbing my head under my cap.

319

"Yes, human scalps, like the American Red Indian!" the policeman says seriously, ghoulishly enjoying our discomfort.

"Oh my God!" I gasp. "It sounds like something out of a horror story!"

"Scared you, didn't I!" the policeman chuckles, looking down at us with a mischievous grin. "Don't worry it's only a ghost story. The old woman lived there hundreds of years ago if it's true. It was said the place was haunted. But like I said, it's only a ghost story. Created by the locals. I don't believe it myself!"

Open-mouthed, Franz and I stare at him.

Is this man joking? Having us on? Of all our luck we meet a comedian in the middle of the road in the middle of a war. Go figure!

But the village did feel strange, like it was haunted. Maybe the locals were right!

The policeman stops both sides of the street to let the cross-traffic flow pass.

"Do you need a lift?" he asks, changing the subject.

"Yes! That would be great sir! Thanks!" answers Franz, taking off the rucksack.

The policeman waves to a truck to stop.

"Are you going to Völklingen?" he asks the driver.

"Ja! Ja," replies the man. "Only to the outskirts."

"That'll do. Jump in boys!" he commands. "And be careful."

We thank the policeman, climb into the cab and the driver takes off, crunching the gears. Glancing at each other, we can't believe our luck. We got away easily from the creepy village and now we're warm and dry. The truck is a lot faster and easier than walking.

I glance over to the driver. He is a scrawny thin man, unshaven and filthy, with greasy brown hair hanging over protruding ears. He glares back at me, then at Franz. Clearly displeased about something.

We thank him for the lift, but he keeps staring at our clothes, mumbling under his breath.

Shortly, we both fall asleep only to be startled by loud blasts of the truck's horn.

Another truck has pulled in front, narrowly missing the front fender. Our driver swears then accelerates, jerking our bodies backwards as he swerves the truck to the other side of the road. He grates the gears, slamming down his foot as we pass the offending vehicle, and gesticulates with his fist at the hapless driver. I clutch the door frame as Franz holds on tight to the rucksack.

Safely past, the driver relaxes, settling himself into his seat and bringing the speed back to normal. My mouth is dry, and I ask for the canteen. Franz hands it to me. I take a long swig, then pass it back. I glance at him.

He glances back, lifting an eyebrow as he takes a couple of mouthfuls. He shrugs, then screws on the cap, stuffing it into the rucksack.

I look through the grimy window, noticing the daylight fading into twilight as more snow begins to fall.

The driver glowers at us through blood-shot eyes, then goes back to watching the road.

"So, what do you two thinks about Hitler's war?" He asks in a wheezy voice.

I jerk my head in surprise and glare at his profile.

What the hell! How do I reply to that? Maybe he is a Nazi.

Will I take a gamble?

I glance at Franz who slightly shrugs as if to say it's my call.

I proclaim in a high-pitched voice, "It's our war! We support it! Like every good German does!"

The driver growls. He jams on the brakes and swerves to the verge of the road. Breathing heavily, he kills the engine.

There is a moment of silence.

Ah shit! Wrong answer!

"Out!" he screams, making us both jump.

He abruptly scrambles out of the truck, storms round to the passenger side, wrenches open the door and pulls me out. Franz swiftly pulls himself along the seat and leaps down.

"This so called *our* war has destroyed us all!" The driver bellows, throwing me to the ground. "I have no farm left. The bloody Reichsmark is worth nothing. I might as well wipe my ass with it. My only son is at the Front, God knows where, while Hitler and his cronies hide in an underground bunker somewhere, away from all this!"

He waves his arms about indicating the devastation around us. "The Nazis are bloody insane, the lot of them!"

He tries to kick me. Franz pushes him away, making him fall into mud. Snow melts on his face. Dirty rivulets run down his neck.

I suddenly feel sorry for the man. I get up and extend my hand, but he fiercely pushes it away.

"Piss off!" he snarls, climbing to his feet.

He spits on the ground and walks briskly around the front of the truck, climbs back in the cab, slams the door, and starts the engine.

Crunching the gears, he skids on the icy road and speeds

away.

We stand in the middle of the road, watching the receding taillights in silence.

"Sorry, Franz," I apologise in a whisper.

Franz shrugs and begins to plod through the sludge. Feeling wretched, I trudge behind him, bending my head into the bitterly cold wind.

Approaching the outskirts of Völklingen, we forget the last few hours and stop to gaze at the city. It's lit up by the ironworks, a strange sight these days. I'm surprised it's still operating. Usually, the cities are covered in darkness since the onset of air-raids.

Franz points to a blue light shimmering in the far distance. We head towards it.

It appears to be a hospital. I carefully open the glass door, welcoming the warmth inside, and creep in with Franz following close behind.

The foyer is deserted. Large oil heaters are placed on either side of the walls, radiating a wonderful heat. Taking off our coats, caps, and jackets, we drape them over the hot pipes and sit on the floor.

"I don't think we can stay here for long," I sigh, rubbing my back against the hot pipes, feeling the delicious penetrating warmth against my chilled skin.

"You're right, but let's get warm first." Franz breaths out contentedly, as he leans his head back.

A nurse appears, standing near our reclining bodies. Peering down, she places her hands on her hips.

"What are you two doing here?" she asks. In a half daze, I slowly open my eyes to squint up at her.

"We're just getting out of the cold, Madam."

"Wait here," she commands and walks into another room.

"Ah shit Rys," Franz murmurs as he pulls himself up.

I sway with fatigue as I get up and grab the windowsill.

The nurse returns. We start to reach for our coats, but instead of asking us to leave, she hands us two mugs of hot milk laced with sugar. We look at her in surprise, thanking her as we place our hands around the hot tin mugs and breath in the aroma. Taking tentative sips, we lean back onto the oil heaters. I feel heat spreading into my body and the milk and sugar replenishing my energy.

The front doors suddenly slam open, letting freezing air spill into the room. Startled, we all look towards the noises coming from outside. The nurse runs towards the medics carrying in a German soldier on a stretcher.

More wounded pour in, behind them, supported or carried by their comrades.

Franz and I stand motionless, our hands clasping the warm mugs. We stare at the horrific scene in front of us, totally forgotten by the nurse in the ensuing pandemonium.

More nurses pour out of an adjoining room, giving aid wherever possible and shouting out orders to the medics. A doctor ploughs through a swinging door and jogs next to the stretchers, checking the wounded men.

Some of them have terrible wounds. A soldier has his whole leg blown off and another is missing an arm. Blood is all over the men and the medics alike. The room is full of loud moans and agonising screams.

"Let's get out of here!" Franz yells above the noise.

Quickly, we drink the milk down, place the mugs on the

windowsill and put our warm, but still damp, coats back on.

Dodging the remaining soldiers, as they push through the glass doors, we slip outside, only to find the place crawling with Krauts. We take off, steering clear of the army trucks parked in the hospital's forecourt, and run through the gates. Heading for the centre of town, we slow down when we hear the thumping of the steel works and the sound of traffic on the main road again.

"That was a close call," I pant.

"Sure was." Franz replies.

"It must be terrible at the Front." I shudder, wishing we were heading in a different direction.

"I believe you're right," Franz huffs. "Hopefully we will find the Americans first and never see it."

CHAPTER

33

Following the pounding from the steel works, we arrive in the centre of town, about a kilometre away.

The main street, where the shops look poor and unkempt, is deserted. A few have their windows boarded up. We turn into a road pitted with potholes, where narrow houses blackened from soot, cram together on small allotments. Fences made of rusty tin or wooden palings separate each small house. Slivers of light flickering under doorways and around blackout curtains guide us along the uneven path.

At the end of the street is a cul-de-sac with houses backing onto an industrial area. One of these dark houses, standing apart from its neighbours, looks deserted. Franz and I run down the narrow lane and jump the fence. We creep up to the door, finding it locked. So is the back door when we come to it.

Franz fumbles in the dark, finding a rock and smashes one of the small panes of glass set in the back door. He carefully places his hand through the jagged opening and unlocks the bolt from the inside.

Stepping into the gloom, we feel the kitchen surfaces with our hands. I start to look in the cupboards for food while Franz guards the back door.

I hear a sound and stand rock still.

Franz stiffens and looks down at the floorboards.

We hear a baby's muffled cry from beneath our feet.

Franz quickly lies down, putting his ear against the floor as I fall to my knees. We listen intently.

A baby wails again.

There's a shuffling behind a closed door leading to the rest of the house. The door slowly opens, revealing the dim grey outline of a figure holding a gun. The figure suddenly ducks back, aiming the gun through the doorway. I lie flat, my arms over my head. Franz is rigid beside me.

"This is my house!" a woman cries out in alarm. "What do you want?"

With shaking hands, she points the gun towards our heads.

"Get up! Get up!" she demands in a shrill voice.

Both of us slowly stand, holding our hands up in surrender. Careful to make no sudden moves.

"We are so sorry Madam," I say apologetically, "but we thought the house was abandoned."

Franz lowers his hands, then unsheathes his knife. The woman's eyes widen with fear, and I suddenly realise the gun might not be loaded. But we can't take the chance.

"We mean no harm Madam!" I say quickly. "We were looking for food. We'll go … We'll go right now."

I start to back away towards the back door.

The baby cries again, but this time urgently and for longer. The woman slowly lowers her gun squinting through the dim light. She hesitates, biting her lip, and flicks on the safety catch.

"I need to tend to my baby. We're sheltering in the basement in case the British start bombing again. They have been bombing us for days." She pauses, "I'm in two minds to kick you both out, but I'll take a chance here and take you down to the basement." She nods towards Franz, "you need to leave your knife in the kitchen drawer."

She indicates the open drawer near the sink with her gun. Franz hesitates for a moment then puts the knife in, closing it softly.

"Come. It's warmer downstairs."

We enter a small room lit by a kerosene lantern. The basement has been made into a tiny living area. It has a stove in one corner with a table and three chairs against a wall. A single bed is against another. A baby, wrapped in a knitted shawl, whimpers in a pulled-out drawer being used as a crib.

I walk over to the child. Dimpled arms reach up as if it is asking to be picked up. A beautiful little face smiles up at me.

The baby makes a dovelike cooing noise as little hands reach up once more. Awed, I touch tiny soft fingers and smile. The baby gurgles and smiles back.

"I haven't seen a baby for such a long time." I say, totally engrossed.

The woman comes to my side, introducing herself.

"My name is Monika, and this little darling is my baby girl, Lena."

She picks the baby up, adjusting the shawl and carefully puts her into my arms. I look down at her beautiful face and feel a sudden surge of pure joy go through my chest.

"Hello Lena," I whisper, and she coos back at me. I smooth the soft down of fair hair and kiss her forehead.

I glance up at Franz. He puts out his arms and I reluctantly give him the child. He holds her close, looking into her eyes, talking in soft whispers as he rocks her back and forth.

She reaches up and touches his face. He kisses her hands, tears welling in his eyes. Reluctantly, he hands her back to Monika who carefully lies her back in the narrow crib and tucks her in. Franz quickly wipes his eyes.

I take a better look at the lady. Monika. She is around thirty or so, but it's hard to tell. Dressed in a worn housecoat over a brown wool dress, she looks frail and thin. Her lank brown hair, pulled into a low ponytail, is dull and lifeless. Her gentle face is tired and drawn. But brilliant blue eyes the colour of the sky, light it with an inner beauty.

She smiles at us and moves towards the stove.

"I haven't got much to offer, but I can share the soup I made."

"That would be wonderful Madam!" Franz says, dropping the rucksack near the small table.

She places a pot on the stove and lights the gas. It gives off a little warmth, enough for us to take off our coats and drape them on the backs of the chairs.

We sit around the table while Monika serves a thin potato soup, not nearly enough for all of us. Franz retrieves bread and cheese from the rucksack, giving it to her to slice.

Monika tries to give the food back after slicing both in half, but Franz holds up his hand and tells her to keep the rest. She nods in appreciation while we eat in silence.

At a knock on the basement door, Franz and I lower our spoons. I swallow my mouthful of cheese in a big gulp.

Monika casually stands, walks to the door and pulls it open to reveal a policeman, leaning on the doorframe. He looks dishevelled with his black tie pulled down low and his shirt unbuttoned at the neck. His uniform needs a good clean.

The policeman is tall and solid, with dark eyes and thinning brown hair, swept back from his forehead. Lines are etched around his eyes and mouth. His top lip sports a trim moustache. He looks to be around forty.

Tucking his cap under his arm, he is taken aback when he sees us. His thick eyebrows gather in a frown as he straightens and reaches for the long baton hanging from his belt.

Warily, we get to our feet.

Monika leans towards him as he urgently whispers to her. She reassures him that we are travellers in need of food and shelter, then kisses his cheek and pats his arm.

He steps into the room, glowering. The woman, a bit bewildered, stands behind him.

"I don't like this Monika," the policeman growls.

"They mean no harm, Gunther. They are just hungry," says the woman, giving us a warm smile.

"Did one of you smash the backdoor window?" Gunther asks sternly.

"I did sir," Franz answers, "We thought the house was empty."

The policeman studies Franz and frowns again, noting his appearance and then mine.

"Where are you two heading?" he asks.

"Prum. In Belgium," I hastily confess. Franz turns and glares at me. I ignore him.

"The Front?" asks Gunther, astonished.

"Yes Sir," I reply.

"Where do you come from?" he questions, looking at our faces suspiciously.

I know then he's seen through our disguises.

We are silent for a full minute, staring at the two of them, ready to bolt.

"We come from Berlin," Franz finally discloses.

Gunther seems to relax and talks to us in Polish. "You don't have a German accent. I think you are escapees, maybe from a labour camp. Ah!" he exclaims. "I see from your expressions that I am right!"

We say nothing. I sneak a look at Franz. He is staring straight ahead, his stance rigid, as if he might spring upon the man at any moment.

I must defuse the situation before it gets out of hand, so I blurt out, "You are right. We are Polish and come from a slave labour camp in Oranienburg. We are trying to get to the Americans at Prum!"

Monika slowly sits on the bed staring at us in disbelief. The baby starts to whimper.

Gunther limps over, picking her up. Kissing her cheek, he looks back at us, the expression on his face becoming serious.

"If this war is ongoing, in the next few years we're all kaput! This precious girl is our only future."

He gives the child to her mother as we stand perfectly still, wondering about his next move.

He hobbles to his rucksack near the door. Our eyes remain fixed upon him as he takes out a package and places it on the table.

"This is only a small amount of food. I'll give it to you for your journey. I can get more later for my sister. Spend the night here. I don't think the British will bomb us tonight. There is a spare bedroom upstairs."

Gunther asks us more questions. At first, we answer

hesitantly, not knowing how much we should really tell him. He assures us he is not a Nazi, but a Polish sympathiser with a Polish heritage. We finally relax and tell them about the camps, finding the uniforms, and our journey so far.

It's late in the night when Gunther takes us upstairs and shows us a vacant bedroom with two single beds. Falling upon them, wrapping our overcoats and blankets around ourselves, we face each other.

"I thought we were caught," whispers Franz.

"I was bloody sure we were," I breathe. "But miracles do happen."

"I never thought I would get so emotional seeing a baby," mutters Franz, changing the subject, "I don't cry easily. I feel a bit embarrassed doing it in front of a woman!"

"Don't be, my brother," I murmur, "I felt the same way."

I roll on my back and nestle into my pillow, looking at a flickering silver pattern reflected off the ceiling.

The light is from outside, piercing torn slits in the old curtains hanging at the window. It is from the full moon high in the sky. I pull the blanket up to my chin.

"Franz?" I murmur.

"Yep," Franz mumbles sleepily.

"Have you ever wondered if we have a guardian angel?"

"Guardian angel?... No!... Christ Rys, you think of the weirdest things!" he chuckles softly, then turns to lie on his back.

"I think we have." I whisper emphatically. "You think of it, Franz! We escaped being shot. Kapo was a decent bloke and not a murdering maniac. I wasn't shot by that SS idiot. We found the uniforms and escaped. And so far, a lot of people have helped us. I think a guardian angel is looking after us!"

"Well, maybe he or she is," Franz mutters with a yawn. "But I'm too tired to think about it now. Go to sleep."

I sigh and face the wall, thinking about the WW1 soldier with the robin red breast on his shoulder. I wonder if he is my guardian angel. I remember his kind face resembling Pa's. He could be related to me somehow.

I smell a whiff of cigarette smoke. Maybe Gunther has come up the stairs to check on us, but I didn't hear any footsteps. The smell becomes stronger as I turn to look at the open doorway, but no one is there. I feel a presence as if someone else is in the room.

Shafts of bright moonlight suddenly spread across the ceiling and down the walls. I'm amazed and totally mesmerised at the same time. It's like a light show, full of glitter and sparkle. The twinkling lights dance from one corner of the room to the other.

"Franz, Franz! Look up to the ceiling," I whisper excitedly, but he's softly snoring under his cap.

I lie there, my heart pounding, knowing it is more than a trick of light. It could be my angel. I reach up and touch one of the lights along the wall. A tingling sensation spreads down my arm, lasting only a split second. I quickly pull my arm back under the blanket.

Soon the smell of tobacco fades and the lights dim. I pull the blanket around my head and stare at the remaining small soft lights dancing down the wall, until the last of them disappears.

Thinking about the soldier for a long time and wondering if he'll be with us for the rest of our journey, I yawn and rub my face as sleep takes hold of me. I dream of wearing a four-pointed military hat with a small, red-breasted bird sitting on my shoulder.

#####

The next morning we're greeted by a wonderful smell from downstairs. We hot-foot down the stairs into the kitchen, to find Monika frying bread in a pan.

She looks up and grins, "Gunther managed to get a half a block of lard from the black-market. I'm using your bread to make *Frittiertes Brot*. I haven't made it for ages!"

Fried bread! My mouth waters.

Monika turns the slices in the melted fat. "They should be ready soon."

Baby Lena is sleeping in a cane washing basket full of soft baby blankets. Bending down Franz smooths her soft blonde curls and I caress her hand, being very careful not to wake her.

Sitting at the kitchen table, I see Franz's knife lying on the scratched surface. He picks it up and sheaths it in its scabbard, as Monika serves the bread onto our plates.

"Thank you so much Madam!" Franz says appreciatively, as he tentatively picks up the hot, sizzling slice.

I just bob my head in agreement as I eat the bread with gusto, washing it down with sips of steaming black tea.

"I'm sorry about your window," Franz says apologetically.

Monika nods as she leans back against the sink and sips from a chipped cup.

There is a grating noise outside as if someone is dragging his feet on gravel. Through the broken glass I see a figure in a plaid shirt. Both Franz and I jump to our feet, ready to bolt.

Monika puts out a steady hand. "It's my brother ... It's Gunther. Today is Sunday, so he isn't in his uniform."

We both relax, breathing out pent up breaths.

Monika puts a kettle on the stove and takes down a tin mug from a cupboard.

Gunther inspects the gap in the window, then opens the door and limps in. After kissing his sister's cheek, he pulls a map out of his trouser pocket and lays it open on the table.

Monika quickly clears the plates and hands him a mug of tea.

"Have a look here," he suggests as he takes a sip of the scalding liquid.

We study the map as he points to a couple of towns.

"This is Völklingen and there is Prum," he taps his finger on the map. "I say you have about one hundred fifty kilometres to go. You will have to head north again along this road. I can get you a lift to Bitburg." We watch as he traces a line with his index finger. "It's about thirty-five kilometres to Prum from there. You'll have to find other transport for the rest of the journey."

Ah shit, we still have a long way to go.

I glance up at Franz and he seems to have the same thought.

A lot could happen between here and Prum.

Gunther straightens. "I can't give you this map, but I've sketched a couple for you."

He takes two small sheets of paper out of his shirt pocket and hands them to Franz. The sketched maps are very good with all the names of the villages and some of the minor roads.

On the second sheet, in great detail, are drawn the main

streets of Bitburg. We look at him in astonishment.

"I once lived in Bitburg, so I know it pretty well," he explains, smiling.

"Thank you, sir!" exclaims Franz. "These maps are excellent and will be very helpful."

Gunther grins his appreciation as Franz shakes his hand.

I also shake Gunther's hand while Franz crouches down and puts the maps into the rucksack along with the food parcels and gun.

Gunther folds up his map, putting it into his pocket, then leans on the table. His damaged leg is bent at the knee, suspended in the air for a short moment.

"A truck is waiting to be loaded with army supplies at the warehouse behind us," he says, grimacing. He lowers his damaged leg to the ground.

"The driver is a friend of mine and can be trusted. He will drop you two off before he drives into Bitburg to make his delivery. I'll take you to him now."

Monika stands at the backdoor, with the sleepy baby in her arms. We gently stroke Lena's head and thank Monika for her hospitality. Gunther waits at the bottom of the steps, gesturing to us to hurry. Quickly, we walk towards a gate in the fence and pass through its narrow opening, Gunther, his limp more pronounced this morning, leading the way.

We pass through a large iron gate leading to an old warehouse and move briskly to the side of the building.

Standing against the brick wall, I asked Gunther a question that's been playing on my mind.

"Why are the steel works still standing?"

He shrugs. "I've wondered about that myself and I don't

really know why. It could be the British have bad aim, but I doubt it. Maybe they want it still running for some reason. I know most of the workers are slave labourers. Perhaps that's why they haven't bombed it."

Furtively, Gunther looks around the corner of the building, then signals for us to follow him.

Leading us to a canvas covered truck that's just pulled up in the driveway, he tells us to get in the back. We quickly clamber aboard and settle amongst the first row of crates.

"Don't open any crates," Gunther warns in a hoarse whisper. "It could cause trouble for my friend. And don't get out of the truck until Neele tells you to! He is the driver! All the other trucks have already gone so you should be okay. Just keep your heads down!"

Peeking around a crate, we thank him for his help. He smiles, moves to the side door of the truck, and talks to the driver for a couple of minutes, then hobbles along the truck's side, hitting it a couple of times with the palm of his hand.

The driver revs the engine and reverses down the driveway.

I peer around the crates and watch Gunther limping back to his sister's house, stopping now and then to rub his injured leg.

As he mounts the back steps, he stops at the doorway and watches us disappear around the corner. I lean back against a crate and wonder how Gunther got his injury. It might have stopped him from being conscripted. I hope his little family survives and his beautiful niece grows up into a better world.

I hope we all do.

CHAPTER

34

Jolting and bouncing over the potholes keeps us awake. Sitting on a piece of folded canvas at the back of the truck, I huddle in my coat, wrapping the collar around my ears and covering my mouth to keep warm.

Franz dozes with his back against the driver's cab, his lips slack with exhaustion. I crawl to the tailgate and lift the tarp to watch the passing countryside.

Rays of sunlight dance over the dazzling snow, revealing a beautiful alien land. The livestock are gone. The farmhouses seem deserted. I look up towards the winter sun in the clear blue sky then back to the shimmering white fields surrounded by fir trees, dipping low in their snowy blanket.

My thoughts drift to the decorated Christmas trees at home placed behind shop fronts and bay-windows, twinkling in the winter gloom. I remember helping Jo and my sisters use paper decorations and coloured baubles to decorate a tall fir tree Pa cut from the forest. It stood near our front window.

Standing back to admire our work we watched Pa, wearing one of the girls' knitted beanies in red and green stripes, put a star on the very top as Ma laid out delicious food on the dining room table.

We pass a frozen lake, snow drifts spilling down its banks. It brings up memories of the civic park in Sochaczew next to the department store where Pa worked. The pond in the centre of the park freezes over every year creating a large ice rink.

How excited we were strapping on our wooden skates and venturing onto the ice, feeling the chill wind on our faces. Jo would madly skate around and around, showing off as usual, while Ma stood on the sidelines watching the girls learning to skate. They'd hold onto each other's arms, slipping and sliding, their free arms flailing about like a windmill.

I remember laughing, it looked so funny.

Ma would eventually skate out onto the ice and grab the girls' hands, guiding them around the rink.

I usually skated with my mates. Twisting and turning until one of us landed on our bum. This led to hysterical laughter, by us all, especially if the boy couldn't get up. Eventually one of us dragged the embarrassed lad to his feet, and we continued skating.

Smiling, I tie the canvas flap back with a rope and look up into the sky. My smile slowly fades as I think about my family. *Are they okay? Are Pa and Uncle Tomasz still in the army or were they captured by the Nazis, like I was? Are Jo and Helena still alive?*

I begin to pray for them. I pray for Ma, Zaneta, Angelika and Auntie to be safe; for Franz and me to finish this dangerous journey and find the Americans. And for the bloody war to end! I grip the top of the tailgate in frustration. Bloody Nazis! I watch the receding road for a long time. Lost in thought. Numb with cold.

Loud engine noises make me peer into the distance. A convoy of vehicles appears over the crest of the hill behind us.

Quickly, I drop and secure the flap and shake Franz awake. Bleary eyed and grumbling, he rubs his face as I whisper urgently, "Army trucks. Behind us."

Braking, Neele pulls over, allowing the convoy to pass.

A vehicle slows and stops.

Doors slam and a voice demands for Neele to get out and show his papers.

Terrified, I stare at Franz. He crawls to a couple of crates, gesturing to me to follow him. He wedges himself into a gap barely wide enough to squeeze through.

I back in on my ass and screw myself into a ball. Putting my head between my legs, I try not to breathe.

"What's in the crates?" demands a loud voice.

"They contain medical supplies for the hospitals at The Front," explains Neele.

"Open one. Now!"

The truck lurches. Someone has climbed into the back.

I hold my breath and keep very still. I sense Franz doing the same.

I hear one of the crates being prised open and the top torn off. There is rustle of straw and paper. Neele grunts as he pulls something out. The truck rocks as he jumps off the tailgate.

"Like I said, they all contain medical supplies."

"All these crates need to be inspected immediately," the officious German insists.

The truck sways as more men climb aboard and more crates are ripped open, the lids carelessly thrown onto the road.

The Germans work their way towards us as they rummage through the straw and tear open boxes. Crouching further down, I feel Franz tense.

From outside, the German officer suddenly shouts a command.

"Out! Out! We leave immediately!"

Franz and I cling onto the crate in front of us, as the soldiers leap from the truck, making it bounce and jump.

A truck revs its engine. Commands are shouted above the noise.

We sit still and silent for a few more minutes, listening till the German vehicles are out of hearing.

We sense Neele climbing in once more. He curses as he drags the crates along the truck floor, reordering his load.

Franz and I crawl out and stand facing the poor man. He sighs with frustration and asks us to help him with the crate lids. He takes out a hammer from a toolbox and nails a lid back on, while Franz and I jump down from the truck, picking up the rest.

"Why did they leave so abruptly?" I ask, handing him a lid.

"They got an order through their radio about an attack somewhere," he replies.

He shakes his head, "Christ we were lucky! I thought for certain they'd find you both and we would all be arrested!"

"I thought the same," I say, nervously raking my fingers through my hair.

Franz bends down and picks up two more lids, carrying them back to the truck.

He's silent for a long time.

After reassembling the crates, Neele pulls out a lunch pail from under his seat and offers us his salami sandwiches, saying he will keep the apple. Thanking him we sit back down out of sight in the truck and share the food. Franz reaches into the rucksack for the canteen. He takes a swig then offers it to me. "I've got a feeling we are going into dangerous territory," I claim, while wiping my mouth with the back of my hand.

Franz gulps down more water.

"I think the whole bloody journey so far has been bloody dangerous," he growls, shoving the canteen back into the rucksack. He seems upset or worried. Maybe both.

I begin to worry.

What if Franz is having second thoughts about finding the Americans? Perhaps he regrets ever teaming up with me in the first place.

I glance at him, noting his vacant stare and the firm set of his mouth. My heart sinks. He could easily leave me at the next town.

An hour passes.

Both of us remain silent.

The truck stops near the outskirts of the city.

"You can get out here! The army trucks have long gone, and it looks safe," reports Neele as he lowers the tailgate. "But be careful! Bitburg is full of German troops heading for the front."

We jump down onto a grassy verge, near a couple of oak trees, their trunks buried in snow drifts. I look towards the crossroads and see a sign saying Bitburg, pointing north.

Neele pats our shoulders.

"Be safe and I hope you find the Allies" he says in Polish.

We thank him then shake his hand.

He gets back into his cab and drives away. We move behind the trees and wait for night to fall.

Splitting an apple, we munch it down fast. Franz peels open the parcel given to us by Gunther. It contains a block of cheese, a pickle gherkin and a boiled sausage.

"We'll keep this for later," he mumbles, stuffing it back into the rucksack.

"Are you okay Franz?" I ask, unable to contain my worry any longer.

"Yeah... I'm okay," he grumbles, facing away from me. "I'm just worried about this whole trip. Wondering if we will make it."

"Are you having second thoughts on escaping with me?" I ask hesitantly. "I don't blame you if you do. I know I can be an idiot sometimes."

Astonished, Franz swings round to face me.

"Christ Rys, I've never thought of leaving you. We're in this together. We always have been. I will not, and could not, leave you. Don't you ever think that!"

I smile weakly.

"Sorry Franz. I thought you might want to part when we get to Bitburg."

"Never Rys, never!"

Grinning, he gives me a headlock.

I wiggle free, losing my cap in the snow. I pick it up and nervously fiddle with the brim.

"Franz, I know we'll find the Americans! We have too!" I try to sound reassuring, but my assertions lack conviction.

Franz pats my back. "I hope so, Rys. I really do."

We start to walk along the icy road, heading for the city, but hide in a ditch as another German army convoys heads our way.

"It looks like a big push to the Front," I whisper.

"I hope we can pass them unnoticed." murmurs Franz.

"I think we should find a hiding place soon and keep out of sight until it's late, then we'll try to get on the road to Prum. Hopefully without these German convoys."

We climb onto the road once again and continue our way north.

CHAPTER

35

Darting along the deserted streets, the cold biting into our faces, we enter a block of dilapidated warehouses looming in the darkness. We are both edgy, starting at every sound.

"Shit Franz, it's dark here. Anyone could be lurking about."

Franz is about to answer when he suddenly skitters to a stop in front of an old building, holding me back with his hand.

"Hold on! Hold on!" he whispers excitedly. "Have a look in there."

He points through a grimy window. By the light of the halfmoon I can just make out army trucks lined up in rows. Lots of them.

A mischievous grin lights up Franz's face, "I have an idea. Let's do a little sabotaging. Like in the old days!"

"Franz, that would be too dangerous," I hiss, fear and excitement vying for supremacy. "What if they're guarded?"

"The place is deserted. We'll keep an eye out for anyone lurking around. I need to do this, Rys. I need to fight back. Do something to stop these bastards!"

Finding a loose nail, he pulls it out with his knife, then picks the lock. He slowly slides the door open a fraction to reveal army trucks lined up in rows, then slides it further open. We slip inside and Franz eases the door shut.

"We're going to disable all of these trucks." Franz whispers.

"How?" I ask.

"We will take the distributor caps off and take out the rotor. The trucks won't be able to start without a rotor."

I stare at him, amazed.

"How do you know that?"

He makes an exasperated sound.

"Remember, I told you, I worked as a motor mechanic. I've disabled lots of trucks for the Resistance."

"Oh yeah, that's right!" I exclaim, as I recall the trucks, he dismantled in one of the Nazis' warehouses.

"Now let's get started," he whispers excitedly, patting my back.

He leans into the cab of a truck and pops the hood. I light Frau Schmidt's matches to light his work.

When all the trucks' hoods are up, we remove the distributor caps. Franz pries off the rotors with his knife, putting them in his pockets or handing them to me. I help him to clip the distributor caps back on.

"I have a question. Why are we bothering to do this?" I ask as I push the clips down.

Franz smirks.

"This is so the Germans have no idea why the engines won't start."

"It's going to take them ages to figure it out!" he chuckles.

The last match dies in my hand.

"Are we going to throw the rotors in a garbage bin outside?

"Yep," Franz replies as he picks up the rucksack.

I follow him onto the pavement, waiting as he relocks the door behind him.

At the side of the building, we empty our pockets into an old bin. I pat myself down, making sure I haven't missed any bits, and look around the dark, abandoned street. Franz covers the rotors with rubbish.

"Let's find shelter, fast," whispers Franz, his teeth chattering, "before we freeze to death."

I point to a building across the road.

"There's a basement window over there. I'll check it out."

Jogging over, I peer through the window, seeing a room full of old furniture covered in white sheets. I wave Franz over.

"It looks fine," I murmur.

Franz jemmies it open and we climb through.

As I pull the window shut, Franz takes the sheet off a cabinet and settles down against the wall, where we'll be least noticeable if anyone looks in. I join him, pulling the sheet over us.

Just before dawn there's a loud commotion outside. Creeping to the basement window, we squat down low, listening to every word. There is a lot of shouting.

"Shyster! The trucks won't start!" A door slams. "Colonel Fischer is going to have my guts for garters," growls a voice. "I don't understand. They were fine yesterday!"

"The cold weather could be the cause. Sometimes extreme cold plays havoc with the fuel lines," suggests another man.

Franz stands and peeks through the small window.

He ducks back down to my level, grinning from ear to ear.

"Two German sergeants are scratching their heads while the other drivers are running around like chooks with their heads cut off. I think they're in a lot of trouble. A German Colonel just drove up. He's swinging his arms over his head like a mad man."

I grin back.

Scurrying back to our corner we celebrate by sharing some of Gunther's food, washing it down with water from the canteen. As I'm taking another swig, the air-raid sirens scream their high-pitched wail outside the building. Startled, I drop the canteen, spilling the rest of the water over the floor. I cover my ears to block out the wailing.

Muffled shouts come from the Germans outside.

Our building shudders when the first bomb explodes. Dust falls all around us. Panicking, Franz scrambles to the window, trying to open it. I grab his arm, pulling him back, yelling at him over the pounding noise.

"It looks like the city is getting bombed. We can't leave yet! Besides, those bastards outside would see us."

Crouching down on the floor, we cover our heads as each explosion rocks the very foundations of the building. We could be trapped if the whole thing goes up, but it's too late to run.

I grip Franz's arm and bellow. "Shit, Franz, we could die here!"

"Ya reckon?" He shouts back. "But what can we do about it? Let's hope that Lady Luck is still with us!"

Bombs fall in rapid succession.

We dive under a sheet covering a table. Franz holds the backpack over his head. I'm crouched down low, covering my head.

The building above us makes a 'whomp' sound and seems to lift then fall. Chips of concrete cover the white sheets and tumble to the floor. A large piece of plasterboard ceiling falls onto the table, showering us with chalk dust.

There is a tremendous crash inside the building above us. I cringe, tightening my grip around my head as more explosions erupt. I wait for the ceiling to cave in.

Bang! Bang! Bang! Thump! Thump!

The noise stops.

I lift my head.

The air is still.

I let out one long pent-up breath and pull the sheet back.

The sirens end their wailing, their noise replaced by the clanging of fire engine bells.

Clambering towards the window, we break out the glass with the grip of the gun and push and pull ourselves out. We look around, amazed. The building that was above us has disintegrated into a pile of rubble.

"How was that for luck!" grins Franz.

I shake my head in wonder as people, frantically running past, knock us aside. The warehouse full of army trucks still stands amongst the ruins while every building around it has been destroyed.

"Bloody hell! Would you believe it?" exclaims Franz. "Everything is flattened except for that bloody warehouse. Christ, I'm glad we did our little sabotaging stunt. It's going to make the bastards' war effort a lot harder without those trucks, now that the war has turned against them!"

I grin at him, "There is no doubt about you, Franz. You're a lot brighter than you look!"

"I know," he says, returning my grin.

He turns and starts jogging down the road. I follow close behind.

Covered in dust, like most of the people around us, we take

advantage of our anonymity and run into a lane which leads into a wide street.

Dodging jeeps, trucks, and tanks, we manoeuvre a path through the scattered rubble and broken glass. We skid to a stop at a crossroad. Thick smoke billows all around us filling my mouth and nostrils, making it hard to breath. I spit on the ground, my eyes streaming with tears.

"Where are we Franz? I wheeze.

"How should I know," retorts Franz, wiping his stinging eyes. "We could be anywhere.".

He takes out the map and studies the pencil lines for roads out of Bitburg.

"Ah shit, I can't make head or tales of this!" he shouts against the chaotic noise. "We need to see a street sign!"

Scurrying across the road to a small roundabout, I peer up a street pole through the smoke.

"I think it says Kolner Street." I callout as I trot back to him. I take the map and trace a pencil line with my finger.

"Look, it's the main road. I can see it on the map here. If we follow it north, we will be going the right way!"

Pocketing the map, Franz and I run through the frenzied mob.

Many buildings are destroyed and many more are on fire.

Bodies are strewn along the road, with people tending to them, crying out in grief, or calling for help.

An overturned cart burns, a horse lying dead in the traces. Blood pumps onto the road from where its head is nearly severed from its neck. I look away from the sight, my gut churning.

We run around a wall reduced to ruins and slow down. A lot

of trucks and cars are turning into another street. "I think they know a better way out!" yells Franz, grabbing my arm.

Running full pelt, we race down the road, following the exodus.

CHAPTER

36

Panting, I slow to a stop.

Gasping. Gulping air, I put my hands on my knees.

I don't seem to have much energy anymore... How will I ever play soccer again?

"Help! ... Help! Someone, help me!" A voice screams out. "For god's sake, someone get me out. I'm stuck here! Help me!"

"Someone's in trouble," I wheeze, pushing myself upright. "A woman. We should help her."

"Not bloody likely!" snarls Franz as he continues up the road.

Hands on hips, he stops and looks back as I climb over a pile of broken bricks, covered in smouldering timbers, heading towards the desperate shouts.

I turn to face him.

"I can hear a woman shouting, Franz! There's a woman trapped somewhere!

What if she's like Frau Schmidt, a decent woman who deserves our help? I'm going to help her, with or without you."

Franz trots back to me, shaking his head.

"Okay. Okay Rys, but remember, you're not a fireman!"

We scramble over the remains of a large house until we come to a bedroom. Most of the furniture is destroyed except for a large wardrobe overturned in a corner, its doors facing the floor.

Angrily, the woman's voice calls out again as she bangs on the inside of the wardrobe, rocking it to and fro. I knock on one of the sides telling her we're here to help and to calm down.

Urgently, she cries out to hurry, and believing she is injured, we quickly clear a space, throwing bricks and plasterboard to the side. Finding a long piece of timber to use as a lever, we push and pull until the wardrobe wobbles into an upright position, allowing the doors to be flung open.

A half-dressed young woman tumbles out, the hem of her skirt riding up around her thighs, exposing the tops of her stockings. Her full breasts, barely covered, bounce up and down as she gasps for breath. Franz extends his hand, but she knocks it away.

"I can get up myself, thank you!" she says curtly, as she pulls herself up from the ground.

At first glance, the girl is very attractive with light blue eyes and a fair complexion. Her dishevelled blonde hair is pulled into a tight bun which she smooths back into place with her hands. But when I look closer, I see selfish arrogance in her eyes and a certain harshness to her pouting lips. Her prettiness is all on the surface.

Complaining in a whiney voice, she bends down to straighten her skirt.

"You took your time! Ooh," she glares at me, "look what you made me do. I've laddered a stocking!" showing us her thigh. A long ladder ran from above her knee to her ankle. "Have you no idea how expensive they are?"

Aghast, I look at her exposed leg.

Franz lifts an eyebrow and smirks.

She peers up, snarling, "Take your eyes off me!"

Franz sniggers. His eyes roaming over her body.

I obediently avert my eyes, staring at the charred beams above me.

While adjusting her slip under her skirt she grumbles, "I heard the bombs while I was getting dressed, I had nowhere to hide so I jumped into the wardrobe. The house was hit, making the stupid wardrobe topple over. I do not need an unstable wardrobe. I need one that can withstand a bomb blast and stay upright. I'm going to complain to my father and insist he gets me a better one."

"I wouldn't complain, Fraulein. I think that stupid wardrobe saved your life," says Franz, ignoring her nasty manners and forgetting his own as he stares at her breasts.

She has on a silky top with thin straps tucked into a tight-fitting skirt. She scowls at him and snatches her blouse from the wardrobe and puts it on, buttoning it quickly, but leaving a tantalising glimpse of her cleavage.

"I need to get to the Army barracks immediately. I am Kommandant Wagner's, secretary. He will need me. Go and stop a car to take me there."

Flinging her hand, she gestures towards the road.

"Go! Go!"

We don't move but keep staring at her.

Tucking her blouse into her skirt and reaching into the bottom of the wardrobe for the rest of her clothing, she allows her skirt to roll up once again to reveal her long legs.

I can't take my eyes off them. Franz whistles, which makes her quickly straighten up.

"How dare you!" she hisses, and slaps Franz on the cheek. He rubs his face, grinning.

"Well? What are you waiting for?" She shouts in a shrill voice, slipping on her shoes. "Get me a car! Now!"

Franz and I scramble back over the rubble, heading for the road.

She shrieks after us.

"Quickly! I need to reorganise the schedule for my father, for Kommandant Wagner!"

"We'll be quick." Franz answers back, but then murmurs to me, "Especially when we get back on the road and run like hell."

An army staff car, flying swastikas on its antennas, skids to a stop on the icy road, right in front of us, cutting off our escape. The stupid girl suddenly appears behind us as the driver rolls down the window and leans through it. She stumbles and grabs Franz's arm to steady herself.

"Are you alright Fraulein Wagner?" The driver calls, getting out to help her.

She still holds onto Franz's arm.

"I'm fine, Wolfgang, but I'm complaining to my father. You should have been here sooner."

Fraulein Wagner clutches us both by the arm. "You are to come back to the barracks. My father will have questions for you both, then I will arrange your transport."

"It's not necessary Fraulein!" I chime in, pulling my arm away, loosening her grip.

She grabs my arm tighter.

"No! No! No! I insist! Get in the car!"

The driver scrambles to open the door for her.

He gives Fraulein Wagner a smouldering look, his eyes travelling all over her body behind her back. She doesn't notice his sleazy smirk. She opens the back door of the car, gesturing for us to get in.

There is a holstered gun in Wolfgang's belt, his hand resting on top of it. I hesitate, but only for a moment. Our options are not good. If we bolt, the chances are he'll shoot one of us. I get in and slide across the seat.

Frowning, Franz stands on the sidewalk, his fists clenched.

Fraulein Wagner glares at him.

"What are you waiting for?" She snarls. "Get in!"

Franz plops down on the back seat and she slams the door. Fraulein Wagner slides into the front seat. The driver bangs her door shut, then runs around the front of the car. He dives behind the wheel and turns to face her, giving her a lecherous smile.

Wolfgang glances back at us.

"Have you picked up a couple of strays, Fraulein Wagner?"

"In a way," she replies. "They helped me out of the wardrobe I was trapped in. Now, get me back to the camp at once! Come on, step on it!"

Scared, I glance sideways at Franz. He stares straight ahead as the car skids on the ice, spinning the wheels.

We drive through a city in chaos. Buildings are still burning. The injured sit on the roadside in shock, or stumble aimlessly around.

Desperate men and women clamber over rubble, looking for survivors.

It reminds me of when the Germans bombed my street. It gives me savage satisfaction to see them finally getting a taste of their own medicine.

Fraulein Wagner seems oblivious to it all, speaking casually to the driver as if nothing has happened.

A crying child, blood running down its face, runs towards the car. Neither German seems to notice.

I lean forward and ask them, "Don't you think we should stop and help these people?"

She turns to look at me in utter amazement, as if she had just heard the most ludicrous suggestion. As if the child's plight means nothing.

"What? ... No! Of course not. I can't get my clothes dirty or even worse, covered in blood. I need to be presentable. My father, Kommandant Wagner, will need me straight away. I have a very important job in his office. Those people can fend for themselves! I have no time, or any inclination, to help them. I'm only taking you two back out of courtesy for getting me out of that faulty wardrobe."

I give her an incredulous look. She turns back to the front, calmly observing the chaos outside.

"I think we will win this war Wolfgang," Fraulein Wagner comments as she settles back into her seat. "The British have no idea about bombing cities. They've missed the Hospital and the Primary School. I heard my father say that our air force bombed London until it was razed to the ground. I expect their casualties would have been much higher than ours."

"Anyway," Fraulein Wagner adds "Only common working-class people live here. No big loss."

"Just so, Fraulein. Just so," agrees Wolfgang. "Here, let me brush those brick fragments off your jacket. They are making you look untidy."

His smarminess makes me feel ill.

He carefully removes each piece with his free hand as he steers the car with the other, sliding his hand down her arm. She seems totally unaware of his actions.

Franz glances at me, frowning.

After a moment of silence Franz leans forward.

"We live on the outskirts of town and need to check on our families. Could..."

Urgently, I finish his sentence. "Could you just drop us off here, please, at the end of this block?"

"Where did you both come from, anyway?" Fraulein Wagner snaps, suspicion now tingeing her imperious voice. She slowly turns right around, taking a proper look at us for the first time, checking our uniforms and examining our faces.

"What barracks are you stationed at? Who is your commanding officer?" she demands.

We remain silent.

Her eyes narrow.

"Who are you two? Answer me! Now!"

Wolfgang slams on the brakes, narrowly missing a woman running across the street with a baby in her arms. We all lurch forward.

People scatter as screams come from a burning building. The fire brigade has blocked the road up ahead. Flames reach ten metres up into the sky, engulfing more buildings.

In a panic, I shove open the car door, yelling in Polish for Franz to do the same. But I trip on the car's running board, ploughing into a fleeing man. He pushes me back. I tumble onto the pavement.

Before I can get up, Fraulein Wagner leaps out of the car.

She kicks me hard in the stomach as I struggle to rise.

With little muscle or fat and my thick army coat no barrier, I double up in agony.

Her face twists into a hideous mask. Spittle flies from her thinly stretched lips as she lays into me.

"You son of a bitch! You bastard!"

Kick.

I curl into a ball, covering my face.

She frantically searches the ground and grabs a fence paling. Wheeling it above her head with both hands, she slams it into my shoulders.

"You are...You are! From a camp!"

Wallop!

"I just know it! I can tell! You are a filthy Jew. You should be hanged!"

She clobbers my arms, hitting an elbow. The pain is excruciating as the wood hits the bone.

Desperately protecting my face, I try to crawl away.

"No! No! Not a Jew!" She snarls, swinging the plank once more.

"You are a filthy, escaped cabbage head. I saw it in your face! I will tell my father and he'll have you shot!"

Whack! Whack!

Under this intense assault, I writhe in pain, my body roaring in agony.

Gasping, I peer into the bitch's contorted face. Ugly with hatred, she is unrecognisable. She raises the plank again, her eyes protruding from their sockets. Her nostrils flare with malevolent loathing. Her skin turns a mottled red. Snarling, her mouth reveals the tip of her tongue flicking back and forth. She looks like a demon I once saw in a book of fairy tales. It scared me to death then, as this bitch scares me now.

I grab the wood before it clouts my skull.

I call out to Franz, but he's struggling with the driver in the car, grappling in the front seat for the gun. I'm on my own.

Wolfgang bursts out through the car door. Franz follows, landing a punch to the man's head, knocking him down. The German drops the gun. Hitting the ground, it fires, then skitters across the sidewalk as Franz pins Wolfgang down.

The bullet grazes Fraulein Wagner's leg, just above the knee. She screams and collapses on top of me. I yank the paling from her grip, hurling it into the air.

Shoving her off, I scramble for the gun, clutch the grip with both hands, and with a mixture of fear and power, turn back and aim it between the bitch and the sleaze.

"Get the rucksack, Franz!" I yell.

He reaches into the back seat of the car and pulls it out.

"Get up, you Nazi bastards! Back in the car! Drive! Or I'll shoot you both!" I roar.

I feel in control.

I feel I could end these bastards.

Franz moves behind me. His eyes wide.

Fraulein Wagner and her driver sit on the ground, staring in disbelief.

"Get up! Get in the car! Now!" I yell, waving the gun.

Squinting, I aim the gun above their heads and fire two bullets, hitting the car's door.

That gets them moving.

Wolfgang scrambles to his feet and pulls the bitch up, watching me warily. He urges her into her seat and slams the door. Fraulein Wagner yells obscenities through the closed window, winding it madly, trying to force it down. Wolfgang dives into the front seat and starts the engine. Wheels screeching, he makes a U-turn, accelerating away, the tires squealing.

I breathe deeply.

My hands begin to shake.

I lower the gun, putting the safety catch on.

Warily, Franz comes to my side.

"What the hell, Rys! Are you out of your bloody mind?" he hisses.

Shaking, I turn to face him.

"What?"

"First you get in that car, where we are exposed. Then you threaten them with a gun, shooting bloody bullets through their car door!" he yells back, angrily.

Why is Franz shouting at me? Did I do the wrong thing? I stare at him, wide-eyed. My mind is in a whirl.

"Should I have killed them?"

"No, no, no! Of course not," Franz says, his voice lowering, his anger dissipating.

"It's just... Rys, what the bloody hell were you thinking?"

"We had to get into that car, Franz! Don't you see? If we didn't, the driver would have smelt a rat and started shooting before asking questions. He was just as crazy as that evil bitch."

I grit my teeth, looking back to where the car turned the corner.

"I really wanted to shoot them dead!" I seethe.

Franz grips my arm and I stare into his eyes. He looks worried. I calm down and draw a steadying breath.

"Only, I'm not a cold-blooded murderer, or a maniac." I try to reassure him. "Not like those two, and all the other damned Nazis who've killed our friends and destroyed our country."

Franz slowly nods his head, appreciating my point. I watch him grip my hand holding the gun.

"Give me it to me, Rys," he says softly. "Give me the gun."

I release my fingers slowly, as Franz takes the Luger and places it carefully in the rucksack.

"Now. Let's get out of this bloody town," he says calmly, "before all hell breaks loose and 'Daddy' comes looking for us."

37

Avoiding the main street with its proliferation of German army vehicles, we hide in deserted back alleys, trying not to get lost. It takes most of the day to reach the outskirts of town.

Franz pulls out the map and studies it. "Almost clear of '*Bitchburg*'. We need to find shelter."

I snigger at his joke.

His lips twitch as he quickly folds the map and puts it in his pocket.

"You're right, Franz. I think it's best to lie low and rest until it all settles down," I suggest, sobering up quickly. "It'll be safer travelling at night till we're well clear of dear old Bitchburg."

In a darkened alleyway full of rubbish, we hide behind a couple of large oil drums. Squatting down to rest, our backs leaning against a wall, I pull my coat over my ears, trying to drown out the screeching of tank track-plates on the concrete road. The noise seems never ending.

Franz peeks around the drum and whispers, "There are a lot of tanks moving out of town and a lot of soldiers on the street searching buildings."

Still squatting on his haunches, he looks around, then points to a door at the end of the lane. We creep up to it and I try the handle. The door scrapes back on the stone floor and we scurry inside to find the cluttered room dark and dank. It's full of car parts and old tires, like a garage, which explains the oil drums outside.

We move slowly around the room, trying not to knock anything over. Engine parts are strewn over the floor and clutter the benches. Everything is layered with grease and grime.

Franz grunts, "Bloody untidy workshop. My boss would tan my hide if I left the shop like this."

Booted footsteps crunch on the debris outside. We can hear a couple of men talking.

Franz drags me into a broom closet and secures the door. As we stand behind mops and buckets, he takes out the guns from the rucksack and hands me one.

"Get it ready to fire Rys. We can at least shoot the bastards before they shoot us."

With trembling fingers, I release the safety catch. I hear someone entering the garage.

"Christ Otto, that Fraulein Wagner is a right bitch!" says a voice.

"She has us all running around like chickens with their heads cut off, over a couple of escaped POWs. I mean, what the hell! We have more important things to do than be at her beck and call!"

Another voice pipes up.

"You should have seen Kommandant Wagner. He was bloody mad. I've never seen him go purple before. Oh! I take that back! He went purple when we caught that British officer who spat in his face. The poor bastard was tortured for days. I can still hear the screams." There's a thump and a crash of tools. "Anyway, I thought Wagner was going to have a bloody heart attack."

I jump when a couple of crates slam to the floor, close to where we're hiding. Sweat beads on my forehead. My hands gripping my gun are damp. Franz stiffens and points the Luger at the wooden door panelling.

"I agree with you, Leon!" continues the second voice as a body leans on the broom closet. "This is a bloody wild goose chase! We have better things to do than dig around empty buildings, looking for Polaks who'll be long gone if they've got any sense."

Cigarette smoke drifts into the closet. Franz carefully rests the muzzle of the gun against the door.

The wood creaks as the body lifts off. "Let's get out of here. I've got to be at the Der Gasthof Inn by nightfall to meet a sweet fraulein, who has pretty green eyes and a body to match. I don't want to be late."

The other soldier grunts in reply as they give the room a cursory search. I hear bins being overturned and things being kicked around.

Then the room is quiet. The only sound is our own heavy breathing.

After a few minutes, Franz opens the closet door and scans the room. He jogs to the open doorway and peeks outside, moving back quickly.

"It seems okay," he whispers, gesturing with his hand to hurry.

I dart towards him, jumping over the mess strewn on the floor.

Outside is now dark and quiet with long shadows lining the abandoned street. We leave the building and briskly walk along the road. A black car drives around a corner and slowly idles next to us, making us walk faster.

A gravelly voice calls out. "Hey! Boys!" The driver calls through the open widow. "Can I give you two a lift?"

We turn to face him.

Looking like a banker, a middle-aged man in an expensive suit, leans across the passenger's seat.

I hesitate, looking left and right, but, unfazed, Franz says calmly, "How far are you going?"

"Out of the city, up to my villa further to the north," the man replies.

"We're heading north as well," Franz says with a smile.

The man smiles back.

"Well, jump in lads."

We hop in the back. In case we need to escape in a hurry, I make sure the car door is unlocked.

"Are you stationed at the barracks? Was it damaged at all?" he asks.

Franz leans forward. "It's a miracle it's still standing! The canteen blew up as well as a storage shed. We got leave to visit our families to see if they are alright and will head back tomorrow." As an afterthought he adds, "We are very grateful for the lift."

The man nods, appreciating Franz's deferential manners.

"Are you going to the Front?" he asks.

"Yes of course, we will fight for our Fatherland and for the Fuhrer!" Franz answers so assertively I almost expect him to add 'Heil Hitler!'

He's taking a gamble that this man is a Nazi, unlike the truck driver.

The man glances over his shoulder. "Good, good. We will win this war and show the world we are truly the superior race!"

The arrogant pig!

I grimace, peering out the car window at the passing countryside.

After fifteen minutes of him giving us the rundown about the war and his beloved Fuhrer, I can't stand it any longer.

He drives through a small village where a few houses look occupied. Slivers of light peep through the blackout curtains, but a couple of houses look deserted. It looks like a good place to hide.

"This is our home," I say, and reach for the door handle.

As we jump out, he winds the car window down and thrusts his arm through the opening.

"Heil Hitler!" he bellows.

"Heil Hitler!" Franz and I cry as one, throwing up our hands in unison.

"Nazi pig," I snarl, watching him drive away and turn the corner.

Franz smirks, then pulls my arm to move me on.

We creep around a couple of houses, dodging those looking inhabited and spot an old cottage at the end of the street which looks unoccupied.

A shed out the back has its doors wide open, and in the failing light we spot two lady's bikes, covered in snow, propped against the doorframe.

The old cottage is made of river stone with a decaying thatch roof and small glass windows facing the overgrown front yard. Franz tries the back door, finds it unlocked, unsheathes his knife and ventures inside. After a few moments he steps into the doorway.

"It's okay, Rys. No one is here."

I quickly climb the steps, closing the door behind me.

We search the kitchen for food, finding two tins of sauerkraut in the dark recesses of a cupboard then plates and spoons in a drawer. Franz opens one of the cans with his knife.

"We'll have the other one in the morning," he tells me when I cast a hungry look at the second can. He shares the cabbage out very evenly.

We sit on the floor to eat instead of the kitchen table.

After our meagre meal I lean against the cupboard, exhausted. I tentatively touch the bruises forming along my ribs and close my eyes.

The day has been taxing.

"Shit Franz, thank God we found these uniforms." I say in a hushed tone.

Franz leans back, placing his plate on the floor next to mine.

"I know. We've been so bloody lucky. But rescuing Fraulein 'Stocking Tops' could have been disastrous. We might have been caught and shot or sent back to the camp. I don't know which would have been worse."

"Don't worry Franz. I won't be rescuing any more crazy dames. They can find their own way out of overturned bloody wardrobes."

I look up at the ceiling.

"Did you see her face when we first met?"

"Who? Oh, you mean 'Stocking Tops'. No, I had my eyes on other places," Franz sniggers, folding his arms.

I smile weakly . Normally I would have joked with Franz

about the girl's semi-nakedness but I'm not in the mood. I think aiming the gun at the two Nazis then firing it into the car affected me somehow.

"She is a cruel bitch!" I snarl. "She and that sleazy bastard, Wolfgang. They didn't care what was happening around them. The bombing of their city or the people dying. The selfish bastards didn't stop to help anyone! It was as they didn't *see*! As if it was just a normal day for them."

My voice becomes louder. Franz hisses, elbowing me and I drop my voice to a hoarse whisper. "I'll tell you what this world will be like if the Nazis, like that bitch, and the bloody bank manager, have control of it! It will be a world deprived of human decency. A world where you're allowed to commit murder every day! And torture innocent people whenever you like! A world of slaves. Where no one will care if you live or die. Did you notice, Franz? No-one came to their aid. Not one person! It was as if they were invisible. As if *we* were invisible! I don't understand them Franz. I just don't understand these people."

I turn to look at Franz and can just make out his profile by the light of the rising moon.

He's staring into space, then looks fixedly at my face for a long moment.

He pats my arm. "I've never understood them either, Rys. But it's only human to do nothing. It's called self-preservation. Shit, I did the same thing back at the camp. I let that German bastard point a gun at your head!"

"That was different Franz."

"No, it wasn't. I was bloody scared for you, Rys. But I was more scared of getting shot if I interfered."

I grunt, then look through the window at the moon in the sky with its silvery beams piercing the tattered curtains and dancing along the ceiling. I'm quiet for a long time gathering my thoughts.

"I really wanted to shoot to kill. I really did," I murmur through a hiss. "I wanted to kill them for all my dead friends. For the Jews and the Russians in the camp. For Helena and her family. For Pa and Jo, and especially for Poland! ... Kapo was wrong. The German people know about the camps and what's going on. The stench of burning bodies travels for kilometres. They must have noticed thousands of people going in and not many coming out.

They can't all be bloody stupid. How is it going to look for them when the rest of the world finds out about the killing of thousands of innocent people? They will never be forgiven. Never!"

Franz puts his arm around my neck and gently squeezes.

"Rys, don't be too hard on the German people. It's in our human nature to be that way. If you look back in history the Ancient Romans slaughtered and crucified thousands and took thousands more as slaves. Genghis Khan invaded Asia and showed no mercy to the people who didn't 'bend the knee' to him. Even Napoleon, who had good intentions at the beginning of his reign, became power hungry, made stupid mistakes, and let his troops freeze in Russia. The Russian Czars didn't care about their people either, and in the future, nor will the Communists. The French Revolution was caused by much of the population starving and the aristocrats not giving a damn. The Americans slaughtered the American Red Indians nearly to extinction to take their land and build a railway. They enslaved black Africans to work their land and grow their cotton and sugar cane, causing a lot of suffering so they could become wealthy, respectable men in their society. The white colonials in Australia did the same. Tasmania's Aboriginal tribes were practically wiped out and the South Sea Islanders were enslaved to work the cane fields. The human race will always take what doesn't belong to them, like the Germans are doing now.

Did you know it was the British in the African Boer war who created the first concentration camp?" he asks.

I shake my head.

"Wars, massacres, murder, torture, starvation, suffering and killing the innocent have been going on from the beginning of time," he adds. "Even cavemen fought against other tribes, taking prisoners as slaves or in some cases eating them.

So, you see, Rys, the Germans are just normal human beings with human faults like the rest of us. I'm not saying the Nazis aren't evil bastards. They are. But they believe they are on the side of the right and will make the world a better place, under the leadership of their beloved Fuhrer."

He pulls out the canteen from the rucksack and takes a swig, then hands it to me.

"It's normal for humans to hate, persecute and be cruel to each other, especially in a war," he continues as he leans his head against the cupboard. "I once read a Latin proverb, 'Homo Homini Lupus.' It means 'Man is wolf to man'. I believe the Nazis are wolves at this moment in time. Cruel, predatory, and inhuman. And there is a high probability, as history has shown, that in the future another country will make the same mistakes the Germans are making right now. Allowing a crazy sociopath to rule them, creating chaos and death because of their leader's insanity."

He begins to pull himself up from the floor.

"Now, let's see the condition of those two bikes!"

I pull him back down.

"Can I ask you a question first?"

"What?"

"How come you know all this stuff?"

"I read a lot of books. My home was freezing in winter, and I used to go to the library a lot. It was warmer there. I would read books about all kinds of things, but I like history the most."

He stands and walks outside into the freezing night. I get up wearily to follow him and at the doorway notice Franz scooping the snow away to examine the tyres. He looks up.

"Rys, come and have a look! I think these bikes are still usable."

At a sudden commotion, Franz, cursing under his breath, slowly stands. Frowning I turn towards the noise.

38

Engines roar, shattering the still, cold air. Trucks are on the move.

Franz sticks his head around the corner of the cottage.

"We need to be careful," I whisper behind his shoulder. "Should we find another house?"

Franz backs away from the corner.

"No, I think we'll be safe," he murmurs. "The Germans are further up the road. Heading out of town. They must be rushing troops forward to the Front. We'll stay the night and head towards Prum in the morning. It's too dark to ride at night, anyway."

Crouching low, we watch as German army tanks and trucks, followed by German officers in jeeps, drive through the crossroads two doors up. The convoy turns left onto a main road.

Waiting a few more minutes, until the noise of the trucks fades away, we trot back to the shed to continue examining the bikes.

I find a shovel leaning against the wall and start to dig them out of the snow drift. They seem to be okay. Their chains are still intact.

"This one has a basket screwed on the front with a dog lead

tied to it," Franz says, examining one of the bikes, "but it has a flat tyre. I'll look in the shed for a pump."

I reach for the other bike. "Mine has a carrier rack on the back," I say in a hoarse whisper as Franz searches the back of the shed. "If we find anything else that is useful it will be easier to carry."

Finding a pump on the bench along the back wall, he pumps up the flat tire, then walks his bike up the path for a test run. I follow with my bike skipping over the ice.

We adjust the seats and push off onto the road. Mounting my bike, I press down on the pedals. And hit a pothole filled with sludge. The bike bucks, swivelling the front wheel to the side. I fall onto my ass. Brushing myself off, I mount the bike again but keep driving into the hidden holes.

"Christ this is hopeless. Let's go back!" I grunt, after slamming back down on the seat once more.

Franz hits a big pothole, staggers, and falls off sidewards.

"Shit!" he snarls as he pulls himself off the road and lifts up the bike. "We're going to break the bikes or worse, injure ourselves! You're right. Let's go back to the house and rest till morning. We'll make an early start. As soon as there's light enough to see these bloody potholes."

Bringing the bikes into the kitchen for the night just in case someone else decides to borrow them or it snows overnight and buries them once more, we wander upstairs to find beds. A double bed, bare of all coverings, is the only bed in the house, so we sleep head to toe as if we were back in the camp.

Waking up to daylight shining into my eyes, I peer down at Franz. Snoring, his head is nestled in his arm.

I wander into the kitchen to see if I can find more food. The bikes are propped against the cupboard where we left them. I examine them closely. Boy! Franz is in for a big surprise. Mine is painted yellow, just like Helena's, which is not so bad, but Franz's is pink with half a dozen blue and red ribbons threaded through the cane basket, and a green dog lead dangling from the frame.

I chuckle at the thought of Franz's reaction to such femininity.

Just then, he stumbles bleary-eyed into the kitchen and swears when he notices the pink bike.

"Looks like you'll have to put up with the ribbons Franz!" I snicker.

"Not bloody likely!" he growls, pulling them out and throwing them on the floor. He unsheathes his knife and slices the dog lead, throwing it on the kitchen bench.

"At least my bike isn't yellow," he laughs. "Looks like you'll have to put up with the pretty, sunshine-colour, Rys!"

I smile back at him, not bothering to comment. Little does he know I like yellow. It was Helena's favourite.

Franz opens the second tin of sauerkraut, dishes it out and we bolt it down. He stands at the sink and fills up the canteen and our mugs, passing one to me. Thirstily, I drink the freezing water as Franz lets out a ripper of a fart, making us both laugh.

He belches, wheezing out an apology. "Ah, sorry Rys. Sauerkraut always gives me wind! Good roughage though."

Franz gulps down his second mug of icy water and releases another loud fart.

The air around us is rank.

I bolt for the open door gulping in fresh air.

"You smell like something dead!" I grumble.

Franz sniggers as we look for more food. Finding none, we wash our faces instead.

"Let's get going," he says as he slings the rucksack on his back, deciding not to use the basket in case it falls out.

Wheeling the bikes outside, we venture onto the road. Dodging the potholes, now clearly visible, we set off on our bikes.

Franz pedals behind me.

"You look so sweet on that yellow bike, Rys!" he teases.

Glancing back at him, I smirk. "You look like Zaneta riding to the shops!"

Both of us grin, then burst out laughing. The bikes sure beat walking.

We ride for an hour, then stop at a farm gate to drink from the canteen. Between gulps, Franz belches loudly.

"So far, so good," he says when he's recovered. "At this rate we'll get to Prum in a day or two."

"I don't think the sauerkraut agreed with you," I exclaim. "I've never known you to be so full of wind!"

"Christ, I agree," he rasps and belches again. "I've always hated anything ending in kraut!"

I snicker, then look past him to the road ahead.

"Looks like a big hill ahead! We'll have to pedal fast for a run up!"

Franz jumps on his bike and swivels around to face me.

"Let's have a race!"

I jump on and level my bike beside his.

Both of us steadily pick up speed.

Standing up and pedalling like mad, I race past Franz and fly down the other side of a steep hill. I suddenly realise I have no brakes. I plant my feet firmly on the ground, only for them to skid and scrape over the gravel without gaining traction. I can't slow down. I'm going too fast. Hastily, I lift my feet up and belt down the road with my head down, my bum up, hoping for the best.

I hiss as my cap flies off. The freezing air whips over my head. I close my eyes as I hit a bump in the road. Catapulting over the handlebars, I land on my ass as the bike wobbles and slams into my back.

Franz rides up, laughing. "Oh Christ, Rys! Are you alright?"

I grunt and push myself unsteadily to my feet, then pick up the bike to examine the damage. The front wheel has a couple of broken spokes and a flat tyre. It's a total wreck.

"Unscrew the carrier and you can ride with me on the back," Franz says, still laughing.

It takes me a minute or so to get my breath back and examine myself for injuries. Fortunately, I've suffered nothing worse than a few bruises and mild gravel rashes, although the knee of my trousers is torn. Using the knife, I unscrew the carrier and attach it to the pink bike.

Meanwhile, Franz retrieves my cap and jams it on my head. He gets back on the seat, balancing with both feet, as I straddle the carrier with the rucksack on my back.

Franz pushes down hard on the pedals, then zigzags over the road until we both find our balance.

As we ride along the road into a forest, I hear the growling of a truck engine and the revving of gears behind us.

"Shit! Shit! We need to get into the trees!" I yell.

Franz quickly glances over his shoulder.

"Get off Rys! We'll make a run for it!"

Dumping the bike in the undergrowth, we bolt under the branches and scoot down into a wide ditch. Lying on the bottom, we frantically cover ourselves in fresh snow. I take a chance and peep over the top, spotting a large convoy of army trucks, towing heavy artillery. The guns are followed by German troop carriers. I pull Franz's sleeve and he slowly rises to take a look.

The last truck has gone. We are about to crawl out of the ditch when a jeep suddenly pulls up ten metres down the road. We duck back into hiding. An officer climbs out and slips behind the nearest tree. He fiddles with his fly, then pisses against the bark, staining the snow yellow at his feet.

Hearing a low growl behind us, we slowly turn our heads. A large grey wolf trots to the edge of the ditch, sniffing. I cringe, pulling my head further down. The wolf looks up and snarls as he spots the Kraut. Tilting its head back, it howls an ungodly sound, sending a chill down my spine.

Startled, the officer pulls out his gun, taking a couple of pot shots. His bullets whizz above our heads, making us hunch even lower. The wolf flattens to the ground, spoiling the German's aim. I peer up and the canine's snout is very close to mine.

It sniffs again. I pull back in shock and watch in amazement as it bounds over the ditch, in one gigantic leap, landing steadily on its paws.

It charges towards the Kraut, who scrambles behind the tree for cover. But the wolf grabs his lower leg and trips him face down into the snow.

The crazed animal savagely shakes its head from side to side until the Kraut's boot flies off. Snarling between clenched teeth and spraying saliva in a wide arc, the wolf is distracted from its prey. The screaming man desperately clambers on all fours to the jeep. As he leaps up, diving into the back seat, the vehicle takes off, slipping and sliding along the icy road.

The wolf leaps into the middle of the road. It runs a few steps after the jeep, then gives up, flinging the boot at the retreating vehicle. It howls again. Long and loud.

Shots are fired from another German truck. The wolf turns and bolts in our direction.

It leaps over the ditch once again, skidding to a stop, metres away, where it's sheltered from the Germans' view. It swivels around to face us. Holding our breaths, we both face it as it calmly moves to the edge of the ditch, peering down with its brilliant yellow eyes. Shaking its coat, it sets snowflakes spinning in the air and swirling around our heads. It quietly sits on its haunches as I quake in fear, waiting for it to pounce.

The animal is magnificent. Its grey coat is thick and sleek, shimmering in the dappled winter sunlight. A loud rumbling of approaching tanks makes the animal prick its ears forward. It rises quickly, sniffing the air. It turns, leaping into the undergrowth, disappearing amongst the branches.

We sit in the ditch until the tanks are well ahead and the wolf long gone. Marvelling at what just happened, we climb out and look around, brushing snow off our clothes.

"That… that was… bloody amazing!" I stutter. "I've never seen such a beautiful creature. Did you see what it did? It just stared down at us but didn't attack!"

Franz stares at the undergrowth, his eyes wide with astonishment. "I know! I know! I thought we were his next meal. He was incredible!" He looked at me, smiling, "I believe he was an omen, Rys. A true omen. He reminds me of the Latin proverb I quoted in the cottage, *Homo Homini Lupus* - Man is wolf to man."

"What do you mean by omen?"

"It means the German bastards will be defeated," says Franz, dusting off the snow from his cap.

"I didn't know you believed in omens, Franz?" I laugh, swiping the snow off my shoulders.

"I do now." says Franz, pulling his cap firmly over his ears.

"And how do you know that wolf was a *'he'*?" I query.

Franz answers with a sly grin. "I looked up when he jumped over us."

I burst out laughing again. "You would!"

We retrieve the bike and continue our journey, stopping every few kilometres so I can flex my legs, rub my ass, and relieve Franz for a bit.

As twilight drifts into night, we park under a fir tree, its branches laden with snow, and eat the last of the sausage and cheese.

Beside the trunk we dig a snow cave and crawl in. Lying close together, back-to-back to keep warm, we talk about the wolf and the fleeing Kraut. Laughing at the way he screamed and dove into the jeep.

The next morning Franz pushes the bike back onto the road as I shoulder the backpack.

For over an hour we take turns peddling and straddling the carrier, until we reach the base of a large hill. We get off to push the bike up the steep slope and stop at the top to look at the scene below us.

Nestled in the valley is a town showing signs of recent

bombing. Brilliant sunshine reflects off the remaining rooftops and melting ice glints on the streets. Distant artillery fire can be heard to the North. Another long German army convoy on the main road is heading towards the sounds of battle.

The bike has a flat, the same tyre Franz pumped up. He pushes it to the edge of a steep incline and we both salute in homage as it skitters away, landing on its side then sliding over the sheer bluff into the trees below. Franz takes out Gunther's map and studies it. I look over his shoulder.

"Prum," he announces, looking back down at the town. I slap his back and start to walk down the hill.

CHAPTER

39

Burnt out tree stumps line the sides of potholed streets with the occasional bomb crater. We trot along the roads, dodging collapsed brick walls and fallen power lines.

A few of the bombed houses still have front gardens intact. Small spears of green push through where snow has started to thaw. Now and then a swallow flutters to the ground and pecks between the shoots.

Franz and I skirt the valley floor using narrow side roads. We move cautiously between houses, peeping around the corners before venturing on. Scuttling behind a church, we catch sight of men working on the road, clearing away rubble. They are watched over by a German guard. Making a wide detour, we cross the northern outskirts of the town and emerge onto a main road.

Skirting a corner, a school comes into view. Its large iron gates are open to a sweeping driveway lined with fir and oak trees.

Two men squat near the front entrance of a large school building, stirring a pot over a small fire. Stomachs growling, our pace slows.

"I'm bloody hungry!" mutters Franz as he comes to a stop.

"Let's see if these two will share their meal."

Standing in front of the crouching men, I notice each is wearing a filthy woollen coat over a tattered Russian air force uniform. They look up. One man keeps stirring the pot, the aroma from which makes our mouths water. The other man rises to his feet. He towers over Franz and me.

I gaze up, my mouth agape. He is huge. Thick-bodied and muscular, his shirt straining at the seams, he stands over six feet tall. His dark hair, cropped short under a dirty Russian air force cap, frames an angular face hidden behind a thick black beard. From beneath thick, dark brows, slanting dark eyes indicating Mongolian ancestry, peer at us menacingly.

Aghast at his threatening size and his unusual appearance, I stumble back. Regaining my footing, I step forward and ask politely, "Excuse me sir, is it possible we can have some soup. We are hungry and have come a long way?"

With a very strong Russian accent the big man shouts in broken German, "Get lost ... You are Krauts. Go now. Before I thump you both!"

"No! ... No! We are Polish... Polak... You understand?" I articulate slowly, pointing to Franz and myself. "Polak," I repeat.

"You are Kraut, you have on uniform of Kraut, and so you are Kraut!" he bellows.

"Christ man, we are Polish!" Franz yells back in Polish.

I change to Polish also. "Yes. Yes, we are Polish! We come from Poland!"

He glares, refusing to believe us.

"No! You are Kraut! Piss off! Before I thump you silly!"

"We are not German, you Russian moron!" Franz shouts back in German.

The big man must have recognised the word moron because he suddenly charges, knocking Franz down with a whoomph. Franz slides about ten metres along the ground and lands under a tree. Bouncing up quickly, Franz takes a running jump and head butts the Russian in the belly. The man grunts and stumbles back, still on his feet.

Franz staggers, shaking his head, twisting it from side to side.

The big Russian grins at Franz and charges again. I leap onto his back, wrapping my legs around him and smacking both his ears with the palms of my hands. He bellows with rage, throwing me off with one hand and rubbing one of his ears with the other.

I land on the other Russian who is rising to his feet. He slips on the icy ground, landing on his ass, accidently kicking the soup pot over. Hot broth and vegetables spill onto the fire, which hisses and billows smoke, then goes out.

The smaller man leaps up in a fury and gives me a kick to the stomach, winding me. But when he tries again, I manage to grab the back of his knee and squeeze the soft flesh behind it. He makes a weird throaty noise and falls on top of me.

I kick him off and slowly stand to face him. He is black haired and bearded like the bigger Russian, but his face is less angular, and his beard is not as bushy. His eyes are a different colour, too. A steely blue. He stands to face me, and we circle each other, looking for an opening.

He has the advantage as he's at least a foot taller than me, but I'm quicker and easily dodge his lunges.

As I'm circling slowly, I glance at Franz to see him straddling the back of the big Russian, tightly gripping the back of his shirt collar inside his coat and screwing it into his fist. The man roars, trying desperately to get Franz off by twisting and turning his big frame and bringing his huge hands above his head to get a grip of Franz's head.

Franz clings on for dear life, wrapping his legs tight around the man as he throttles him.

Yanking the door open at the entrance to the school building, another man runs up to Franz grabbing him by the back of his coat. He pulls him off the Russian and drags him along the ground, like a sack of potatoes, towards me.

The man grabs the back of my collar and roughly pulls me onto my toes, yelling in German, "What the hell is going on here?"

We stop struggling and go very still. This man has a firm grip on both of us.

The two Russians stride towards him.

"They are Krauts, they wear Kraut soldier clothes," the large Russian gasps, gulping in air and tugging at his collar.

He changes to Russian and quickly speaks to the man again, pointing at us.

"We're not German! We are Polish!" I shout, frustrated.

I wriggle frantically out of the man's grip and run to the rucksack which has upended beside the driveway. I dig in, tearing the lining. The two guns fall out onto the snow.

Shit ... Shit! We are screwed!

The new arrival darts over and snatches both guns from the ground.

"Bloody hell!" he yells as he points them downwards.

"Please sir... Please sir! We are Polish prisoners of war," I beg. "We escaped from a camp and stole the guns from

Germans we met on our journey. Here are our identity cards. Please look at them!"

I pass the ID cards to him. He pushes the guns into his belt, and inspects both cards, looking up now and then to study our faces.

"Is your name really Muszynski?" he asks, confusing me.

"Yes. Why do you ask?"

He doesn't answer.

"Mm... Alright," he mutters to himself. "Both of you. Follow me."

He hands back our papers. Franz stuffs them in the rucksack and swings the bag over his shoulder.

"No bloody way! We're going nowhere!" he shouts, backing away. I get ready to run.

The man pulls out a gun from his belt, pointing it at our chests.

"Yes, bloody way," he growls, waving the gun towards the front doors. "Inside!"

"Where are we going?" I ask as we reluctantly climb the stone steps.

He doesn't reply, only aims the gun at our backs as the two Russians begin to rebuild the fire and scrape the soup vegetables off the snow.

The man marches us through the front doors and into a school room. Desks and chairs are still lined up in rows. A mathematics lesson is written on a blackboard. Papers are strewn all over the teacher's desk. An overturned inkpot lies on its side. The ink, long dried, spreads a dark patch across the wooden surface.

Franz and I step into the middle of the room, turning to face our captor. He is tall, with a thin, wiry frame and slightly stooped shoulders.

I notice swarthy skin, a high forehead and pronounced cheekbones. His thick, grey-streaked brown hair and scruffy beard are cropped short. I guess he's aged between thirty and forty, but it's hard to tell these days. He isn't wearing a Russian uniform like the others, but civilian clothes. Grey pants, worn at the knees, and a matching grey overcoat a size too big.

He must be strong to pull Franz off the back of the Russian. Franz is tough, and it would have taken considerable strength to overpower him.

He looks hard at me, his grey eyes studying my face.

Apparently satisfied, he lowers the gun.

"Stay in this room for the rest of the day, until I come back. I won't be long, I promise you. Now, I am going to lock the door."

"What! No! No!" I plead. "Please sir! Don't do that!"

"Calm down! You will not be sent back to the camps, and I certainly will not be telling the Krauts. I am not a German. I am Russian and lived in Germany for fifteen years. Kaminski is my name. I lead a work party here to clean up and fix the roads. We're also prisoners of war. As I said I won't be long, but you both need to stay in this room. I promise you both, I will not bring the guards. You will not be harmed. Please trust me."

He turns to Franz. "Give me your knife."

Franz reluctantly unsheathes it with the handle facing Kaminski, who takes it and threads it onto his belt.

Having no choice but to stay in the room and wait, we sit on the desks as he shuts and locks the door.

"We are so screwed," mumbles Franz. "You know, I thought we would make it. I really did. It just seems so bloody unfair, coming all this way only to be nabbed so close to freedom! Life can really be a bastard! That's a lesson I learnt a long time ago."

I slip into a chair behind a desk and rest my cheek on my hand. "I just can't believe it... I just can't!" I murmur. "We will die here! I know it! I don't believe Kaminski. He'll probably tell the Germans about us for food or grog. We should have shot those two Russians and stolen the soup!"

"Ah Rys, you told me once you're not a murderer and I'm certainly not one either, unless it's in self-defence. Maybe Kaminski is genuine. Let's see what happens in the next few hours. Then we'll make an escape plan!"

Franz sits down beside me and pats my shoulder, offering silent comfort.

Sitting for a long time, we wait for the return of the man in the grey overcoat.

CHAPTER

40

I'm exhausted. I doze as Franz prowls around testing all the windows. But they are nailed shut. He soon gives up, picks up a book and starts to read, reclining on the teacher's chair.

The smaller Russian comes to the door, opens it slightly and slides two bowls of soup, spoons and two slices of bread on a tin plate, along the wooden floor.

We scramble to our feet and pepper him with questions.

"Why are we being kept here?"

"When will we be released?"

"When is Kaminski coming back?"

He shakes his head and quickly shuts the door.

Franz rushes over, tries the handle and curses. He carefully picks up our meals and puts the food on the desk. I arrange the bread in the middle between us and lay the spoons beside the bowls, as if I'm setting the table at home.

We eat in silence. This soup is better than the typical camp soup. It has a lot more vegetables and the broth is tasty.

"Mm, this is alright!" mumbles Franz, slurping enthusiastically.

I nod, my mind drifting, "have you ever wondered why we never got a cold while we were in the camp?"

I dip the hard bread into the soup and take another bite.

Franz looks up. "What? ... Oh. Yeah, we never did, did we?" He slurps soup off his spoon.

"I think it was the soup," I say with conviction, "I think something in all those carrot tops and outside cabbage leaves stopped us from getting a cold."

"Oh Christ Rys!" Franz chuckles as he bites into a piece of bread. "You think of really strange stuff sometimes."

"I know ... I know," I agree, chewing a piece of turnip. "Thoughts just come into my head for no reason."

I stare out the window, noticing a tall fir tree growing in the schoolyard. It reminds me of my school at home. I push the empty plate away and watch the leaves rustle in the breeze, showering snow onto the ground.

I don't leave the chair for the rest of the day.

I'm tired and, in spite of being fed, have given up all hope of getting out of here.

It's late afternoon by the time the schoolroom door opens and Kaminski strolls in.

We scramble to our feet and stand impatiently beside the desks. He nods and gives us a broad smile. Turning towards the door, he gestures to someone to come in.

A young man walks through and stands beside him. I quickly glance at the lad and back at Kaminski then back to the lad.

"Oh my god! I can't believe it!" I cry out, not trusting my eyes.

The young man standing next to Kaminski is my brother Jo. My brother Jo! It's a bloody miracle!

Laughing, he runs up to me and grips my arms, kissing my cheeks. We hug tightly.

"Oh my God, Jo... Jo!" I sob as I look into his eyes. "I can't believe you're here! I just can't believe it! You're here and you're okay!"

"I'm here, Rys. I'm here." he whispers hoarsely.

Tears stream down our faces as we hug each other again. We part and hold each other at arm's length. I study his face as he studies mine.

He's thin, like all of us, but his face looks different. His eyes reflect something I can't quite put my finger on. I squash the feeling of dread in the back of my mind and grab him once more to kiss him on the cheek.

He pats my face affectionately.

I glance over to Franz, who is watching us, amazed. Walking up to him I put my arms around his shoulders.

"Jo, meet my other brother, Franz."

Jo steps forward and shakes Franz's hand then pulls him into a hug as well. Franz looks surprised then hugs him back, patting his back.

The Russians stand near the door, smiling, as Kaminski wipes his eyes and nose with a rag.

"You can come out of this room now, lads. We need to talk."

We crowd into a small staff room dominated by a large desk and five chairs, two against the wall. Kaminski makes 'camp coffee' in a pot on a small kerosene burner and as it begins to boil, we produce our own mugs from the rucksack. Kaminski pulls out four mugs from a cupboard near a small sink and places them on the desk. The coffee is strong, and we all have a small measure of the thick liquid.

Franz and I sit at the front of the room, Jo alongside us. The Russians, slouch on chairs against the cracked wall. Kaminski squats on the edge of the desk, facing us. He asks us a lot of questions, so we tell him about the capture, the escape and our journey. Now and then he translates our answers to the two Russians, who look at us in surprise. Jo is silent, his eyes switching between Franz and myself as the story unfolds.

Kaminski tells us the four of them are in a sub-camp, attached to the Hinzert Concentration camp. The other work gangs are quartered in the school grounds in different buildings, loosely guarded by the German home army. He and the other Kapos pay the guards off with homemade alcohol.

In return they allow the prisoners more freedom to do what they like.

He sips his coffee then adds. "We are still organised by the guards to repair and maintain the roads, but they leave us alone most of the time. They still give us food, but only the basics like bread and this shit coffee, so we scrounge around and find what we can to make our own soup. That's why Popov and Volkov," he points to the two Russians, "were making soup out front. We don't work as hard as we used to, and we go in shifts to work on the roads. That's where Jo was. He is in another gang."

"I am Yuri Popov!" the big Russian suddenly bellows. "My comrade is Ivan Volkov." He points to his friend. The smaller Russian nods and salutes.

This is strange. Why doesn't Volkov talk?

Franz tells them of our plan to meet up with the Americans in Belgium.

I sense a subtle tension in the air as Kaminski shifts his backside along the desk, moving towards us.

"I think we will leave this place and join you," he whispers. "I know you'll be taking Jo with you. So, I think we," pointing to the Russians and himself, "should also go." He settles back on the desk, folding his arms. "The next twenty-four hours are critical. I overheard from the guards that the Allies are advancing over the border. I think we should try to make it to Saint-Vith on the Belgium border, not far from here. That's where the Americans are stationed."

He repeats the conversation to the Russians who stare at us, then bob their heads in unison.

Jo beams at me and pats my arm.

"We will be a lot safer with Boss and the Russians!" he says.

"Okay. We need to work fast," orders Kaminski, standing up. "We'll leave in the morning at dawn, carrying shovels and picks as if we are on a road gang and walk north. If we get stopped, you let me do the talking. Now, Ryszard and Franz, you both need to find something else to wear or we'll have trouble.

I think there are clothes in a cupboard in the next room, find jackets, coats, whatever you can, but nothing new, it must look old."

He speaks in Russian, "Yuri, you and Ivan, find as much food as you can carry."

"I'll get rid of these guns," he says in German then pats his belt. "If we are caught with them, we will be shot. I think even *our* lax guards will shoot us. It's a shame to ditch them but that's how it's got to be. I'll keep the knife, Franz, and hide it in a secret pocket in my coat. You can have it back one day, I promise. Jo, look for food also and get shovels and picks."

Jo bobs his head.

"Now we must hurry! Rys and Franz keep yourselves hidden for god's sake!" is Kaminski's final order.

Franz and I find old jumpers with holes in them, a couple of wool caps and two old overcoats. But we still wear our wool pants. They are already filthy and look the part.

I discover two pairs of gloves and we stuff them into our pockets. We shove the Hitler Youth uniforms and the German overcoats into the bottom of the bin, piling old clothes on top of them. I rummage through another clothing bin and find another pair of gloves for Jo.

We hide in the office, wrapping ourselves in our newly acquired coats and using extra coats from the bin as blankets.

Kaminski wakes us before dawn and gives us coffee. Everyone is quietly moving around packing the few items they have. We venture outside into the freezing morning air where Jo, shivering with cold, is waiting with picks and shovels.

Franz is still carrying the rucksack with three loaves of bread, two onions and a piece of sausage inside.

Tramping down the driveway with our picks and shovels over our shoulders, we set off along the main road.

A grey dawn lightens the sky. There is the distant booming of artillery to the North.

Now and then, we hear the rattle of machine-gun fire. A battle is in progress. My heart sinks with every boom-boom-boom. I hope the Americans can withstand the barrage. They need to defeat the German bastards, or we are all lost.

"How did you get away from your work gang?" I ask Jo.

"The guards were drunk," he answers, adjusting his shovel along his shoulder. "They found some Schnapps from somewhere and were sound asleep when I snuck out and got the gear."

"My gang didn't care if I left," he adds. "I didn't have many friends in that group anyway. Kaminski looked after me in the camp. I kept close to him and some of the other lads."

He falls silent.

Out of the corner of my eye, I stare at him. He chews his lip, his face overwhelmed with sadness for things he hasn't shared with me.

We have both seen and experienced a lot of horrific things and I realise I'm not ready to share my most terrible memories with him either. Not yet. So, I don't question him. Jo will talk in his own time.

We walk a couple of kilometres and stop at the side of the road, to sip from our water bottles.

Trucks speed past us. We move to the side of the road and start to shovel sludge mixed with dirt into the holes around our feet. The Russians grab their picks and start to dig into a mound of snow exposing a heap of gravel.

Army transport trucks slow down. German soldiers glare down at us as they pass. A jeep from behind veers to a stop along the edge of the road, allowing the convoy to pass.

A German officer leaps out, holding onto the open car door.

Scowling, he shouts above the noise of the trucks.

"You lot! You should not be here! You're too near the front! Turn around and head back into Prum. There will be plenty of work for you there. Turn back! Now!"

"Yes sir!" Kaminski yells above the revving of engines. "Thank you for the warning!"

Kaminski orders us to turn around. Swinging our tools back over our shoulders we march the same way we came, back towards Prum. The officer nods his approval, jumps back in and the jeep drives off, disappearing around the corner. It's followed by a long convoy of tanks with soldiers sitting on every spare part of the metal hulls. Huge artillery guns, pulled by supply trucks, grind their way along the icy road, churning up dirt and snow. In the opposite direction, ambulances drive towards Prum, followed by jeeps with wounded men strapped on stretchers.

"Seems a lot of wounded going one way and a huge amount of weaponry going the other," comments Franz.

"I hope the Americans are kicking their asses," I reply.

Jo suddenly grabs the sleeve of my coat, fury leaping into his eyes. "I hope the Americans tear them apart.

Slaughter every last one of them bastards until all of them... all of them ... are dead. Not one left alive! Not one!"

Frowning, I study his face, noting something there that makes me uncomfortable. I pat his hand gripping my sleeve.

"It's okay Jo! I'm sure the Americans will give the Krauts hell!"

He releases his grip and trudges ahead. The convoys are never-ending. Kaminski decides to detour across farmlands and head to the Belgium border that way.

Between the farms we discover narrow lanes, linking up to other properties. Along the way we search abandoned farms for vegetables hidden in cellars or food stored in cupboards, and anything else we can use.

It begins to snow. Although I pull the cap over my ears, I can still hear Franz grumbling under his breath. Walking becomes difficult. We plough through the snow drifts and skid on the ice, slipping and sliding on our knees and asses. By nightfall we're sore and exhausted. To top it off, the wind begins to strengthen, turning the snowstorm into a blizzard.

"We have to find shelter," mouths Kaminski, the sleet beating into his face as his words are lost in the howling wind. Bending our heads and backs, we force our way through to the nearest farmhouse.

Half the roof is missing, tiles and timber are strewn on the floor of what was once a living room. It is abandoned. The Russians scout around arriving back in the kitchen with pieces of wood to make a fire. Huddling in the kitchen, we share our canteen of water as Kaminski makes a small fire in the kitchen stove.

Volkov discovers a pot in a cupboard, inspects it closely for any holes and cuts up one of our onions. We hand him turnips, potatoes and a few herbs and he throws them in. Venturing outside, to collect some snow, he scoops it into the pot and carefully sits it on the hot plate.

"It's a good job we found these extra supplies in the abandoned farmhouses," Kaminski comments over his shoulder as he stokes the fire. Grinning, he stands and pulls out a vodka bottle from one of his deep pockets.

"I found it in the last house we raided. Take out the mugs, Jo, and I will give everyone a nip."

Jo pulls out the mugs from the rucksack. Kaminski pours a drop in each, and we take tentative sips to allow the fiery liquid to warm our bodies. Sighing, we sit on the floor and wait for the soup to boil.

I notice the smaller Russian, Volkov, still hasn't spoken a word.

Later that night, I ask Kaminski about Volkov's muteness.

Kaminski sits on a chair in the corner of the kitchen, having a quiet smoke. I pull up a chair and sit next to him. He offers me a cigarette. Taking one out, I place it between my lips as Kaminski lights it up with a match. I suck in the smoke and cough and cough, water streaming from my eyes.

"Not a smoker, Rys?" Kaminski chuckles, patting my back.

"Not really," I wheeze. "I smoked once with Tomek, my friend, who gave me one behind the camp's canteen, but if we'd got caught, we'd have been beaten, so I didn't smoke much in the camp.

Once I saw a man get beaten to death because he was smoking around the back of his hut. His Kapo was a total bastard who seemed to like caning men to death."

In silence, I wipe my eyes, remembering the terrible scene once more.

"What's wrong with Volkov?" I ask, changing the subject. "I've never heard him speak."

Kaminski pauses for a moment, staring into the dark. "He has no tongue. An SS guard cut it out and fed it to one of the guard dogs."

"Shit!" I whisper in shock., forgetting the burning cigarette.

"He and Popov were caught later in the war, that's why they weren't executed. The SS left shortly after their capture. I think it was the same day they arrived at the camp that Volkov lost his tongue. Apparently, he said something in Russian to the SS Commander, who didn't like the tone of his voice, so he ordered his tongue to be cut out."

Kaminski takes a drag from his cigarette, "I think their transport plane went down somewhere near Luxembourg. I heard there was a battle between the Krauts and the Russians. Most of the air crew and Russian military were killed. They were the only ones to survive. I think Popov was wounded in the side and Volkov had a head injury."

"Why do they follow you?"

"I speak German and Russian, so they need me to interpret for them. Mind you, Popov is trying to learn German. He's getting there."

We are silent for a while and I observe the smaller Russian, while Popov whispers to him in the hallway.

I think of Jo and his reaction to the Germans. I take a puff at my cigarette.

"Is Jo, okay?" I ask, blowing out smoke.

Kaminski considers my question and breathes deeply.

"He's okay. He's seen and experienced a lot of terrible things, just like the rest of us. We are all affected in some way by this war. The camps destroyed something in all of us."

He changes the subject.

"How old are you, Rys?"

"I'm eighteen," I say, squashing the cigarette butt under my boot.

"Here," Kaminski hands me his hip flask. "Have a drink."

I take a swig, then sputter and cough again.

"Hell! That was foul!" I gasp "What is it?"

"Something the guards cooked up. I swapped it for a packet of cigarettes. He chuckles, "and you thought I was enjoying it."

He finishes his cigarette, crushing it on the bench top and leans his head against the wall, taking another swig from his flask. He grimaces and gives a little shudder.

"Your right Rys, it's shite," Kaminski growls. And proceeds to pours the contents of the flask onto the kitchen floor.

He retrieves the vodka bottle from his coat pocket, and with a steady hand, pours the clear liquid into the small flask.

I wander back to Jo and Franz, who are now fast asleep. I nestle behind Jo, lying my head on the crook of my arm.

Gently, I rest my hand on Jo's shoulder and close my eyes, hoping my brother really is okay.

CHAPTER

41

The next morning we're into the rich farmlands of the Rhineland-Pfalz.

I stare at the wintry sun, piercing the snow clouds banked up along the horizon. Its light streams down onto the fields highlighting burnt-out buildings looking like blackened, broken teeth silhouetted against the sky. I hear, once again, heavy machine-gun fire and artillery, but this time it's much louder.

Closer.

"We need to find a safe hide-out," says Kaminski. "It's getting too dangerous to travel on the road."

On a nearby hill, we spot a solid, stone farmhouse. Intact. It's a large two storey building, with a sloping roof, nearly reaching the ground. A big red barn stands twenty metres away, next to a group of trees.

Trudging up the slope, we split up and scout around, aware the Germans could be near.

"Look about," Kaminski orders. "If you come across anyone or anything, give a whistle."

Ten minutes later, we enter the house via the back door into a large kitchen. A big wood stove stands against the stone wall. A small window, facing east, lets in a soft morning light which spills over dusty benches and a dirty sink. Torn and tattered curtains blackened with mould, hang limply against the chipped windowpane. A crystal vase holding a bunch of dead flowers sits on the kitchen table, the dried petals scattered along its surface.

The kitchen opens into a parlour from which a staircase leads to the upper storey. All the walls are made of thick river stones painted white. Dust-covered heavy furniture, carved in beautiful patterns of scrolls and flowers, fill the two rooms. A huge kitchen dresser, in the same floral design, stands alone along one wall.

We separate and search the house for food and supplies, including the cellar where the door opens to the outside.

"Looks good, Boss. No-one around," Jo reports as he walks back into the kitchen.

Kaminski rubs his hands together. "Alright. I think this is the place we'll hide and let the war flow over the top of us!"

"What do you mean, flow over the top of us?" asks Franz.

"We're going to hide in the cellar with food, clean water from the pump and anything else that's useful," he explains. "Then we'll block the cellar door with anything we can find. It's going to be hard living in the dark, however, it's the only choice we have. If we are caught by the Germans, we will be shot for sure. The Americans, on the other hand, might let us live."

"Are you suggesting we do this now or can we wait a few days?" asks Jo. "I'm not that keen on being buried underground."

"I'm suggesting it now," answers Kaminski. "The war is getting closer. We could be caught in a crossfire any time now. I know it will be hard for you Jo, but this is our best chance."

Jo looks worried but reluctantly nods his head.

I'm puzzled. What happened to Jo to make him scared of

being locked in a cellar?

"Okay let's get started," orders Kaminski, then explains to the Russians what is happening.

The Russians search for food, Jo and I fill two buckets with clean water from the kitchen pump over the sink, and Franz and Kaminski scout around the house for anything useful left behind by the owners.

We meet back in the kitchen, piling everything on the table and the floor, including what is left in the rucksack.

"Let's see," says Kaminski, lifting the vase and putting it in the sink. "We still need matches and spare buckets. We can't light anything that will show too much light to the outside. Did you find any food, Yuri?"

"Ja, ja," he says in broken German. "We found turnips in cellar... only for...for five days." He holds up five fingers.

"Okay. Let's scrounge around and see if we can find anything more!" orders Kaminski.

I look at the straw mattresses strewn along the floor with moth-eaten horse blankets piled on top and buckets of water near the kitchen door.

The table holds Volkov's saucepan with a small knife he found in a drawer, six odd bowls, six battered tin mugs, two being from Frau Schmidt, and a kerosene lantern with a full reservoir. Franz comes back with matches he found at the back of a cupboard. Jo searches upstairs and finds another two buckets, hidden behind brooms in a cupboard.

Kaminski has brought his small fuel stove, which he separated in pieces before we left, hiding the parts in the pockets of his overcoat, making his hips bulge and clank when he walked.

He quickly assembles the stove and places it on the table amongst the tin mugs.

Kaminski looks over the pile of supplies.

"Come. Come. Be quick and move these to the cellar."

We carry all the food and equipment out in the yard and into the cellar, above the kitchen. The whole room is dug out of the ground. Its earthen walls and floor packed down hard. The room is about eight metres by six and a half metres. Quite a large cellar, but it makes sense seeing the farmhouse is so big.

We make room for the bedding. The mattresses, with the horse blankets, are pushed together in a corner, making one big bed. The water and food are placed in another corner next to a wooden crate.

Kaminski glances around the dark room, satisfied.

"Jo, can you put the empty buckets in the far corner? We'll use them as a latrine."

Jo nods and places the buckets side by side.

The wooden crate becomes a table and Franz and I place the bowls, mugs and small stove on top followed by the lantern. Kaminski nods his approval and digs out a pack of dog-eared playing cards from his topcoat pocket, placing them on the crate.

"Okay. I think this will do. Now, find as much rubble, bricks, stones, whatever is suitable and block the cellar door."

"When I was scouting around, I saw broken bricks, bits of timber and smashed concrete behind the barn," I tell the others.

"Good. We'll use as much as we can," says Kaminski.

Franz finds a wheelbarrow in the barn, its wheel bent and

wobbly, but still serviceable. Jo finds an old wooden sled strapped to the barn's rafters.

We all pitch in, hauling the debris round to the cellar. Popov pulls the cellar door off its hinges, and we spend the rest of the day bricking in the doorway. Franz suggests we have a loose brick in the right-hand corner so we can see outside. Grinning, Kaminski pats him on the shoulder.

"You're a smart lad!" he says.

"Ah Kaminski don't say that. It will make his head swell!" I say, grinning at my friend who gives me the one figure salute. But deep down I know Kaminski's right. Franz is smart.

By nightfall we're entombed in the dark cellar.

"I think it's safe to light the stove and lantern tonight." says Kaminski, "I don't think the light is strong enough to show through the cracks."

Using Franz's knife, Volkov cuts up a couple of turnips and the last onion, putting them in a pot with water to make soup. He adds herbs from the rucksack and a bit of salt he found in one of the abandoned houses and lets it boil until the turnips go soggy.

He dishes it out into the bowls with a thin slice of bread left from the work camp, and we eat in silence. By the small flame from the lantern, I notice everyone is staring into the gloom between slurps, maybe contemplating what lies ahead.

After our meal, Kaminski turns the lantern down low, plunging the cellar into near darkness.

Jo makes a strange throaty sound, and I hear Kaminski reassuring him, then asking him to be the first lookout. Jo crawls to a plank of wood, covering a ledge in the rubble, and looks through the peephole.

The night outside is pitch black. He won't be able to see anyone, but he can certainly hear them approaching. We laid gravel in front of the doorway and along a path leading to the house, just for that purpose.

Talking in whispers about the war, I recall what Kapo found out from the informant at the concentration camp. Kaminski listens with interest then relays it to the Russians.

Kaminski turns off the lantern as we lie, head to toe on the mattresses, and settle down to sleep. He takes the next watch, occasionally swigging from his flask. He wakes one of the Russians later in the night for the next shift.

We all take turns to be lookouts throughout the next four days. With nothing to do, we mostly sleep, wrapped tightly in our coats and horse blankets.

We eat and drink sparingly, sometimes play cards by the filtered light from the peep hole and make turnip soup at the end of each day. And each day, we hear the Front drawing closer.

CHAPTER

42

After five days, the cellar really stinks. making us all feel wretched. Apart from our body odour, the latrine buckets are overflowing. The stench is so overpowering, we take turns in putting our faces near the peephole to gulp in fresh air.

I've had enough.

"We need to get rid of the shit, right now," I mumble through the crook of my elbow. Trying to stop the foul smell assaulting my nostrils "I'll find a place in the cellar somewhere to bury it."

"Ah, I don't think the hole will be deep enough," splutters Franz. "I think one of us will have to go outside and get rid of it!"

"Ah shit!" says Jo.

"Yes exactly," Kaminski chuckles.

"I'll go," I say with resignation. "I'm the smallest one here!"

Jo and I take turns clearing away the rubble, using the peep hole as a starting point and making an opening large enough for me to squeeze through.

I drop down to the other side, knocking a few bricks over with my feet. Quickly, I look around to see if the coast clear.

The farmyard is quiet, the air around me, still. Not a creature stirs.

The only sound is the thunder of artillery fire. Much closer than before. I look towards the horizon and see plumes of black smoke billowing above the treetops. The Front is almost on top of us.

Popov carefully hands me one full bucket then the other.

I waddle towards the barn to dump the putrid mess but change my mind. It could give us away to the Germans, so I struggle towards a thicket of trees on the edge of the field, spilling the stinking mess in a trail along the snow.

Dumping both buckets in a ditch behind the bushes, I wipe them out with handfuls of snow then clean my hands. I run back with the buckets slamming against my legs, reach the opening, and in a hoarse whisper, call out to the others to be ready.

Passing the buckets back into outstretched hands, Popov hands over the two clean buckets to fill with drinking water. I quickly fill the buckets from the outside pump and hand them back through the gap.

Throwing in the broken bricks that spilled out when I climbed out, I scramble back through the opening into the dingy, foul-smelling room.

Franz and Volkov fill in the hole carefully as Jo return the water buckets to our kitchen corner.

It is a blessing to drink fresh water. For the last two days we've been collecting it from the cellar's walls. Using Franz's knife, Kaminski dug grooves along the seepages, then constructed a funnel with tin sheeting he found wedged in the ceiling beams and directed the slow dribble of water into one of the water buckets. In one day, he only managed to produce three cups, dividing it equally among us.

As I sit on the filthy mattress, I think back on the last couple of days.

We'd talked in whispers, about our previous life, and what we believed would be the outcome of the war. Kaminski interpreted our stories to the Russians and through him, they told us their stories.

Popov told us he is from a hard-working family, where his father worked in a steel mill and his mother in a co-op. When he was a teenager, he took up weightlifting and became a regional champion. He isn't married but had lots of girlfriends and took them dancing every Saturday night at the local dance hall. He liked dancing the Russian Gopak, a traditional dance, where he and his mates would form a circle as they bounced and squatted, kicking out their legs. It was all to do with balance and stamina he stated proudly.

Popov told us Volkov was in an Olympic rowing team. Their aim was to win in the next Olympics.

But the war put an end to that dream. He is married to a beautiful woman named Olga, and they have a little girl named Magda, who is three years old.

I remember Volkov turning from the peephole, tears running down his face. Popov stopped talking and crawled to Volkov and gripped his shoulders. I recognised the Russian words for 'not to worry' and 'everything will be okay' as I've heard these words before in the camp.

Volkov signed, "I'm okay, but I miss my family and am worried about them."

In the last couple of days, he had developed sign language, using hand signals and scratching pictures on the earthen floor. Yesterday he made a signal for 'screw the Germans', pumping a clenched fist in the air. We snickered, knowing full well what it meant.

When not sleeping or talking, we filled in the time playing cards and teaching Popov German. We slept cocooned against each other's backs at night, to keep from freezing.

I smile as I think back to two days ago. I woke up with a start, Popov snoring into the back of my head, his arm slung over my shoulder, pulling me in for a cuddle. Straight away, I moved to the side of the mattress. Oblivious to it all, Popov loudly grumbled and turned to face Kaminski, their noses nearly touching. Kaminski stirred and pushed the Russian away. Popov sat up and rubbed his face.

"I had a weird dream," Popov said, yawning. "I dreamt my Magdalena was next to me and I was cuddling her."

"That was me you stupid bastard!" I hissed.

"Voo?" Popov said in disbelief.

"Yes, me!"

At the time, Franz was peeing in the bucket, stifling his laughter. He glanced back at me as I gave him a one finger salute. His shoulders shook with mirth as he tried to concentrate on what he was doing.

Popov flopped down on the mattress with a smile on his face.

Frowning, I got up and pissed in the bucket as well.

"One word from you," I snarled in Franz's face, "and you'll find a fist in your nuts."

Still grinning, Franz returned to the peephole for his turn as lookout.

As the memory fades I stand and walk to the crate, filling my mug from the saucepan Kaminski warmed on the stove.

I sip the hot water.

I slump on the mattress again.

I feel so tired.

My head swims.

Venturing outside took more out of me than I realised.

I glance at Jo sitting against the wall. He's been acting strange.

The last few days he sat with his head in his hands and rocked back and forth, mumbling to himself. In his sleep he cried out, his legs twitching violently. I woke him a couple of times and tried to soothe him, reassuring him as best I could.

I finish my drink and lie on the mattress. Jo joins me while the others play cards.

Volkov is now on lookout duty.

Facing each other, Jo and I speak in low whispers.

"I don't think I can stand another day of this," Jo murmurs.

"You have to, Jo. The bombing and gun fire are very close now."

"I hate the dark," Jo mutters and turns his head, staring into the gloom. "I never used to, but now it frightens me."

"You must be strong, Jo. It won't be long until the Americans arrive. Then we can get out of here."

I pat his arm. "Try to get some rest."

The day drags on. We sleep most of the time. Kaminski, snoring on the far mattress, suddenly curses and sits up.

I watch him scratch his legs, then his back. With all six of us hiding in the cellar the body lice have become rampant, driving us mad, especially at night.

Yesterday we stripped off our clothes and tried to squash the bugs between our fingers, but we succumbed to the cold and quickly dressed again.

Now they're crawling all over us.

Franz is playing cards with Popov. Disgruntled, he throws his hand onto the ground and gestures for us to have a quiet talk in the corner. I follow him behind the crate.

"I think your brother is unwell," whispers Franz.

I glance over to Jo, who's curled into a ball.

"I know. I'm really worried. I'll have a talk with him. I might be able to help."

Jo, awakened by another of Kaminski's outbursts, sits up wide-eyed and confused.

I move back to him and place my arm around his shoulder. He looks into my eyes as if he doesn't recognise me.

"Are you sick Jo?" I ask with concern.

"No, no. I just don't like being here. It reminds me of a dark wet grave. I'm afraid we will be shot. I don't want to be killed. The Krauts killed all my friends in the camp, did you know that? All of them who were in my unit."

His face distorts with hatred, his eyes glaze over. I've only seen this once before while leaving Prum.

"The Krauts must all die!" he seethes viciously. "I hope the British and the Americans kill them all, destroy their homes and murder their loved ones."

I peer into his face.

"Christ Jo," I say in a hoarse whisper, "don't say that. You're worrying me. Not all the Germans are bad and not all of them deserve to die. Our Kapo in the camp was German and was a decent man. A beautiful German woman fed us and gave us warm clothes. A German policeman and his sister gave us shelter. They are not all like the Nazis. There are many normal people who care about others."

I grasp his shoulder, "I didn't know about your friends. I'm sorry, but you have other friends with you now. You have me and Franz. Kaminski and the Russians. We are all your friends."

I pause and arrange a moth-eaten blanket over his shoulders.

"Go back to sleep Jo," I suggest.

I lie him down and stay by his side until his breath softens into a slow rhythm.

I turn to Kaminski.

"What really happened in the camps?" I ask.

I rest my hand on Jo's thin shoulder as Franz and Popov move away from the card game and lean against the earthen walls, facing Kaminski.

Volkov is still on lookout duty but glances back now and then.

Kaminski takes a swig from his flask. He winces as the raw vodka burns his throat.

"I've known Jo for three years. We were both caught earlier in the war. I wasn't executed by the Nazi bastards, due to the fact I'm a civil engineer and lived in Germany most of my life. For two years we worked in the armament factories in Buchenwald concentration camp. I was a Kapo in that camp. Jo and his unit were put in my hut.

"However, most of the men in his unit were killed. Some were experimented on by doctors in the camp's hospital. They were injected with typhus, typhoid and cholera, to see if they could be cured with experimental drugs. Most of them died. Others were executed by the SS.

"Later Jo, myself and what was left of his crew, were sent

to another concentration camp called Hinzert. It is situated in the Rhineland-Palatinate, thirty kilometres from Luxembourg on the Hochwald Plateau.

"It's a bastard of a place, with gale force winds all year round. It's wet in summer and bloody cold in winter. A lot of men died from the cold in that place, especially when forced to stand and face the flagpole for hours.

"Compared to the rest of the camp, our area was quite small, about 200 metres square. Over time it became very overcrowded.

"We were housed in four huts that contained two rooms each, harbouring about two hundred men, then later, five hundred. Some men slept on straw pallets on the floor. The conditions were very bad, and disease was rampant.

"The brick buildings near the main gate, were used as Gestapo offices. There was a central roll-call area in the centre of the camp where a pole held up a loudspeaker, bellowing orders night and day. This is how crazy these SS bastards were. They ordered prisoners to plant a flower garden in front of their huts, and when the job was finished lined them up to be shot. One of my friends was murdered that way."

He lowers his head and rubs his forehead. Breathing out slowly, he looks up and continues.

"Just before dawn, the roll call area was used for drills and exercises. We had to jump up and down to the sound of a beating drum. The SS guards were cruel bastards. They would flog anyone who faltered or fell over. Sometimes to death."

He stares into the gloom.

"Jo, I, and the rest of his unit were put in a sub camp called 'The Cart Camp.' We hauled unearthed roots and other materials back to the camp. It took eighteen men to pull a cart. Sometimes, for fun, the SS released the brakes on the cart as it travelled downhill, running over the prisoners. They took bets on how many were killed.

"One day I was in the forest cutting lumber and Jo was digging out a stump near the side of the road. He saw one of the guards release the brake. Two of his friends were killed under the wheels. When he got back to the camp, he attacked a Kapo, a right bastard. I don't know why. But I think Jo just lost it.

"Anyway, Jo was badly beaten by the Kapo and put in a drainpipe set in the ground. It was made of concrete, over a metre and half in length and about a metre wide. It stood upright with its full length dug into the ground. It had an iron lid with a small trap door on top."

Kaminski takes a long breath. "Jo was left in it for two weeks. I used to feed him soup by lowering a mug attached to a string, through the trapdoor. He was lucky it was summer and surprisingly dry for the season, so he wasn't too cold or wet. But when he came out of the drain, he was very ill.

It took me weeks to nurse him back to health. You see, he couldn't stand in the pipe. It was only tall enough to squat, sit or kneel in. We called it 'The Shit Hole' because that's what you did, you squatted where you shat. Plenty of men died in that pipe, but not Jo. He is a tough son of a bitch."

I cringe when he uses this term, but I keep quiet. He intended no insult to our mother.

"So that's why Jo is so afraid of dark holes in the ground," he adds. "Like the one we are in now."

Kaminski leans back against the crate and folds his arms.

"Later we were sent to a marsh drainage and forestry sub camp, where we met the Russians. Finally, we were all sent to another sub camp, east of the German border, to repair roads. That's where we met you two."

Smiling broadly, he nods towards Franz and myself, displaying a couple of broken teeth. We glance at his mouth briefly and he taps his remaining teeth.

"Compliments of the SS bastards!" He chuckles.

"How come you're not in striped uniforms?" I ask.

"When working on the roads, we scavenged around. One house had a lot of men's clothing. We couldn't believe our luck!"

I glance at Jo, noticing his mismatched clothing under his dirty overcoat with his pants cut off to fit his height.

We fall silent for a long time.

Jo stirs and sits up and notices our glum expressions. Thinking we're still worried about him; he slings his arm around my neck and looks at Franz grinning. I feel a little better at seeing him smile again.

He asks Franz if he would retell the story about the 'Bitch in the wardrobe'.

Franz nods, stands, and begins the story in hushed tones, with Kaminski translating in Russian. We smother our laughter at his facial expressions and silly gestures, like the way the fraulein straightens her stockings, to which he adds extra flourishes for a more dramatic effect, even slapping his own face.

He describes how I fell out of the car, mimicking Frau Wagner jumping after me, her face a mask of intense hatred, kicking and hitting me over and over again. He raises his hand as if to shoot the imaginary car and mimics how I threatened to kill them if they didn't leave.

Jo glances at me with admiration. I look away remembering how I felt that day, and how close I was to committing murder.

Being a true friend, Franz never mentions this, or our conversation in the cottage, and I silently thank him for that.

43

"**K**rauts! Krauts!" Franz snarls in a low whisper, shaking us awake.

Sitting up and breathing hard, I hear a commotion above our heads and the sound of vehicles driving into the farmyard. In the dark I peer helplessly towards the ceiling, hearing heavy footsteps, furniture being pulled around, and loud voices speaking in German.

"Shite," Kaminski growls, getting quietly to his feet and moving to the peephole. He peeks out and scans the yard.

An hour passes.

In total silence we listen carefully to snatches of conversations above our heads. I hear two men talking to each other and another who sounds as if he's speaking into a radio transmitter. The smell of coffee brewing and something delicious frying in a pan is torture. I bow my head, clasping my bent knees in despair. We've hardly eaten for the last two days.

The voices grow louder, and I can catch snatches of conversation.

The 506th heavy Panzer Division destroyed the American positions a couple of weeks ago ... Tiger tanks have destroyed American army vehicles ... then ran out of fuel.

There is a bloody big traffic jam on the roads ... Mainly our tanks and trucks. They are jammed together in two feet of mud ... 18th division ... General Lucht tried to cut units from the American line ... He's used thrust troop tactics ... Special shock companies ... Seize key bridges ... Combat engineer ... Self-propelled assault guns ... Clear roads ... Allowing flank attacks ... Communication is down for Americans ... We're engaged in a battle with the Americans in a forest at Boscogne ... They have been too slow ... LXV One has overrun St Vith ... The Americans have sustained our artillery fire ... Have denied us the road ... Bloody bad weather ... The final attack at St Vith was on the 21st of December ... 1st Panzer division and 1V Eleven Panzer Corps ... Pincer around St Vith ... We looted American supplies ... The British blocked the advance ... The Yanks escaped us due to ice on the roads .... The bloody mud became frozen!

One of the men is a German officer the other men call 'Herr Captain Muller'. He seems to be in charge.

Captain Muller goes outside and orders four machine guns to be placed in strategic positions and the rest to be stored in the barn.

Kaminski reports back to us.

"They are an SS Panzer division," he whispers as he faces us.

I rub my scalp, grimacing. This could be bad. I remember Pa talking about the Panzers to Uncle Tomasz. He said they are a special German army unit made of SS soldiers and are the most disciplined units of the German army, well organised and known for their strategy in warfare.

The Panzers troops stay for three days. For seventy-two hours we hardly move. There is no food, and only a little water left in the buckets and seepage from the walls. I'm worried the stench of the latrine buckets will creep through the floorboards and give us away.

On the third morning we hear the captain issuing orders to his men.

None of us moves a muscle, listening hard as a soldier reports the sighting of American troops.

This could be it!

We grin at each other, Kaminski giving a thumbs up and Volkov pumps his fist in the air.

But then all hell breaks loose outside.

A volley of gun fire rips through the air around the house.

Instinctively, we duck for cover, even though we're safe in the underground cellar. A German machine gun rattles round after round from somewhere near the farmgate. As it ceases fire to reload, we hear rifle shots further up the road.

Artillery shells hit the farm, making the house shudder.

Bits of timber fall from the ceiling.

Thick dust falls around us, coating our heads and shoulders.

An artillery shell explodes very near to the house, making it rock on its foundations.

We press ourselves against the walls, crouching low with our arms over our heads.

Jo suddenly leaps to his feet, screaming, his mouth wide.

He yells obscenities to the ceiling, flailing his arms above his head. He scrambles for the cellar door, pulling the bricks away.

"Oh my God! Jo! No!" I cry out in a hoarse whisper and scramble after him.

Grabbing his arm I growl in his ear, "Bloody hell what are you doing? Stop! Stop now!"

He looks at me disoriented, his face twisting in rage.

"Let go of me, you German bastard!" he shrieks. "I'll kill

you! You bloody Nazi! You're not going to bury me again. I'm not going back into that hole!"

Savagely, he pushes me back.

I collide with Kaminski.

We both fall flat to the floor.

Jo keeps screaming, kicking my legs.

Franz springs to his feet and grabs Jo around the waist, silencing him with his hand across his mouth.

Jo squirms and twists, elbowing Franz hard in the ribs. But Franz holds on tight.

Popov leaps up but Volkov holds him back with his hand. He races up to Jo and grabs his head, pushing it into his shoulder in a kind of embrace, sandwiching Jo between himself and Franz. All three of them career around the room, banging into the crate and nearly toppling the lantern. Popov steadies it, placing it back while Volkov maintains his grip on Jo and Franz.

Jo struggles desperately with the back of his head wedged into Franz's throat and his face pushed into Volkov's chest. His screams are muffled by Franz's hand clenched around his mouth. Determination is written on all their faces as they perform their strange dance around the room.

For a brief moment the shelling stops and the gun fire ceases.

We hear loud voices above us.

"There is something under the floorboards!" exclaims one of the Germans.

We freeze, wide-eyed, and gawp at the ceiling.

I hold my breath.

Volkov and Franz grip Jo harder, keeping him still.

Someone else in the kitchen says, "It could be rats. I've seen a few around the house."

Another voice mumbles an inaudible reply.

Kaminski stands and calmly walks to the clenched threesome and murmurs into Jo's ear.

Jo loosens his grip on Volkov's jacket and drops his arms.

Franz and Volkov peel themselves away. Kaminski leads Jo to a mattress and lowers him to the ground. Sitting beside him, he wraps his arm around Jo's neck and whispers in his ear.

"You are safe here, Jo. You are safe. You are with friends. With your brother and with me. Nothing and no one will harm you. You need to be very still now, and very quiet, or we will all die. Do you understand me, Jo?"

Jo dips his head, acquiescing as Kaminski pats his head and pulls out his flask, ordering him to drink. He takes small sips then slowly lies down as Kaminski strokes his forehead. Closing his own eyes, he places his other hand lightly on Jo's chest.

Jo's breathing becomes calm and even.

While the war rages above us, we stare in amazement at Kaminski. His hand moves slowly over Jo, centimetres away from his body.

Jo is sound asleep.

Outside, the SS Panzer troops are calling to one another and we can hear the injured crying out for help. Men are yelling for the Medics to attend their comrades.

I look through the peephole and see German boots running past. Captain Muller shouts orders to three soldiers, who run inside the barn and come out hefting another machine gun and rounds of ammunition.

"Go to the creek that crosses the farm road and guard that area at all costs! We cannot allow the Americans to take that road, do you hear! They are not to take that road!" he shouts.

The soldiers disappear into the dark. I can see the red tracer of the machine guns as they open fire and hear the intermittent boom of artillery shells somewhere in the distance.

The battle continues for the rest of the night. We sit against the walls and listen to the sounds of war. I lean my head against the damp earth willing it to be over. I glance often at Jo. His still form is covered in a horse blanket. His chest rises slowly with each laboured breath.

Will he wake and start screaming again?

Around dawn I look through the peephole and see one of the soldiers returning from the machine gun emplacement at the creek.

Captain Muller, who is standing near the cellar's entrance, turns to face him. I notice his boots need a polish. *No Polish slaves to keep them clean, here at the Front!*

"Herr Kommandant, my two comrades are dead, and the Americans are now advancing on the farmhouse!"

"Shyster!" barks Muller, thumping his fist against his thigh. "You will report to Corporal Berger. He is on the radio transmitter. Tell him that all units are to prepare to evacuate."

He turns to another soldier running past. "Private Meyer! I want men to set land mines along the southern road!"

The young man stops and faces the captain.

"Well, what are you waiting for! Go! Go!" Muller growls with irritation, waving his hand about.

I hear the first soldier report to the Corporal in the kitchen then see him jog to the barn. Moments later, more men pour out with the wounded being carried on stretchers to waiting trucks. I crawl back and whisper what I have just seen and overheard. Kaminski translates this to the Russians and in hushed tones adds, "The Germans are moving. That means the Americans might be here soon."

We hear the Germans stomping around the house. Chairs are scraped on the floor in haste and words quickly spoken into the radio transmitter.

I peep outside. Soldiers are piling into army trucks with ammunition and guns thrown into the back with them. Shouting orders, Captain Muller leaps into a Jeep with his two junior officers. With the engine revving, a corporal swerve the Jeep out through the farm gates onto the mud-churned road, heading south.

Twenty minutes later, an unearthly silence has settled all around us.

"The Germans have left," whispers Kaminski, peering through the peephole "I can't see a living soul."

We slowly stand and look at each other in amazement. Bursting into laughter, we dance wildly around, throwing our arms in the air, cheering at the top of our voices.

I grab Jo's face with my hands and kiss his forehead. Franz wraps his arms around us both, making us dance around in a circle. The Russians grab each other around the neck and kiss each cheek, while Kaminski takes a swig from his flask, laughing between gulps. Draining his flask, he throws it into the air, letting it land at his feet, then dances around with the rest of us.

We shake Kaminski's hand, and, with tears running down our faces, thank him for saving us and coming up with the plan to hide in the cellar. Unable to contain our exuberance, we once more dance around in joyful abandonment. Slapping each other's back.

CHAPTER

44

I sit near the peephole, anxious, my stomach churning.

It's been two hours. Still no Americans.

What if the Americans don't come? They might bypass us. Go somewhere else. Then we'll be on our own, and it won't end well. We're too weak to go any further. We'll end up dying.

I put my eye to the hole and study the farmyard for about the hundredth time. The whole place is still, quiet, only a faint booming can be heard in the distance. The day is bright and full of sunshine. The snow reflects brilliantly off the barn's roof, melting along the edges and forming icicles that slowly drip to the ground. It's a day to be outside. To breath in the fresh air. To celebrate at being alive. But we don't dare venture outside in case the Germans double back.

Exhausted from the shouting and dancing around we sit in silence. Franz and the Russians slump against the wall, Kaminski shuffles his cards, resting against the crate and Jo, sitting on the mattress, his chin resting on his knees, stares into space.

Waiting.

Waiting.

The growl of engines breaks the silence.

They're getting closer.

I twist around to see the road leading to the farm.

Army vehicles drive through the open gate and pull up to the house. Unsure if they are American or German, I duck-down and hold my breath. Turning my head slowly towards the others I place a finger to my lips, indicating the need for silence. Everyone is still. All eyes, wide in apprehension or anticipation, are staring at the barred door.

Outside, voices call back and forth.

The words we hear are strange. Not German. It is the same language Kapo used when talking to the British in the camp. I tentatively look through the hole once again to see a pair of different boots walking past. Not German boots.

"It's the Americans! They're here! The Americans are here!" I whisper hoarsely.

Kaminski quickly stands, his forgotten cards tumbling to the ground. "Pull those bloody bricks down and let's get out of here!" he growls.

I frantically tug at the bricks. Everyone rushes to the door and claws at the rubble, desperately pulling away the rocks from around the peephole.

The larger gap allows the cold morning light to seep into the dank gloom and move over our faces.

Being the smallest, I'm the first one to scramble up and out. I lift my face to the winter sun, squinting my eyes against its soft glare, and breathe in a couple of deep breaths. But being so weak I stumble, buckling at the knees, and sink into the snow.

I hear the clicks of rifles being cocked.

I put my hands over my head and slowly raise my eyes. Six American rifles are aimed at my head.

Behind me, Jo quickly climbs out, followed by the others.

Ignoring the Americans and their guns, he lifts me to my feet. The soldiers stare at our filthy clothes and skinny frames. Warily, we place our hands on our heads. Our stench must be heinous as a few of the men screw up their faces and spit on the ground in distaste.

One of them growls "Krauts!" And spits again, disgust written on his face.

Fingers tighten on the triggers of the rifles pointed at our chests.

We stiffen. Despite the cold, sweat rolls down my face.

After all we've been through, is this how it ends? Being shot by the Americans.

I tightly close my eyes.

Kaminski shouts in German. "No, no! I am Russian, I am Russian!"

I shoot a glance at him, then the Americans, who shout words I don't understand, aiming their rifles higher.

Jo pleads, his hands lifting from his head and reaching up. "We are Polish! Polack! We are Polish! Please, please don't shoot!"

Franz copies him, "We are Polish! Polak! We come from Poland!"

"Russian! Russian!" Popov bellows, pointing to Volkov, then himself. "We Russian!"

We are all speaking in German, so we switch to Polish and Popov to his own language. Volkov keeps his hands on his head, staring at the Americans, nodding, and smiling. We repeat ourselves over and over again, until the Americans realise, we are not the enemy.

They lower their rifles. We slowly let down our arms.

Kaminski tries to make them understand who we are and where we come from. As he speaks. I study these American soldiers. The first I've ever seen.

They're dressed in khaki uniforms with saggy pockets on their jackets above and below their belts, even their pants have large side pockets. Some have thick overcoats on, but each has a brown leather utility belt packed with canteens, pouches, small clip bags, grenades, and a large, sheathed knife.

They all carry canvas rucksacks on their backs with a few carrying small ones on the front as well. Their helmets are round and dome-like with a small lip around the edge. A white insignia is painted on the side, and they are covered with camouflage mesh, threaded with dead leaves. They all look scruffy, untidy, with soot smeared on their faces. Most are tall. The shortest one being Franz's height, making Jo and I look like children.

They look tough and dangerous.

A jeep with a circled white star painted on the hood pulls up and a Sergeant steps out, favouring his left leg. He is a large muscular man, with a freckled face and red bushy eyebrows. He hobbles towards us, and as he comes closer, I see his eyes are a piercing blue.

Red stubble covers his jawline. He takes his helmet off and runs his hand through short red hair. Studying us, he jams his helmet back on. He is so intimidating we lift our hands high above our heads again. Kaminski begins to speak in Polish, repeating who we are.

The sergeant grunts loudly, then bellows to his men.

"God damn it! … God damn it! Where in God's name is Corporal Dabrowski? Someone get him here now, ya hear!"

One of the men peels off and runs to a couple of soldiers walking our way. An American with a sling on his arm runs forward and talks to the American Sergeant.

He then speaks to us. In Polish.

"My name is Corporal Charles Dabrowski, but everyone calls me Chuck. This is Sergeant Cooper." He points to the tall red haired American. "Who are you and why were you all in this cellar?"

His American accent is strong with each word stretched out. He sounds like a movie star I saw in a Cowboy movie. He is tall and lean with dark brown eyes and the shadow of a beard.

Kaminski moves forward, lowering his arms and speaks for all of us.

"The Germans have laid mines on a road leading out from the farm! I think it is the one going south!" He nods to me. "Ryszard saw them planting them before they left."

He takes a deep breath. "We are prisoners of war and have escaped the slave labour camps. We came here to be rescued by you, the Americans!"

The Corporal translates all this to the Sergeant who then orders his men to the south road.

He turns once again to Kaminski and frowns.

"Now hold ya horses! Where the hell y'all from?"

He looks at Chuck. "Did he say slave labour camps?"

The Corporal translates to Kaminski who quickly relates back to him about the camps in Germany, giving him a summary of the extermination of the Jews and some of the horrors he has seen.

Chuck translates it to the American soldiers. They all stand still in shock.

I asked Chuck if I could get our ID papers and show them to the Sergeant.

Chuck translates my request and Sergeant Cooper dips his head in approval.

I retrieve the rucksack from the cellar and hand him the small, folded documents.

Looking at them carefully, the Sergeant is silent for a few moments.

He sniffs loudly and studies our malnourished bodies.

"Yes'm, this is a hell of a thing! A hell of a thing! I guess y'all need to be fed," he adds.

He looks at one of his men. "Jack, would ya get these poor bastards some food!"

Kaminski asks for a cigarette. Chuck offers him one and lights it. Then offers the rest of the packet to us, but I decline.

The rest of us, including Franz, each take one out of the packet and let the Americans light them. They all inhale the smoke deeply, waiting to see what happens next.

Sergeant Cooper hands back our papers, shouts orders to his men, and with his gun raised, limps to the front of the farmhouse. Soldiers follow him, raising their rifles. They burst through the back door in search of Germans. The barn and the surrounding farmyards are also scoured but nothing is found. All the machine guns were taken, leaving only the spent ammunition cases in the dugout ditches.

The Americans guarding us pull out chocolate bars from their packs and hand them to us. Starving, we quickly unravel the foil wrappers and wolf down the chocolate, only to vomit it up a couple of minutes later.

Chuck comes over to us as I'm spitting on the ground.

"Are you all okay?" he says with concern.

I wipe my mouth. "We've all been starving so long; our stomachs can't handle rich food like chocolate. It makes us sick."

He nods in understanding and orders a young soldier to find Jack.

"Tell him to heat up some canned soup and to give them some bread," he orders.

Near the entrance to the cellar, we sit wearily on a log. A few soldiers stand around us offering water from their canteens. We gulp it down greedily. The lanky soldier, no older than Franz, returns and hands out slices of bread and mugs full of steaming soup. We eat slowly, scooping up the small bits of vegetables at the bottom of our mugs with our fingers.

After our meal, Chuck takes us to see the platoon's medic. On the way he asks us our names and where we're from, so we answer him in turn. Chuck asks the Russians a few questions, but Popov only shakes his head.

"The big fellow, Popov can only speak Russian and some German. Volkov, the smaller one, is mute. He has no tongue," Kaminski tells Chuck.

Chuck winces.

We all grow silent as Kaminski quickly retells their capture and about Volkov getting his tongue cut out.

As we pass through the big barn doors a medic is sorting out medical supplies on a hay bale while other men are setting up tables. The medic talks to Chuck who introduces the man as 'Doc'. Chuck translates as he asks about what we've been through, shaking his head in disbelief as he hears our abbreviated stories.

Doc checks our throats and feels around our necks for any swelling. He looks into our eyes and ears, then rests his ear on our backs, listening.

He checks the inside of Volkov's mouth and shakes his head. Turning, he talks to Chuck. Most probably about Volkov's injury as he keeps nodding towards him as he speaks.

Finally, he addresses us through the Corporal.

"You all seem okay, but extremely undernourished. I can't find any symptoms of disease. You are all lucky to be alive. I know you are hungry, but we must be careful what we feed you. It will be soup and small amounts of bread for a while, until you can stomach something more. It will take time, but eventually you can have a decent meal."

"You are all infested with lice," he adds. "So, let's get you all cleaned up and dressed in clean clothes."

He walks towards a medical bag, "I'll also give you antiseptic cream for your sores."

I breathe in a ragged breath, my tears freely flowing. Shaking, I slowly sit on a straw bale. I find it all so hard to believe. We are finally liberated. We survived the camps, the journey to the border and hiding in the cellar.

I can hardly believe we are okay. Thin and starving, yes, but okay.

Franz extends his hand. I grasp it as he pulls me up into a hug. I feel his shoulders shake. I pull away and to my surprise, tough, resilient, no-nonsense Franz is crying. Really crying like a child. His tough facade disintegrating with each sob. I pat his shoulder, then his head, like he used to do to me in the camp, making him laugh. He wipes his face.

I look around and see we're all crying.

I hug the two Americans and kiss the doctor on the cheek.

Chuck wipes his eyes with his sling then speaks in a husky voice.

"Let's get you all cleaned up. We'll give you combat overalls to wear."

Sitting on bales, waiting for the Corporal to return, we watch two soldiers file in carrying buckets of water, soap and clean clothes. We strip off, shivering with cold, and use our shirts as wash-clothes to scrub ourselves.

One of the soldiers points to a bundle of clothes he's put down on the bales, so we dress quickly in woollen underclothes, then thick overalls. Disregarding our filthy clothing in a pile.

Chuck walks back into the barn and sees us shivering in the icy breeze.

"I'll get men to bury your coats in the snow. I heard this gets rid of the body lice. You can get them back soon," he tells us.

He orders his men to hand out pairs of warm army socks and as I'm putting them on, I notice the Corporal speaking to Sergeant Cooper near the barn door.

The Sergeant calls Kaminski over to join them. The conversation becomes intense. Kaminski rubs his forehead, then nods. Sergeant Cooper pats Kaminski's back.

An agreement has been reached which will probably involve all of us.

CHAPTER

45

Chuck approaches, rubbing his injured arm.

"I know you need to rest," he says, "but we need help in recovering our wounded men outside the farm. We don't have a stretcher to get the men off the field. The rest of the platoon will arrive shortly with extra supplies, but we need to get the wounded back here quickly for medical treatment. The Sergeant asks if you could scout around for a temporary stretcher to transport them back and more importantly if you could help to retrieve them."

Kaminski translates the request to the Russians as Chuck and the Sergeant leave us to discuss our options at finding a stretcher.

"Maybe there is a wardrobe in the house. We can use the doors," I suggest.

Kaminski nods. "Yes, that can work. Good idea Rys!"

Climbing the narrow staircase in the farmhouse, I find two bedrooms near the landing. A small one with a single bed with no mattress, and a double bed in the larger room, made of the same dark wood as the furniture downstairs, also missing a mattress. We must have used them in the cellar. Both headboards are carved beautifully with swirling scrolls of poppy flowers with the foot of the bed having the same floral, decorative pattern, but smaller.

Jo runs his hand along the carved wood admiring the texture and craftsmanship.

"This fine work is all through the house," he claims. "I think the owner may have been a craftsman. It's a shame to see it left here to rot. I would take it back home if I could."

I spot a wardrobe along the far wall with its doors flung open. It looks empty apart from coat hangers haphazardly hanging in a corner. The outside of the wardrobe doors has the same ornate designs as the bed head, however inside the panels are smooth.

I call Jo over and he inspects the wardrobe running his hand once more over the timber.

"Well, I suppose we'll have to sacrifice these doors," he says through a long sigh.

Franz begins to prise off the brass hinges using his knife.

"Try not to damage the wood too much Franz," says Jo, "It would be a shame."

"I'll be careful, Jo."

After all that's happened, I'm surprised to find it's still important to us to keep such things in good condition. Maybe we are looking towards a future at last.

"Try lifting it with me on top!" Kaminski orders.

Franz and Jo place the doors on the floor while Kaminski lies on top of one. We all crouch and lift it unsteadily and manage to balance it with the two Russians at one end, Franz and myself at the other.

"When you two get tired you can rotate with me and Kaminski," Jo suggests looking at me then Franz, "I think the Russians are in better condition than any of us and should last the distance."

The door is lowered, and Kaminski gets off with a grunt.

"Okay. Let's get started," he says, straightening his overalls. "Time is of the essence."

We manoeuvre the doors down the small stairwell, angling them sideways through the narrow opening, and march outside to meet the Americans near the barn.

The Sergeant looks at the doors with approval.

"Well done boys! Well done! I sure appreciate your help."

We lean the doors up against the barn as Doc walks out and hands us all clean bandages. and syringes to. He shows Kaminski and Franz how to inject the morphine in a thigh by pretending to jab his own. Satisfied they know what to do, he gives them each a box of filled syringes.

Through Chuck, Franz asks a couple of questions, which Doc answers. He then demonstrates the jabbing of the needles again. Franz and Kaminski carefully place the small boxes in their pockets, and we're ready to go.

Sergeant Cooper shows us the positions of his men on a map, with the nearest location about half a kilometre away. Franz and I grab one end of the door, the Russians the other.

The tall, red-head sergeant stands near the barn door, his hands on his hips.

"Now get out there and get our lads back. Y'all come back, ya hear!" he shouts at our retreating backs, as we briskly trot out of the farm gates, towards the first wounded soldier.

A few hundred metres from the farm, a bullet whizzes above our heads.

We dive for cover as more rounds pepper the ground behind us.

The Krauts are somewhere in the forest, and we have nowhere to hide. Crawling into a shallow drain, we prop up the door for protection. To our right a sudden barrage of gunfire hits the trees. A German sniper tumbles from the higher branches, landing in the snow as American soldiers run into the forest.

"Get up! Run!" Popov shouts in broken German.

Scurrying the rest of the way, towards the wounded American, we approach cautiously and put the door down near his feet. Franz quickly bandages the wounds on his legs as we move the door parallel to his body, easing him onto the improvised stretcher. The poor man groans in agony, painfully grasping the door. Franz injects a shot of morphine into his thigh. It calms him enough to look up at our faces.

He murmurs something in English. Not understanding him Franz places his hands on his chest, then slowly says "Polish." The soldier nods and closes his eyes.

Squatting, we grab the door and grit our teeth.

"Take the weight on the count of three. One...two... three, lift!" Franz orders.

We grip the door and lift. Grunting, we wobble a few steps to get our balance, then surge ahead towards the farm, slipping and sliding in the sludge. I look around nervously, feeling vulnerable out in the open.

"Take him into the barn!" Chuck orders, as we trot through the gates.

Resting the door on hay bales and relieved to be free of the weight, we back away leaving Doc to quickly examine the wounded man. We look at the map for the next soldier's position and pick up the spare door. Doc has the wounded man transferred to a straw bed on the floor, leaving a door free to give us a quick turnaround when we bring in the next man.

Franz and I change with Jo and Kaminski on every second rotation with the Russians helping in all the rescues. Some of the Americans are large men with serious injuries and it takes us longer than expected to get them stabilised and onto our makeshift stretcher.

By mid-afternoon we've rescued all seven of the American soldiers. Bending our heads, exhausted, we sit on the log, breathing hard from the unaccustomed exertion.

It's been an enormous effort for all of us. We haven't had enough time to recover from the days of starvation. But we couldn't say no to the Sergeant's request. If it wasn't for him and his men, we would have died in that cellar. Unfortunately, most of his platoon are still engaged in a battle further up the road, where pockets of Germans are holding out in the surrounding forest.

Basking in the late afternoon sun, we slowly sip sweet black coffee, real coffee, savouring the taste. Chuck and the two soldiers from the barn walk towards us and hand back our coats. He dismisses them and sits down.

"I think your coats are free of vermin," he says, taking off his helmet and rubbing his cropped black hair with his free hand, making it stick up in all directions. "And I know you are all tired, but the Sarge has spotted another wounded soldier on top of a low hill about two clicks away. It's about a hundred feet from a double storey building which we believe to be a storage shed of some kind. Could you do one more rescue?"

Franz and I volunteer, throwing the dregs of our coffee into the snow while Kaminski asks the Russians, who also agree. We put on our coats and pick up the door as Kaminski and Jo head for the mess tent, erected beside the farmhouse.

Quickly moving through a thicket of trees and over a field, stopping twice to get our breath, we pass a narrow two storey building. We come across the hill further up with a margin of trees behind us.

A soldier is lying on his side and has somehow burrowed himself into a shallow trench in the snow. We approach him, calling out softly that we are Polish. He is extremely tall, maybe over six feet and is badly wounded. He lifts his head and smiles.

We hurry over and carefully peel his overcoat away, revealing his back, which is a bloody ruin. Franz packs the wound. The soldier pants and moans in pain, as we gently turn him from side to side, allowing Franz to wrap the gauze and strips of linen around him.

Positioning the door near his back, we carefully roll him on. Even so, he cries out in agony. Due to his size, Franz quickly pulls out two syringes of morphine and injects both into his leg.

We lift the door cautiously with his arms and legs hanging over the side, skimming the top of the snow.

He's just too long for the length of the door.

Carefully, we put him down again and secure his hands inside his coat to keep them from flopping about, but let his legs drag on the ground. The Russians move towards the centre of the door, taking the heavier weight, while Franz and I take the lower half.

We all lift at the same time, swaying with the effort and scurry along a path towards the narrow building.

I peer up at the second storey and am surprised to see a German soldier sitting at an open window, looking down at us.

He waves his gun about threateningly, pretending to shoot.

"You dirty bastard!" I snarl up at him. "I bet you shot this American!"

Without thinking, I release one of my hands and give him the one finger salute. It was an instinctive response to all we've been through for the last four years.

The Kraut opens fire. Bullets whizz around us, pelting the ground. One hits Volkov's arm. He makes a horrible grunting noise and starts to pant, gripping the door with all his might.

Franz swears, Popov bellows.

We all dive for cover in a ditch, pulling the door, with the injured man, down with us.

"You stupid bastard, Rys!" Franz yells at me. "I saw the Krauts up there! They were letting us pass! Now we're stuck! You're an idiot!"

"I'm sorry! I'm sorry! I couldn't help it! It just happened. I know. I know it was stupid, but I couldn't help it!" I plead in a high-pitched voice.

"You … You are stupid Polak!" Popov roars in my ear. "You made Kraut shoot and he shoot Volkov!"

He grabs me by the neck and pushes me headfirst into the snow, leaving my ass sticking up in the air. A bullet tears through my overcoat, narrowly missing my bum, so I plaster myself flat against the ground.

The wounded American screams out in pain as Franz and Popov slide the door further along the ditch and pull it behind a thicket, growing in the shallow gully.

Volkov, clasping his bicep, scrambles behind them.

"Ah shit! I'm sorry Volkov!" I cry out as I crawl around a small bush and grab the back of his coat.

I pull a bandage out of my pocket and press it against his arm. Popov grabs it off me and begins wrapping it around the wound, swearing in Russian as he does so. The ditch is strafed with machine gun fire, from the building.

We're trapped.

"I'm so sorry, American soldier!" I whimper, patting the man's arm. Eyes glazed he stares into my face and mumbles in his own language.

Two American soldiers suddenly appear in the trees behind us, and in a commando crouch, move swiftly to the lip of the ditch. They jump down and rapidly assemble a machine gun, placing it on the ground above them. They return fire. One of the soldiers gestures with his hand for us to keep down.

The Germans retaliate by pulverising the thicket above our heads and along the tree line, splitting the bark and shredding pine needles. The snow billows into the air and onto our heads.

The Americans duck back and wedge themselves against the bank. There is lull in the firing. One of the Americans pops up and mans the machine gun again, firing back. He takes out the German machine gun as well as the two Germans manning it. One of them tumbles out of the window into the snow below.

The American soldiers stop firing as we wait in a tense silence.

Finally, there are calls of surrender and three more German soldiers emerge from the building, throwing their rifles to the ground. As the Americans run up to them, Franz and I peer over the edge of the ditch and watch them retrieve the Germans' weapons, ordering them in broken German to put their hands on their heads as they search through their pockets. They push them into a line and lead them back to the farmhouse.

Franz and I scramble back and help to pick up the stretcher. Popov takes the full weight at the head, as Volkov has no strength in his injured arm, and slides the stretcher over the edge of the ditch, as Franz and I shove and push. Climbing out, we heft the door once more and follow close behind the Americans and their prisoners.

I'm shunned for the rest of the day.

My comrades sit apart from me, not saying a word. Occasionally Jo looks over and shakes his head, embarrassed by my stupidity.

An hour goes by. I sit with my head bowed and my knees pressed together, clutching my outstretched hands as if in prayer. I am miserable. I could have got us all killed.

Without warning my back is thumped, making me fall off the log. I clamber up in shock, only to see Chuck and Sergeant Conner behind me, smiling. The Sergeant pats me on the back, but this time with less force. He must have realised the first clap was too hard.

He smiles again.

"Goddammit boy! Ain't you somethin? If it wasn't for ya blessitt stupidity, those Nazees were fixin' to be around for some time! Now, ya remember this son, as far as I'm concerned, Mr Hitler and his buddies can all go to hell, ya hee-yur!"

I don't understand a word he is saying.

Noticing my confusion, he pats my arm reassuringly. "I'd have given those Krauts the same one finger salute boy. The same salute!"

His tone softens a little. "You did good today, mah boy. You did good."

Chuck translates and then adds. "You've saved American lives today, Rys."

I stare at the Sergeant as he bobs his head, grinning. They both shake my hand.

I'm stunned. I watch them in disbelief as they walk to the farmhouse.

Jo overhears Chuck's translation and tells the others. They all stand up, totally bewildered, and walk over to me.

Volkov is sporting a sling and I ask him about his arm. He signs that he is okay. I sigh with relief and in broken Russian tell him I'm truly sorry. Volkov pats my back with his free hand indicating all is forgiven. However, Popov hasn't forgiven me. He is still scowling as we sit back on the log. In silence we watch more American soldiers arrive at the farm.

Several officers arrive in jeeps with a large group of soldiers in trucks and sitting on tanks. More soldiers march into the farmyard, bedraggled and filthy. The farm is filled with noise and commotion. Men yell at each other as tents are erected, trucks unloaded and soldiers march to and fro from the kitchen, carrying boxes and radio equipment. The farmhouse is now an American command post.

At sunset we're shown into a mess tent and served a larger portion of soup with lots of potatoes, a small amount of meat and two slices of bread. We wash it down with black, sweet tea, then play a game of euchre.

Later in the evening we're ordered into the farmhouse. Sipping from a mug, an American Major sits on a carved dining room chair that's been recently occupied by an SS officer.

We stand at attention. The Major stands and salutes the

two Russians then wave for us to sit down at the table. *That's a bit odd I thought! Why salute the Russians?* Interpreting through Chuck, he states, "My name is Garry Jones, Major Garry Jones."

"What's your story and how did you get here?" he asks. We retell our stories. We've told them so many times now the words roll off our tongues without having to think about them.

Major Jones, like Sergeant Conner, is stunned by our accounts of the German camps, the treatment of POWs and the annihilation of the Jews. When Kaminski finishes with the Russians' story, the Major swings back on the kitchen chair, forgetting the tin mug and takes out a flask from his jacket and unscrews the top. The contents smell like cognac.

He offers it to Kaminski, who takes a gulp and smiles, then offers it to the Russians. They take it in turns, draining the flask. Major Jones stands, walks to a crate near the door and produces another bottle and cups off a shelf, pouring us all a couple of fingers, including the Corporal.

We drink greedily. I splutter and cough, making them all laugh. Jo slaps my back.

The Major places his cup down on the table, regarding us with his dark eyes.

"You lads have had a tough time and I won't forget what you have told me. I'll draft a report tonight for the General informing him on the situation in Germany. Then I'll make arrangements for you three," he turns towards Jo, Franz, and I, "to join the Polish army nearby. But these Russians," and he nods towards them, "are very important, high-ranking officers and will be transported to headquarters tomorrow."

He looks at Kaminski. "You on the other hand will become a Russian interpreter for us."

Chuck translates and Kaminski seems pleased, taking another sip of his drink. We all look at each other in surprise. We had no idea the Polish army was so close or that the Russians were that important.

Kaminski translates to the Russians, who both stand and shake the Major's hand, while the rest of us gape, open-mouthed.

"What does the Major mean by very important, high-ranking officers?" I ask Chuck. "I thought the Russians were just Russian Airmen, the same rank as a Private in the army."

"They had to lie about their ranks to the Germans as well as all of you. That's why they swapped uniforms with their fallen comrades. Popov is really a Major and Volkov is a Colonel."

"What the hell!" we say in unison and stare once more at the two Russians in disbelief. Kaminski sits back with a sly smile on his face. The bastard must have known all along.

Shocked, I look at Jo and Franz. Stunned, they look back, and we begin to laugh. The Russians smile in confusion, not understanding they have spectacularly played us as well as the Germans. I pat the now 'Colonel' Volkov's good arm as he and his co-conspirator sit down.

"Good joke. You fooled us," I say in stilted Russian.

He understands and gives the thumbs up, grinning.

I reach behind Volkov's chair and tap Popov's arm.

"So, Popov, I mean Major Popov, all the stories about you and Volkov, I mean Colonel Volkov, were a lie?"

"Nein! Nein! Story is true. "Popov says in a thick German accent. "But Colonel has family safe in Russia. He put on a... a, how do you say it, a good performance. He good actor! Da?"

"Yes, 'he good actor'," I chuckle. "So are you!"

Popov smiles broadly, showing his large white teeth.

I think back to when we were in the cellar and before that, in the farmhouse. Popov was forever having these secret conversations with Volkov. Probably scheming their next move. Come to think of it, I did notice that the uniform on Popov was too short and too tight on the first day we met, but didn't think much of it, until now. It's been years since any of us have had clothes that fit.

I glance back at the American Major who is discussing the Polish army with Jo and Franz. Realising what he is saying, my smile turns into a broad grin.

We're going to join the Polish Army! I can't believe it!

I suddenly stand to attention and salute Major Jones, throwing the remaining cognac down my throat, and slamming the mug on the table. The fiery liquid burns my windpipe. I turn red, choke, and cough my heart out. Everyone breaks into laughter. Looking on, the Major grins as everyone stands and down their drinks, slamming their mugs down.

The gruelling day and the cognac take their toll, and we slump down in our chairs until Major Jones stands and opens the kitchen door, indicating the meeting is at an end. He sympathetically pats our shoulders and shakes the Russians' hands as we pass by him. Chuck salutes and follows us down the steps.

He takes us to our tents on the edge of the camp.

"You need to make up your own minds about who sleeps where," he says.

Jo, Franz, and I camp together. The Russians share with

Kaminski. As we enter, three army stretchers, with pillows and blankets, are lined up together in the centre of the tent. In one corner is a small stove, which Jo lights immediately. Soon the tent is cosy and warm.

I lay my head down on the pillow and wrap the blanket around my body, briefly thinking of the day's events. I grimace to myself at my stupidity but being so tired I yawn and close my eyes.

I fall asleep to the soft snores of my brothers, and the wind rustling the canvas. For the first time in four years, I sleep deeply and soundly, and without nightmares.

Marcia Wakeman

Part 4

1945

46

"Viel gluck! Good luck! Good luck!" Major Popov bellows, slapping our backs.

Smiling openly, he clasps Kaminski firmly by the hand, grips his shoulders and kisses him on both cheeks. In Russian, he pours out his gratitude for keeping him and the Colonel alive.

With a broad smile, Colonel Volkov shakes Kaminski's hand, slapping him on the back, signing, "I will miss you."

He turns to us and signs, "I will miss all of you."

Jo signs back, "We will miss you too."

The colonel smiles, playfully grabbing Jo behind the neck and ruffling his hair. He then stands to attention to salute us, his movements as precise as if on parade. We return his salute, although with not quite the same precision.

During our farewells, an English officer and his driver stand patiently, smoking cigarettes. Finally, the Russians climb into the back of the jeep. Major Popov wriggles his large frame into the back seat, squashing the Colonel into the corner as the driver crushes his cigarette beneath his boot and climbs in the front. The engine kicks into life.

After speaking to Kaminski for a few minutes, the English officer swings his leg over the jeep's side and settles next to the driver. He barks an order. The driver crunches the gears and speeds off through the gate. Major Yuri Popov's head and broad shoulders dominate the skyline while Colonel Ivan Volkov, looking like a schoolboy next to him, sits upright holding onto the jeep's frame. We give them a final wave, but the Russians never look back.

Later that afternoon, we're sitting on the log near the cleared cellar door, talking to Chuck and drinking coffee, when a British army truck drives up to the farmhouse and parks in front of us. A Polish soldier climbs out and asks if we are the new recruits. We throw the dregs of our coffee away as we get ready to leave, taking turns shaking Chuck's hand and thanking him for his help. He stands at the tailgate as we climb into the back.

It's already full of men. Poles. Like us.

Settling on the bench, we introduce ourselves and shake a few hands. Some of the men look very frail, no more than skin and bones. They've been propped up on the floor, leaning against wooden planks with hessian sacking cushioning their backs. Only a couple of men sit along the bench next to us.

I peer out through the canvas flap and see Chuck turn and walk to the mess tent. I notice he has Franz's knife strapped to his utility belt. Franz whispers behind my back.

"When Kaminski went back to the cellar, I got him to give it to Chuck as a gift. It occurred to me, without him translating for us, we could have been in real trouble."

I smile at the Corporal's receding back, "You're damn tootin' we would be in trouble."

Franz chuckles.

I grin at Franz. He grins back.

"You can be thoughtful sometimes, Franz, even though you

act as if you didn't care."

He grunts and leans back on the seat as the truck takes off.

Arriving at an army camp, near the American command post at Saint Vith, the truck stops at a guard post where the weaker men are helped down and put onto stretchers. The rest of us jump off, about the same time as a soldier with a clipboard, walks up and asks us our names, ticking them off with a pencil.

A Polish officer approaches Kaminski speaking in Russian and points to a brick building. Curiously, I watch them walk down a stone path and wonder where the officer is taking him. Jo trots after them but soon turns back. Before he leaves, I see Kaminski pat him on the shoulder, giving him a reassuring smile.

"The lieutenant says Kaminski is going to the Russian side of the camp and will join us soon," Jo pants as he joins us back at the truck.

Just before Kaminski goes into the building, he turns and gives us a short wave. I half-heartedly wave back with a sinking feeling in my stomach.

More trucks pull up. We're ordered to form lines and wait.

This gives me a few minutes to take a good look at the camp. Guarded by Polish soldiers, a set of iron gates in a wire mesh fence stand open to the road leading into the camp.

In a field are army green camouflage tents, two larger ones flying both British and Polish flags. Narrow metal chimneys poke out of canvas roofs, allowing grey smoke to drift into the clear sky. Small piles of patchy snow lie alongside planks of wood, used as walkways to keep from walking in the sludge. Soldiers walk to and fro, weaving between rows of tents, some entering the two larger tents. Behind the tents a tank drives out of a large barn and stops near a fuel tank. Half a dozen men climb all over it, doing some kind of maintenance.

I peel my eyes away as a Polish corporal walk towards us and introduces himself as Jan Symanski.

Blond, and of average height, with wide, hooded blue eyes and prominent cheekbones he has the typical Slavic appearance. He smiles broadly, welcoming us. His uniform is like the British, only he has Polish insignias on the sleeves and wears a brown beret, pulled back from his forehead.

He tells us to gather round and offers cigarettes, lighting them with a silver lighter. Leading us through the gates, he chatters non-stop.

"There is a contingent of British and Polish army personnel stationed here to help you assimilate into army life," he explains. "Also, a large field hospital to help with the sick escapees. The camp is designed to collect prisoners escaping from the German camps who are making their way to the borders of Germany. There are hundreds like you finding their way towards the British and American army camps every day."

Stopping in front of the two larger tents I saw previously, a group of us are led through the tent flaps while the rest wait outside.

Standing in line, I observe a Polish Officer behind a large trestle table. Immaculate in his uniform, with his brown hair slicked back and his moustache neatly trimmed, he looks up briefly then back to his notes. He throws out his arm with his fingers clicking for the three of us to come closer.

"Papers!"

Franz and I hand him our ID papers. Jo hangs back. The

officer hands them back to us after making notes in a ledger. He glances up at Jo. Jo shakes his head.

The officer nods and asks him some questions, writing the answers down.

We stand at attention as he fills in three small brown books and holds them out to us.

"They're your new ID papers, the 'Soldiers' Service and Pay Book' in which your army pay will be recorded. It is important to keep them on you at all times in case you're asked to show them to an officer, military or civil policeman, or any military authority."

He gestures for us to move towards a short soldier with a close haircut. The private asks us to get on the scales one by one. He adjusts the weights along the rods and measures us as we step down, then writes his findings down in our books. He hands them back.

We thumb through the books quickly, not understanding the written language inside.

The private smiles.

"I wrote it in English because you are now under the English command."

Grinning, I glance up at Jo and Franz.

"We're getting paid for being here!" I exclaim, excitedly waving the book around.

They smile broadly. Franz smartly salutes the officer and the private. Jo and I follow suit with exaggerated salutes and pulling stupid faces. The men behind us laugh, some having a coughing fit. The Polish officer looks up from his ledger and waves us away with a humorous grunt, commenting that we're just as idiotic as Laurel and Hardy from the Hollywood movies.

We laugh. I love those two goons. Jo and I used to imitate them when we clowned around with our mates.

Corporal Symanski, still chuckling, directs us to the supply tent where the quartermaster soon kits each of us out with a combat uniform, overcoat, underwear, socks, boots, beret with a Polish insignia and other equipment. We even get a duffle bag, toilet gear and a sewing kit.

Symanski pats his own uniform.

"Wear your uniform with pride," he says, looking each of us in the eye, his glance lingering sternly on me. "We have the same uniforms as the British, but with a special insignia of our own. As you can see it's the helmet and wings of the Polish Hussars." He shows us the sleeve of his jacket. "The Hussars are very important in Polish history. They represented a Polish Cavalry as far back as the 1500s. Be proud of your heritage!"

No longer feeling the urge to clown around, we fill the duffle bags, heft them onto our backs and trudge along a muddy track towards a row of tents.

Corporal Symanski stops in front of one.

"Gather around boys! This is your tent. The washroom and showers are down the track. They're easy to find.

There is a sign on a tent pole. You all need to visit the camp's barber. He has a tent next to the shower tents and the mess tent is further down near the centre of the camp. I'll leave you now and let you get settled."

Entering our tent, I see it has three canvas stretchers, each with a neatly folded blanket and pillow. Three metal lockers are lined up against the opposite wall.

A wood burning stove, its flue piercing the canvas roof to the outside, stands in a corner with a wood box and kindling alongside.

Jo and I dump our gear on the beds, while Franz lights the stove. It burns bright. He adds a small log and closes the grill. We gather towels, underwear, socks, pants and shirts, and, with toilet bags in hand, head to the washrooms.

Undressing quickly, I place my clothes and kit on the benches provided, and step into the cubicle. I stand on the wooden pallets on the floor of the cubicle and study the spray nozzle, hanging from a pole, trying to figure out how it works. I fiddle with the taps until I get a generous flow of hot water jetting out from the nozzle. Adjusting the two taps makes the water warmer or cooler. I stand there, amazed, and let the hot water run through my fingers. I've never seen a shower before.

I hear Franz and Jo laughing, also adjusting the water flow. Jo pops his head over the partition, grinning.

"What do you think, boys? Have you ever seen anything like it?"

The other men in the washroom, including Franz and myself, laugh and cheer.

"It's fantastic!" I shout with excitement, doing a jig under the flow. I twist the taps again, making the water luxuriously warm and lift my face into the spray, then turn around to let the water pound on my back.

It's like massaging fingers on my scalp and body. It's the most incredible experience. I scrub all over with soap and stand under the water for a long time. I can hear Franz whistling and Jo singing a Polish folk tune. I hum a hymn that Alek once sang.

We dry off, our skin a bright red with our hair standing on end, then quickly dress in our underwear. I face a small mirror over a sink and search my toiletry bag for a razor. Lathering my face with soap and with careful and precise strokes, I have my first shave.

Smiling, I turn to Jo and Franz with the soap still clinging to my skin. Franz glances over, still in the middle of his shave, and ruffles my wet hair.

Quickly, we dress in our uniforms, jog back to our tents, and store our gear. Stepping outside into freezing temperatures, we run along the boards to the barber's tent where a line of new recruits waits inside, chatting excitedly. The barber clips our hair very short, and I notice lice dropping on the cape around my shoulders.

Grunting, he flicks the cape now and then, tossing them onto the dirt floor. I remind myself to use the stuff Doc gave us when he checked us over.

Franz insists on an American buzz-cut, just like Chuck's, which leaves more hair on the top of the head. However, Jo and I choose a crew-cut, which is a short length all over, just like the private who weighed us.

Back in our warm tent, we put on our khaki jackets, buttoning them up to the neck and adjusting the belt around our waists. I touch the red 'Poland' badge on my sleeve, above the insignia of a helmet with a wing, and pull it around to take a better look. I'm now a Polish soldier.

Enormous pride swells in my chest. I put on my beret, and overcoat and turn to look at Jo and Franz. We look very smart.

Grinning at each other, a sense of achievement mirrored on our faces, we venture outside to find the mess tent.

Men we met in the army truck emerge from their tents, looking like us in their fresh uniforms. They offer us cigarettes and as we smoke, we ask them questions. Most were from sub-camps. Only two escaped a concentration camp and were forced to walk in a 'death march.'

One of these men introduces himself as Artur Wojcik and the man next to him as Szymon Kowalczyk.

Artur recounts their story.

"The SS marched us to a camp a hundred kilometres away without food or water," he begins, "knowing full well they were killing us."

He wipes his eyes, "Many died on that march. When men fell and were unable to get back up, the SS guards shot them in the head."

"Szymon and I," Artur nods to his friend, "would lift our friends up by the arms and carry them as far as we could, but in the end, they begged us to put them down, so they could die."

He swipes his tears with the palm of his hand.

"I saw my friends keel over to never get up," Artur murmurs.

He swallows and resumes his story in a louder voice.

"A lot of the time the SS wouldn't waste a bullet. An opportunity came our way when a man dropped at the front of the line.

With the screaming and all the confusion, Szymon and I ran into the forest and hid in the undergrowth until it got dark. Then we walked to the nearest town and hid in a cellar.

The next morning, an old man found us trying to steal food from his kitchen.

Taking pity on us, he fed us and hid us in the back of his hay cart, then drove to the nearest American army post.

The old man put a white tablecloth around the old nag's

neck to show he had come in peace.

The Americans laughed when they saw the horse and gave him a block of chocolate and were surprised when Szymon and I spilled out of the back of the wagon. Szymon had to convince them we weren't German."

Szymon grins, picking up the threads of the story.

"They fetched a soldier who could speak a little German," he says.

"I had to tell him we were Polish not Krauts. It took some time as the American's German was very limited, but with a lot of hand signals and pointing to him, and each other, he finally understood. One of the guards, ... What was his name, Artur?"

"Bedo, I think it was Bedo," answers Artur. "A strange name!"

"Oh yeah, Bedo," continues Szymon. "Bedo took us to an American field hospital where we were examined by doctors and fed a weak soup for days.

We stayed in the hospital for two weeks to recover, then they sent us here."

We listen in silence. I stare at the Polish flag on top of the flagpole, flapping in the breeze and begin to think. What if this happened to the men left in our work camp? Or perhaps they we're all just lined up and shot? I begin to realise not a lot of men had escaped the concentration camps. Most of the men we've met have come from sub-camps.

I also realise just how lucky we are. I shudder, thinking what might have been our fate.

Dinner is a serving of meat and vegetable stew followed by a bread pudding and a cup of coffee with lashings of carnation milk. I relish every mouthful and sit back with my hand on my full stomach. At least I can keep the richer foods down now. Although, I still need to be careful not to eat large amounts.

As I'm sipping the sweet coffee, I make a promise to myself that I'm going to eat everything on my plate from now on. In memory of the starvation in the camp.

Szymon pulls out a packet of cards and we have a game of euchre before heading back.

#####

The army allows us two weeks to recover from two years of malnutrition, deprivation, and cruelty. I believe a lot of the POWs took longer, and in some cases actually died.

We're allowed to sleep throughout the day, eat plenty of food, read magazines and play cards. Franz even finds a book which he reads out in snippets.

A doctor examines us at the end of the second week. He measures and weighs us and seems pleased with our progress.

"You're doing well lads," he reports, "I'll give you to the end of the month before you become active servicemen.

Late one afternoon, Jan visits and tells us we will be fighting at the Front. I'm excited, but also fearful. This could finish us off. I could lose Jo and Franz or even be killed myself. Being killed after what we've been through in the last four years seems kind of ironic.

I offer Jan a cigarette. "Jan...," I say, hesitating in case I'm about to do something else stupid, but decide to ask, anyway. "What do you know about our friend, Kaminski? Do you know where he is?"

"Kaminski?" He looks curiously at me. "I'm sorry, Rys.

I know nothing of him, but if you like, I'll see what I can find out."

That night he finds us in the mess hall.

"Kaminski is an interpreter for the Russians," Jan reports, as we look up at him expectantly.

He sits down on the bench and slouches off his coat, lying it beside him.

"He was sent to Berlin on the same day you arrived. General Zhukov recruited him," he says unbuttoning his jacket.

"Did you know Kaminski was fluent in four languages, Polish, German, French and Russian?" he asks.

We shook our heads.

"No wonder he was snatched up as soon as you arrived." Jan adds. "He is a valuable resource."

"Damn. Damn," Jo curses despondently. "I never got the chance to say a proper goodbye

Or thank him for saving my life."

Jo bows his head, clasping his hands together on the table. I pat his shoulder.

"Maybe when the war is over, we can find him, Jo."

He nods his head.

I looked back at Jan.

"Kaminski really helped us. Without him we could have easily been caught."

The following day we march to a field tent and are issued helmets, ammunition, and army rations, then instructed on how to load and fire a rifle. Before we know it, we are in trucks heading into the war zone.

CHAPTER

47

The Front Line is chaotic. Terrifying. All at the same time.

A mixture of Polish and British forces manoeuvre tanks, set up machine gun posts and dig foxholes amongst the trees in a vast forest. Most of the morning we dig trenches deep enough to crouch in to fire a rifle.

The Polish and British artillery bombard the Germans to the North, but the Germans are getting closer. Their artillery shells are unremitting with troops from an SS Panzer division attacking us with machine gun fire. Bullets rip through the air. We duck lower as the foliage above our heads is shredded, pelting us with sharp twigs, splitters of wood and smouldering pine needles.

Our platoon returns fire, launching grenades. I hear the rat-a-tat-tat of our machine gun to my right. I spit grit out of my mouth and keep my head down. Gripping my helmet, I swear under my breath, thinking all the while how stupid this war is.

What a waste of human lives. Men killing men for what reason? For a piece of forest? To make a stand?

To regain honour? I can't see any Generals cowering in these trenches. That would be too dangerous for the bastards. It would spoil all their fun in planning the whole stupid thing. Bloody idiots, the whole lot of them.

The noise is deafening. Men cry out in alarm and pain. Trees are blown apart and land on top of them. The sickening creak of wood and booming thuds of falling tree trunks is as bad as the mortar shells exploding around us.

I press my forehead against the mud and desperately gulp in air, rancid with smoke. I glance sidewards at Jo, who is staring back at me, his eyes wild.

Franz peers over the trench, aiming his gun, and begins to fire.

Jo lifts his head and begins to shoot, swearing at the top of his voice and grinning from ear to ear.

I follow suit, without the swearing and grinning, firing from side to side.

But I can honestly say I don't think I killed anyone. I'm too busy keeping my head down to aim properly. My shots go wild. Ricocheting off branches, embedding into tree trunks and the ground. I even shoot the mound of soil in front of me.

Franz swears loudly.

"For Christ's sake aim your shots higher!" he shouts in my ear.

The battle is intense. Men die around us. A trench blows up behind us, showering us with dirt. A German tank, sweeping a wide arc left to right, fires into our ranks, decimating our artillery. Red hot shrapnel rains over our heads as we crouch down further.

Smoke swirls around us. The bombardment is unrelenting.

I start to pant, clutching my rifle even harder. *This is it! This how I die!* I cringe, shutting my eyes tighter.

The bombardment abruptly stops.

I cautiously peep over the edge. Through the haze I see a

huge impenetrable machine ploughing towards us.

Jo shouts in my ear, "It's a German Panzer IV Infantry Support tank! A smaller version of the German Tiger Tanks we saw on the road coming from Prum!"

It rolls straight over fallen trees and dugout trenches. German infantry, in a crouching run, hide behind it, using it as a shield as they fire their rifles. Jo and I duck down, burying ourselves into the mud, as a barrage of bullets slams the earth around us.

"Bloody stupid! The both of you!" growls Franz, "you'll get your heads blown off!"

We crouch in a ball, gripping our guns.

"Get back! Back into the forest!" yells a corporal crawling along the ground towards us.

We don't need to be told twice!

Leaping out of the trenches, running like madmen back towards a dense part of the forest, with the Panzers in pursuit, we twist and turn, trying to dodge the barrage of bullets sprayed between the trees and flying over our heads.

Amazed we're still all together and running at full speed, we flee through the undergrowth into a ploughed field. A Polish Sherman tank grinds towards us. We fall behind it and dive into bushes on the opposite side of the field, under a clump of oak trees. The Sherman tank now fires into the pursuing German infantry, pushing them back into the forest we just vacated.

The Panzer IV tank roars into view, a black iron cross painted on its six-metre-long hull. Its tracks and road wheels grind and squeal over the dead lying in the churned-up mud. Swivelling its turret back and forth, it fires its KwK 40 L/48 gun. The muzzle spurts red flames, followed by a grey tendril of smoke. Sitting in the gun hatches on either side of the huge barrel, German gunners fire MG34 machine guns at the fleeing Polish army.

Men dive into the undergrowth, heaving with exertion.

We're pinned down, as the battle rages around us. The tanks fight it out with our men taking pot shots at the German gunners. Their bullets ping off the metal hull with no effect.

The Panzer IV fires round after round at the Sherman tank, which is no match for the Panzer IV accuracy. Our tank takes a direct hit and blows up with a horrific boom, shaking the earth around us.

Men tumble out of the hatch half crazed and screaming as the flames engulf them. Most are ripped apart by a spray of German bullets.

The Panzer IV swivels its gun towards our position. We scramble backwards into the thickest part of the wood, our bodies pinned low as a shell explodes behind us. The German gunners rake the oak trees with machine gun fire. Two men die in front of us.

I drop my head to the dirt, panting hard, breathing in the damp earth. I pray out loud. "Mother Mary please help me! I can't take much more."

At that moment, the land suddenly shakes with an almighty explosion. The air becomes thick with smoke. Intense heat sears everything around us. I gaze up in disbelief to see the German tank engulfed in flames. Billowing black smoke spews out its open hatch and the engine air intake, then the tank explodes into a massive fireball. Its iron cladding buckles and screeches.

Men cheer around me. I just lie there with my mouth open.

Dazed.

#####

In the late afternoon, Franz, Jo, and I trudge back with the medics, carrying stretchers, to help bring in the wounded.

"How did the German tank get blown up?" I ask one of the medics as he checks a soldier's pulse, nods his head, and starts to wrap bandages around his bleeding leg.

"A rifle grenade. It stopped the German tank from further decimating our troops," he answers, glancing at me. I squat down beside him and dig inside the medic bag for a clip.

"Apparently, the tank's gunners were killed by a sniper," he adds, cutting the bandage away and securing it with his hand. I passed him a clip. "Who also shot the tank commander as he scrambled up the hatch to man one of the MG 34 machine guns. The sniper hid somewhere in a spruce tree, away from the action. Corporal Adamski, who fired the anti-tank grenade, found a ditch, and used a grenade launcher, sending a No. 68 AT grenade into the Panzer IVs open hatch, blowing it up, and killing all inside."

We grip the unconscious man under his arms and carefully lift him onto the stretcher.

"It was pure luck and an unbelievable aim that won that battle," he grunts as he takes the weight. "It would have been a very different outcome if the German tank was left to fight on."

As we carry the injured men back towards the waiting ambulance, I look around me. Most of the men on the battlefield are dead. Polish and German alike. I feel sad, seeing their vacant stares and their bodies lying twisted on the ground, amongst the acorns and fallen leaves. Until now our men had survived the horrors of this bloody war. Most survived the camps. But in the end the Germans got them anyway.

After this battle, our platoon is sent back to the main camp, shell shocked and weary. My nightmares return. But instead of a snake around my neck I dream of a German tank running me down. Jo begins to twitch and call out in his sleep, waking in a sweat. When I wake through the night, I see Franz sitting on the edge of his bed. His head in his hands.

One afternoon, Corporal Jan Symanski visits our tent with a bottle of Polish Vodka. How he got it I have no idea. As he pours us a shot, he talks about the Polish Army, telling us he's been in the Polish 1st Armoured Division 26th Infantry Battalion for some time.

He sits on my stretcher and takes a sip of his drink, then recounts his story.

"The armoured division we're in is commanded by Major General Maczek. It was formed in Scotland around 1942.

But before that, we were guarding two hundred kilometres of the eastern British coast.

We remained in Scotland when the Polish forces regrouped in France and the Soviet Union hoping to re-enter Poland and defeat the Germans. With the help of the Allies of course."

I thought of Pa. Maybe he was sent to Scotland.

Jan pours more shots.

"We came late to this campaign, landing at Caen on the 1st of August. Then we fought a major battle against the Wehrmacht to claim Mont Ormel and Chambois, losing a lot of men."

For a moment he's quiet and stares into his drink.

"It so happens we closed a pocket of land and trapped the German Panzer divisions. They couldn't break through. The fighting was brutal. The 2nd Polish Armoured Regiment supported by the infantry took the brunt of the German attack. Running out of ammunition, we had been surrounded for 48 hours, until we were relieved by the British and the Canadians.

We fought the Germans right up the Belgium and Netherlands coast and one of our last battles was last November, at Moerdijk, when we liberated the town of Breda in the Netherlands. All the civilians came out of their houses and cheered, waving their flags, and hanging orange cloth out of windows. The Dutch partied for days. We got a lot of kisses from pretty girls and ugly old women!"

We all laugh, the horrors of our battle loosening their grip. I think everyone must feel as we do after their first battle. Jan smooths back his hair as I study him. He seems to be in his late twenties and is reasonably fit. I notice his forearms bulge when he takes off his jacket and rolls up his sleeves.

"I came to Scotland in 1941, in the earlier part of the war," he explains. "I've been in the army for a couple of years now.

I still have family in Poland, but when this is finished, I'd like to resettle in the UK. I've seen a lot of Scotland and some parts of England too. I've met a Scottish girl I'm keen to marry."

He pours us another drink, then leans back on his elbow, smiling.

"Now, tell me your stories."

We talk for another hour, then follow him back to the mess tent.

At the end of the week, we are deployed once again, but this time to French towns and villages to flush out small, isolated pockets of the German Army.

The Nazis are trying to keep their strongholds in France and Belgium in a desperate, last-ditch effort to win the war. It has changed from open battlefields to street battles, making it very dangerous for us all.

We are deployed to a small French town near the German border.

The Krauts barricade themselves in the Town Hall, firing for thirty minutes, until a Polish tank fires into the building. Through the smoke a white flag at the end of a rifle slowly comes into view.

We stand in a semi-circle as the Krauts file out and throw down their weapons then put their hands on their heads. Two Polish soldiers grab their discarded guns as we push them into lines and search for cigarettes and anything else of value. A Polish soldier pulls a German officer to the side and shoots him in the head.

I grimace. I feel no gratification in seeing the Kraut killed. He probably was following orders like the rest of us.

A British lieutenant reprimands us.

"I understand your hatred for the Germans," he says, "but they can still give us vital information. So, I'm ordering you not to execute any more German prisoners."

However, despite his order, some soldiers still kill the Germans whenever they get the chance.

A week later, our unit is scouting an empty street lined with trees. It's eerily quiet, the buildings abandoned.

Franz and I fall back to light cigarettes when a grenade is

thrown out of a two-storey building, blowing up a large fir tree. Unfortunately, Franz and I are under it.

It splits in half, raining huge branches, knocking us to the ground. Splinters fly through the air. A large branch thumps the back of my head, sending pain shooting through my skull.

Stunned, I lie on my stomach, my ears ringing, my face being ground into the hard pavement. Sounds around me are muffled as if I'm under water. I hear a faint voice, telling me not to move. My head throbs. My vision is blurry. I lift my hand slowly to my scalp. It feels sticky. Raising my head slightly, I squint at my fingers, seeing blood.

Slowly turning my head, I can just make out a blue cross on a soldier's helmet. He's talking to someone next to me.

I think he's talking to Franz.

Oh shit! ... Franz!

There is more gun fire. I feel hands lifting me. I think I speak to someone, but I'm not sure. My mind is foggy, and darkness clouds my vision. I sink into oblivion.

I remember no more.

Marcia Wakeman

CHAPTER

48

Slowly, I open my eyes. The pain is excruciating. My head feels like it's on fire. I hear a soft snore, then a grunt and carefully turn my head towards the noise. I can just make-out Jo sitting in a chair, his head nodding as a snore escapes his slack mouth. I try to say his name, but it comes out as a croak. He wakes, wiping drool with his sleeve, and looks at me. Quickly he leans forward and grasps my hand. I try to smile at him, the injury on the back of my head throbbing.

"How are you, Rys?" he asks softly.

He looks tired. There are small cuts and long scratches along his forehead and neck.

"I've got a massive headache!" I croak as I tightly shut my eyes.

"I'll ask the nurse if you can have some painkillers," he says soothingly, patting my arm.

The pain in the back of my skull is agonising. I tentatively touch the bandage wrapped around my head, creeping my fingers to the back.

I don't feel any soreness until I finger the wad of gauze near the base of my skull. Where the pain is the worst.

Ahh... shit!

From the next bed I hear a muffled voice. I slowly turn my head to that side and see Franz's face squished into the mattress. His mouth contorts into funny angles as he tries to speak.

"Thank God you're okay Rys," he mumbles. "I thought you were dead!"

"The Krauts can't get rid of me that easily!" I chuckle, but then regret it as fresh pain seizes my skull. I groan, and slowly face the tent's ceiling, my least painful position.

"Ah shit, Rys! Don't move your head!" Franz hisses through his teeth.

I take a deep breath and speak slowly, trying not to move any muscles in my neck.

"How bad are your injuries, Franz?"

"Not that bad. I had a large splinter lodged in my back, below the ribs, just missing my spine. The doctor operated to remove it and a bigger splinter that stabbed my butt. I have two holes in that area now!"

I cringe. "Ah, shit Franz!"

"I bloody hope so!" he chuckles.

I try not to laugh.

"I have to lie on my stomach for two weeks so the nurses can dress my wounds," he continues. "It's bloody uncomfortable."

He wiggles around, nestling into the bedsheets.

"Where are we?" I ask, confused.

Gritting his teeth, Franz winces as he puts pressure on his back.

"In a field hospital near Saint Vith. It's a hospital for the badly injured."

Jo returns with a nurse, and together they help me to sit up. They raise me slowly, just enough to swallow two aspirin with water, then carefully lay me back down. The nurse gently supports my neck with her hand as I am lowered to the pillow. She looks into my eyes, and I notice hers are a striking blue.

"Can you hear me?" she asks.

"Yes, nurse," I reply then realise she's speaking Polish.

Her face comes close to mine, "You have a severe head injury and a damaged eardrum. And grazes along your forehead and nose, which isn't serious."

I can smell her floral perfume. It smells the same as the talcum powder my mother used. A tear rolls down my face.

The nurse wipes it away with her fingers, straightens and smiles.

"You're going to have terrible headaches for a few days, and a sore head. You'll have a nasty scar on the back of your head, but your hair will cover it. You have a fractured skull, and you are suffering from concussion, so be careful when you finally sit up. You could feel dizzy and nauseous. I'll leave a pan near the bed if you need to be sick."

She puts a thermometer in my mouth and rests her slender fingers along my wrist as she looks at a watch, pinned to her uniform. She asks more questions about my vision then writes on a chart.

Placing it at the end of the bed she moves towards Franz. I turn my head very slowly to watch her.

She is very pretty. Her red hair is pulled back in a neat bun under her nurse's cap, with escaping curls forming a halo around her freckled face. Her lips are soft and full. She has a beautiful smile. Of average height, her figure is curvy, but not buxom and she moves gracefully, like a ballerina.

Removing the dressings, she examines Franz's back and his bum. He winces in pain as she re-dresses both his wounds and, surprisingly, pats his good bum cheek.

Franz tries to get a better look at her but gives up due to the way he's lying. He drops his face into the mattress and sighs.

She bends forward and whispers in his ear.

Franz grins and goes a little pink.

Smiling, she writes in his chart and hangs it at the base of his bed and moves to the next patient.

I smile ever so slightly, realising I've never seen him blush before.

"I think Franz is in trouble!" Jo chuckles under his breath.

My smile changes to a grimace as I take a good look at his face. He has small puncture wounds near his eyes.

He looks down at me, noting my concern.

"I was lucky I didn't lose my eye!" he admits as he tentatively touches his face.

"You sound like Pa when the store got bombed!" I wheezed.

"That was so long ago Rys." Jo whispers through a sigh. "Looking back, he was lucky he didn't get badly hurt or, even worse, killed."

I change the subject. "What happened in the street battle? I just remember an explosion."

"Our unit opened fire and took the bastards out! No prisoners this time!" Jo gloats.

Inwardly, I cringe. I expected a bloodbath, but I still didn't like the way Jo bragged about it. Most of the Germans captured were just kids, about the same age we were when we joined the Resistance.

Jo senses I've gone quiet

"I'll let you sleep now," he says, patting my leg. "I'll come back tomorrow."

When the pretty nurse returns on one of her rounds, I smile at her.

"What is your name?" I ask.

"Mary. What's your name?"

"Rys. The ugly one on my right is Franz," I mutter in reply.

"Oh, he's not that ugly," Mary says softly as she tucks the bed clothes around me.

Franz mumbles something incoherent into the mattress.

"Are you Polish?" I ask in a whisper.

"No, I'm British," she whispers back, carefully adjusting my pillow.

"But my parents are from Poland," she admits. "They have lived in England for a long time."

She marks the chart on the end of my bed.

Grinning cheekily, she adjusts the blankets on Franz's bed.

"I'll come back later and give you a sponge bath. I think you both need one!"

Beaming with pleasure, Franz and I face each other and quietly chuckle as she moves away.

#####

After two weeks Franz is more mobile. Mary helps him to walk around the tent and, weather permitting, venture outside to take in the fresh air. It becomes a regular outing.

One night, as the lanterns are dimmed, and we settle down

to sleep, Franz whispers to me.

"When Mary and I went outside today, we strolled around the hospital grounds and found a quiet spot under a tree. We talked for a while about our lives. She was telling me how her sister died. I took her hand and kissed it. Then she kissed me. It was only a brief kiss, but it took me by surprise. She allowed me to kiss her properly. When we came up for air, I looked into her eyes and my heart skipped a beat and did something strange. It began to unravel. All my life my heart has felt like a tightly wound ball of string, as if it's been this twisted thing behind my ribs. Somehow, Mary's kiss tugged it loose, as if her beautiful fingers had threaded themselves in between the tight strings and pulled them free. I felt incredibly alive and unbelievably free. As if I could finally breathe. It was wonderful. She told me she usually doesn't fall for a patient, especially a Pole, but she just couldn't help it this time. I kissed her again and knew then I love her."

He smiles and stares whimsically into space. I look at him through the soft light and grin. I've never seen him like this before.

During the week, even though he is leaning on one butt cheek, Franz manages to get himself into a padded chair.

Leaning on his crutch, he watches Mary do her rounds, glowing with love.

Occasionally, Mary smiles back at him as she tends the other men. When she makes her way back to us to check our wounds again, her hand lingers on Franz's shoulder as she chats to us. Taking her hand gently, he kisses her fingers, making her blush.

Jo and Jan visit regularly and entertain the whole ward with

476

their silly antics. Jo is always telling us lame jokes and Jan impersonates one of the British officers by stomping around with a stick under his arm.

Throughout the two weeks we both heal quickly. I soon become restless, wanting to do more than sit in a chair.

By the end of the third week a Polish officer walks into our ward and asks the nurses to gather all the able-bodied men, from the other wards, and meet him here. He stands before us as the wounded men congregate around him.

Mary moves closer to Franz as he stands beside a chair, holding it for support. She secretly takes his free hand.

I'm happy for Franz. He deserves to have a beautiful girl to love him and for him to love her. I don't think his Pa cared for him as a father should. I believe he had little or no love from anyone else, except from me. I love him as a brother. Without him, I would never have survived.

The Polish officer looks around the room. Some of the men are in wheelchairs others lean on crutches. For a long moment, he stands with his hands behind his back.

"I am Lieutenant Safranski. You might have seen me in the mess tent, especially when it's serving placki."

A few of the men laugh.

The officer smiles.

"I have seen how courageous and brave you all are. I have seen how you fought against the Germans with tireless tenacity and selflessness. I am honoured to be amongst you."

He takes a breath, "I believe you have done enough in serving our country, our beloved Poland, and I also believe you have been through enough hell!"

We all cheer and as the whooping fades.

He continues. "We are in the final stages of this war. It could be over in a couple of months. The British government needs our help in dismantling war fortifications surrounding the Scottish coast. Every available Polish man, who wishes to go to the UK, will be sent to the Scottish Isles to help with dismantling these fortifications."

The men around me begin to clap.

He clears his throat. "But I'm here to make an official announcement."

We grow quiet and pay attention.

"You will be recuperating for the rest of the war in the Orkney Islands, north of Scotland.

There is an audible gasp around the ward.

Franz and I look at him in surprise.

Scotland!

"Company Three and Company Four will also be deployed to Scotland," he states. "They mainly consist of men just like yourselves, ex-POWs."

Thank God, Jo will be going as well.

Utterly relieved, I sit quiet and still in my chair. I'm going to leave. I'm partially deaf in one ear and the back of my head sports a large round scar about the size of an English penny. I feel tired, worn out. I've had enough of this war and being in a safe place will be a welcome change.

Lieutenant Safranski shakes hands with the men. I look over to Franz. His eyes meet mine. He flashes me an exuberant smile. A silent message pass between us.

We've made it. We have survived.

CHAPTER

49

The hospital orderlies help the wounded into the waiting trucks, pushing and pulling them over the tailgate. I'm one of the last to climb in. I steady myself by gripping the truck's frame. Taking deep breaths to combat the dizziness, I heave myself onto the nearest seat. And wait for Franz.

He takes his time.

I gaze through the opening in the canvas to see Mary lifted onto her toes with Franz's arms encircling her waist, holding her tight. Mary clings to him as they kiss, then slowly pulls away and buries her head in his shoulder. I look away. I feel I'm intruding on something intimate and personal between them. I am sorry for them. It's a shame Mary can't leave with us, and it's hard for Franz to leave her behind. I know it would be for me if I had such a girl.

I look back as one of the men yells out for them to hurry up and the rest start to wolf whistle, calling out rude remarks. Franz ignores them as he gently strokes Mary's hair, loosened from its bun and cascading over her shoulders in soft curls. It gleams with red highlights in the bright morning sunlight.

Gripping her nurse's cap in one hand and Franz's lapels with the other, Mary weeps into his jacket as Franz stares into the distance, his face wet with tears.

When he approaches the truck, I take a closer look at Franz, realising he has grown over the last couple of months. He is taller, and broader through his shoulders, losing his thin, gangly shape. He even has the beginnings of a moustache. He is a man, not a boy.

Franz is helped up by two orderlies and winces as he sits down, wiping his face with his sleeve. Empathising, I pat him on the shoulder as he gazes forlornly through the canvas opening.

The truck slowly pulls away leaving Mary standing in the middle of the road, her pretty face a mask of misery.

Franz pulls the canvas flap back to let in some fresh air. Side by side, we look silently at the war-torn landscape. I study what we're leaving behind and wonder what the future will bring. I realise I'm actually leaving Europe, with all its horror and death. I inhale sharply. I'm leaving my homeland and my family! Maybe for ever. Am I doing the right thing? But true optimism lifts my spirits for the first time in years. Scotland could be a good place to start a new life.

Whatever it takes, I'm going to make the best of it.

Franz finally drops the canvas and carefully leans back. I look at him as he glances my way, both of us wearing the same determined expression.

"I think the UK could be a good thing!" I say with some conviction.

Franz crosses his arms, "I think you're right, Rys. I'm not ever coming back!"

After some time, under a dark and threatening sky, the truck pulls up to a harbour packed with naval ships. I locate a ship with its hull painted white and a long red strip painted along its sides. Port holes are above and below the red line with more cabins on deck. Tied to the wharf, the ship bobs and sways in the stiff breeze, looking more like a cruise ship than a man-o-war.

We all climb off the trucks with the help of waiting sailors.

A strong wind, carrying the scent of the sea, blows in our faces. I haven't seen the ocean before, so I stand on the wharf for a long moment, marvelling at the waves lapping along the ship's hull and the huge expanse of water reaching to the horizon.

Wounded men climb up the gangplank, hobbling and shuffling along its swaying length. Franz and I follow them, Franz walking stiffly on his crutch and I steadying myself on the rail.

I glance back and see trucks pulling up with more men on board. Soldiers jump onto the wharf with Jo amongst them. He looks up, as if on cue, and gives me a wave, and trots towards a transport ship.

A sailor meets us on deck, directing us to a large hold full of steel bunks suspended from the ceiling and secured to the floor with steel pipes. The bunks are end-to-end from one wall to the other, leaving a narrow corridor for us and the nurses to walk through.

The mattresses are covered in white sheets and thick blankets. I'm shown a bed and sink down into its heavenly softness where I can smell the freshly laundered pillowcase and sheets. I adjust the pillow to accommodate the soreness of my scalp.

Franz heaves a sigh of relief when he finally manages to

swing his legs up onto the bunk across from me.

"What's Mary like Franz?" I ask, after a while.

"She is the love of my life, Rys!" he exhales in a soft whisper. "After what we've been through, I can't believe I've fallen for a beautiful girl, who loves me back. Mary is marvellous. Did you see her hair shining in the sunlight with so many red and orange colours running through it?" he asks but doesn't wait for my reply. "It's like the sunset over the Polish plains."

He pauses for a while staring into space, but then carefully moves to his good side. He adjusts his pillow and looks at me.

"Mary is very intelligent and reads all the time," he says enthusiastically. "She's teaching me English and when I get to Scotland, I'm going to learn the language properly and surprise her. Her parents came to the UK years before the war and her father is in the Polish embassy. He is involved in the Polish government-in-exile.

When the Polish army came back to Europe, Mary joined the nursing corps and asked to serve in the Polish Command. She was snapped up because she could speak the language."

He grins.

"We have agreed that when she comes back to the UK, we'll get married."

Franz, married?

I stare at him, open-mouthed. I don't know what to say.

He chuckles, adding. "And Rys, you're going to be my best man!"

I smile, relieved that I feel truly happy for my friend.

"Franz, I'll be honoured!"

"And Jo is going to organise the catering!" Franz continues, "I'll ask him when we get to Scotland."

He prattles on, sharing his dreams with me.

"I'm going to get a good job and earn a lot of money. I'll get an education and become a mechanical engineer. Mary said there are universities in Scotland where I can get a degree. I'd like to do that. I'll buy her a house with a backyard and a flower garden. We would like to have children, Rys. A boy and a girl would be nice. I'll take them to the ..."

Lulled by the rocking of the ship, I close my eyes. Franz's voice gradually fades, murmuring in my ear, as I fall into a deep dreamless sleep.

It takes a week to arrive in Kirkwall, one of the largest towns in the Orkney Islands.

Nestled in a green valley, among snow-capped mountains, Kirkwall is a small city with a church steeple peeking above grey tiled roofs.

The surrounding land is lush, with sheep grazing on the fields and mountain slopes.

Fishing boats, tilted on their sides on the mud flats at low tide, are anchored in the harbour.

Huge gulls hover above the fishermen cleaning their catch. A raucous flock squabbles along the pebble beach, demanding offerings which occasionally come their way.

The island has a wild, rugged, breathtaking beauty.

Standing on the wharf, I gaze, awestruck. It's as if I'm in a different world, totally alien to the one I have just left.

The army barracks, situated on the outskirts of Kirkwall, are built in neat rows with tarmac roads separating the buildings and flower gardens planted near the entrance and around a flagpole.

As we climb out of the ambulance trucks, the cold sea air

whips around the parade ground, smacking into our faces. I take in a deep breath then exhale, enjoying the salty taste.

Energised, I heft the duffle bag onto my back, and we march up to the administration building where, yet again, we're met by a corporal. He ticks our names off on a clipboard and directs us to the hospital for a check-up by the doctor. There is a certain sameness about armies, whatever their nationality.

Franz and I are still in the recuperating stage and are put into a hospital ward, while Jo is stationed in a hut with other men from our company.

I unpack quickly and decide to have a look around the hospital building.

Shuffling towards the nurse's office and holding onto the wall in places, I peruse the notice board where I spot the name 'Muszynski'.

Muszynski!

I stare at it, not quite believing what I'm seeing.

Yes! It is the same name as mine!

Muszynski. My heart beats faster. Could this be a relative? Thinking, I tap the list of names, *Muszynski is a common name in Poland. I could be lucky! Who knows!*

I follow the sound of laughter further up the corridor and enter a recreation room. Gazing around the room with its warm, crackling open fireplace, a dining table and soft leather lounges, I see a man I recognise, playing cards. Grinning, I stand behind his chair, hardly able to believe my luck. He looks up at me then back to his cards, then looks up once more.

"Can I help you?... Do I know you?" he asks, studying my face uncertainly.

"I think you are my uncle... My Uncle Jon!" I say, smiling.

"What the hell!" He blurts out, rising unsteadily to his feet and tossing the cards onto the table.

"Oh my God, you're Wladyslaw's son, Ryszard! Bloody hell! It's so good to see you lad! I didn't recognise you! The last time I saw you, you were just a small boy counting jellybeans in a paper bag."

He suddenly wraps thin sinewy arms around me, pulling me into a hug. Stepping back, clutching my arms, he searches my face and notices the bandage wrapped around my head.

"What happened to you?" he asks as he releases his grip.

"I was injured when a tree blew up and a branch smacked the back of my head," I answer, touching the bandages. "But I'm recovering every day. I don't have as many headaches now." I add, "Jo's here as well. He's in the barracks."

"I don't believe it, both Wladyslaw's boys!"

Uncle Jon leads me to two chairs and sits facing me.

"Have you seen Pa?" I ask excitedly.

He clasps my forearm. "Yes! Yes! I saw him when the Polish army regrouped at Coetquidan in Brittany. He was with Tomasz. I was so glad to see them.

From that camp we moved around a fair bit as conditions were poor. We finally settled in Cecile-les-Vignes and your father Tomasz were sent to fight the Germans in a French region called Basse-Normandie. I lost track of them then.

I got word in August last year they were fighting in the 1st Armoured Division and were making ground, trapping the Germans in Mace and Chambois, hemming them in. They drove tanks which is a long way from riding horses, aye! But I'm sorry. I haven't heard anything about their division for a while."

I look at him in amazement. *Pa and Uncle Tomasz operating tanks! What the hell!*

But I keep quiet, remembering what happened to the Polish tank in our battle. I say a silent pray, hoping they're still alive.

After a while, I ask, "What about you Uncle Jon? What happened to you?"

Wincing, he carefully leans back on his chair.

"I was deployed in the Polish 2 Corps 5th Kresowa Infantry Division in the battle of Monte Cassino in Italy. We were to capture an abbey high on top of a mountain. It commanded the approaches of the Allies in the valley below. My division was sent to Colle Sant' Angelo and the surrounding hills to cover the advance of another brigade.

"I was so looking forward to this battle. It would be a chance to confront the German bastards and regain some honour for Poland. But we ran into heavy fire and all three of our battalions were engaged along Phantom Ridge. We were pretty much wiped out. I got badly wounded in the back. Then I was shipped here to recover, but I'll never recover fully.

I'm thinking of going back to Poland, when the war is over, to live out my days."

"I'm sorry to hear about your back injury," I say sympathetically.

"Don't be, Ryszard, I fought hard for Poland, and the Allies have pushed the German bastards back to Germany. The Nazis are losing this war and that's all I hope for."

"Now tell me what has happened to you?"

So, I tell him my story, including Jo's.

Uncle Jon leans over and grabs my shoulders giving them a gentle squeeze.

"Ah Ryszard. You and Jo are tough lads. I'm so glad you both came through this."

"My friend Franz is tough as well, but I think Jo might be even tougher."

We hear shouts and cheers from outside. Peering through the window we see men slapping each other on the backs and dancing around, throwing their arms into the air.

"What the hell! What's going on?" I ask excitedly.

Uncle Jon limps to the door and retrieves a cane leaning against the wall.

"I think there's good news, Rys!"

He looks back, grinning. "Are you coming?"

We hobble outside, with Uncle Jon holding onto his cane and me clinging to his other arm.

Looking baffled, Franz limps out of the ward and joins us. Jo runs out of a hut, followed by other men and they all look around in amazement.

"Hey! You! What's this all about?" Uncle Jon calls out to a soldier.

"The war has ended! Hitler is dead! The Germans have surrendered!"

"Holy shit! ... Holy Shit!... Yes, yes!" Franz shouts, pumping the air with his fist. I stand there like a stunned mullet, crushed in a bear hug from Jo.

We all begin to laugh and hoot with the rest of the men as Uncle shakes hands with his friends, slapping their backs. Others kneel on the tarmac, weeping into their hands.

I look up into the sky and pray to God that all my family, including Helena, have survived.

We make a wide circle and sing the Polish national anthem

at the top of our voices.

It's at that point I start to cry.

The celebration goes well into the night. We're allowed to go into the town and join with the Orcadian people who are cheering and dancing in the streets.

The pubs are full of rowdy patrons. We squeeze in and join in the merry making.

It's at this pub I have my first taste of English ale and my first kiss from a Scottish girl.

However, the next day I find myself lying in my bed with a massive headache, not knowing how I got back there.

I have a terrible hangover. I sit up and look slowly around finding at least half of the stretcher beds are occupied by snoring soldiers.

Throughout the day I rest, sitting in an armchair near a window, looking at the mountains and thinking of home.

In the afternoon I return to my bed to sleep it off.

Around teatime, I finally enter the mess hall and devour a big meal of roast lamb and vegetables. Everyone else is there so we have a game of euchre. Not much is said as we play. Most of us are nursing sore heads.

Later, I return to my bed, lie on top of the blankets fully clothed and think of the last twenty-four hours.

I can scarcely believe we got through this bloody war. I begin to worry again. I hope my family is okay.

Worrying is pointless. I will have to wait till I can find out what happened to them. After some time, I yawn, carefully turn on my side and pull the blanket over my shoulders.

I dream of fishing along the river and catching a long, silvery pike. Old Billy is eating the lush grass at my side. Walking back to Auntie's house, with the pike in a bucket, I watch the setting sun disappear below the horizon, the last of its rays warming my face.

I meet Ma at the door as I hand her the bucket. She hugs me tightly and Auntie offers me a plate of paczki.

CHAPTER

50

With the war ending, I feel amazingly light and free. For days I can't wipe the smile off my face. I laugh at any silly joke and keep whistling tunes. We all do. We're all excited about starting a new chapter in our lives.

Franz, Jo and I make a lot of friends in Kirkwall. Mainly ex-POWs, who, like us, escaped the camps. We are different from the typical Polish soldier who fought in the war. We endured and saw terrible things in the camps, which is a lot different from fighting on a battlefield. We have difficulties relating to the regular troops, and there are lots of fights.

Both sides sport blackened eyes and bruised jaws for days. The Commanding Officers, seeing this as a problem which needs to be addressed quickly, devise a plan for soccer matches to be played on the weekends. Anyone causing trouble during the week is automatically banned from playing or attending the matches. This rule keeps us soccer mad Poles in line.

Our team, called 'Koniks' or 'Wild Horses', consists of Franz, Jo and me, and our mates from our barracks. The opposing teams are the big shots from the regular army.

Altogether, we make up four teams which rotate every Sunday. Our uniforms are a mishmash of sweaters and under shirts with coloured armbands, representing our teams. We are lucky our team colour is red, one of the colours in the Polish flag.

The games soon sort out the hotheads from the steady players. Determined to win, we become disciplined, play fairly, and look forward to the matches. Although, shouting for ninety minutes is thirsty work. So, after the game, it's not unusual to end up at the local Pub to lubricate our dry throats by downing a few ales.

A few weeks later we're told the Polish army is to play the British RAF team barracked at the Mainland Aerodrome.

The COs select the best players from the teams and it's to be the best of three matches against the RAF, with the winning team receiving a bronze trophy. If one of the matches is a draw, we'll play an extra ten minutes, hoping to score. If not, the team with the highest combined scores of all three matches will be the winner.

The COs ask the locals for help. They donate old soccer shirts, blue and green stripes, from one of their own soccer clubs. The colours are not that great, but at least we look like a team.

We play the following Saturday, on a school soccer field in Kirkwall. Being Polish foreigners, we're the underdogs. The British lads from the RAF are the favourites.

The RAF run out in brand new uniforms, red, blue, and white, which are the colours of the British flag. With matching socks and new soccer boots they all look the part.

It puts us on edge. Our play is downright awful. The refs send our men off for illegal tackles, dirty play and swearing in Polish and broken English. Yellow and red cards shower down on us like confetti.

I'm sent off for a nasty tackle when I try to kick the ball away from the opposing wing but collide with his shins instead. Landing on his back, the airman clutches his shin in pain with blood running down from a cut to his knee. I lean down and I try to help him up.

"Piss off!" he hisses, slapping my hand away.

I apologise to him and plead with the ref, but to no avail. The ref shows me a red card, and deservedly so.

We lose the game one-nil.

After the game, our coach gives us a pep-talk on not letting the opposing team get under our skin. It didn't matter how we look, playing the game well is all that matters.

In the next round we prove to ourselves we can outsmart the Poms. We slaughter the smart asses four to three. Franz, a striker, kicks two goals. I managed to land one and Adi, one of our mates who plays forward, the other.

The following Saturday is the last and final game. We're all tense, talking loudly, warming up by stretching and jumping up and down in the changeroom. Our coach, Captain Dabrowski, runs in with a cardboard box.

"Get your gear off, we have new uniforms!"

We stare at him.

"Come on! Uniforms off!" he shouts, ripping the tape off the cardboard.

He pulls out soccer shirts in red and white stripes, the colours of the Polish flag, with black numbers printed on the back. We cheer, hands pumping the air as our coach hands them out.

"Sir, how did you get these jerseys?" Adi asks.

"From the Polish embassy. They arrived just now!" He pulls out more shirts. "What a gift!"

I look over to Franz. He's pulling a jersey over his head and emerges, chortling.

"My Mary!" Franz exclaims loudly. "She must have written to her father about the game!"

He kisses the air. "Oh, I do love that girl!"

We play hard and fast but are on the defence most of the time. The opposing team is excellent. I notice a few of the RAF players have been replaced. Their goalie is a taller man, red haired and freckled, looking like a Scotsman. Their forward is well built and strong and plays with terrific skill. The airman I injured in the last game is nowhere to be seen. I feel a little guilty for that.

It's a one-all draw at full time when Adi manages to equalise just before the whistle when the RAF team leaves an opening.

Our team goes ballistic for a couple of minutes, then regains some order and concentrates on the next ten minutes of extra time. In the last two minutes the score is still a draw.

Kacper, who's in the regular army, passes the ball to Franz who runs with it to the goal mouth, but quickly passes it to Jo on the wing. Jo dodges the big Brit barrelling towards him and passes it back to Franz, who dribbles the ball for a few seconds then kicks a terrific shot.

It's so powerful, he lands on his ass. The ball passes over our heads, escaping their goalie's dive, and lands in the top right-hand corner of the net. The ref's whistle blows, ending the game.

There is a stunned silence. Then our team erupts. We whoop and shout, running around the field, waving our shirts over our heads.

The crowd in the stands goes wild.

Captain Dabrowski runs onto the field slapping us all on our backs and shaking our hands. Some of us are crying, prostrate on the ground, as if we just won the FA cup final. The rest of us hug and dance.

Hooting with laughter, Franz collapses on the grass, his arms spread out wide as the whole team piles on top of him.

The airmen shake our hands, and with heads down, trudge off the field.

We sing and dance in the showers and dress in our best to celebrate in the local pub. The trophy is placed on the bar and the CO shouts us drinks.

There is a lot of back slapping and laughter. The pub's piano begins to play. We gather around and try to sing a Scottish song which results in most of us rolling on the floor in hysterics.

I sit at the bar and watch Franz wrapping his arm around the neck of our goalie, Paul, a regular soldier. They're in fits of laughter.

I smile. It was a good idea, mixing our teams. We all got to know the army men and they got to know us.

#####

The next day is a beautiful summer's day.

Franz, Jo, Adi and I climb the steep hills around Kirkwall and walk around the headlands.

We stop and look at the amazing scene before us. The great expanse of the ocean glitters in the sunlight. Seagulls hover and screech above us. Cormorants dive among the waves like shooting arrows.

We walk up a mountain path through rolling grasslands dotted with grazing sheep. Rugged, snow-capped mountains dominate the blue sky, reflecting the morning sun. Along the mountain slopes are rocky outcrops, covered in moss. The usual chilly wind, which can turn into a gale at any moment, blows from the sea, numbing our faces.

I breathe in the fresh air. I've never felt so alive.

We walk up the summit, taking in the incredible vista. The whole scene seems to shimmer, like the sea. The sky is a brilliant blue. The mountain slopes and hills are a blanket of purple from the flowering heather.

After a while, we trudge back down to the valley below.

Wind burnt and tired from the previous day, we stroll, stomachs growling, to the fish and chip shop, where we meet up with some of the regular army guys. Sapped by our long hike, we slouch on metal chairs pulled up to a wooden table to discuss the match.

"Christ, that was a good match!" Derek, a corporal in the army, exclaims. "I didn't think we had a chance against those stiff-necked Poms! But we did it! All because of Franz's brilliant goal!"

"Kacper and Jo made it happen," says Franz, settling in his chair.

Kacper suddenly appears, dumping a hot paper parcel on the table.

"Get stuck into this!"

We unwrap the butcher's paper to reveal a mound of battered fish and greasy chips. A feast. We greedily shake vinegar and salt on top and tuck in. Eating with gusto and talking with our mouths full, we lick our fingers, absorbing the salty flavours.

Some of the men joke around, putting cooled chips in their ears and making stupid faces. We bellow with laughter, becoming far too loud.

"Noo! Noo! Laddies!" says Joyce, the shop owner, a rotund woman with mousy brown hair pinned back from her round sweaty face.

She scowls from behind the counter, wiping her hands on her grubby apron. "Oot! Noo! A canna hiv ye here, makin a rackit. Ithe up n' be on ye way!"

Stumbling out and teasing each other with easy banter, we make our way to the pub.

From that day on, it becomes a tradition for us.

Every Sunday afternoon, we visit the Fish and Chip shop followed by a couple of ales at the local pub to wash it all down, then head back to the barracks.

#####

The summer weather is surprisingly warm in the islands. The whole place is bursting with life and colour. Yellow primroses grow beside well-worn tracks with small birds flying among the blackberry bushes. I love walking around the island and lying on the grassy slopes.

Franz joins me if he isn't writing love letters to Mary.

Adi comes occasionally, but Jo is always busy in the army kitchens cooking meals with a team of army cooks. I've resigned myself to the fact that Jo and I are steadily drifting apart, pursuing different lives and different interests. Jo is developing his skills as a chef, while I want to explore all my options and see where they take me.

Even though the war is over, the British government still needs us to dismantle gun emplacements around the islands.

They're mainly in large concrete bunkers facing the open sea or around an inlet called Scapa Flow, which lies between the Mainland and the Isle of Hoy. There, a long concrete causeway, called Churchill's Barrier was constructed at the beginning of the war to keep the German subs from sneaking in.

Polish teams are sent all over the Orkney Islands to dismantle these large guns and anything else they can unscrew, prise open or dislodge with drills and crowbars.

Cranes are used to lift the guns and any scrap into the backs of trucks and ship it to mainland Scotland. It can be hard, tough work, but we believe it's important. It's our way of repaying the Brits for being our Allies.

I like the physical work, and I like the army life. I eat good food. I'm clean and warm, with a clean bed. I wear a smart uniform and have great friends. Also, every weekend I play soccer, called football by the Scots, and drink beer at the pubs. I also get invited to the local dances.

The Orcadian community holds dances in a church hall every month.

There, we meet a lot of pretty girls from the islands and Scottish girls from the mainland.

At the start of each dance, before the band sets up, vinyl records are played on a turntable on the stage. The music is wild and fast to a new dance called the jitterbug, which originated in the U.S.A and was brought into Britain by the

American servicemen.

It's a crazy dance.

You dance fast with your partner, throwing your legs out and swinging the girls around. It's like hopping around from one foot to the other. When you pull your partner in, she jumps up and straddles your waist. A lot of us land on our asses in a tangle of legs, skirts, and petticoats. There's always a lot of screaming and laughter. Like I said, it's crazy.

The dance organisers are mortified when we dance the Jitterbug. They think it is unseemly, a dance created by the Devil.

Orcadians are very religious.

Fearing the dance will get out of hand, they take the needle off the record. It makes us all stop, only to boo and hiss. Some of the men physically manhandle the culprit, pulling him off the stage, or if it's a lady, gently escorting her down the steps.

Later, a band, usually with a fiddle, a set of drums and piano accordion, sets up their instruments as we recover on seats set around the hall. They begin by playing a polka which gets us all hopping again.

Pumping the girl's arms madly and swinging them around, we gallop around the floor until we're all out of breath. This is followed by the Scots trying to teach us a Scottish reel where we swap partners, hooking our arms and swinging around to another girl. It usually ends badly, the men colliding with the girls or each other.

Finally, they slow us down with a couple of barn dances. We don't mind as the slower pace allows us to talk to the girls.

After a few more different numbers the music leads into a slow, romantic waltz, which is always the last dance of the evening. I don't know why, but I always end up with a tall girl in my arms. I don't really mind as I can place my head on her bosom, and she can place her chin on the top of my head.

Franz always excuses himself, sneaking outside for a smoke and a swig of booze from someone's flask. He misses Mary when he sees us smooching with the local girls.

But the best part of the dance is at the very end of the evening, when the older ladies lay out cakes, custard tarts, cheese sandwiches and big pots of tea on trestle tables. We pile our plates high, sit around the edge of the hall and stuff ourselves as if there's no tomorrow. We talk to the girls in our limited English and go back for second helpings, washing it down with sweetened tea.

I don't really fancy any of the girls, even though I do snatch a few kisses behind the church hall. However, the girls seem to like me. They say I'm a gentleman when I kiss their hand after each dance, and that I look like Mickey Rooney, the Hollywood film star. Some say I'm just as cute and just as feisty.

What the hell do 'cute' and 'feisty' mean?

Often the dances end up in a fight between the locals and the Poles.

It's due to jealousy over the girls' interest in us. We're just more attentive towards them. It's common to see an Orcadian girl, wearing a new hat or fashionable coat, walking arm in arm with a Polish lad.

Anyway, the fights can be violent, ending in a brawl. Usually, the MPs break it up, if not the local police. Many times, Franz and I return to the barracks sporting a split lip or black eye.

Once a week we attend an English class organised by the

Polish army. Franz grasps the language like a duck to water, learning it quickly and confidently. I struggle with it as it doesn't make any sense.

Why is the 'k' silent in words like knot and knitting and why does the 'ph' sounds like 'f' as in photos. In the Polish language you say what you write, but not in English. It's so damn hard. 'Caught' could be 'court', 'fare' could be 'fair' and 'threw' could be 'through'. I tend to pronounce the silent 'k,' always getting a smile from my teacher, Mr Drinkwater.

One day, Mr Drinkwater, an old man who once taught in a boys' school, decides to translate our names. He writes on the blackboard that mine is Rich, Rick, or Dick my full name being Richard, Jo is spelled Joe, his full name being Joseph, Adi is Eddie, his full name being Edward and Franz is Francis. He turns to face us and tells us it can also be a girl's name then writes it Frances.

We laugh, making Franz go red.

I think Mr Drinkwater is teasing him.

"There is no way I'm going to be called Francis! No way!" Franz shouts out.

"Don't worry Franz," Mr Drinkwater, chuckles. "You can also be called Frank."

"Frank is fine. I can live with Frank," Franz, becomes a lot calmer and settles in his chair.

I can't help but snicker throughout the lesson, murmuring 'Francis' under my breath. Franz glares at me, until he loses his temper, punching me hard in the arm.

This makes me stop. But the banter reminds me of when I was a small boy, always teasing the goofy kid in class. I think his name was Bogdi. The poor kid! I gave him hell! Ah! Come to think about it, I was a brat and deserved the cane from Pan Zaleski, my third-grade teacher. I smile at the thought. I really was a mischievous kid.

I persevere with the English language, talking to the locals whenever I get the chance. I'm determined the pretty girls at the dances, Joyce, the fish and chip shop owner and the publican will understand me. But most importantly, I want to read the newspaper and learn what's happening in Europe.

CHAPTER

51

Summer in 1945 brings a lot of changes.

Uncle Jon, whose back injury has worsened, leaving him crippled, returns to Poland to live with his daughter. The last time I saw him, he was in a lot of pain, walking with a cane in each hand. Christina, his daughter, arranged through the Red Cross to get him transported to Kotobrzeg, a Polish port on the Baltic Sea. She met him there, then took him by train to her home in Warsaw.

Jo is transferred to London to become a sous chef for the British Army, catering for the dignitaries, generals, and other high-ranking officers. Looking to the future, he applied for the transfer when he heard the head chef needed more experienced workers.

Franz and Mary plan their wedding, although Mary won't arrive in Edinburgh till August. She needs to stay longer in mainland Europe to help the thousands of people still suffering from the ill treatment in the camps and the soldiers with severe injuries, who can't be moved.

Makeshift hospitals were built by the British and Americans in most of the main European cities.

Mary is stationed in Poland, now occupied by the Russians,

under the British flag. But she is leaving the services as soon as possible to marry Franz and to find work in the UK.

I write to Jo every week, telling him what I'm doing in Scotland and any news I hear or read concerning Poland.

He does the same.

Then one day I received a letter from Ma, via the Red Cross.

23ʳᵈ of July 1945,

Dear Ryszard and Jozef,
I'm writing to you both at last. I have been so worried. I believed you both. were killed, and I have been lighting candles for you every Sunday in church.

I got news, through your Uncle Jon, that you are in Scotland of all places. I can't believe you are both on the other side of the world. I am so blessed you are both well and I have lost neither you nor your father to this terrible war.

Your Pa has returned uninjured, thanks to the Blessed Mother. I prayed to her every day for his and your safe return. However, Uncle Tomasz never came back. He died fighting the Germans somewhere in France. Your Pa is still struggling with his loss.

Jon said you were injured, Ryszard, but are recovering well. I'm so glad, my dearest boy!

Auntie Alicja is very ill. She has the wasting disease and will not live long. I will miss her when she passes, but I know she will be with Jesus and our beloved Virgin Mary.

She has given us the farm, so now we have a home of our own again. She got sick after the last of her cats went missing. It broke her heart when Old Tom disappeared. All her cats mysteriously vanished over the years.

Your sisters have found jobs in the city.

They make army boots for the Russians, in the same factory where Helena made boots for the Germans. Pa can now repair our shoes with the leather pieces they sneak out. I still wear the boots you took from the train all those years ago. They have served me well and never had a hole.

When the Germans occupied Poland, a lot of slave labour was brought into the factories and a lot of Germans came over to Poland to steal a business, a house or land. Auntie and I were so lucky no one were interested in her farm. One look discouraged them. We made the front garden untidy by not cutting the grass for months and throwing rubbish around. We even tied up Old Billy to the front gate. He would bleat loudly if anyone tried to open it. A really good watch dog was Old Billy.

But Pan Tolinski lost his home. He was tossed out with all his possessions strewn all over the front yard. He sat in the middle of the road and cursed the new owners. He was so loud I thought they would get him arrested. Luckily, he wasn't. We helped him collect his belongings and moved him into the attic. I took down Helena's picture of the little bird and kept it safe...I know you and Jo thought it was special. Anyway, Pan Tolinski was lucky. His old truck was parked outside our place. So, the Germans never took it.

He slept in the attic for a couple years, until your Pa came back. The girls moved into his room and Pan Tolinski moved to the barn, making it into his home. He even put in a wood-burning stove.

Nevertheless, we insisted he have his meals with us.

Our people have a lot of work to do to rebuild Poland. Warsaw was raised to the ground when the Jews fought back in the Warsaw uprising. In reprisal, Hitler made sure not one building in our beautiful city was left standing.

There was little food in the last years of the war. The Germans took our old horse, the remaining two goats and even poor old Billy. One day only the rope he was tied to was left at the front gate. I hope he gave the mongrels hell.

We struggled to find enough to eat.

Pan Tolinski helped when he could by cutting and selling timber and Auntie and I sold vegetables. Between us we all survived somehow, but we're all so skinny. I now look like the scarecrow in Auntie's turnip field. However, it's not all doom and gloom. I have some good news!

Helena has survived the camps. I got a letter from her through the Red Cross. She had given our address as her own and wrote a short letter to me asking if she could stay until she found somewhere to live.

Pa and I drove to the railway station using Pan Tolinski's old truck. She came off the train and I could hardly recognise her. Her lovely hair was cut short, and she was so pale and thin. But she still had her beautiful smile. There were a lot of tears and even Pa, who didn't know her, shed a few.

I made an extra bed in the girl's bedroom and told her she could stay as long as she liked.

She has grown into a lovely young woman. We talk often about the past and future, but hardly about the camps. Whenever she does, she becomes very quiet and starts to cry. I know it was terrible. I have heard stories from my friends about the camps. I cry at night when I think about what you two must have gone through. It breaks my heart!

My main job is to find enough food to feed us all, since food is still scarce. I kept your grandmother's jewellery throughout the war but had to sell it a few months ago. I managed to buy a few chickens and a goat so we can have fresh milk and eggs. I have planted potatoes and turnips in the garden, and I've been able to barter with the eggs for extra meat. Ironically from the German family living on Pan Tolinski's farm!

I will ask Helena if she can write to you two as she did before. I'm sure she will.

Please! Please! Don't come home!

Polish boys who returned have been killed by the Russians. They are afraid the returning men will become a Resistance and cause trouble for them like they did for the Germans. Pan Tolinski's nephew was to return, but he has not been seen since he wrote a letter from Warsaw.

The Russians are just as cruel as the Germans, and now we are under their rule life is still very hard. The Polish people are not happy the Russians are here. I fear we will never be a free country.

If you can find work in England, it would be better for you both. You could send medicine or money to help us.

So please make a new life for yourselves and be happy. I will always love you and will pray for you both every day.

Love Ma xxx

I show Franz the letter that afternoon.

After reading it he hands it back.

"Well, it's a no-brainer. There is no way I'm going back," he says with certainty. "I'm staying here and making a new life with Mary."

I read the letter again, thinking I would like to do the same if I'm allowed.

I post the letter to Jo. He sends me a quick note telling me he has written to Ma and Helena about returning to Poland. I write a letter to my family telling them I'll try to stay here and help them whenever I can. I include the army wages I have saved and a letter to Helena.

52

On a cold, rain-swept autumn day, I accompany a very nervous Franz to Edinburgh, to meet Mary's ship.

After being held up in Poland for weeks, due firstly to the slow rate of patients' recovery, and next, to having her ship delayed by a storm in the English Channel, Franz is quietly frantic, worried something else will happen to keep him and Mary apart.

With a weekend pass, we travel across to the mainland by ferry, then by train. Arriving at the wharf in a taxi, we spot the hospital ship steaming up Granton Harbour, sliding into the berth and docking with barely a bump. The sailors on the wharf secure the ship's lines to the huge bollards as two gangplanks are lowered to the wharf and secured.

Frowning, Franz scans the decks in search of his fiancée. I see Mary on the bow, waving frantically and blowing him kisses. I point to her. Franz follows my gaze. Waving madly, he calls out her name. She hurries along the deck with her suitcase clutched to her chest and down the gangplank.

Franz runs towards her, forgetting altogether about the umbrella he's holding. It whips inside out in the turbulent wind, looking like a deformed bat wing trailing behind him.

Then, totally forgotten, it tumbles to the ground.

Mary drops the case, flinging herself into Franz's arms.

Soaking wet yet completely oblivious to the rain, they kiss passionately, locked in each other's arms. Wounded soldiers toting duffel bags, shuffle awkwardly down the gangplank, trying to manoeuvre around the couple. There are loud complaints and some lewd comments. The lovebirds are oblivious to it all.

Surfacing at last, they gaze into each other's eyes. Franz smooths Mary's wet hair from her face and kisses her again.

Looking up at the ship's hull, idly studying the rust marks along its side, I stand back. Waiting. I pick up the discarded umbrella, vainly trying to straighten the spokes while still holding mine upright. Finally, I give up and tuck the mangled thing under my arm. Discreetly, I step forward and pick up Mary's abandoned suitcase.

Finally, Mary notices me as they come up for air. She reaches for my hand and pulls me into a hug, kissing my cheek.

The three of us make our way to the main road to hail a cab, ending up in a small pub in the middle of the city. Starving, we order fish and chips with our drinks and sit in a quiet corner, waiting for the meal. Mary and Franz begin to discuss the wedding plans. I listen attentively, but soon lose interest, leaving them to sort matters out between themselves.

I stare out the pub's window, watching people bustling past in the dreary Edinburgh weather. It's a grey city on such a dark day.

Constructed from grey stone and soot-stained brick, the buildings look dull and dirty. Sleet and rain flood over slate-coloured cobblestones, mirroring the pedestrians splashing along the pavements. Most are wearing grey overcoats and holding up black umbrellas, adding to the overall greyness.

But now and then, a lady wearing a red or a green coat and holding up a colourful umbrella walks past, giving the city a sparkling ray of colour. I smile at the contrast.

My thoughts drift to Helena, wearing a red coat a lifetime ago. She always brightened the day, too.

We book rooms and, deciding to explore the city before it gets too dark, I leave the lovebirds upstairs. Strolling around the wet streets glistening as the streetlights come on, I dodge people hurrying in all directions, wrapped tightly in their coats. They hold their umbrellas up high, jostling for position at a bus stop. A red double decker bus rounds the corner and stops near the curb.

I run up to the bus, jump on and climb the stairs to the top level. There I settle into the back seat and allow the bus trip to show me the sights. I peer up at an imposing hill, noticing a castle perched on the very top, with its guns facing outward to repel Scotland's enemies. A British flag flies on a flagpole, whipping in the wind.

I suddenly feel sad, realising I miss Franz's company. I'm not jealous he's with Mary, not the least.

I just feel lonely without him in this strange place. I have no one to talk to about the sights or strange people around me.

In all this greyness, I look at one man sitting in the next row, who stands out. Instead of trousers, he wears a kilt, as we've learnt to call these men's skirts, made from the colourful thick checked material the Scots call tartan, and a white frilly shirt under a black velvet jacket.

He has what looks a bit like a lady's purse made of fur, hanging on a large leather belt near his groin. His hair is orange, not a soft, pretty red like Mary's, and pokes out from under a green beret with feathers pinned to the side. His muscly legs, splayed apart, are covered in long socks in the same tartan design as his skirt.

He looks strange, peculiar, and intimidating at the same time.

He is very big with large biceps bulging under his jacket.

I wouldn't want to get in a fight with him.

I divert my eyes in case he notices me staring.

The bus finally returns to its original stop and as I disembark into a freezing wind, I make up my mind to return to the warmth of the old pub and have a decent meal.

I don't see Franz or Mary until the morning, and feeling like the third wheel on a bicycle as they sit close together at the breakfast table, holding hands and whispering, I head back to base early.

I take a slow train trip, getting off at a few stations, to explore the Scottish townships and have some lunch.

Finally, I end up on the ferry which crosses the strait to the Orkney islands.

There, I catch a bus to the pub and meet up with Adi for a few ales.

#####

Autumn turns into a bitterly cold winter. Since Mary's father can't attend the wedding in October, due to Russia's involvement in Poland, Franz and Mary delay their wedding until Spring the following year.

Franz visits Mary in Edinburgh whenever he has leave, and I'm invited to spend Christmas with them at the home of long-time friends of Mary's parents, Mr and Mrs Mackenzie.

The festive meal is delicious with heaps of crispy potatoes, my favourite dish, and roasted meat with steamed vegetables. And it's the first time I've tasted haggis, a type of savoury pudding composed of minced liver, heart and lungs of a sheep, mixed with mutton suet and oatmeal then seasoned with spices. The whole thing is packed into a sheep's stomach and boiled. It sounds unappealing but it's quite tasty.

Festively dressed in red and green plaid, Mrs Mackenzie, a tiny, thin lady with sparkling blue eyes and curly blonde hair tells me the recipe so I can write it in my next letter to Jo.

We drink a lot of whisky on Christmas day, getting very drunk and I spend most of Boxing Day in front of a blazing fire, nursing a sore head.

Franz and Mary plan to visit one of Mary's friends and ask me if I would like to tag along. But I decline their offer, feeling far too seedy to talk to anyone.

Despite my hangover, I enjoy hanging out with Mr Mackenzie, a short, portly man with thick grey hair and an impressive moustache.

He talks extensively about his beer stein collection, showing me every single one and describing the history of each. He speaks in his broad Scottish accent, about his life before the war, when he was a baker and owned a shop in the city which he inherited from his father.

After a while, when I surprisingly feel a lot better, he offers me a fourth ale and starts to lecture on the wars between the Scots and the English. He becomes quite agitated with his arms flying about and I laugh at his silly antics. His Scottish accent broadens as the ale is exchanged for Scotch, finally becoming too hard to understand. Except for the words 'bloody English' and the Scottish word 'sassenach'.

Franz and Mary return to find me once more very merry and dancing around the small living room. Mr Mackenzie is showing me how to dance the highland fling. Mrs Mackenzie calls the couple over, clapping in time and stamping her foot.

They fall about laughing, as Mr Mackenzie and I jump and swivel to and fro, tripping each other and knocking into the furniture.

CHAPTER

53

On a warm spring day with the fragrance of jasmine floating in the air, Franz and Mary are married in St Mary's Cathedral in the centre of Edinburgh.

This towering gothic church, with its carved spires and tall stained-glass windows is one of the most beautiful buildings I've ever seen.

The interior is even more spectacular, with arched windows stretching along the top of the sandstone walls, letting in soft light over the pews. A huge mural painted over an enormous arch, depicts Jesus blessing the Virgin Mary as angel hosts drift gracefully up towards them. The cathedral is large and spacious with a high timber ceiling and one wall displaying 'The Way of the Cross' in low-relief sculptural panels.

We stand waiting at the altar, Franz, Adi and I, very smart in our dress uniforms. Franz nervously fidgets with his tie and smooths down his jacket, as he glances down the aisle, waiting impatiently for his bride.

Mary's mother arrives with a handful of flowers and pins a white rose onto Franz's lapel. He kisses her hand, making her blush under her face powder.

She pins pink Carnations onto my jacket and Adi's.

We also kiss her hand, making her very flustered.

She pats her chest as she walks unsteadily back to the pew

and slowly sits down. Peeping across at us, she smiles shyly.

I murmur out the side of my mouth to Adi, "I think we still have a knack with the ladies."

He chuckles as he glances back to Mrs Delekta, fanning herself with her hanky.

I look towards the open doorway at the far end of the aisle and see Mary, more beautiful than ever. Her lovely hair gleams red in the sunlight shining through the windows, her tiara twinkling in its rays. Her head is covered in a veil over a white silk dress that reaches the ground.

As she moves into position, with her father at her side, one of the bridesmaids hands her a bouquet of white roses and pink carnations that cascades down to her knees. Radiant, she stands patiently, the bridesmaids fussing over her veil to ensure it lies smoothly, meeting the long silk train flowing behind her.

The two bridesmaids, in pink flowing dresses, move to the front and start the slow walk down the aisle as the organist launches into Richard Wagner's bridal march.

Everyone stands as Mary's father takes her arm and leads her towards the altar. They smile as they glide past, her father dipping his head to people he knows, while Mary fixes her eyes on Franz.

Mary's mother suddenly bursts into tears, which I don't understand at all. I glance at Franz, but he hasn't noticed. In fact, his eyes shine with tears of his own as he takes in Mary's beauty in her elegant wedding dress, her face radiant as she glides towards him.

Mary reaches Franz, and her father gives him her hand and steps back. Franz faces his bride and kisses her hand as she smiles up at him.

At a quiet 'Humph' they both turn to face the priest.

He is a tall thick set man with a large bald head, resplendent in white and gold vestments.

"We are gathered here...," he begins, his hand on a page in the bible.

Suddenly a light, powerful and strong, shines around Franz and Mary. Amazed, I looked up to find its source. A beam of sunlight penetrating a stained-glass window, falls on the couple, highlighting their faces. It creates sparkles in the air as they exchange their vows. I look at the whole scene in awe and wonder and make a wish. I wish to fall in love with a beautiful girl and feel the same joy Mary and Franz do.

At the 'I do' part, with Mary and Franz holding hands, I glance above their heads and notice a small bird is part of the design in the stained-glass window. It makes me think of Helena and how much I loved her. I realise it wasn't the same love Franz and Mary share, but the innocent love of children. Drifting into a daydream of how Helena and I met, I'm suddenly snapped out of it when Adi pinches my arm.

"Wake up!" he whispers hoarsely. "It's the ring part!"

I jump at his voice and act as if I lost the rings, patting myself down and making a fuss.

Franz pokes me on the shoulder, making Mary laugh and sending a muted ripple of mirth through the front pews.

I flamboyantly pull out a handkerchief from my top pocket to wipe my brow, dropping the rings to the floor. Taking a very deep bow, I pick them up and examine each of them, reluctantly handing them to Franz.

The congregation bursts out laughing as Franz murmurs in

my ear, "I'm not surprised. I was waiting for one of your stunts!"

After the bestowing of the rings and the groom kissing the bride, they are led to the back of the church to sign the register with all four of us in tow.

Arm in arm and smiling radiantly, Franz and Mary lead the way down the aisle towards the open doors of the cathedral. I link arms with a tall bridesmaid and follow the happy couple, waving to Jo and the lads as we pass. Some of the guests are already outside, showering the bride and groom with confetti as the cathedral's bells peel joyously.

A wedding photographer hassles the bridal party for photos while Jo gets a lift into the city, to take charge of serving the hundred guests for whom he has catered, who will soon be arriving.

I look across to Franz as we stand on the steps, realising this is the most important moment of his life. He grins back at me and gives a slight nod.

The photographer asks us to look ahead as he shoots yet another photo.

I give him my best smile.

As soon as the last picture is taken, we all pile into the waiting taxis, laughing and jostling on the seats. Adi and I accidentally sit on the bridesmaids' dresses, dragging the fabric under our bums. We apologise at the same time, making the girls giggle as they adjust their dresses and straighten their tops. Adi and I smile at them as they both reveal a little cleavage.

As soon as we arrive at the reception, Adi and I go straight to the bar, leaving the bridesmaids to attend Mary.

I order a couple of beers and look around.

The room is magnificent. Glowing mellow light is cast off from chandeliers hanging from the ceiling, making the walls glimmer in rich tones. Deep red drapes hang from full length widows, each tied with fancy golden sashes. Large, framed mirrors hang on the walls, reflecting the tables draped in white tablecloths. Pink roses in porcelain vases sit in the centre of each table. Gleaming silver cutlery is placed beside gold rimmed plates with folded napkins perched on top. The crystal wine glasses reflect the glow of candles, standing in silver candlesticks. The whole room looks almost as grand as the interior of a French chateau I once saw in a history book.

The wedding reception is an impressive affair. There's plenty of wine and vodka and the meal is a delicious combination of Polish and English food.

When it comes to the speeches I stand to praise and toast the beautiful bridesmaids, saying it all in English.

I straighten my tie and announce I will recite a poem.

Franz groans, rolling his eyes. Mary smacks his arm and looks at me expectantly. *I hope she doesn't think I'm the next Shakespeare!...* I clear my throat.

"*Roses are red, violets are blue.*
Mary plus Franz equal the perfect two.
Franz is smart but also quiet plain,
Mary is sweet with a beautiful mane.
Together their love is great and strong,
May their marriage be wonderful and long.
I do love them both even when the moon is blue,
And I hope you both live to a hundred and two."

It brings the house down. Mary is laughing so much she quickly dashes to the ladies' room followed by her bridesmaids. Franz bellows with laughter and, standing up, gives me a crushing hug, tears rolling down his face. Adi grins, shaking his head in disbelief. Jo, sitting at the table nearest to us, suddenly stands and claps madly, beaming at me. I smile back at him, uncertain, thinking he is being sarcastic, but then realise he is genuinely pleased by my recital. He raises his glass, proposing a toast to my great poetry. Everyone stands.

I bow deeply, thinking I will certainly publish my poems one day.

Mary and her bridesmaids soon return to the bridal table, still dabbing their faces with handkerchiefs.

Franz finds his speech difficult. He takes a couple of deep breaths then, slowly exhales before he utters a word.

He begins to speak in English with every word perfectly pronounced while Mary beams up at him. I sit there amazed. It must have taken him months of practice to speak so well.

After the speeches, the band plays a slow waltz. Franz leads Mary onto the dance floor and takes her into his arms.

They gracefully dance to the music as Adi, and I lead the bridesmaids onto the floor, followed by Mary's parents and the rest of the guests. The four-piece band changes to a Quick Step and Aldi and I change partners. Lilly, who is shorter and prettier, seems to enjoy dancing with me, so I dance with her most of the night while Adi danced with Jean.

Later in the evening, I manage to grab a dance with Mary when Franz is talking to Mr Delekta, his father-in-law, at the bar.

"Thank you for making Franz so happy!" I whisper in her ear.

"He's been through a lot!"

"I know. And so have you! He told me all about the camp and your escape." She whispers, "Franz is wonderful, and I truly love him." She kisses my cheek. "I hope you find a girl who loves you too."

Franz suddenly cuts in, wagging his finger, making us both laugh.

It's a fantastic night with plenty to eat and drink, and lots of dancing. We even romp through a Polish folk dance, where we all go around in a circle, holding hands, singing and kicking up our legs in time with the music.

Jo meets me at the bar, and we have a quiet drink together.

"Did you know I wrote poetry?" I ask as I take a sip of the beer froth.

He bobs his head in reply as he takes a swig of his drink and wipes his mouth.

"I knew for a long time. Ever since Helena was in the ghetto. I once saw your poem in a letter you left open on your bed. But I never mentioned it, as I knew it was somehow important between you and Helena."

Perplexed, I gaze at him.

"Why didn't you say something?"

"I thought it was not the right thing to do! I knew you would tell me eventually. But I was surprised at how funny your corny poems really are. That was a good one tonight, Rys."

We both laugh and give each other a brotherly hug.

Franz joins us with the rest of our army buddies, and we chat about the dismantling work in the islands. He tells us he has decided to leave the army and has a job waiting for him when he and Mary come back from their honeymoon. He'll work as a motor mechanic and Mary will have a job at Edinburgh Hospital as a theatre nurse. They will be moving into an apartment Mary's parents have bought them as a wedding present.

He's still keen to go to university and Theo, Mr Delekta is helping him enrol in Edinburgh University to study engineering.

We all shake his hand and wish him good luck for the future.

At the end of the night, all the guests make a circle and sing a farewell song in Polish. Franz and Mary walk around the inside, saying goodbye. When Franz comes to me, he regards my face with affection and places his hands on the side of my neck, planting kisses on my cheeks, like the Russians did in the cellar. I look up at him, tears rolling down my face and utter a sob. He holds me tight, my head against his shoulder.

"You'll always be my best mate," I mumble into his jacket.

Choking back tears, he whispers hoarsely, "You'll always be my brother."

We stay like this for some time, then Franz pulls back and smiles.

"But I wish Frau Schmidt was here today, to see me married. I think she would have liked the wedding," he whispers, and adds, "I think about her now and then."

"Me too!" I say, smiling up at him.

He shakes my hand, pats my shoulder and moves on to Jo and our mates from the army, hugging each one, even the CO. He says his goodbyes to the other guests, kissing the ladies' hands and shaking the men's.

I watch Franz as he talks to his other quests, and think back to our moments together – grinning and running like hell when we blew up a train , – our grim faces as we stand in the

Infirmary, clutching the tail ends of his shirt as we held up Alek, – stuffing the uniforms into the rucksack and using the toilet to wash our faces, – sleeping in a barn with the dead for our bedfellows, – sharing the pink bike and watching the wolf fly over our heads, – fighting the Russians in the school grounds, – hefting the wardrobe door and being fired upon by the Germans, – chuckling at the prospect of Mary giving us a sponge bath, – winning the soccer game against the RAF. And lastly, sharing this special day with him where his handsome face, full of joy and love, watched Mary walk down the aisle.

I'll cherish these memories and more, knowing full well our lives will never be the same. We won't be together, as before, but we will be together in our hearts.

I take a staggering breath and wipe my tears with a handkerchief and blow my nose.

I will miss my friend. My second brother.

Mary walks up to me, and I kiss her hand. She in turn kisses my cheek and holds me tight as she whispers in my ear.

"Thank you for being Franz's best friend. He told me, without you he wouldn't have known what true friendship is and how to love a man like a brother. He is so grateful you came into his life, and I'm so grateful he came into mine." She kisses me again and I hold her tight.

Franz is a lucky man.

Franz waits patiently while Mary says goodbye to her parents and takes her hand as they move through the open doors to a waiting car. They disappear into its dark interior as we all rush outside to wave them off. The car takes off, making a horrid racket as it drives up the road, tin cans trailing from its fender.

Adi and I stayed in Edinburgh for the rest of the weekend, taking in the sights and visiting Edinburgh Castle.

Trudging up the steep ramp to the castle gates, we wander around the courtyard, admiring the huge black guns. It reminds me of the castles in Poland but better restored. Most of the Polish castles are in total disrepair and I wonder if any of them are still standing.

We also try out the Edinburgh pubs. In one old inn we have an exciting game of darts with the locals, with us buying a round of drinks after the game.

It's an enjoyable weekend and I look forward to visiting again when I call upon the happy couple.

The next day, late in the afternoon when we arrive back at the camp, a thick envelope from Poland is waiting for me. I lightly touch the handwritten address.

The writing looks familiar. My heart skips a beat. I haven't seen this neat flowing script for a long time. Years. I take a slow breath.

It's from Helena.

CHAPTER

54

Darkening shadows creep up the slopes of the mountains, as the sun dips behind the rugged peaks dominating the darkening sky.

I look outside, holding the thick envelope in my hands, my heart beating faster as I consider what it might contain.

Putting off opening it, I study the postmark, realising it was sent six weeks ago from Tomaszów Mazowiecki.

Lying on my bed, I prop the pillow behind my head, then reach over to the bedside table to switch on a lamp. I can't put it off forever. I exhale a pent-up breath, break the seal, pull out a neatly folded wad of paper and begin to read.

16th April 1946.

Dear Ryszard,
I'm so glad you are alive and well. I thought about you and Jozef often when I was in the camps. At times, my memories of you both kept me alive. But now I need you to convince your brother not to return to Poland!
It is too dangerous!
He writes in his letters that he will be boarding a boat to Poland as soon as possible. I am so worried he will be imprisoned when he gets here, or even worse,

shot by the Russians. A lot of men have been.

I beg you, Ryszard, to talk to him! I would die if anything happened to Jo, or you for that matter.

I'm really sorry for not replying to your letter sooner, but it's been very difficult for me to talk about the camps or even write to anyone about them.

But now I'm ready to tell you what happened after Levi, and I left the ghetto. In fact, I need to tell you. I know you'll understand having experienced the horrors in the camps.

We had no idea about the terrible conditions in the cattle wagons until we were ordered to climb into them. There was very little light or fresh air, and we were all crammed in like farm animals going to the market. Levi and I couldn't move. It was awful. We had to pee where we stood as there weren't any buckets provided for a toilet. The stench was overpowering.

It was so hot people were fainting and we had to leave them where they fell.

When the train finally stopped and the doors slid open, the SS guards ordered us to get out immediately, but my legs were numb from the lack of movement, and I found it hard to walk. A surge of bodies pushed Levi to the carriage door. I scrambled after him, clutching the air, screaming his name and pulling people back to get to him. Everyone was doing the same thing. It was bedlam.

Jumping out onto the railway tracks, we were pushed and pulled into lines by the guards. Some held whips and led Alsatian dogs, who pulled against their masters, barking and growling savagely, snapping at our legs.

We were all terrified and huddled together while the

guards kept yelling 'Raus! Raus!' at the stragglers in the wagons. There were hundreds of people milling about with more and more spilling out onto the road.

Moments later, screaming filled the air. Families were being torn apart. Children were being separated from their parents.

Mothers and children alike were wailing hysterically, desperately clinging to one another as the SS ripped the children away from their parents' arms.

I noticed an Officer standing quietly in the midst of this pandemonium, randomly choosing children to be put into a line behind him. Their ages ranged from five years to thirteen with a large selection of twins amongst them.

Levi was chosen by this man and was pulled away from me. He held on tight as I tried to pull him back. But our hands were reefed apart.

I called his name over and over again, but my voice was lost in the frenzied uproar. He stood in the line totally bewildered, crying, desperately looking around for me. I was so distraught I screamed his name again, but I was shoved back into line and made to move along the track, until he was out of my sight. I knew in my heart I would never see him again.

I wept bitterly. It was unbearable.

It was as if I lost my family all over again.

I sometimes dream about that terrible parting, waking up in a cold sweat, screaming Levi's name.

The SS Officer I saw selecting children was Dr Josef Mengele. A corrupt, evil bastard. Much worse than the Gestapo, we discovered later. A depraved, barbaric man, who committed the most horrific atrocities on children.

He experimented on them in the name of science, injecting them with terrible diseases and lethal poisons just to see the results. He'd operate on twins, trying to determine why they were twins and if they had similar organs. If one died, he would murder the other. During the war years he mutilated and murdered thousands of children.

He murdered my Levi.

I feel sick when I think about it.

I hope he is captured soon by the British and brought to justice.

But I digress.

I was led, with other young women, through an iron gate, manned by guards, to a washroom and told to undress.

Leaving our clothes in piles we were met by women prisoners and ordered to stand still.

They began to shave our heads then our private parts, spraying a strong chemical over our bodies. A group of three SS guards wandered in and made us stand naked in front of them. They leant on the washroom walls and sneered at us, shouting out lewd comments to women who had large breasts.

I was so embarrassed. I stood there rigid, covering myself as best I could. The men were vulgar, gesturing with their fingers, one ordering us to turn around and bend over. A woman refused and was shot in the face, her head half blown away. We screamed and cowered in fear. The guards laughed, ordering us to get up and bend over again. We did what they asked.

Eventually, we were moved to another room and given uniforms to wear, shapeless grey calico dresses buttoned to the neck and belted at the waist. There were very few undergarments so only some of us got underpants. Instead of proper shoes, we were given wooden clogs which gave us blisters.

Later, I managed to get a pair of old shoes when I worked in the 'Kanada', a factory where you sorted out clothes from the gassed victims. I think the clothes were shipped out to be sold somewhere. I was surprised the guards did not take the shoes off me. Mind you they were extremely worn with holes in the soles.

All of us were branded with a number, tattooed to the inside of our forearms. I was always referred to as this number, 185056. The guards or the SS never called me by my real name.

In the barracks there were a lot of girls my age or a little older. But there weren't any young children, or old women.

Most of the women and children from the cattle train were sent elsewhere.

I was told later they were all gassed in communal showers and cremated in large ovens.

Over the months thousands died this way. The stench of burning bodies filled the air for days, weeks and even months. It would seep into our hair and clothes, making us reek with it.

The name of this concentration camp is Auschwitz, and it was hell on earth.

The barracks were cold and damp. A small stove was centred in the rec-room, giving off very little heat.

There was hardly any food and what was given out was unbelievably bad. We were given a bowl of a bitter drink made of burnt grain for breakfast and at lunch a dish of thin grey soup made from vegetable peelings with very little meat. At teatime, a slice of bread with a little bit of margarine. This is all we had to eat for one day!

In the winter months, the SS gave us warmer clothing to wear. Old coats, dirty scarves and sometimes thick stockings. Most probably from the gassed victims.

We had to sleep four to six women in one bed in a three-tier bunk, on a stinking straw mattress, without pillows or a blanket. So, we wore our coats to bed, and wrapped the scarves around our shorn heads to ward off the bitter cold. We never slept well, due to the lice and the women crying out in their sleep.

There was no soap or any feminine products. We had to barter and make do with what we had or make things with what we could find.

When I was working outside the camp, I once tore down small green branches from a tree and hid them under my dress. When I got back to the camp, I cut and frayed one end with a rock, making it into a kind of toothbrush. I remember how to do this from a book I once read from the school library. I bartered these toothbrushes for items I needed.

I had to be careful though. If I was caught, I would have been beaten.

I shared a bunk with a girl called Katarina, who preferred to be called Kat, her sister, Anna and their friend from school, Eva. Both parents and younger siblings were gassed the day they arrived.

They became my 'Camp Sisters'.

Kat was selected to work in an ammunition factory but convinced the Block Overseer we were all trained in making bullets. I had no idea how to make them, but with luck we were re-trained to make triggers for a machine gun instead.

We were moved to a sub camp, outside Auschwitz, attached to an ammunition factory. The barracks in this camp were just as cold, the punishments just as brutal and the food no better but it was less crowded. It was here Kat taught me German, which was very important for survival in the camp.

We stayed there for six months until we were transported to a women's camp called Ravensbruck, ninety kilometres north of Berlin.

Our camp dresses were exchanged for ridiculous baggy striped ones, and we were made to wear these stupid bonnets that covered your ears. A lot of women pulled the sides up, tying the straps on top of their heads. So, we did the same.

We all wore aprons, making us look like milkmaids, but they had pockets which allowed us to keep our eating bowl and spoon safe. If the bowl was stolen or lost, you could die of starvation.

The camp was brutal, the work extremely hard, especially if we were clearing land. If we were lucky, we worked in the kitchens where we stole a little food, maybe a potato or a turnip. If we were really. lucky and two of us worked in the kitchens at the same time, we'd make a thin, watery soup on the small wood stove in our hut. We used an old tin pot Kat found in the forest and was allowed to keep.

The pot was borrowed frequently not just for soup, but to sponge a fevered brow or clean a wound. Sickness was widespread. Everyday some poor soul lost their life, either to the 'Starvation Disease', caused by the lack of nutritious food, making your legs and stomach swell, or to Typhus or Cholera. In fact, if you were sick and the guards noticed, you were taken away, never to be seen again.

I saw prisoners with terrible wounds on their legs. They were experimented on by the camp doctors, evil mongrels, who wedged glass or wood into the women's leg muscles and administered certain drugs to judge their efficiency. These women, who volunteered in the hope of better food and to be released early, were called 'Rabbits'. They never got the rewards, instead they were disfigured for the rest of their lives or died from the infections.

A lot of them became insane and were executed.

The female guards, called Aufseherin and Block Führerinnen (Block Overseers), were vile, cruel, evil bitches who flogged us with whips and canes.

At roll call or when distributing food, the Block Overseers would be accompanied by male SS guards and their Alsatian dogs. Every day someone was attacked by the dogs or beaten by the overseer.

It was common for women to be raped by the guards, so we avoided them at all costs. If we had our monthlies, they never touched us, seeing us as 'unclean'. Nevertheless, as the years went by our periods ceased altogether. Somehow being so malnourished stopped our bodies from being normal. (I'm sorry Ryszard. I shouldn't have told you all that.)

The pretty, older girls were taken by the Aufseherin to entertain the bastards in the evenings. For payment they returned with items of food or things we could use, like threads and sewing needles or pencil stubs wrapped in small pieces of paper. We never called these girls whores. They went to stay alive and help the rest of us.

On rare occasions women gave birth in their bunks.

Their babies were whisked away and disposed of. It was heartbreaking for the new mothers, but they knew they would be executed if found with a newborn child. One woman explained to me she could have more children when the war was over, and the camp was no place to bring up a child.

If she was executed for keeping a baby, her future generation was lost. I understood her logic, but it still made me feel sick.

As the months became years, I met some amazing women who would swap stories, exchange recipes and look after each other, but I also met some truly blackhearted ones.

A malicious bitch took a fancy towards a book Kat painstakingly made over the years and stole it from her. Most of us created these keepsakes, like a book made from stolen paper or a necklace with a matching bracelet made from wire stolen from

one of the factories. These items were very important to us. They made us feel less like an animal and more like a human.

Kat risked her life trying to get her book back. She followed the big woman into the washroom, and they fought over it.

The black-hearted bitch grabbed Kat by the throat, throttling her. We tried to pull the woman off her, but she was as strong as an ox and wouldn't release her grip. It was only when the guards kept beating her with their batons, that she finally let go. Kat slumped to the floor unconscious. My 'camp sisters', Eva and Anna helped me to take her back to our bunk. It was a miracle she was still breathing. Although, when she regained her senses, she couldn't speak.

She finally got her voice back a week later, but it was very raspy. Her larynx was damaged and still is. Kat got her book back though.

With all the confusion, I snuck around the legs of the bitch, who was too busy committing murder, to notice she had dropped the book to the floor. I slowly backed away on my hands and knees and hid the book in my apron. I returned it to Kat that night when she recovered a little.

Soon after, the crazy woman got into strife with a guard and was never seen again.

In June 1944, my sisters and I were transported to the Neuengamme Concentration camp and then to a sub camp in Hannover-Limmer. It was a factory that made gas masks.

Kat found out about the factory and once again lied to the SS, claiming we could all make these masks. Being a German Jew, she could speak the language fluently and was very persuasive.

It was at this factory we met a wonderful woman by the name of Klara Schmidt.

Klara Schmidt! It couldn't be! Could it? Not our Klara Schmidt! Incredulous, I read on.

She worked there as a private secretary to the owner.

We formed a secret friendship with her and to this day I don't know why she befriended us. Maybe she found it too difficult to relate to the French girls, who made up most of the factory's slave labour.

Anyway, she would sneak small parcels of food to the four of us, Kat, Anna, Eva and myself. It would be wrapped in cloth, which of course we could use, and placed in our work baskets as she walked past to see the manager or speak to a guard. She would distract them as we snuck the parcels into our underpants.

Late one afternoon in February of 1945, Frau Schmidt saved our lives.

Night had fallen early. The air raid sirens started to wail, and we ducked under our worktables as the Allies bombed Hannover. Then the factory was hit. There was a lot of screaming and a lot of dust in the air. Bodies and debris were strewn everywhere. A fire flared up near a machine that made the rubber moulds. The smoke was very thick. It was hard to see and there was a lot of confusion. The guards were shouting to get out. Klara managed to find us all huddled together under one table, coughing and choking from the smoke. She grabbed Kat's arm and pulled.

"Come quickly!" she yelled.

In the darkness she led us to a section of the factory which was still intact and unlocked a door that led to the outside. It looked like a delivery area with a ramp leading up to a loading dock.

I could just see at the end of the driveway, a large fire blazing in a bombed building, and people running everywhere. We were very scared and clung desperately to each other.

At the back of the factory, Klara, still gripping Kat's arm, pulled her into a small shack full of old machine parts, with myself and the others following close behind. She lit a lantern and dug behind a large disused engine, pulling out two canvas bags and spilling the contents onto the floor. Women's coats, scarves and shoes fell around our feet.

We all stood there, dumbstruck. Klara must have planned this for months. Noticing our confused faces, she told us she would explain later. She ordered us to dress quickly and cover our heads with scarves and to change our boots for shoes. She quickly applied makeup to make us look less pale and adjusted our scarves to cover our shorn heads.

Klara unlocked the gate with a key and led us outside as a small farm truck rumbled up the road with its headlights on. It shone into her face as she stood in the middle of the road, waving both her arms above her head.

The driver had no alternative but to stop.

Smiling, Klara walked up to him and leant on the window. She secretly gestured for us to move towards the truck.

We came to her side and smiled sweetly at him.

He peered at us and grinned, revealing his yellow stained teeth.

Klara pulled out a full packet of cigarettes, which she had in her pocket and handed it to him. He pulled one out and Klara lit it with her lighter then gave him the lighter as well. He nodded with approval and told us he would give us a lift. Leaving him no chance to change his mind we scrambled in the back of the truck and sat amongst his farming tools.

Meanwhile, Klara climbed into the cabin and sat with the driver.

After some time, the man drove down a dark street where the streetlamps were unlit due to the blackout.

It was a street of elegant, granite buildings. The apartments were untouched by the raids, but many appeared abandoned.

Klara hustled us out of the truck, telling us to be quiet.

We hid in the shadows as she thanked the driver. He put the truck into gear and slowly drove away.

As Klara climbed the marble steps to a glass door, masked with paper, she scanned the area to see if it was clear, unlocked the door and quickly ushered us through.

Crammed in, we stood in a hallway as she fiddled with her keys to unlock her apartment door, gesturing for us to hurry.

We entered a small foyer, leading into a living room. Klara rushed around, drawing the blackout curtains over the windows and turning on an electric light. Meanwhile, we all moved slowly into the room and collapsed onto a rug on the floor, our bodies shaking with fear.

We held onto each other, sobbing, as Klara assured us, we were all safe. She left the room and returned carrying a tray with a teapot, cups and saucers, and a pile of jam sandwiches. Placing the tray on the rug, she sat down with us, and poured the tea. We ate in silence as she explained about the clothing.

"I've been planning this for two months," she said as she sipped her tea. "I would bring my suitcase to work regularly, telling Herr Kohler, my employer, I was taking the train to Berlin to visit my family. I did this regularly. Always on a Friday afternoon. Inside the case would be canvas bags and later coats, scarves and shoes. They are mostly from my sisters

and myself."

She set her teacup down.

"After work, before I went home, I would slip back to the shed and fill up the canvas bags, hiding them behind broken down machinery. Taking the suitcase, I caught the train to Berlin, got off at a nearby station and returned to my house later that night."

So that was what she was doing when we met her. This had to be our Klara Schmidt. There couldn't possibly be two women of that name helping escapees. Excited and happy, I read on as fast as I could.

She smiled and said excitedly "I waited for an opportunity to smuggle you all out and today it finally came!"

Still smiling, she stood up, and stretched out her hands towards us. "Come, I'll show you where to wash and where to sleep. But not a sound. I still have a couple of neighbours."

We looked up at her amazed. She was an angel from God. Kat clasped her hand with hers and kissed it. Klara smiled as she pulled her up, then led her to the stairs. The rest of us stood and followed. We climbed the steps to a landing.

Not a word was spoken. We took turns washing in her bathroom, drying ourselves on clean, soft towels. Klara then led us back to the living area to reveal a corridor which had been blocked off to create a secret room. The bookcase was the door, and an air vent was hidden behind a large picture frame. There were mattresses inside on the floor. Blankets and pillows were neatly stacked in a corner and at one end was a small desk, a milking stool and a kerosene lantern. This was to be our hiding place. It was a small space, but comfortable. There were books to read and writing materials.

As the weeks passed, I sketched animals I had seen when clearing a forest near Ravensbruck. Some of the animals sat quietly and watched us dig out tree stumps, before scurrying away. I always paused for a few moments to study the little creatures.

My sisters read books, talked in whispers or slept. We kept very quiet throughout the day, especially if Klara had visitors, and only ventured out at night to wash, or prepare the food for the evening meal.

Klara still worked in Hannover, at another factory owned by the same Germans who owned the gas mask factory.

She managed to buy food on the black market and sulphur powder for our weeping sores.

On one rare occasion, she managed to buy soap. All of us, including Klara, took turns to have a bath. It was a special night, we huddled together beside the fire, dried each other's hair and whispered stories about our previous lives. I told them my story about you and Jo. They couldn't believe I loved you both and still do.

Klara Schmidt was the kindest and most generous woman I've ever known.

We lived like this for about two months. Until Klara came home early one day and pulled the bookcase open. She stood there, beaming, and in a loud voice, full of excitement, announced that the war was over. Speechless, we looked at her, then burst from the small cell, laughing, crying, hugging and dancing. I kissed Klara over and over again, we all did. Dropping to our *knees, we kissed both her hands. Klara went very quiet. She stood there with tears rolling down her cheeks and lifted us up one by one, saying we were to never kneel down to anyone again.*

Ryszard, I will never forget her. She saved our lives.

She is a wonderful woman, Helena," I whispered.

Through her work, she found out the Nazis led death marches from one concentration camp to another, causing thousands to die. Apparently, if you fell down you were shot. It was the Nazis' final solution for ending us. I imagined those poor starving souls finding it so hard to put one foot in front of another, terrified of being killed. If any survived it would have been a miracle.

Our dear friend rescued us from that fate.

Klara also found out that the Red Cross were organising for letters to be delivered all around the world. So, I sent one to your aunt's house. (It was amazing I remembered the address). It was only a short time later when I received a letter from your mother.

Klara bought train tickets to wherever we wanted to go. I went home to your family. Kat was determined to migrate to Canada, taking Anna with her. Eva had relatives in England and wanted to find them. I just wanted to find you and Jo, then decide about my future.

So, my dear Ryszard, that is my story.

It has taken me a while to put all this down, at least a week. I found it hard at times to write it down. I had to stop, especially when a lot of terrible memories flooded back. But I must admit, I feel relieved, as if

telling you what happened to me in the last three years
has lifted a weight off my shoulders. I'm glad I wrote to
you.

Once again, please talk to Jozef. I don't want him to
end up in prison.

Please write to me soon.

Love,

Helena xxxxx

For a long time, I lie on my bed holding the letter against my chest. Helena has changed. She is tougher, more worldly, as if the war has taken away her child-like innocence and made her into a strong woman. But it's not to say she isn't affected by the war. We all are. Like Jo and I, she 'll live with it for the rest of her life.

Leaving that thought behind, I chuckle to myself.

Helena met Frau Schmidt! Who in hell would have thought that!

I wonder, did Frau Schmidt have people in her secret room when we were there? Christ! Frau Schmidt was a people smuggler!

I must write to Franz!

Refolding the letter, I carefully place it on the side table and sit on the edge of the bed. I pick up the envelope, tapping it against my fingers. I need to decide about sending her letter to Jo, warning him once more of the dangers in Poland. But, in the end, it will be his decision to return or stay.

Gazing at the rising moon, drifting above the horizon, I realise I need to let Helena go. In my heart I know this is the right decision for all of us.

I certainly don't want to return to Poland, and I know Jo loves her more than I do. Her leaving for the camp showed me how deep his feelings were. I'll write to him and Franz in the morning and put Helena's letter in with Jo's.

I take a shower and retire early for the night. Picking up Helena's letter, I tuck it carefully into its envelope and kiss her neat handwriting and turn off the lamp.

Lying my head against the pillow, I peer into the darkness and think about her and what she wrote. Even though she pleads for Jo not to return, she needs one of us to be with her. I really can't help her. I think maybe Jo will.

CHAPTER

55

The phone rings in the corridor.

Adi answers it and runs into the rec-room, calling my name.

I panic, thinking something terrible has happened to Jo or my family.

Running to the phone, I hastily pick up the receiver.

"Hello! Hello!"

"It's me, Rys."

"Jo! Jo! Is everything okay?"

"Yes! Yes! Everything is okay.

"How are you?" Jo asks.

I sigh with relief.

"I'm fine. You?"

"I'm good."

There is an awkward pause between us. I stare at the scribble on the wall, beside the phone, wondering why he has called.

"I'm going back to Poland, Rys!" Jo blurts out, breaking the silence.

I take in a long breath.

"What about the dangers there? Helena and Ma have warned us about returning men disappearing!"

"I'll take my chances," answers Jo. "I might be lucky. Chefs are hard to come by. Anyway, I must go back to Helena. I'm going to marry her!"

He pauses.

"Is that okay with you, Rys?" he asks, tentatively.

"Yes Jo! Yes, that's okay with me!" I say with ease, knowing in my heart I'll always love Helena, but need to put the past behind me.

"Are you going to return to Poland?" he asks, hesitantly.

"No, no! I'll stay in the UK and make some money."

"I think that's a great idea," Jo says, sighing with relief. "I wish you all the best, my brother, and maybe you could send money to Ma and Pa when you can."

"I'll do that Jo!"

For a long beat we both fall silent. I tap on the wall with my fingers.

"When are you going?" I ask softly.

"Next week. I board a ship from Plymouth on the 23rd."

"I don't think I can get down there in time to see you off. I'm sorry," I say, apologetically and add quickly, "I'll miss you, Jo, but I'm glad you are going back to be with Helena, so give her my love and tell her I'm looking forward to being her brother-in-law."

We say our goodbyes and Jo hangs up.

Slowly, I put the phone down, wondering if I will ever see my brother again.

Two months later, I receive a letter with wedding photos. Jo wears a tuxedo belonging to Auntie's first husband and Helena wears Auntie's wedding dress. I remember seeing the dress and the suit in a wedding photo on the mantelpiece.

Helena looks beautiful. She has matured into a lovely

woman with her hair a mass of short curls. She sits on a high-backed chair with Jo standing by her side, both smiling radiantly.

I notice she wears a jewelled brooch of a small grey bird with a red breast pinned to her shoulder. It looks like the one Frau Schmidt wore on the day Franz and I met her, but with a slight difference, this bird is sitting on barbed wire made from gold.

I smile at the photo.

They both look so happy.

I read they are all well and living with Ma and Pa for the time being. Auntie died a week before Jo arrived home. She left the farm to Ma as she promised.

My sisters are living together in a flat in the city, learning to be typists for a Russian government agency. Pa has a job in a big warehouse that distributes food to the co-ops, and Mother has bought a huge pregnant sow, hoping to sell the piglets at the markets.

But Jo also writes, "...life is not the same. There is no incentive to own a business or to make a lot of money. The Polish people have resigned themselves to being under the Communist thumb, so they drink a lot of vodka and smoke a lot of cigarettes."

I feel relieved that I now live in a free country. I sit on my bed and read the rest of Jo's letter.

He writes of the struggle Pa and Ma have running the small farm and that Pa needs medicine for a war injury. It's not serious, but it gives him trouble now and then. He finally asks if I could send money.

The following day, I take a bus to Kirkwall and buy a silver tea set for Jo and Helena. I include half my wages inside a wedding card and write 'Best of luck to two people I hold dear, Yours, Rys.'

Jo soon replies with a telegram.

'The tea set arrived intact. Thank you for the money. We are planning to move to Warsaw. I have a new job. Will write soon.
Jo

I received a letter from Jo a month later. He writes that Ma and Pa have decided to sell the farm and move to the city as Pa has got a job as a manager in a wholesale warehouse.

The girls both have boyfriends and are now secretaries. He and Helena have finally moved to Warsaw.

I write back I'm still dismantling fortifications around the Orkney islands. Still waiting to see what the future will bring.

#####

In September 1946 I'm formally discharged from the regular army and enlisted in the Polish Resettlement Corps, the P.R.C. The British Government realises it would be difficult and down-right dangerous for us to go back to Communist Poland, so they organise a holding unit for the Polish armed forces. It's designed to ease our transition to civilian life and help us adjust to the British way of living.

We're asked to choose between two types of work.

Farmers or tin miners.

"I think the tin mines are the way to go." I claim, as Adi and I drink coffee in the mess hall. "The pay is good. I heard about seventeen pounds a week."

"But it all depends on the tin lodes," warns Adi, "and how

large they are. It can be very dangerous with cave-ins, explosions and the like."

"I think I'll take my chances." I say, touching the scar behind my head and thinking back to when the grenade split the tree.

A week later, I'm sitting on a bus waiting to be transported to the ferry, heading for mainland Scotland.

As I look out through the window, I notice a little bird, sitting on a wire fence.

I take a harder look, realising it's a robin red breast. It fluffs-up its feathers and quickly looks around. I watch it for some time, noticing the rust-coloured plumage on its breast and its small grey wings. I think of how skilfully Helena had captured this little bird in her drawing.

It becomes startled, madly beating its tiny wings as it lifts into the sky. I follow its flight, until I see a tall figure, amongst the heather. I can just make out his WW1 army uniform and the four-pointed hat. It's the same man I saw years ago, standing in the field of death, with the robin red breast on his shoulder. A ghost, or my guardian angel? I think the latter. Slowly I lift my hand and place my palm against the window.

The man lifts his hand as if in farewell.

Past Images suddenly flash through my mind.

Jo kicking the paper ball; Mother digging in her garden; Helena's smile; Franz's grin; the Major patting my head; Alek singing; Kapo stoking the fire; Frau Schmidt measuring our waists; the wolf howling; Kaminski taking a swig from his flask; Jo's amazement when he sees me in the schoolroom, the colour of Mary's hair and the sea crashing along the cliffs of Scotland.

I have an aha moment. I realise I really do love life!

But life can be strange. I could have easily given up and lain down to die like a lot of the men in the camp, but for some reason I didn't.

I kept going, because hope never really left me, even though at times I felt it had. I now understand that without hope you simply perish. I saw this time and time again in the camp.

The survivors of the war, like Franz, Jo, Helena and my family didn't give up either.

So, despite what the Nazis threw at us, the horror they brought into our lives and the destruction of our homeland, we were all determined to cling to life and to build a new, and better, future.

But I do believe the Nazis must be punished for what they did.

I remember the cruelty in the camp, the murders committed and the blind hatred of the SS. I remember men dying from starvation and the cold. I remember the beatings, the hangings on the gallows and the cruel laughter of the SS as they watched. But most of all I remember the SS Commanders and how they looked at us, as if we were nothing, not human at all, even lower than the rats that ran in Berlin's alleyways.

They should be hung by the neck or shot like they did to my friends.

I grit my teeth, clenching my hand into a fist.

As for those Nazi bastards who escaped Germany, I hope every night they wake up drenched in sweat, haunted by the atrocities they committed.

When they stand before God, I hope all the suffering they bestowed upon us rips their very souls apart.

But I also remember the camaraderie and kindness in the

camp. The way the men sheltered Alek when he was sick and collected bread to feed the Russians. How Kapo protected us, and Tomek sneaked in 'treasures' behind the barracks. Just the little things, like Wapasha placing a kind hand on Alek's head or Kapo giving us an extra spoon of soup.

It makes me realise there is good and evil in all of us. As Franz tried to tell me, it isn't dictated by race, creed, political idealism or even culture. But by the heart!

I cast my mind back to the German people giving us scraps of food when we were filling in potholes. How Frau Schmidt fed and clothed us. Gunther, Monica and Neele who helped us in Völklingen. The warm milk the nurse gave to us in the hospital and Kaminski's leadership that led us safely to the Americans. These people represented the good people in Germany. Without them Franz and I might not have survived.

Smoothing back my hair, I breathe out a deep sigh.

I suppose the horrors of the war will be forever in my shadow and will occasionally grip my shoulder to remind me of the past.

Still staring out the window, I follow the flight of the robin redbreast disappearing into the distance and the soldier slowly fading away.

Adi plonks down on the seat beside me.

I turn to face this tall, solid man with his dark curly hair cropped short, sporting a black moustache under his long nose. He told me his story when we first met, which is similar to Franz's and mine, except he escaped a camp in Poland and then fled through Germany to the French border.

But his story can be told another day.

"Well, what's the plan when we get to Cornwall Rys, apart

from mining?" Adi asks as he takes off his cap, placing it on his knee.

I smile, speaking in English.

"We are going to play football!"

He grins back, unbuttons his jacket and gazes around the bus, nodding to a couple of his mates sitting at the back.

"I think I would like to be called Eddie from now on," he says, settling into his seat.

"That's okay with me if you call me Dick," I say, unbuttoning my grey jacket as well.

He nods in agreement as the bus starts up and drives out of the camp.

I focus ahead as we round the corner. The snow-covered mountain tops, glowing in the brilliant sunlight, are a backdrop to a group of fishermen hauling in their catch. The seagulls screech above them, as families walk on the promenade around the harbour. It's a wonderful sight.

"What a nice day," I say to no one in particular.

"It be a bonnie dey, me laddie!" replies Eddie in an awful Scottish accent.

I smile at his colloquialism.

The bus turns a sharp bend, following the robin redbreast's flight.

Gazing once more through the window, I see my reflection in the glass. I look happy and excited to be starting a new life. I sit back in my seat and laugh at one of Eddie's jokes. When he asks me to recite one of my poems, I happily agree. He shouts out for everyone to be quiet. I stand, steading myself against the seat in front of me, and taking a deep breath recite a poem about life in the army barracks. Everyone laughs and cheers.

Gesturing with a flourishing wave of the hand, I smile and take a bow.

Epilogue

I slowly surface from my memories of the war.

Groggily I sit up, bleary eyed. The back of my head is sore from leaning on the brick wall. I rub it, making my sparse grey hair stand on end. I hear footsteps along the porch and look up to see my daughter walking towards me.

"Are you okay Dad?" Marcia asks as she gently places her hand on my shoulder. "You look sad."

"I'm fine Marchinka. Just tired," I say, patting her hand. "I've noticed my orchids aren't doing so well. I could lose them to that bloody mould again!"

"Oh, that would be terrible!"

My daughter responds, offering a solution as she usually does. "You have such a wonderful display this year. I'll look on the internet and see how we can fix the problem."

Barbara, my wife, comes to the front door and calls Marcia in, describing the trouble she's having with one of her new-fangled kitchen gadgets.

I smile, thinking I'm up for another 'Biz-Whiz' or whatever they call it.

"Come in Rich, the pasties are ready," Barbara calls from the doorway. She has been making them all morning, using her mother's recipe.

Taking my time, I rise and stretch, feeling all my aches and pains. An unwelcome familiarity in my old age. I will be ninety-two soon.

I follow Barbara through to the dining room, where I smell

the most amazing aroma of golden, crusty Cornish Pasties filled with potato, turnip, meat and onion, steaming on plates on the dining room table.

I slowly sit down and peer up at the wall where the robin redbreast drawing, done over seventy years ago, proudly hangs. My mother sent it to me before they left the farm. Silently, I say a little prayer for my now deceased brother Jo, his wife Helena and my best friend Franz, who passed away last year. His wife, Mary, now ninety-one, still sends a card every Christmas with photos of her great grandchildren.

I look at my family photos of my son, his wife and children, and my daughter, husband and their growing family. Now I also have great grandchildren. I look at my wife making a cup of tea, marvelling that she is still as beautiful as the day I met her under a town clock, in Saint Just, seventy years ago.

I pick up my pasty, take a bite, closing my eyes as I chew and promise myself not a morsel of food will be left on my plate. It's a promise I made long ago and have kept ever since. I sigh with delight, at every delicious mouthful.

Despite the war, I realise I'm a very lucky man indeed. I've had a wonderful life. Still do. It was tough in those war-torn days. *'Those days.'* So long ago. A lifetime ago. I was lucky to be surrounded with love then and now. I glance up at the robin red breast once more and make a wish.

I wish for of a better world. A world without war and cruelty. A world that will always contain love and hope.

Author's notes

This story is based on Dad's life when he was a boy in Europe during the Nazi occupation in WW2. However, I fleshed it out by introducing new fictional characters and events based on his stories.

Many of the characters are fictional, including **Franz**.

Dad was alone in his adventures, until meeting up with **Kaminski and the Russians**. With all that happened to him, I like to think of Franz as Dad's guardian angel, believing he had one to guide him through the perils he encountered.

As for Jozef, the family and **Helena**, they were real. My oldest daughter, Elizabeth, suggested the love triangle between Jo, Rys and Helena. Not that it really happened. But I'm glad I wrote this part as I'm sure it hit home with some of my readers when it comes to adolescent love.

Helena's name was different. I never did find out what her true name was due to Dad having Dementia while I was drafting this book. She was his Jewish girlfriend, and he did ask her father if she could live with his family. But as in the story he was refused. Unfortunately, the whole family was shot earlier in the war, and she was never sent to a ghetto. Extending her life and giving her a voice was important to me.

It gave me reason to research the conditions in the ghettos and the treatment of women in the camps.

Helena had a significant purpose in the story as she

represents all those women.

*Jozef, **Jo**, Dad's brother, was a chef and an artist. He returned to Poland after the war and married a very attractive lady. There are photos of them in Dad's photo album.*

***Alek** is fictional. I even doubt such a fragile boy could survive the camps. But I like to think a boy, like Alek, who could sing like an angel, could give comfort and peace to the men left in these horrific circumstances. Even for a short time.*

***Tomek** did exist. Dad met him on the train as the book suggests but the rest of his story is fictional. I have no idea what happened to him.*

***Kapo** was real as well, and he did look after the younger men. But as for his character I created that part too.*

The story line, and most of the events in the book are actual, although I had to manufacture conversations between characters. I also had to manufacture, as well as tweak, some of the scenarios.

*Sachsenhausen concentration camp required no tweaking! It was, and still is, real. I received most of my information from a book called **'Sachsenhausen Concentration Camp Events and Developments'** by Gunter Morsch and Astrid Ley. I picked up this book when I visited the camp site in 2014, and believe me, there was no way Dad could have escaped that camp.*

In my research I discovered satellite slave labour camps surrounding the bigger camp, and Dad was interned in one of these. I believe most of the prisoners who escaped the Nazi occupied countries would have been from this type of camp.

***Frau Schmidt** is fictional. But a German lady did help Dad by making him winter trousers and giving him a meal.*

***Fraulein Wagner** (the bitch in the wardrobe) is also fictional*

I wanted to create a chapter portraying the fanaticism in Nazi Germany.

*Helena's imprisonment in the ghetto was based on true accounts. I read an amazing book by Abraham H. Biderman called **'The Word of My Past'**. His true account of his life in the ghetto and the concentration camps helped me understand the politics and conditions the Jews had to endure.*

I relied on the internet and Dad's book collection for most of my research. He was obsessed with WW2 and especially Adolf Hitler. In his later years, his collection of war books was extensive.

Any mistakes are all mine.

Dad never did get over the war and looking back I realise he suffered from depression most of his life. The actions of Hitler and his cronies, especially Himmler, not only caused people to be physically maimed or killed but also contributed to the deterioration of their mental health.

Throughout his life, Dad was a clown, always pulling faces and chasing the grandchildren around as a gorilla.

He loved to be the centre of attention, and he did write poetry that was hilarious. He'd try to rhyme words that don't rhyme. He loved to dress up and put on Christmas concerts with the grandchildren. He was a dear soul with a big heart, but he lived a long time with his demons.

In his later years, he was awarded the Polish Medal of Valour, which he proudly wore every Anzac Day.

*As for my dad's storyline, I referred to a book written by Michael Hambrook called **'On the Front Line,'** about expatriates from other countries living in Australia. It gives true accounts and testimonials of war experiences. I'm glad my dad* *was able to recount his story to Michael before he got fourth stage Dementia. I believe his story needed to be told.*

Acknowledgements

I would like to thank my friend Helen West for being my editor for the last three years. She is a marvel. I have learnt so much! Thank you, Helen.

Helen, writing as Lena West, is an author herself in the Australian Romance genre.

I would like to thank Jenny Dobbie for illustrating the book cover and being one of my readers. Jenny is an amazing artist, and you can find her on Instagram.

Thanks to you also, Erin Syddall, my graphic designer for the book cover and creating my webpage. You did a fantastic job.

I'd like to thank Meredith Wakeman, my sister-in-law, for being one of my readers as well. Input from Helen, Jenny and Meredith has made this story flow, and their advice has been immeasurable.

I would also like to give special thanks to my husband Kevin, for putting up with my constant distractions and very early starts in the morning, when I woke up with ideas for the book or to correct the mistakes I'd made. Thank you, Kev, for supplying the glass of red at 5pm!

My daughters have been wonderful. Helping me form ideas and develop scenes.

My father died in 2020 right in the middle of the Covid 19 pandemic. He was 93 years old. I believed he was looking over my shoulder when I wrote this book, whispering in my ear about all the adventures he had, telling me what was 'veediculous' (ridiculous) and what should be taken out. I also believe he encouraged me to keep going when I had doubts of ever finishing.

I dedicate this book to Dad's memory and his absolute determination to live his life to the fullest. To eat everything edible on his plate, (I kid you not, he would line up his cleanly picked chicken bones), and his ability to love his family and friends unconditionally.

To Ryszard Muszynski, may your memory live forever.

About the Author

Marcia Wakeman was born in England in 1956, migrating to Australia in 1961 with her family. She attended Newcastle Teachers College in the latter part of the 1970s and was an Art teacher for 26 years.

Happily married, Marcia has three daughters and six grandchildren. She decided to write this story about her Polish father, Ryszard, when he passed away in 2020, aged ninety-three.

Connect with Marcia!

Be the first to know about it when Marcia's next
book is released!
Write to

www.marciawakemanauthor.com/

Bibliography

'World War II, No. 10 'The Death camps' based on the original text by Lt.-Col Eddy Baur Published by Orbis Publishing Ltd. 1972
'The World of My Past' written by Abraham H. Biderman. Published by Random House. 1996.
'Sachsenhausen Concentration Camp, 1936-1945 Events and Developments'. Written by Günter Morsch and Astrid Ley (ed.). 5th edition 2013. Schriftenreihe der Stiftung Brandenburgische Gedenkstätten Band 24
'On the Front Line' written by Michael Hambrock. Published by New Holland Publishers. 2012

Website Links:
SS and the camp system. The holocaust Encyclopedia
http;//encycolpedia.ushmm.org/content/en/article/ss-and-the-camps-systems

Camp leader in a slave labour camp-google search
Www. enclopedia.ushmm.org>article

Survivor Reflections and Testimonies – United states
https: www.ushmm.org/remember/holocaust-reflections-testimonies
Echoes of Memory – United States Holocaust Memorial Museum

https:www.ushmm.org>collections

Albert Speer-Wikipedia
https://en.m.wikipedia.org/wiki/Albert_Speer

The Phenomenon of the Polish Underground State
https://warsawinstitute.org/phenomenon-polish-underground-state/.

Heinrich Himmler| Biography & Facts Britannica
www.britannica.com>biography

Heinrich Himmler The Holocaust Encyclopedia
www.encyclopedia.ushmm.org>article

https;//orkneyuncovered.co.uk/wartime-orkney-explorer/?doing   wp
cron=1593934435.0816121101379394531250

Polish armed forces in the West
https;//en.m.wikipedia.org/wiki/Polish Armed Forces in the West

Tomaszów Mazowieki
https://pasazepamieci.pl/en/tomaszow-mazowiecki-2/

http://en. m.wikipedia.org/wiki/Sochaczew

Printed in Australia
Ingram Content Group Australia Pty Ltd
AUHW011222050124
388545AU00004B/15